The Cowboy Who Spoke Softly

A Single Dad Friends to Lovers Christian Cowboy Romance

Three Rivers Romance™
Book 6

Liz Isaacson

Copyright © 2025 by Elana Johnson, writing as Liz Isaacson

All rights reserved.

No part of this book may be reproduced in any form or by any electronic or mechanical means, including information storage and retrieval systems, without written permission from the author, except for the use of brief quotations in a book review.

ISBN-13: 978-1-63876-429-8

Reader Note

Hello Fabulous Christian Cowboy Readers!

There's very little I like more than a single dad. And a secret baby—and this book has BOTH!

It makes my author and reader heart so dang happy.

I don't get to write the secret baby trope very often, and I've never once done a secret baby that came from a couple who wasn't married...

But life is messy sometimes, right? And there's so much room for improvement and repentance and forgiveness, and as I started to conceptualize Conrad, he needed to go through all of those things.

So when I wrote The Cowboy Who Called Back (the previous book to this one), and it was time to start getting you to connect to Conrad...the secret baby came out of nowhere.

And Sari is wonderful. Conrad is wonderful. His journey back to his faith and God is absolutely amazing, and I hope it'll provide hope and healing for you, whether you're dealing with your own issues or you have to sit quietly on the sidelines as someone else wrestles with their own faith and journey to God.

As Glory Rose tells her parents in this book, "He's repenting of the things he's done. Isn't that all we're expected to do?"

Yes, we're all trying to do the best we can. We're all dealing with things—maybe not as big as a secret baby!—but we all need and deserve our Savior's sacrifice and forgiveness.

Anyway, I hope you love Conrad and Glory Rose, the Walkers, the Glovers, and the band of ranching/farming cowboys brothers in Three Rivers!

xoxo

~Liz

Get free books!

Get a new free book every month, access to live events, special members-only deals, and more when you join the Feel-Good Fiction newsletter. You'll get instant access to the Book Club area on the Feel-Good Fiction website, where my books are now hosted and where all the goodies are located, so **join today!**

Join the Feel-Good Fiction Reader Community on Facebook.

Want to read books as I write them? Join the hundreds of other Feel-Good Fiction subscribers on **Ream** (online or in-app) or **Substack** (online, in-app, or direct to your email!)!

Join Liz's NEW texting list!

Text COWBOY to 801-618-2114

The Small Town of Three Rivers

Welcome to Three Rivers! There have been three complete series here already - Three Rivers Ranch, Seven Sons Ranch (Walker Brothers), and Shiloh Ridge Ranch (Glover Family).

That's 37 books. Loads of characters. I'm going to list them here, but you don't need to know them all comprehensively for this book. I just know some of you like seeing these amazing small towns and who lives here!

Seven Sons Ranch:
Momma & Daddy: Penny and Gideon Walker
1. Rhett & Evelyn Walker
Son: Conrad - 29
Triplets: Austin, Elaine, and Easton - 23

. . .

2. JEREMIAH & WHITNEY WALKER
    Son: Jonah Jeremiah (JJ) - 26
    Daughter: Clara Jean - 23
    Son: Jason - 22
    Daughter: Emily - 29
    Daughter: Hattie - 18

3. LIAM & CALLIE WALKER
    Daughter: Denise - 33
    Daughter: Ginger - 29

4. TRIPP & IVORY WALKER
    Son: Oliver - 39 (and married to Aurora Glover)
    Son: Isaac - 29

5. WYATT & MARCY WALKER
    Son: Warren - 26
    Son: Cole - 24
    Son: Harrison - 23
    Daughter: Rachel - 19

6. SKYLER & MALLERY WALKER
    Daughter: Camila - 26
    Son: Sawyer - 24

Son: Gideon - 21

7. MICAH & SIMONE WALKER
    Son: Travis (Trap) - 25
    Daughter: Daisy - 23
    Son: Jensen - 19
    Daughter: Laurel - 17

Coyote Pass:

Alex Baxter, wife Nikki (twin boys - Shane and Hank, age 5)

Three Rivers Ranch:

Frank and Heidi Ackerman - patriarch and matriarch. Frank died 17 years ago; Heidi is remarried to Malcolm Rust.

Squire and Kelly Ackerman

Son: Finn - 37, wife Edith, Theo (son, 7), Bubba (son, 3), Dustin (6 months)
    Daughter: Libby - 32, married to Rusty Jackson
    Son: Michael - 29
    Son: Samuel - 26

. . .

Pete and Chelsea Marshall (Chelsea is Squire's sister, and they own Courage Reins, which is housed at Three Rivers Ranch)

4 sons:

Paul - 33, married to Brielle

Henry - 31, wife Angel, son, Wrangler (18 months) **(Lone Star Ranch)**

John - 28

Rich - 25

Reese and Carly Sanders: They're the admins for Courage Reins, Pete and Chelsea's equine therapy unit at Three Rivers Ranch. They have no children.

Garth and Juliette Ahlstrom (former foreman; vet technician)

Son: Jake - 31

Son: Carson - 28

Cal and Trina Hodgkins (he's the full-time vet at Three Rivers Ranch)

Daughter: Sabrina - 40

Daughter: Abby - 32

Daughter: Olive - 28

. . .

Ethan and Brynn Greene (they own Bowman's Breeds, which is housed at Three Rivers Ranch)
> Daughter: Carolina - 29
> Son: Tyson - 28
> Son: Bryan - 25

Beau Peterson (foreman at Three Rivers Ranch) and Charlotte Wisenhouer
> Son: Walter - 13
> Daughter: Michelle - 9

Bennett and Ellie Peterson (he's a cowboy, she works on the finances on the ranch with Kelly)
> Daughter: Joy - 14
> Son: Jaxon - 12

Tad and Sandy Jorgensen (he's a cowboy, she owns the pancake house in town)
> Son: Nathaniel (Nate) - 28
> Daughter: Helen - 25

Kenny and Taryn Stockton (he's a cowboy, she works for a local online newspaper in town)
> Daughter: Joelle (Jo) - 27

. . .

Jon and Grace Carver (he's a cowboy, she helps Heidi run the bakery in town)

Andy and Lawrence Collins (he's a cowboy, she owns a clothing boutique in town)

Summer and Tanner Wolfe (he's a cowboy, she's a nurse at the hospital in town)

Gavin and Navy Redd - they own their own single-family ranch on the northeast side of Three Rivers

Boone and Nicole Carver (Squire's cousin) - they own and operate the full time veterinary clinic in town

Camila and Dylan Walker (he's a cowboy and an electrician, she owns a plumbing shop in town)

Shiloh Ridge Ranch:
   Lois & Stone (deceased) Glover, 7 children, in age-order: (Lois is now married to Donald Parker)

1. Bear — Sammy, wife

- Lincoln (33), adopted son, married to Misty / Dallas (nickname: Diesel, son 5), Scout (son, 2)
- Stetson (Smiles, 23), son
- Russell (Rock, 21), son
- Heather (19), daughter
- Sunnie (18), daughter

2. Cactus — Allison, ex-wife / Bryce, son (deceased) // — Willa, wife

- Mitch (34), adopted son
- Cameron (29), adopted son
- Kyle (27), adopted son
- Charlie (Chaz, 23), son
- Lynn (22), adopted daughter
- Melissa (20), daughter

3. Judge — June, wife

- Lucy Mae (39), step-daughter
- Birch (20), son
- Willow (18), daughter
- Linden (15), son

4. Preacher — Charlie, wife

- Betty (22), daughter

- Hank (19), son
- Daisy (16), daughter

5. Arizona — Duke Rhinehart, husband, living at the Rhinehart Ranch, just south of Shiloh Ridge

- Shiloh (22), daughter
- April (19), daughter
- Dwayne (17), son
- Dallas (14), son

6. Mister — Libby, wife

- Belle (19), son
- Marley (17), daughter
- Hazel (14), daughter
- Brantley (11), son

7. Bishop — Montana, wife

- Aurora (39), step-daughter and married to Oliver Walker
- Robbie (27), son
- Georgia (21), daughter

Aurora and Oliver have 4 children, who are Bishop and Montana's grandchildren:

- Jewel (12), daughter
- Laramie (Lara, 9), daughter
- Mason (7), son
- Lennon (5), son

Dawna & Bull (deceased) Glover, 5 children, in age-order:

1. Ranger — Oakley, wife

   - Wilder (25), son
   - Fawn (23), daughter

2. Ward — Dot, wife

   - Glory Rose (24), daughter
   - Silver (21), son
   - Flint (19), son

3. Ace — Holly Ann, wife

   - Gunnison (23), son
   - Pearl Jo (21), daughter
   - Ashton (18), son

4. Etta — August Winters, husband

   - Hailey (31), adopted daughter
   - Joey (21), son
   - Nash and Nellie (twins - 18), son and daughter

5. Ida — Brady Burton, husband

   - Johnny and Judy (twins - 25), son and daughter
   - Riggs (19), son

• Sonora (16), daughter

Bull and Stone Glover were brothers, so their children are cousins. Ranger and Bear, for example, are cousins, and each the oldest sibling in their families.

Rhinehart Ranch:

1. Dawson, wife, Caroline / Colt (son, 4), Joy (daughter, 4 months)

2. Brandon (36)

Chapter One

Conrad Walker pulled up to his parents' house, deep gratitude instantly striking through him as he drank in the colorful banners, streamers, and balloons that had taken over the entire front porch.

"Oh, my goodness, Sari," he said. "Look at Grandma's house."

His daughter was turning three this week, and Conrad had decided to have a family birthday party on the weekend so that his aunts and uncles and cousins could attend. Her late February birthday meant that everybody had school and work, and since this was the first birthday that Conrad had gotten to celebrate with his daughter, Sarina, he'd wanted her to have his entire family there.

Truth be told, Conrad needed his whole family with him as well. As the gratitude drove deep through him, it left a hole for the guilt to fill. He shouldn't have asked his mother to host the party here. He should have done it at his own house so that she wouldn't have to clean things up afterward. Not only that, but he certainly didn't deserve such an amazing party for his daughter, the daughter that no one had known about until last summer—not even him.

Just as quickly as the guilt chased the gratitude, Conrad was able to reason it away. He'd been working on making things right between him and God for a long time, even before he found out about Sarina, as he knew he'd done some things wrong in his past that he needed to repent of—whether those things had produced a baby or not. And in this case, they had.

He thought of his ex-girlfriend and how she might be feeling this year not having their daughter with her. So he got out of the truck, and before he moved to the back to get his little girl down, he snapped some pictures of the house so that she could see how much his family loved Sarina.

Then he turned his attention to the back seat, where Sarina giggled and kicked her legs to get out of the seat.

"All right," he said with a chuckle. "Come on, let's go see what she's got."

"Boon boon," Sarina said, and Conrad would take that, because his daughter didn't talk very well or very much. He'd been taking her to an early childhood behavioral specialist for the past couple of months. When he read her books with dogs and frogs and pigs and cats, now she said all of the animal noises. She'd always called him "Dad," but now she called Grams "Gams," too, and he was pleased with the progress she'd made in her speech.

He set her on her feet, and she ran laughing toward the

house. Conrad's heart filled with joy too, and he took a picture of his little girl running toward the house so he could send it to Chloe too.

He knew things between him and Chloe were irreparable. Had he known about the pregnancy in the beginning, he probably would have married her. But since he hadn't, she'd left town and hadn't told him about their child. She hadn't wanted him, and that hurt Conrad, but he'd been over her by the time she came back into his life with a little girl bearing all the Walker features, from eyes to nose to chin—all of *his* features.

He jogged to catch up to his daughter as she took the steps one at a time, both feet on each one before she went up to the next. The door opened, and his daddy came out, already bellowing, "Happy birthday, Sari!"

He carried an enormous stuffed sloth that made Sarina freeze and then shriek, "Sloth! Sloth!" She pronounced it with an "F" sound at the end instead of "TH."

Daddy laughed and scooped her up off the top step and into his arms. She grabbed onto his face and laughed as he tickled her with his beard and pressed kisses all over her face.

"How are you, my darling girl?" he asked.

Sarina started to talk as Conrad ran up the stairs too. He caught a few words like "Gams" and "balloon," but not much else. When Daddy looked over to him to interpret, Conrad just said, "Yeah, Grandma and Grandpa got you a lot of balloons, didn't they, baby?"

His mother came out onto the porch too, carrying a purple balloon in her hand with a matching tie that she put around Sarina's wrist. She took the little girl from Daddy, already talking to her about cake and presents and how she was going to be the best three-year-old in the world as she took her back into the house.

Chatter and laughter leaked out of the house before Momma closed the door behind her. Conrad knew he and Sarina were the last to arrive. In fact, he'd staged it that way on purpose, so that he didn't have to greet everyone as they came in. He could simply greet everyone once as he arrived.

"How you doing, son?" Daddy asked.

Conrad turned his attention to his father. "Just fine," he said, his voice somewhat guarded.

He used "just fine" all the time, because he was just fine.

How's the farm?

Just fine.

How was church today?

Just fine.

How's Sarina doing with her potty training?

Just fine.

Okay, that last one wasn't really true, and Conrad had given up the endeavor until she turned three. He'd been reading books on how to potty train for the past couple of months, and he'd simply started too early. But he didn't have to get into specifics when he said "just fine," because in reality, everything was just fine—even if he still struggled some days, even if he couldn't get the mini donkeys to come into their pens at night, even if Grams continued to get older and older, and Conrad worried about the day she might not wake up.

"Sure," Daddy said, clearly disbelieving. "Tell me what's in your head."

He gestured toward the door with one big hand. "It's my daughter's third birthday," he said. "And the first that any of us get to celebrate with her."

"Yeah," Daddy said, almost an implied *And?* at the end of that, as if it was no big deal.

"I don't know," Conrad said. "I feel stupid."

"Why?" Daddy asked.

"You know why," Conrad mumbled. He didn't have to articulate it again. "Let's just go inside."

"Wait just a second," Daddy said, and he moved over to step right in front of Conrad, blocking him from entering the house. He slid his hand along the side of Conrad's neck and to the back of it, holding him there, making him feel loved and valued, but also making it so Conrad couldn't look somewhere else.

"You're a good man, Conrad," Daddy said, pure emphasis in his voice. "You have got to stop believing otherwise."

"I don't know how," Conrad told his father.

"You still seeing that therapist?" Daddy asked.

Conrad nodded. "Every couple of weeks."

Daddy dropped his hand. "So keep doing that. And I think maybe it's time you went back to God and asked Him where you stand."

Conrad ducked his head and looked at his boots. "He knows I need to know," he said. "Why do I have to ask too?"

"I don't know," Daddy said. "But sometimes we do. And maybe if you ask Him how you're doing and where you stand with Him, He'll be able to let you know what I can see—that you're good, that you've repented, that you don't need to beat yourself up about Chloe, about Sarina, about any of it, anymore."

Daddy reached out, put a gentle hand under Conrad's chin to lift it up. "It's time to be done with all that. You're forgiven."

Conrad ached to be forgiven, and he nodded, because his emotions had coiled tight and knotted in his throat to the point where he couldn't speak.

Daddy once again dropped his hand, and Conrad hated that he'd caused any turmoil for his parents at all. Of course, they hadn't known that he'd been sleeping with Chloe. He hadn't told anyone about that, but when Sarina showed up in his life, everyone had found out, and everyone judged, no matter what they said and no matter how they acted.

Conrad had worked through that with the Lord, and he'd learned that everyone had to deal with what he'd done in their own way, that it did have consequences for more than just him and Chloe and Sarina, that sometimes people needed space to grieve or process, that sometimes people needed to talk it through.

Sometimes it took a long time, and sometimes it took no time at all.

Conrad had been eternally grateful for his cousin JJ, who seemed to work through whatever he needed to in a matter of minutes before he'd arrived at pure acceptance of Conrad for who he was in the moment and who he could be in the future.

His parents, particularly Daddy, had taken longer. But as Conrad looked at his father now, he distinctly knew that Daddy loved him, wanted the very best for him, and had worked through any conflicting feelings about Conrad being a single dad who'd never been married.

He yearned for that knowledge and acceptance of himself, and he determined that he'd kneel down and pray that evening and ask God what else he needed to do, if anything, to be made whole and to be forgiven completely.

He nodded. Daddy did too, and then he turned to open the front door.

"Oh, there you are," Aunt Ivory said. She and Uncle Tripp lived just down the road on this same lane. "I was just coming to get you. Evvy wants to do the cake and presents right now."

"Yep," Daddy said. "We're coming." He went in the house without a backward glance at Conrad.

Conrad gave a tight little smile to his aunt, who pulled him into a hug and said, "I love you, buddy," the way she had when he was a little boy, a tween, and a teenager.

Conrad had always loved being a Walker, and he had loved his aunts and uncles and all of his cousins growing up. So he hated that things between them had been strained and silent and just so different since Sarina had come into his life —come into all of their lives.

But now he melted into his aunt's embrace and said, "I love you too, Aunt Ivory."

The interior of the house had been transformed completely into the set of a tiny girls' wonderland, pink and purple and all the shades in between. Balloons, decorations, banners, gifts, and more had been thrown everywhere. Conrad barely knew where to step, as Momma had set up chairs and tied balloons to every single one, almost creating a maze through the living room to the back of the house in the kitchen, where an enormous three-tiered cake sat on the counter, done in bright pink-bubblegum frosting.

Sarina sat on the counter next to it, and Momma lit the chunky candles as Conrad and Daddy moved through the house to join the party.

"Daddy!" Sarina called. "Cake!"

"Yeah," he said in a bright voice. "That's a big cake."

His mother wouldn't look at him, and Conrad had already decided not to give her a hard time about anything she chose to do for the party. He'd asked her to host it, and he'd told her she could do whatever she wanted. He wasn't going to now criticize that she'd maybe gone a little overboard.

He reminded himself that Sarina was her first and only grandchild, that none of her kids had gotten married yet, and that she simply wanted to pour out her love on Sarina.

And by extension, on you.

That thought entered his mind in a voice he didn't recognize, and as Momma lit the last candle, Conrad realized God had just spoken to him.

His mother's enthusiasm and exuberance for this party wasn't just for Sarina. It was to show Conrad that she loved *him,* supported *him,* and accepted *him.* And everyone's attendance meant they did too.

"All right," Momma chirped. "We sing first." She looked around at everyone.

Since they'd celebrated many birthdays over the years in

the Walker family, they all took a big breath and then started singing "Happy Birthday to you..." in tandem.

Conrad tried to join in and found he couldn't. His emotion surged up and down and back around, and he couldn't get his voice to come out of his throat. He also couldn't hold back the tears, and instead he let them stream down his face as first JJ came to stand next to him, then Easton, and then Austin, and then Elaine.

He loved the triplets with his whole heart, even if Elaine could be a little sassy sometimes. Right now, she stood in front of him as if she could protect him from the eyes of his aunts and uncles and cousins, and if they had anything to say to him that wasn't one hundred percent perfect and positive, they would have to go through her first. Elaine had always been a fierce friend to everyone around her, including Conrad, and he loved her so very much in that moment.

The song finished, and JJ stepped in front of him and turned his back on the party. Austin did the same, and Elaine handed him a tissue over their broad shoulders. Easton completed the barrier between him and everyone else as he wiped his eyes, and then he smiled as the room erupted in cheers because Sarina had gotten all three candles blown out on her cake.

"What are you doing tonight?" JJ asked, his voice quiet and yet somehow heard among the crowd.

"Going home," Conrad said. He glanced over to Easton.

"I think the five of us should go out."

Conrad blinked at him, because JJ knew full-well he had a three-year-old daughter he had to take care of.

"I'll ask your mom if Sarina can stay here tonight," JJ said, and he turned and walked away before Conrad could say a single word.

"It's a good idea," Austin said, his voice low and somehow set on growl as well. "Let's just go get burgers and wings and hang out."

Conrad wanted to tell him that single dads didn't get burgers and wings and "hang out." But Elaine muscled her way into the spot that JJ had vacated, and she said, "Yeah, let's do that. Maybe you guys can help me meet a man."

Conrad blinked at her, surprise running across his face. "What happened to you telling us to stay out of your business?"

"I'm a little dumbfounded myself," Easton said.

She glared around at all of them, cocking her hip and folding her arms, looking so much like Momma when she did. "I'm allowed to change my mind," she said. "Surely you guys know some single cowboys our age."

Conrad did, yes, and his brain blitzed through who he could possibly set Elaine up with.

JJ returned and said, "She said she'd love to have her."

"I'm gonna call Beaumont." Elaine stepped out of the circle, once again before Conrad could protest or accept what she'd said. He found himself being swept along by this tidal wave of Walkers that he loved so much. He didn't know how to stop them. He wasn't even sure he *wanted* to stop them.

Thankfully, his phone chimed, and he looked down at it to get away from their gazes. He turned his back on them as he saw Glory Rose Glover's name flash across his screen.

What are you doing tonight, cowboy? she asked. *My uncle just gave me two tickets to the stargazing taste testing tonight. Maybe we could go together.*

Conrad had been flirting with Glory Rose for months now, and he'd asked her out a time or two. They'd even set up dates, and then somehow it had always fallen through.

In this moment, he spun back to his cousin and siblings and held up his phone.

"Glory Rose just asked me out," he said.

"Great," JJ said without missing a beat. "You should go out with her. I know you've been trying for a while."

"It's for tonight," Elaine said, a touch of surprise in her voice.

And Conrad already had a babysitter.

Austin, ever the level-headed one, said, "You should go, Conrad. We can do our thing another night."

"Yeah," JJ said.

He looked at Easton and raised his eyebrows. His brother read the text and then grinned at Conrad. "If Glory Rose Glover was offering me tickets to the stargazing taste test, I'd have already said yes."

That caused several people to laugh, including Conrad, but his thumb still hovered over his phone as he continued to wonder what he should say to her.

"Oh, give me the phone," JJ said, and he swiped it out of Conrad's hands before he could protest. His thumbs flew over the screen, and then he shoved the phone back at him and said, "There, you have a date. Now come enjoy your daughter's birthday."

Chapter Two

Glory Rose Glover stood in front of the full-length mirror in her bedroom, tilting her head as she scrutinized the outfit she had carefully chosen for the night. The sweater hung down a little too far on the right, and she pulled it back left. At least these dark-wash jeans hugged her legs just right, but she second-guessed the ivory-colored sweater with the criss-cross fabric in the front that then hung down past her hips on the sides.

It wasn't too fancy, but she wasn't the neatest eater—and tonight's date with Conrad included a taste test. She'd definitely be eating, maybe even saucy, Texas-type ribs or wings.

She tucked a lock of her long, dark hair behind her ear, her fingers brushing the silver hoop earrings she had decided to wear. A smile tugged at the corners of her mouth as she thought about the man she'd be seeing tonight.

Conrad Walker was quiet, sure, but something about him

intrigued her. Something that drew her in like a moth to a flame. Something that scared her a little, because Glory Rose sometimes ran out of things to say too.

"He's not like the other cowboys around here," she whispered to her reflection. "He's different."

And that difference had her heart doing little flips in her chest every time she thought about him. She had been flirting with him for months now, and while they had danced around the idea of going out, life always seemed to get in the way. Either his daughter needed something, or something had blown up on his farm, or Glory Rose had a family obligation.

But tonight?

"Tonight is so going to be different."

A knock on her bedroom door startled her from her thoughts, and she turned to see her cousin Fawn poking her head into the room.

"How's it going in here?" Fawn asked, her voice full of teasing as she scanned Glory Rose's outfit. "You look like you're about to go on a first date with a really hot cowboy or something."

Glory Rose rolled her eyes, but she couldn't help the grin that spread across her face. "Don't make me more nervous than I already am." She turned back to the mirror, her gaze locking onto Fawn's as her cousin came closer. "What are you doing tonight?"

Fawn was only a few months younger than Glory Rose, and they'd grown up next door to one another here at Shiloh Ridge Ranch. Their daddies were brothers, and Glory Rose leaned into Fawn as her cousin put her arm around her.

They'd been best friends for a long time, so when it came time for them to move out, they'd moved in together.

Yes, still here on the ranch, but into one of the cabins just north of the Top Cottage, where Link lived with his wife and family.

Uncle Bear and Uncle Ranger had both fully retired from the ranch work now, and Lincoln—Bear's oldest son—and Wilder—Ranger's oldest, and Fawn's older brother—both ran the ranch now. There were so many Glovers living and working here, and Glory Rose and Fawn were just two of them.

And really, Glory Rose didn't work on the ranch. She just lived here, as she had a nursing job down in town, at a pediatrician's office. Fawn, however, had earned her vet technician certificate, and she worked with the animals here at the ranch.

She wanted to become a vet, but she hadn't quite pulled the lever yet, as it would take her away from Shiloh Ridge, away from Three Rivers, away from all the Glovers. And Fawn was very much a homebody. She still sometimes drove the five minutes down the road to sleep at her momma's, as they got along so well.

Right now, Fawn reached up and swept her fingers through her own dark hair that fell in waves over her shoulders. "What am I doing tonight?" She sighed. "Helping Pearl Jo with her application to the Animal Science major? Probably that. It's due soon, and I don't have anything better to do."

Glory Rose stepped out of the side-hug and sat on her bed to pull on her boots.

"You're going with the sweater-boot look," Fawn said.

She looked up to her. "Not a good combo? It's February."

"It's really cozy."

Glory Rose glanced down at her outfit again, a flicker of doubt creeping in. "I don't want to look like I'm trying too hard, Fawn. We're going stargazing, not to some fancy dinner."

"But it's Conrad Walker, and you've been pining after this guy for months now."

"I have *not* been pining," Glory Rose protested, though her cheeks flushed. That could be because she couldn't get this blasted boot to go on. She pulled harder, which allowed her to focus on her feet instead of Fawn.

"Oh, please." Fawn's laughter filled the room. "You've been talking about him non-stop. Conrad this, Conrad that. *He's so quiet, you guys, but he's got these dreamy eyes. He texted me back, but he didn't say much. What do you think that means?*"

Fawn grinned as Glory Rose finally got the boot on and looked up to her. "And don't even get me started on his daughter. You're practically in love with her, and you've only met her a handful of times."

Glory Rose huffed, got her second boot on easily, and stood. She crossed her arms over her chest and glared at Fawn. "I'm not in love with anyone, okay? I just—I think there's something special about Conrad. He's been through so much, and I like that he's grounded. He's not like all the other cowboys around here who just want to have fun and flirt."

And Glory Rose needed some excitement in her life. As

one of a great many dozens of Glovers, and since she didn't play a role here on the ranch, Glory Rose often felt overlooked in her own family. She wondered if Conrad did too. He had a lot of cousins, aunts, uncles, and siblings too.

Maybe that was why Glory Rose wanted to get to know him better. Maybe they could create a space for each other where they were each the most important.

"Who's flirting?" Pearl Jo asked as she appeared in the doorway. She scanned Glory Rose down to the boots and back. "You look amazing." She glanced over to Fawn. "What's going on tonight?"

"Our girl Glory Rose here has a date with the one-and-only Conrad Walker." Fawn grinned at her, and Glory Rose's face heated again.

Pearl Jo looked like she'd just come in from the stables, with mud on the cuffs of her jeans and her hair still braided back. Her eyes only got wider as she stared at Glory Rose.

"Stop it," Glory Rose said, and she brushed her hands down the front of her sweater. "Settle a debate for us. Good sweater or too blah?"

Pearl Jo settled her weight onto one foot and cocked her head to the side. "It's seriously cute. Not my style, but perfect for you."

Glory Rose threw a *so-there* look over to Fawn. "Perfect for me."

"You've always been very good at being yourself," Fawn said with a laugh.

Glory Rose smiled over to her and pushed her hair over

her shoulder. "I hope that doesn't come back to bite me tonight."

"Why would it?" Pearl Jo reached up and started to release her hair out of its braid. "I stink. I need to shower."

Glory Rose could've agreed with her, and she had teased Pearl Jo about the...certain smell she brought back to their cabin in the evenings in the past. Tonight, the doorbell rang, and all three of them gasped.

The chime died after only a moment, as the battery needed to be replaced. The higher-pitched bell sank into a low buzz in a way that seemed like the sound was melting.

"That's him," Glory Rose whispered, her heartbeat suddenly a sprint through her veins.

Pearl Jo grinned, rushed toward the window, and peeked through the blinds. "Oh, it's definitely him, all right. And he's looking all cowboy-cool in his jeans and jacket."

"I'll get it," Fawn said, stepping past where Glory Rose had frozen.

Glory Rose took a deep breath, smoothing her sweater down one last time. "The sweater is really okay, Pearl Jo?"

Her cousin turned toward her. "Absolutely." She came over and pressed her cheek to Glory Rose's. "I'm too stinky to hug." She grinned as she stepped back. "Now, I'm going to go get an eyeful of Conrad too."

She left before Glory Rose could tell her not to do that, and Glory Rose stayed where she stood. Pearl Jo had a double name like her, and she was the oldest daughter of her daddy's other brother—Uncle Ace. She was definitely more outdoorsy than Glory Rose, and she wanted to earn degrees in animal science and agronomy. With the rotational ranching Glory Rose's daddy had incorporated here at Shiloh Ridge, the agronomy would be particularly useful at maintaining their crops.

Voices filtered back to her from the front of the cabin, as it wasn't a big space. Glory Rose had her own room, but she could barely take three steps in it. The bigger bedroom across the hall housed Fawn and Pearl Jo, and Glory Rose had never minded the smaller living space.

Her pulse sped even more as she took a deep breath and stepped out of the room. Only a couple of strides put her in the kitchen, and her gaze shot to the front door. Conrad stood inside the house, standing at least a head taller than both of her cousins.

Everything about him made Glory Rose's cells sing. His height, his broad shoulders, his dark hair under that deep, black, midnight cowboy hat. He wore a black leather jacket too, and Glory Rose's hand shot out to steady herself against the fridge beside her.

He held a small bouquet of wildflowers, and the sight made Glory Rose's legs feel like toothpicks that were unable to hold her upright.

His eyes came to hers, and his whole countenance brightened. "There she is."

Fawn and Pearl Jo turned toward her, but Glory Rose couldn't move. Fawn gestured at her with a low hand, and Glory Rose somehow got her feet to walk her closer to the door.

"Hey, Glory Rose." Conrad's voice came out soft and a

little shy. "These are for you." He held up the brightly colored wildflowers.

Glory Rose's smile widened as she took the yellow and orange blooms from him. "Thank you, Conrad. They're beautiful."

He nodded, his eyes lingering on her face for a moment before he cleared his throat. "You ready to go?"

"Yeah, just let me grab my jacket." She turned and reached for her coat, a soft blush creeping up her neck as she felt Conrad's eyes on her.

She handed the bouquet to Fawn, who said, "I'll put these in a vase for you."

"Thank you, Fawny." She gave her cousin a quick hug, then started to put on her jacket.

"Let me help you." Conrad's deep voice tickled all through her, and Glory Rose could scarcely believe this was even happening. She couldn't feel his skin as he helped her put on her jacket, but when their eyes met, pure lightning struck the cabin, struck her vocal cords hard enough to make her mute, struck so deep in her heart, she hoped Conrad could feel it too.

He blinked a couple of times, then reached for her hand with one of his while turning to open the door with the other. He led her outside into the cool February air. The sky had already darkened, and a shiver ran down her spine. Not from the cold, though. Oh, no. More like nerves, excitement, and the way she felt completely unsure of what to expect from the night.

Her skin sizzled where it touched his, and he adjusted his grip on her fingers. "It's good to see you," he said.

"Yeah," she said, feeling completely foolish afterward. Why had her tongue tied itself into a knot? She'd never had a problem talking to boys, and now that she'd become an adult, men. She'd danced with this cowboy last year at a birthday party and had never run out of things to say.

But now, her mind had gone completely blank.

She glanced up at Conrad, her heart doing somersaults in her chest. He didn't say anything, just gave her a small smile as he opened her door for her.

"Come on, Glory Rose," she muttered to herself as he rounded the hood to get behind the wheel. As he got in, she asked, "Who's got Sarina tonight?"

Conrad started his truck and adjusted the air vents as he said, "My mother."

She nodded, not sure why her insides felt like they'd been encased in ice.

"We had a birthday party for Sari this afternoon," Conrad said. "So she just kept her."

Glory Rose looked over to him. "Oh, is it her birthday?" Her pulse broke through the band of ice around her heart. "Conrad, we didn't need to go out on your daughter's birthday."

He rumbled down the tree-lined lane to the main road on the ranch. He glanced up toward the Top Cottage and then made the turn, the big blue family barn now on his left. "It's not her birthday today," he said. "It's actually on Wednesday, but I wanted everyone to be able to attend a party." He cleared his throat, and Glory Rose wondered if he had more to say.

But he didn't go on.

"Okay," she said. "Good." She immediately started thinking about what a little girl would like. "And she'll be three?"

"Yep."

So what would a three-year-old like? Glory Rose had grown up with a lot of children around her, as her daddy had four siblings and seven cousins, all of them living right here at the ranch—or very close to it. She could talk to Aunt Etta and find out what a three-year-old girl would absolutely love, and she started planning to stop by Conrad's farm and drop it off on Wednesday.

"So where are we going?" he asked. "I'm assuming out into the hills, maybe?" He turned to go past the main homestead and under the arch announcing the arrival at Shiloh Ridge Ranch. "Stargazing won't be in town, right?"

"Oh, right." Glory Rose dove into her purse to get her phone, and she tapped to get to the email her uncle had sent her. "This says...." She looked up and out the windshield. "We need to go to the Kingman's abandoned farm. It's that road—"

"Right up here," Conrad said with her.

"I know where it is." He flashed her a smile that made her stomach flip. "My cousins and siblings and I got in so much trouble at the Kingmans."

"Did you now?" Glory Rose tucked her phone away. "Doing what?"

"Oh, me and JJ would make up stories about how the barn

was haunted," he said with a chuckle. "Then tell all the younger kids about them, make them go out there when it was dark, that kind of stuff."

"I'm surprised my family didn't buy it ages ago," Glory Rose said. "They tend to do that—buy up land around Shiloh Ridge to add to the ranch."

"Yeah," Conrad said. "JJ did that last year with Seven Sons."

"It's not a bad expansion strategy."

"Maybe your daddy didn't think you guys had enough people in your family to take on the extra land." He threw her a smile that rose higher on the right than the left.

Glory Rose realized a couple of beats later that he was teasing her. *Flirting* with her. She burst out laughing, because no one would ever call the Glover family small.

"Must be right down here," he mused as he bumped along the dirt road. He drove a nice truck, and while he didn't always have a lot to say, Glory Rose liked his steadiness. She liked how safe she felt with him.

He pulled up next to another truck in the designated parking area, and he peered out the windshield. "The wind is not going to be kind tonight."

Glory Rose looked too, and sure enough, the few tree limbs she could see blew and blustered around. "I guess the tasting is here," she said, though she had no idea what kind of tasting someone could put on at an abandoned ranch. The barns and stables here surely didn't have commercial kitchens in them.

Strings of fairy lights had been hung from the single pole

in the lot, casting a soft glow over the area, and leading along a path, and as Glory Rose watched, another couple walked that way. "Looks like we go along the lights." She cast a quick look over to Conrad, who nodded.

Then he twisted, reached into the backseat, and pulled a blanket over the seat. "I brought this, just in case."

Glory Rose opened her door and slid from the truck, the fairy lights and a couple of floods on the corner of the barn not reaching that far into the night. The air entered her lungs in a cold way, but Glory Rose hunkered down into her coat and took in a long, deep breath of it. "It's so beautiful here," she said.

"Isn't it?" Conrad joined her, once again securing her hand in his. "Should we walk through the creepy buildings, trusting that those fairy lights aren't going to lead us to our deaths?"

Glory Rose looked at him, sure she'd find that glint in his dark eyes that would tell her he was joking. But she didn't find it. "You really think this might be nefarious."

"I can just see the headlines now," Conrad said. "Tourists and locals alike get lured to abandoned ranch and slain." He chuckled then, and Glory Rose relaxed. "I'd send up a drone to see what I was walking into, if it were up to me."

"Do you have a drone in your truck?" she asked.

He looked over to her. "No, ma'am, I don't."

"I'm twenty-three years old," she said. "You don't need to call me ma'am."

"What should I call you?"

"What do you mean?" Glory Rose stepped toward the pole with the lights, taking Conrad with her.

"Well, JJ calls Ruby by a bunch of cutesy nicknames. Maybe, I mean—maybe...." He trailed off, and Glory Rose sure enjoyed the flush that stained his cheeks. In the dimmer, yellow light, it almost looked orange.

"I love the stars," he said, effectively changing the subject, and Glory Rose didn't want to push him to come up with some cutesy nickname.

She smiled as warmth spread through her chest. "Me too. There's just something about the night sky that makes everything else seem smaller. Like all the worries in the world just fade away."

Conrad glanced at her, his expression softening. "Yeah. Just like that."

Around the corner of the front barn, the lights led them to a square of sorts—an open area surrounded by four buildings. A long table had been set up at the back of the barn, covered in trays of appetizers, desserts, and warm drinks. Glory Rose's stomach rumbled as the smell of freshly baked bread and roasted meats filled the air.

"You hungry?" Conrad asked, a small smile tugging at the corner of his mouth.

"Starving," Glory Rose admitted with a laugh. "I don't know if we just dive in, or what." She glanced around and found a woman taking tickets. "Conrad." She nodded in the direction of the woman, and he took her that way.

They got in line to show their tickets, and Glory Rose pulled them up on her phone from the forwarded email from

Uncle Bear. The woman looked at her phone and then her. "These are Bear Glover's?"

"Yes, ma'am," Glory Rose said, because this woman was at least as old as her mother.

She didn't scan the tickets. "This is an invite-only event."

"Oh." Glory Rose didn't know what to say.

"We curate our menu to those who RSVP."

"Uh." Her heartbeat accelerated, because she didn't know how to handle this situation. A crying, squirming baby, sure. She could soothe the infant enough to get the child to cooperate. But this? Uncle Bear hadn't told her anything more than this was a stargazing taste test.

"That's okay," Conrad said, stepping in front of her. "We don't feel like dying tonight anyway."

The woman looked at him, and her name snapped into place in Glory Rose's head. Camille Burke. "Dying tonight?"

Conrad gave her a swift smile. "Come on, Glory Rose. We'll go grab dinner somewhere else." He backed up a step and then turned, taking Glory Rose with him.

She went with him, expecting him to take her back to the truck. Instead, he walked along the buffet at the back of the barn, the scent of sweet-and-spicy barbecue sauce taunting her.

"Conrad," she hissed as they moved further and further from the lit square.

"Come on," he whispered, his hand firm around hers as he moved between the barn and a stable.

"Where are we going?" she whispered back, a thrill of excitement pulsing through her. In two more steps, she'd be alone in the dark with Conrad Walker. Her eyes adjusted with every step, and she could make out shapes now.

He rounded the far corner of the stable and paused, only darkness back here. "We were promised stargazing, so stargazing we will go."

"But...." Her protest faded as he grinned down at her, his face inches from hers. "Are we even allowed?" She drew in a deep breath of him, the scent of his cottony skin, his leather jacket, his woodsy cologne, very nearly causing intoxication.

"We make our own rules tonight." His lips brushed her earlobe, sending a shiver down to her toes. "So come on."

Chapter Three

Conrad could honestly hold Glory Rose on the dark side of the barn for a good, long while. But he tamped down those hormones, straightened, and let his heart pound with a mixture of excitement and nervousness as he faced the moonlight.

He couldn't believe he was actually doing this—sneaking away from an event they weren't supposed to be at in the first place. But something about Glory Rose made him want to be spontaneous, to show her a side of himself he rarely let anyone see.

"So what would they have made for your uncle Bear?"

Glory Rose scoffed, her hand so perfect in his. "Curated menu. Please, they had all the food sitting out. It's not like they'd have a plate just for him and Aunt Sammy."

Conrad smiled at the disconcertion in her voice. "You said you were starving. Maybe we should just go get pizza." He paused and turned back to her. "Or we can look at the stars for a few minutes."

"Stars first," she murmured, and Conrad ducked his head to make sure he didn't lead her off a cliff. "And if I get to pick what we eat for dinner, I want some really saucy Texas barbecue."

"Saucy Texas barbecue." Conrad chuckled. "I can probably manage that."

"*Really* saucy," Glory Rose said, and the path widened, so she came to his side.

Conrad led her up the slight incline, the old barn that he'd told the triplets was haunted on the right. "Hopefully, the loft floor won't have rotted." He sighed, sure he'd be calling an ambulance in the next fifteen minutes, and Camille Burke would know they didn't just leave. Then Conrad would have to deal with the police too.

And his parents.

And Grams.

As if he didn't already have the whole town looking at him.

He led her further into the darkness, away from the lights and chatter of the event. The night air was crisp and clean, filled with the scent of grass and earth. Conrad's boots crunched softly on the ground as he guided Glory Rose inside the barn and then up to the loft.

"Here we are," he said, spreading out the blanket he'd brought from his truck. "Our own private stargazing spot." He pushed open the hay doors to reveal the night sky, that big, bright moon hanging in the sky as if God had personally placed it there just for them.

"Wow." Glory Rose laughed softly as she settled onto the blanket, and he dropped down beside her. She reached over and took his hand. "You're full of surprises, aren't you?"

A flush crept up his neck. "I don't know about that," he murmured, suddenly feeling self-conscious and totally focused on the stars in the midnight blueness beyond the opening. He hadn't even asked her out for this "surprising" date.

His stomach grumbled, and his focus shifted to the feel of Glory Rose's slender fingers in his. "Your hands are cold," he said.

"A little." She looked over to him, and oh, Conrad could push the cowboy hat off his head and lean down, easily kissing her right here in the barn.

On an abandoned ranch.

On the first date.

Conrad swallowed and jerked his attention back out to the moonlight. "We won't stay long. I don't want my truck to get towed."

Glory Rose sighed happily and leaned her head against Conrad's arm. He sure liked that, because she made it seem like she couldn't get close enough to him. That he comforted her. That he could protect her.

He wanted all of those things, and he knew his mother or grandmother would take Sari any night of the week so he could go out with Glory Rose. JJ and Ruby would take her too. Any of the triplets, especially if all they had to do was show up at the farmhouse and let Grams feed them while Sari took a bath and then they put her to bed.

"What's your schedule like next week?" he asked, immediately clearing his throat.

"I work every day," she said. "My evenings are pretty free."

"So maybe we could go out again real soon." He couldn't believe he was asking before an hour had passed since he'd picked her up.

"Mm."

He sure didn't like the sound of that, and he had no idea what it meant. "If you don't want to, I—"

"I want to," Glory Rose said. "Conrad, I don't think it's any secret that I've had this crush on you for months."

"I mean, I haven't thought a lot about it," he muttered. The moment the words touched his lips, he wished he could recall them. "I mean, I've thought about you, Glory Rose. I just have so much other stuff going on right now."

"I know," Glory Rose said. "Plus, I had my birthday, so you're not too old for me now."

He looked over to her. "I never—"

"You told Jo you were too old for me." She gave him a pretty smile that made his pulse accelerate.

He grinned back at her. "You know what happens to me every year too?"

She searched his face, clearly confused, and Conrad leaned closer. Her smile slipped away as he whispered, "I have a birthday and get a year older too." He chuckled, and Glory Rose's grin came roaring back.

She bumped her shoulder against his. "So you're always going to be six years older than me, is that it?"

"Yep, that's it."

"Well, I still have a crush on the whole 'cowboy cool' thing you have going on."

Conrad's stomach twisted at her words. Cowboy cool? Was that how she saw him? He wasn't sure if he liked that or not. He didn't want to be some stereotype, especially not to Glory Rose.

"I'm just me," he said quietly, leaning back on his elbows to gaze up at the stars. "Nothing cool about that."

Glory Rose stayed quiet for a moment, and Conrad worried he'd said the wrong thing. But then she said, "I like just you, Conrad. You don't have to be anything else."

Her words warmed him from the inside out, but a nagging voice in the back of his mind whispered, *She deserves someone better. Someone who isn't so damaged.*

He pushed the thought away, determined to enjoy this moment with Glory Rose. "So, the triplets and I used to come here and lay back like this." He turned around, flashed a smile at her and laid back, his head almost all the way out of the window.

"It scared Elaine. She's always been the most cautious out of all of us."

Glory Rose turned around and lay down beside him, and this time, Conrad reached over and threaded his fingers through hers. "My cousin Pearl Jo is the daredevil in my family."

Conrad laughed, the stars a little brighter with Glory Rose at his side. "So, what do you see up there?"

"There's the Big Dipper, of course," she said, pointing. "And over there, that's Orion's Belt."

Conrad nodded, following her finger. "My dad taught me about the constellations when I was a kid," he said. "He'd take us out to the edge of the ranch, we'd set up a tent, and as the triplets ran around and Daddy made a Dutch oven dinner, I'd just...look at the stars."

"That sounds wonderful," Glory Rose said softly. "My family never really did things like that. The Glovers are so big, and my daddy was one of the foremen. We did a lot of things with my Uncle Ace and Uncle Ranger. And of course, Uncle Preacher—he still works as one of the foremen."

"Your daddy doesn't?"

"He's in semi-retirement. He's phasing out a lot of what he does to some of my cousins."

"So you never did anything with just your core family?" Conrad came from a big family too—not as big as the Glovers, of course, but plenty of aunts and uncles and cousins bore the Walker last name.

"We'd go to movies on our birthdays," she said, the happiness riding in her voice. "My momma would let us get all the candy and popcorn and soda pop we wanted." She laughed lightly. "Which is a big deal, because my momma's diabetic."

"Sounds fun." He breathed in the beauty of the night sky, the stars he loved so well. "I've always been the outlier in my core family. Sort of comes with the territory when all of your younger siblings are triplets."

She squeezed his hand. "My aunt says we all feel like we're the outlier," she said. "She says that Satan wants us to feel like that, and that God wants us to be His and belong to Him and come to Him."

Conrad let what she'd said sink into his ears, then his heart. "I'm sure she's right. I like your aunt's sermons."

Glory Rose turned her head toward him, and he did the same to meet her gaze. "I sometimes feel lost in the shuffle of Glovers, the same way you probably feel insignificant among your Walkers."

"Yeah," he whispered, unable to look away from the beautiful dark depths of her eyes. "Tell me you don't judge me."

She blinked. "Why would I judge you?"

"Because my daughter will be three on Wednesday," he said. "And I didn't know she existed until last summer."

"I can't imagine how hard that must have been for you," she said softly. "Finding out you had a daughter you never knew about."

Conrad swallowed hard, fighting back the emotions that threatened to overwhelm him. "It turned my whole world upside down," he said. "But Sarina's the best thing in my life."

Glory Rose's smile was soft and understanding. "She's lucky to have you as her dad, Conrad." She looked skyward again. "I don't judge you. When you grow up in a family as big as mine, there are lessons about second and third and fourth chances, trust me."

They fell into a comfortable silence, and Conrad let his mind wander as he gazed up at the stars. He became hyper-aware of Glory Rose's presence beside him—the warmth of her body, the soft sound of her breathing, the faint scent of her perfume.

He wanted to pull her close, to kiss her under the starry sky. The nagging voice in his head reminded him of all the reasons that was a bad idea. *She's too young. Too innocent. You're not good enough for her. She's a Glover, and they're all amazing.*

"Hungry?" he asked. "Saucy Texas barbecue is calling my name."

She grinned and sat up. "Me too."

He groaned as he sat up, and he took Glory Rose's hand to help him get to his feet. Then he grabbed the blanket and folded it before he led the way out of the barn. "I think we can get down to the parking lot without going back to the tasting."

"I'm sorry," she said, her hand in his tight as he led her down a semi-steep path toward the parking lot. "I promised you dinner, and we didn't even get in."

"Not your fault," he said. "And hey, we got the stargazing —as promised—and dinner will be amazing." His boots finally touched the gravel in the parking lot, and he managed to smile over to her. "Do you have a favorite barbecue place in mind?"

She swung their joined hands back and forth. "You know what, Mister Walker? I'm going to let you choose the barbecue joint."

"This sounds like I'm being set up." He reached to open her door, easily sliding his hand out of hers and along her waist. "You really want me to pick?"

Glory Rose put her palm against his chest and smiled at

him like he held all the joy in the world. "Yep. You pick. I trust your taste buds."

With that, she climbed into the truck, and Conrad simply stared at her for a moment. Then he snapped back to himself, shut the door, and headed around the tailgate, whispering, "A little help here, Lord, would be much appreciated."

After all, he hadn't dated in years, and never with a daughter waiting for him at home. So he'd take all the help he could get, especially if it came from On High.

Chapter Four

Glory Rose reached out with her fork to take another bite of the chopped brisket in the middle of the table. "Tell me your favorite song," she said, really enjoying being with Conrad and learning more about him.

"You're asking me to pick just one?" He carried plenty of flirtation in his voice, the way he had since they'd left the stargazing behind. He didn't seem to have a problem talking to her, or women in general, and he told her to order whatever she wanted at Better Barbecue.

"Yes," she said. "If you have to listen to one song for the rest of your life, which one would it be?"

"Now I have to pick one to listen to for the rest of my life?" He chuckled and reached for his peach iced tea. He took a drink, his dark eyes never leaving hers.

Glory Rose finally broke their connection by dropping her chin so she could squirt some more of the sweet with heat barbecue sauce on her plate. She liked this man too much, she knew, and she had a cacophony of voices in her head telling her to slow down, to be gentle, not to come on too strong.

Her momma, Aunt Sammy, Pearl Jo, Fawn—even Link and Smiles had their voices in there telling her that yes, Conrad was great, but she had a long way to go before she'd really know him and would really know if she could spend the rest of her life loving him.

A surface crush sure was fun, though.

"Well, I suppose it would be something by Alan Taylor," he said. "That man can pick a mean guitar."

She wrinkled her nose as she brought her brisket to her mouth. She took the bite while his eyebrows went up.

"You don't like Alan Taylor?" he asked. "How is that even possible? He's, like, the most popular country music star in the world."

She finished her bite of brisket and shrugged one shoulder. "He's always talking about dogs dyin' and leavin' his girlfriend behind," she drawled out.

Conrad folded his arms, the teasing quality of his eyes the highest she'd ever seen. "All right then," he said. "What's *your* favorite song?"

"I just want to point out that you did not pick a favorite song." Glory Rose grinned at him, feeling like she was made of stardust and glitter. "You chose an artist."

"Choose an artist," he said. "Can't be as good as Alan Taylor."

"Taylor Swift," she said.

Conrad scoffed, then coughed as if he'd swallowed wrong,

and he rolled his eyes and his whole head. "Taylor Swift." He might as well have put six question marks at the end of his sentence. "She's great and all, but there ain't no way I'm listening to a Taylor Swift song for the rest of my life."

Glory Rose laughed because she wouldn't really pick Taylor Swift. She just really liked teasing Conrad.

"All right, all right," she said. "Your favorite food, then. One thing you have to eat for the rest of your life."

"The *only* thing, or just one thing every day?"

She said, "You have to eat it every day."

He picked up the container of sweet pea salad that had come as one of their sides. "It would be this salad," he said. "I love this stuff." He pushed it closer. He set it down closer to her. "There's only a little bit left. Do you want it?"

Warmth emanated through Glory Rose with the power of the sun, and then the sun's twin. He loved that sweet pea salad, and he wanted her to have the last of it.

"You can have it," she said. "Though I do like it."

"What's your favorite food?" he asked.

He pulled the container closer to him and picked up his plastic spoon to eat the rest of it. "I am so full. I don't know why I'm eating this." Then he put a bite in his mouth.

Glory Rose felt sure that the grin on her face would stay there permanently for the next several weeks. A simple thought of this conversation and this dinner and this date would bring it back, and she'd never have another bad day in her life.

"I'm gonna go with pepperoni pizza," she said. "Pan style, extra cheese, with a little sprinkling of oregano."

Conrad grinned at her. "How very specific, Miss Glory Rose."

"It's my favorite food," she said. "I could literally eat it every day."

"Good to know."

She sat back and placed one hand on her stomach because she'd eaten far too much as well. "All right," she said. "I guess we better head out."

Conrad looked at her. "Oh, yeah?"

She leaned forward, not sure if she should be glad his focus was only on her or worried that he didn't seem to notice anything around him. "They closed twenty minutes ago, Conrad. We're the only ones here." She glanced over to the woman standing at the till. "I think she might actually stab us with plastic forks if we don't leave soon."

Conrad looked over to the manager as well and scooted to the end of the bench at their booth. "I didn't even notice," he said. "I'll get us a box."

"We don't need a box," she said.

"Oh, I'll take that home and feed it to my dogs."

"You have dogs?" she asked as she stood too.

"Be right back," he called over his shoulder, and he hurried over to the till to pay. He came back with a box, where he loaded everything extra from their meat sampler, and then took her hand in his before heading for the door.

Once they were free of the restaurant—and the very loud lock clicking into place sounded behind them—Glory Rose dissolved into giggles. "Did she have any plastic forks on her?" she whispered as they hurried toward his truck.

"I didn't see any," he said. "But let's hurry just to be safe."

She loved this carefree, wild, flirty feeling, and she let him open her door so that she could step up into his truck. He joined her only a minute later, and they left the barbecue joint in their rearview mirror.

"I have three dogs," he said. "They work the farm with me."

"But you don't have cattle, right?"

"Nope, no cattle." He drove casually with one hand on the steering wheel and the other resting on the console.

She reached over and took his hand, tracing her fingertip along the top of his fingernail. "Your hands aren't nearly as rough as my daddy's."

"My farm is far smaller than Shiloh Ridge." He glanced over to her. "Grams feeds the chickens and turkeys while I get the goats in the milking shed. We've got electric milkers for that. Most of my time is taken up with the mini donkeys."

"Oh, yes. I know about those donkeys."

"Sarina is getting real good at gathering the eggs," he said. "I got her a padded basket." He smiled to himself, and Glory Rose sure did like the sight of it.

"That's amazing," Glory Rose said. She wasn't sure if she should or could ask the next question, but she told herself that if she wanted to truly get to know Conrad, she should be able to ask. And if he didn't want to answer, that was his choice.

"Doesn't sound like full-time work," she said casually.

He chuckled and shook his head. "That it is not. I mean, it was for my grandpa. Just taking care of his forty mini donkeys could eat up his whole day."

She felt like he put a light bulb inside her and switched it on. "I remember my family chuckling about his love of mini donkeys," she said. "Do you miss him?"

"Every day," Conrad said seriously. "Every single day." He drew in a deep breath, held it for a moment, and then exhaled it all out. "I bought the farm from my grandparents so that I could help them with it," he said. "My daddy and uncles and I were going over there all the time anyway. I wasn't in school or anything, and it's been a real blessing to be there for my grams since Gramps died."

"I bet it has been." Glory Rose adjusted her hand in his and squeezed. "I really, truly believe it has been."

He nodded as they left the lights of small town Three Rivers behind and headed down the highway toward the hills where Shiloh Ridge sat.

"Anyway," he said. "We raise a couple pigs each year. We have a turkey for Thanksgiving. Grams has me plant a big garden that she mostly takes care of, but she can't plant or harvest it. It's a good life."

"Almost like homesteading," she said.

"Oh, I would die homesteading," Conrad said with a chuckle. "I need reliable power and water. And I sure like having indoor plumbing."

"There are homesteads with those things," Glory Rose said. "I really like the idea of living off-grid."

"Have you ever done it?" he asked, and he didn't seem judgmental or dismissive.

"No," she said. "Not really. But it feels like something I would like."

"It's really rewarding growing your own food," he said. "I do like that—the gardening, the animals."

"We have so many animals at Shiloh Ridge," Glory Rose said, a dry quality to her voice now. "My daddy implemented rotational ranching, so we have every kind of animal imaginable. They help us turn over our fields faster."

"Yeah, I went up there in high school," Conrad said. "Your aunts run an outreach program to teach people about that— rotational ranching, cattle ranching, business stuff, all that. I took that class."

Glory Rose nodded, because Aunt Etta and Aunt Ida still ran the outreach programs for the FFA at the high school in Three Rivers. In fact, Aunt Etta had met her husband through an elementary school field trip to show the kids around the ranch.

"You don't work the ranch, though, right?" Conrad asked.

"No, sir," she said. "I'm a pediatric nurse in town."

"So you're making that drive every day?"

"For now," she said. "I'm thinking about getting a place in town, but rent is really expensive. And I've already put in my year at Shiloh Ridge so I can live there for free."

"Wow, that's nice," Conrad said. "I didn't know your family did that."

"We have to live on and work the ranch for a year," Glory Rose said, as she watched the night sky blur past her passenger window. "We get paid the same as a regular cowhand so that we learn what it really takes to get by. That was not an easy year of my life."

She wasn't sure how much Conrad knew about her

family, but Shiloh Ridge had been in the news plenty of times, and it seemed that everyone in Three Rivers knew they were wealthy. Of course, it wasn't like the Walkers were hurting for money either, though she wasn't entirely sure of Conrad's financial situation.

He didn't ask her about hers, and Glory Rose felt content about all the things that she'd asked him that evening, so she simply let the silence settle between them, wondering how it would feel.

The next thing she knew, cold air swept along her face, along with the warm touch of human hands. "Glory Rose, sugar," Conrad said softly. "We're back."

Her eyes flew open, and Glory Rose could hardly believe that she'd fallen asleep. "Oh, my goodness," she said, sitting up so fast her seatbelt locked. "I fell asleep. I didn't mean to fall asleep."

Her eyes met his as she tried to untangle herself from the seatbelt. "I'm so sorry."

He gave her the most beautiful grin in the world and said, "It's fine, Glory Rose. You must have had a busy day." He reached across her and pressed the seatbelt button to release her.

"Come on now. I'll walk you up to the door." He reached for her hand, and she gave it to him as she slid from the truck.

"I'm so embarrassed," she said. The cool February air felt like ice shards against her heated skin.

"It's fine, sugar," he said. Then he cleared his throat.

Glory Rose thought about kissing him, and something inside her warned her not to do it. She'd kissed on the first date before, and she had a feeling that Conrad needed to go a little bit slower than that, so she stopped at the bottom of the three steps that led up to the front door, as the cement pad there would barely hold both of them.

"Thank you so much, Conrad," she said. "I'm so glad we finally got to go out."

"Me too," he murmured, and in one swift movement, Glory Rose tipped up onto her toes and kissed his cheek. "I'd love to go out with you again, so let me know when you're free."

"Yep," he said, as she tiptoed up the steps. "I'll call you."

"Oh, you don't have to call," she said, with all of the flirtation back in her voice. "You can just text."

He chuckled and ducked his head. He pressed his palm to the top of his hat and said, "All right. Well, I sure had a good time tonight. I'll talk to you later."

He lifted his eyes to hers, and Glory Rose nodded quickly before she ducked inside the dark cabin. With her back pressed against the door, she twisted the lock and sighed the happiest sigh of her life.

She really hoped Conrad would text her again for another date. As she pushed away from the door to go brush her teeth and go to bed, she told herself sternly, "You will not ask him out. You will let him ask you next time."

She'd tell Fawn and Pearl Jo, and they'd hold her to it.

As she knelt down to say her prayers that night, she thanked the Good Lord above for Conrad Walker and that she'd finally, finally gotten her first date with him. Then she quickly asked, "If it wouldn't be too much, Lord, please,

please, let him call me again. I like him so much, and I would love to go out with him again."

She'd have to tell her momma about this date and that she'd been the one to initiate it, and her parents wouldn't be happy about it. But as Glory Rose finished up her prayer and got beneath her covers, it was reaffirmed to her that she was an adult.

She didn't have to do everything her momma and daddy said. "And maybe if he doesn't ask you out again": she whispered into the darkness. "It won't matter."

So she'd wait until Conrad did ask her out on a second date, and *then* she'd tell her parents.

Chapter Five

"All right, sweets." Conrad scooped Sarina into his arms. "How many eggs you got? Let's count them."

She held the padded basket in both hands, and Conrad balanced the bottom of it against her thigh. As she released her left hand, he put his over hers and guided her to the first egg. "One. Now you say it, baby."

"One," Sarina said. "Two."

"That's right, two," he said, and he moved her finger to the next egg. "Three," he said, and she didn't respond. He waited for her, and she said, "Twee."

"Four...."

"Four."

"Five...."

"Five," she repeated.

"Six." His voice pitched up on that number, and she did the exact same thing as she said, "Six."

She looked up at him, and he grinned at her. "That's right, sweets, six eggs."

"Six eggs," Sarina said, and she wiggled to get down. He balanced her on her feet and let her take the basket.

"Take them to the deck," he called as she started toddle-running away from him. Love filled him from top to bottom, and he did think about what Glory Rose had said about home-steading. He and Grams ate eggs almost every day, even on days when they only got six of them. Sarina loved scrambled eggs, and Conrad could eat eggs-in-a-frame for breakfast, lunch, and dinner.

"So maybe that's your favorite food," he mused to himself, his thoughts on Glory Rose. They often strayed there, and he'd texted her plenty of times over the last several days. In fact, they had a lunch date set up tomorrow as Sarina had a speech therapy class at the hospital and Glory Rose worked at a doctor's office only a couple blocks away.

Conrad had been sitting in on Sarina's appointments, but this one was to be an assessment. Now that she'd been doing the therapy for several months, they didn't want him in the room to influence her.

His heart beat faster for a couple of seconds as he thought about turning her over to perfect strangers to do a speech assessment. Then he reminded himself that they weren't strangers; Sarina worked with these ladies every week, and she knew them.

He followed Sarina off the farm at a much slower pace, and he pulled out his phone to text Glory Rose.

We still on for tomorrow at lunch? he asked. *I can pick it up before I get there, so we don't have to wait.*

My lunch hour is all yours, Glory Rose said, a smile and a thumbs up following it. Conrad grinned at her text because he never used emojis and she always did. As he scrolled up through their many exchanged messages, he found some sort of happy, cheerful, rainbow-like icon in every single one.

He wanted to silence his phone and tuck it away for the rest of the day, but he knew he couldn't. "You're not going to text her and tell her that you're a billionaire," he muttered to himself. "Or that you're a wealth manager for all of your billionaire siblings and cousins and aunts and uncles." That was a conversation he needed to have face-to-face.

But it didn't necessarily have to happen on the second date.

What *did* have to happen today was a phone call to Chloe.

Conrad sighed as he climbed a few steps to the deck and sat at the top. "Sweets, come on over here," he called to Sarina, who had put down her eggs on the bottom step leading up to the deck, and then gone over to the sandbox he'd put in for her. He whistled through his teeth, though he knew his daughter had heard him. "Come on now," he called, and he gestured for her to come closer.

His whistle and those words in that gesture always got his dogs to come, and while he certainly didn't think of Sarina as a dog, it did the same thing for little girls. His daddy had always called the kids in from somewhere out on the ranch or their big piece of property with a whistle and a gesture. Conrad supposed it wasn't the worst thing he'd picked up from his father.

"We're gonna call your momma," Conrad said, as Sarina approached. "It's your birthday. She'll want to see you."

"A birf-day, birf-day," Sarina sang as she climbed the steps in a painstakingly slow way.

"Come on, baby doll." He picked her up and settled her on his lap, then he tapped to video-call Chloe. He'd done the same thing at Christmas, on Thanksgiving, and for Halloween, so that she could see what Sarina had dressed up as—one of her favorite cartoon characters from a TV show she loved.

He had to talk to Chloe plenty, though it wasn't nearly as much as if they lived in the same place and he had to take Sarina back and forth to her house all the time. He texted her things Sarina said or did that he thought she might want to know, and he sent her pictures, and he texted to arrange times to do video calls so that he wouldn't interrupt Chloe at work.

It wasn't lost on him that she was a nurse too, and it took her several seconds to answer. When she did, she wore light violet scrubs.

"Hey," she said.

Conrad smiled at her. "Hey, there," he said. "We're just calling because it's Sarina's birthday." As if she didn't know.

"Mom-ma, Mom, Mom-ma," Sarina said, and she waved both hands at Chloe while they both grinned and grinned.

"Hey, baby girl," Chloe's voice pitched up, ripe with emotion, and Conrad focused the phone on Sarina because that was who Chloe wanted to see. She asked her questions, and Sarina answered the best she could. Conrad filled in the blanks for anything else, and twelve minutes later, he lifted the phone to his own face and said, "Let me put her down. I want to talk to you for a second, okay?"

He twisted and set Sarina on her feet. "Go ring the bell, baby. Grams will let you in." She ran off to do that, and Conrad waited until Grams had exclaimed about the many eggs she'd found and closed the door behind her.

Conrad looked at Chloe again and found her wiping her eyes. "She's doing so good, Conrad," Chloe said. "Thank you so much for taking such good care of her."

"Of course," Conrad said. "And I don't need you to thank me. She's my daughter."

Chloe sniffled and nodded. She wouldn't look at him.

"You're doing okay?" he asked, his own emotions making his voice tight. "You don't need anything?"

That brought her eyes to his, an edge in them now that he didn't like. "You don't need to send us any more money," Chloe said.

"Yeah, but I can," Conrad said.

"I'm gonna send it right back," Chloe said, and she leaned closer to the phone. "I mean it, Conrad. You've helped enough; more than enough."

He nodded, his throat tight. "I wish—"

There were so many things he wished. Things could have been so different if Chloe had told him she was pregnant. She maybe wouldn't be separated from her daughter, and Conrad wouldn't have missed two and a half years of Sarina's life.

"Just like you say I don't need to thank you, I'm telling you, Conrad, we don't need any more money."

He nodded and looked over the top of the phone. "All right," he said, trying to make his voice light and airy the way Glory Rose did. "You'll let me know if you do?"

He didn't think she would, but Chloe said, "Yeah, I'll let you know if we do. Thanks for calling, Conrad."

"Yep, talk to you later." He lowered the phone and ended the call, and he wished fifteen minutes and forty-three seconds didn't take so much from him. But he knew exactly how to bury all of the things he was worried about, everything that upset him, and anything that didn't seem quite right in his life.

He got up and went in the house, where Grams had set Sarina in her eating seat while she made breakfast.

"I'm going to work in the office this morning," he said. "And all afternoon."

"All right," Grams said pleasantly.

"I can be interrupted anytime," he said. "I'm just doing easy stuff."

"Sounds good." Grams didn't let her gaze linger on him, and Conrad was glad for that.

"I'll bring breakfast in," she called after him, and Conrad took the stairs two at a time up to the second level of the farmhouse. His office on the main level had been converted into Sarina's bedroom so that the three of them could live in the trio of bedrooms on the main floor.

There were three more bedrooms upstairs, and Conrad really enjoyed his office on the back side of the house that overlooked the farm. He could see the herd of mini donkeys, his goats, his chickens and turkeys, and his two milk cows.

Grams would not bring breakfast up the stairs, but the house had a dumbwaiter, and she'd text him when she put the food in that, and he'd pull it up, get it out in the hall, and eat while he went through this month's numbers.

"What an exciting life you have," he whispered to himself as he sat down at his big desk and picked up the top folder sitting there. His past-self always did his present-self a favor by making sure the files and items that he needed to do that day were sitting right in front of his chair, in the order he needed to do them.

So when he flipped open the folder and saw Uncle Tripp's portfolio sitting there, Conrad knew exactly what to do.

He wished that every part of his life could be as easy as pulling numbers, checking stocks, and making financial decisions. He could do those things like clockwork, even in his sleep, and he never doubted himself. His gut always told him the right thing to do when it came to investments and stock portfolios and managing money.

But boy, it sure would be nice to know what to do when it came to being Sarina's father and possibly Glory Rose's boyfriend.

* * *

Hours later, after darkness had fallen and Sarina had finally gone to sleep in her car seat, Conrad drove the streets of

Three Rivers. He'd learned from his mother to put Sarina in the car and drive around at night when she wouldn't settle down. Apparently, Momma had done that with the triplets, especially Elaine, who had always been the most high-strung of the Walkers in Conrad's branch of the family.

Sarina had tripped outside on the farm tonight. She'd gotten a splinter in her palm. Her anguished cries still filled Conrad's soul, though he had gotten the splinter out, kissed it better, and given her a cartoon character band-aid to make everything good. She'd sniffled and hiccupped in his lap for a good long time, and she cried and cried when he tried to put her down in her bed.

So he'd hugged her close and brought her out to the car, sang her favorite lullabies, and drove around town. She'd fallen asleep about twenty minutes ago, but now Conrad wasn't ready to go home and go to bed.

He turned the corner and saw the little white church with the stained-glass windows where he'd attended services his whole life. Lights shone out the front windows, and he put his blinker on and pulled into the parking lot. He hadn't been planning to come to the church, and he wasn't even sure why he'd stopped now. And he'd have to get Sarina out and take her inside?

What was he doing?

He continued on for a reason he couldn't name, other than it felt like the right thing to do. He gathered his little girl in his arms, and she didn't wake up. Then he headed inside the church, expecting to find people there for a function, an event, or a rehearsal. Inside, music rang through the air, so someone sat at the organ.

He entered the chapel just as the last notes played, and he found only Willa and Cactus Glover in the room. He'd made no noise, but they somehow knew that he had arrived as they both turned toward him.

Willa sat on the bench of the organ, so it was Cactus who made the first move toward him. "Hey there, son," he said, lifting one hand in a friendly wave.

Conrad certainly couldn't turn tail and run now, so he went down the aisle between the pews to the front of the chapel. "I'm sorry," he said. "I don't know why I came in. I didn't mean to interrupt."

Willa stood from the bench and went to her husband's side. "It's fine, Conrad," she said. "We're just finishing up one of the songs we're going to be playing at the Easter services."

Conrad nodded, though he had no idea when Easter was. Coming up, he was sure. In his arms, Sarina whined and started to stir. "I should go."

"Oh, come talk to me first," Pastor Glover said.

"I'll take her," Cactus said, and he stepped into Conrad and easily took Sarina into his arms. As the little girl woke, she whimpered for a moment, and then she curled into the other cowboy's big chest.

"See, we're best friends already." He smiled at Conrad, who had no choice but to go with Pastor Glover now.

"It'll just be a few minutes, sweetheart," she said, and she limped out of the side door, clearly expecting Conrad to simply go with her. After a moment of wondering if he could really leave his little girl with Cactus Glover, he scampered after the pastor. Of course he could. He left Sarina with dozens of people, and the fact that she'd settled right back to sleep without crying against the strange man's chest, told Conrad that she was just fine.

He caught Pastor Glover just as she turned into another doorway, and he lengthened his stride so that he wouldn't be too far behind her.

"There's no one else here," she said. "But you can still close the door if you'd like."

"It's fine," he mumbled as he took one of the chairs in front of her desk. "I really don't know why I came."

Willa settled into her chair too and folded her arms on her desk in front of her. He expected her to say something, to maybe launch into a sermon, to tell him exactly what he needed to know and understand. But she didn't. She sat there silently, a neutral expression on her face while she waited for *him* to say something.

Conrad had never felt so uncomfortable. And he had no idea how to spill all of his sins out loud. Of course, he'd told her brother about some of them, and he'd been working with Pastor Knowlton to get back to a place where he felt like he'd completed the repentance process. He had no idea if Pastor Knowlton had shared anything with his sister as they ran the congregation here on the south side of Three Rivers together.

"How do you know...?" he started, not quite sure how to finish.

Pastor Glover tilted her head and continued to wait.

"How do you know when you've been forgiven of something?" Conrad finally asked.

"Mm." Pastor Glover nodded. "How does the Lord talk to you?" she asked.

"Are you asking me personally, or are you asking me for a general answer?"

"You personally," she said.

"Well, I mean, I guess it's sort of like this feeling," he said. "Like, if I'm not really sure what to do in my life, and I've been praying for help, then I just sort of know. It's just like this feeling, this good...feeling that I have." He ducked his head and shook it. "Honestly, sometimes it sounds like my mother's voice." He looked up again, feeling vulnerable and so weak. "But it's not really a voice. There's no sound," he said. "It's just a feeling."

Pastor Glover nodded, a smile coming to her face. "I get feelings like that a lot."

"So will I just feel that I've been forgiven...maybe?"

"Where do you feel it?"

"In my heart," he said. "It just sort of burns in my chest."

The pastor reached toward the corner of her desk and tapped the book there, the Holy Bible. "When we want to talk to God, we pray," she said. "When we want God to talk to us, we can read the scriptures." She picked up the Bible and set it in front of her, and she gazed at it with a fond look on her face. "It could be, Conrad, that the words that you need to see and hear have already been said." She looked up, her gaze intense and powerful. "They may already be in the scriptures."

Conrad's first inclination was to dismiss her, that it absolutely couldn't be true, that ancient records from thousands of years ago could not hold the answers that he sought today. And yet, that burning feeling in his chest whispered that she might just be right.

"I haven't read the scriptures in a while," he admitted.

"Ah." She smiled and lifted her hands from the Bible. "Well, there's my challenge to you then. Read the scriptures, just a little bit every day. I'm not even asking you to study them. Just read something from Holy Writ every day, and I can promise you that the answer that you want—and that you need—will be there."

Conrad nodded, but he wasn't one-hundred-percent sure he believed her. "I'm not even sure I have a Bible," he said.

"Oh, you don't need one," she said, almost dismissively. "You've got a phone, right?" She smiled at him. "I know you've got a phone. Everyone your age has a phone, and you have a million apps on it. All you need to do is put on the Scripture app. You can have it read aloud to you while you feed your mini donkeys."

He chuckled, and she did too. Conrad got to his feet. Pastor Glover did too, and she limped around her desk to him, but he wasn't sure if he should shake her hand or hug her, and he drew her into an embrace that was only awkward for a moment.

"Thank you," he whispered. "And really, I'm sorry I just dropped by. Sarina was restless, and I needed to drive her to sleep."

"God leads us right where we need to be," Pastor Glover said. "I knew it would only be a few minutes." She released him and nodded, and Conrad ducked out of her office to go get his daughter.

He had no idea what, if anything, Glory Rose had shared with her family about their date over the weekend or their upcoming lunch tomorrow. He had no idea how close she was to Cactus and Willa Glover. He wasn't even sure if he and Glory Rose would make it much past the third or fourth or fifth date.

He wanted to. He hoped for such a thing. But life was twisted and complicated, and he knew that now better than ever. And he also knew that the Lord answered prayers in more ways than one.

Sometimes He put a feeling into Conrad's heart; sometimes a thought would pop into his head. Sometimes his momma or daddy would say something that rang true in Conrad's mind, and sometimes He led lonely fathers to lit-up churches on dark nights.

So as Conrad collected Sarina and put her back in her car seat and headed home, he vowed, "If thou will keep guiding my feet, I will keep walking in Thy way."

And he hoped that his path would also lead him alongside Glory Rose Glover.

Chapter Six

"Oh, this is not fair," Glory Rose said as she entered the waiting room of the pediatrician's office where she worked. Conrad stood there, a white box in his hand.

"What's not fair?" he asked.

"Look at you," she said, as she stopped. "You're wearing those sexy dark wash jeans and that polo." She spread her arms wide and turned in a circle. "Look at me. I'm wearing the ugliest mint green scrubs on the planet."

"I don't care what you're wearing," Conrad said with a smile. "You look great to me."

The receptionist cleared her throat, and Glory Rose grinned over to her. "Be back in a little bit, Melinda."

"Enjoy your lunch," she said suggestively.

Conrad turned toward the door, and Glory Rose went to his side. "Not sure where we can eat," he said. "There's a park a couple blocks over."

"What about the gardens at the hospital?" she asked. "I told you I'd meet you there."

"I think I panicked," Conrad said, and that made Glory Rose giggle.

"You panicked about what?"

"Second date," he said with a shrug of one of his shoulders. "It's a big deal."

"Is it?"

"Well, I haven't been on one in several years," he said. "So yeah, it's a big deal."

Glory Rose didn't want to make light of something that he thought was a big deal. So she said, "Well, we could eat on the tailgate of your truck. I'm fine with that too."

"I didn't know there were gardens at the hospital," he said. "Are they indoor or outdoor?"

"They can open the roof," she said. "But my guess is they have it closed today." She looked up into the sky, and it was a flat gray with the sun trying to break through in places and not really succeeding. So the tailgate would be a cold lunch date.

"We can eat in my truck," he said. "If you give me a minute to fix it up."

"Fix it up?"

"Yeah, I can turn the seats around in the front and we can put the seat down in the back and kind of use it as a table. Give me two seconds."

"Two seconds you shall have," she said, and she went to the passenger side and got in while he put Sarina's carseat in the truck bed and then lowered the bench seat in the back.

He said, "You gotta get out while I rotate the seats."

"Okay." She slid down to the ground again, and Conrad reached into the truck and pushed a button. To her delight and wonder, both bucket seats in the front started to turn. The leather made squeaking sounds against the console, and she thought for a moment that it would catch and not complete the rotation, and then it did.

"There we go," Conrad said. "You can actually get in the back seat now."

"I can see that," Glory Rose said. She closed that door, opened the back passenger door, and climbed up into the seat that now faced the back. "This is incredible. Did your truck come like this?"

"Sure did." He climbed in and set the white box on the "table" in front of them. "I got it from your aunt." He grinned at her with pure sparkle coming from his eyes. "Surely you remember she used to own the motorsports arena." He raised his eyebrows and looked over her. "She's still pretty connected in the car world, and she gets access to prototypes and new stuff all the time."

"Mm, yes, Aunt Oakley. She's a former Formula One driver, you know."

"Oh, I know. My brothers and daddy and I are huge fans of Formula One." He grinned at her and reached to open the box. "This is a truck that GMC makes only for Texas, and I'm pretty sure there's only four of them in the whole world right now."

"Wow," Glory Rose said.

"That's incredible, right?" Conrad opened the box and started pulling out sandwiches and chips and salads. "We've got potato salad today," he said. "Potato chips, turkey sand-wiches on potato rolls." And he lifted a clamshell container of chocolate cake.

"Oh, a cowboy after my own heart," Glory Rose teased as she reached for the cake.

"That's made with potato flakes, I'll have you know," he said. "Apparently, when you go to the Spudalicious, every-thing they make has potatoes in it somehow."

"It's a great place," she said.

"I learned about it from Dawson Reinhart," Conrad said. "You know the Reinharts, right?"

"Oh, yeah, we know the Reinharts," Glory Rose said. "Duke is my uncle. Married to Arizona."

"Oh, duh. Of course." Conrad offered her a plastic fork, and then he twisted and said, "I bet we can even have some music with our lunch." He got the radio playing low—on country, of course—his beloved Alan Taylor picking the guitar in the background. "Oh yeah," he said. "This is the best second date ever."

He smiled at her, and Glory Rose returned it. "Feeling pretty confident already, huh? The hour's just begun."

"So far so good," he said. "As my daddy says." He started to unwrap his sandwich. "Do you work in the hospital some-times? Or how did you know there are gardens there?"

"There are about five million kids in the Glover family," she said as she forked up another bite of chocolate cake. "And we'd go to the hospital every time a new one was born. I'm one of the older ones, so to give us something to do when we were little kids, my momma or daddy or one of my aunts or uncles would take all of us to the gardens. It would burn at least an hour." She smiled at him.

"Mm." He nodded as he took a big bite of his turkey sandwich.

"So Sarina is getting her speech evaluation done today?" she asked.

He nodded as he chewed, and when he swallowed, he said, "Yep, she's been going for six months now, and she turned three, so they want to see how she's doing."

"They might move her to a dedicated team now that she's three."

"Yeah, that's what we're hoping," Conrad said. "I think she's been doing great. She says way more words than she used to, and I can get her to repeat almost anything I say."

"That's great, Conrad," Glory Rose said. "I'm glad."

"So, when did you know you wanted to be a nurse?" he asked.

She gave a light laugh and ripped open a bag of potato chips. "Oh, I've known I was going to be in some sort of health service industry since I was about ten," she said. "I wasn't sure if it would be human or animals at first, but I shadowed my uncle Cactus on the ranch one summer, and I decided it was a little bit too much manure for me to be a vet."

She laughed, glad when Conrad joined her.

"So you work with babies," he said. "No, no poop there."

She laughed. "Babies are some of the messiest humans on the planet, I'll give you that."

"Some of the best, though," he said wistfully, and Glory

Rose reached over and put her hand on his knee. "Yeah," she said. "Some of the best too."

"You want kids then?" he asked.

"Wow." She giggled and reached into her bag for some chips. "What a question for the second date." She checked her watch. "Ten minutes in."

Conrad laughed and shook his head. "I don't mean—like that. I don't mean like, like...."

She waited because watching him blush was absolutely adorable. "I didn't mean *my* kids," he mumbled, and then he shoved another huge bite of sandwich into his mouth.

Glory Rose grinned, and when she was with him, she realized how empty her life was without him. "Yeah," she said, "I want kids someday. I don't think I'd be a Glover if I didn't."

"No? Everyone in your family wants a lot of kids?"

"I didn't say a lot," she said. "But it sure seemed like they all wanted kids, yeah, and you've got Sarina now, so...." Glory Rose stalled, not sure what she was asking or trying to say. She certainly couldn't ask if he wanted Sarina.

"Maybe she's enough for you," she finally said. "Maybe you don't want any more."

"I haven't really thought about it, to be honest," he said. "Most of the time I'm just trying to make it till lunch." He chuckled. "And let me tell you, when you get up at five-forty-five in the morning, it's a long time until lunch."

Glory Rose giggled too. "Ain't that the truth?"

"So ask me something that's less embarrassing than if I want kids on the second date," Conrad said.

Glory Rose finished her chips and tossed the empty bag back into the box. "Oh, I don't know."

"You don't know?"

"Yes, I don't know."

"You don't have some burning question that you need me to answer?"

"Well, I asked you the other day if your farm took all of your time, and you said no, so maybe you're just a dad on the side."

"Well, that's a full-time job," he said. "If anything, the farm is on the side of that."

"Well, sure, sure," she said, her nerves getting the best of her.

"You seem to know I do other things," he said. "So I might as well just tell you." He straightened and dusted his hands of breadcrumbs.

"You don't have to," she said. "It's not that I need to know this moment."

"I'm a wealth manager," he said.

"A wealth manager." Glory Rose grinned at him, sure he was kidding. "Wealth needs to be managed?"

"Absolutely it does," he said very seriously, his face the straightest she'd ever seen. "If you want to keep it and you want it to grow, someone has to manage it."

"So that's what you do."

"That's what I do," he said. "I manage my own money, Grams's money, and anyone in the Walker family who wants me to."

"Would you manage mine?" Glory Rose felt like she just stepped out onto very thin ice.

Conrad blinked and then shook his head. "No, ma'am," he said. "I'm not licensed to do business in the state of Texas. I do it as a favor for my family. I don't have an office or a company or anything."

"Mm."

Conrad's dark eyes bored into hers. "Do you have wealth that needs to be managed, Glory Rose?"

"Oh, I don't like it when you say my name like that, Mister Walker," she said. "I like *Miss Glory Rose* or *Sugar* so much better."

Conrad chuckled, and everything between them felt so easy. That was why Glory Rose had been able to fall asleep on the way home from their date the other night. Conrad was simply easy to be around, easy to flirt with, easy to talk to, easy to tell the things Glory Rose hadn't told very many other people before. In fact, she'd only told one person on this planet that she'd like to homestead, and that was Pearl Jo.

If anyone could keep Glory Rose alive when she moved off grid, it would be Pearl Jo. So someone else needed to know about Glory Rose's dreams of having her own piece of land and getting everything she needed from it.

"As a matter of fact, cowboy," she said. "I do have a little bit of wealth to manage, and I fear I'm not doing a very good job of it."

"Mm," he said.

"What does a wealth manager cost?" she asked.

"Most of them take a percentage," he said. "You know, like a percentage of your wealth."

"A percentage of my wealth?"

"Yeah," he said. "Like, one percent is really standard. So if I manage a million dollars of yours, I would get paid ten thousand dollars a year to do it."

"Oh, I see," she said. "So are you earning one percent from your family members?"

He cleared his throat and shook his head, clearly uncomfortable. "I don't need the money, Glory Rose."

"Well, *needing* money and *making* money are two different things," she said, and she wondered how long she would tiptoe around this elephant in the room. "I don't *need* to make money either, but I *need* something good to do with my life."

Surprise marched across his features. "You don't need to make money?"

"Not really," she said casually. "My family has a lot of money, and even though we have a lot of kids to split it with, it's still a lot of money."

"I'm not going to ask how much," Conrad said. "And maybe if we start dating, and you know, we're six months in, and you want to see my bank account, I'll show it to you. But I would appreciate it if you didn't ask me how much right now, either."

"Of course," Glory Rose said. "I appreciate that." She started to unwrap her sandwich. "How much money does someone need to have a wealth manager?"

He looked at her, though he kept his head down, and she

could barely see his eyes past the brim of that sexy cowboy hat. "That number is different for every person, sugar."

"Oh, there's the *sugar*," she teased. "What if someone has seven figures in a bank account?"

He lifted his head fully, his eyes wide. "In a *bank account*, Glory Rose?"

"Well, you don't need to make someone feel stupid," she said. "I don't know what to do with it."

"You have a million dollars in a bank account?" he said.

"No—yes."

"Glory Rose, that needs to be managed."

"What does that even mean?" she asked.

"Managed—I don't know. Your daddy and your uncles do not have their money sitting in bank accounts," he said. "I can guarantee it."

"How can you guarantee that?"

"If they did, it wouldn't grow," he said. "Certainly not big enough to give you and every kid at Shiloh Ridge seven figures."

"How old are you?" Glory Rose asked, and Conrad opened his mouth and then pushed it closed again.

"How old am I?" he repeated.

"I mean, I know you're older than me, but I thought it was only five or six years."

"It's six," he said, almost cutting her off.

"How do you know all this stuff, then?" she asked. "I don't know what to do with it. I got it when I turned twenty-one. I don't know what to do."

"Well, I went to school," Conrad said coolly. "I took

several business courses and wealth management courses and investment courses. Then I interned at an investment firm for six months."

"Where did you do all of that?" Glory Rose asked.

"Austin," he said. "I was gone for a couple of years, and then I returned to Three Rivers. I helped my Gramps with his farm for a year or two, and then I bought it, and I've owned it for three years, and now here I am."

"Here you are," she said. "You still didn't say how old you were."

"I'm twenty-nine," he said.

"Not even thirty, and he knows how to manage wealth."

Conrad rolled his eyes. "Oh, you're just teasing me now."

"I am," Glory Rose said, grinning. "And I'm not, because now I know I seriously need a wealth manager. My money's just been sitting there for eighteen months."

"In a bank account." Conrad spoke with absolute disgust. "I can't believe it."

"I'll have you know I'm not the only Glover whose money is sitting in a bank account," she said. "We need serious help at Shiloh Ridge, and we didn't even know it."

"I can't believe your daddy didn't say anything," he said.

"They told me that I would figure it out," Glory Rose said. "And here I am, sitting in one of only four trucks that exist in the world, and I am figuring it out."

She smiled at him. "Maybe you can point me in the right direction of a wealth manager that you know and trust."

"Oh, no, no," Conrad said, shaking his head. "I absolutely can't do that."

"Why not?"

"Because I don't trust any wealth managers, except for me," he said.

"But you just said you won't manage my wealth," she said.

Several moments passed between them, and Glory Rose sure did like the way he considered her. She took a bite of her sandwich while Conrad's dark eyes glittered at her like stars in the midnight sky.

"Glory Rose," he said, "I really don't know how to say no to you."

"Good," she said. "You don't need to say no. I won't even charge you one percent."

He chuckled and shook his head again. "I can't do it for free."

"Why not?" she asked. "You do your uncles' for free. You do your daddy's for free. It could just be a favor to me."

"Yeah, and then you'll tell Pearl Jo, and Fawn; you'll tell everyone at Shiloh Ridge. Next thing I'll know, I'll have thirty more accounts. I have to do this part-time, you know." He folded his arms and sat back in his seat and gave her a glare that wasn't very menacing at all.

"Well, I think you're going to die when I tell you this next thing," she said. "And you'll have to take it on, because you'll feel so guilty you won't be able to sleep at night knowing that I have ten million dollars sitting in a bank account in Three Rivers, Texas."

Conrad wasted no time pounding his fist against his chest as if she had just stabbed him in the heart. "Glory Rose," he moaned. "That has to be a lie."

"It is not a lie, mister," she said. "In fact, my parents put it there and then gave me access to it. I didn't even make the account myself."

"Do you know what kind of account it is?" he asked. "Is it savings? Is it money market? Is it a CD?"

Glory Rose swallowed, because this was no laughing matter, at least not to Conrad. "I don't know," she said.

"Oh, my word." he said. "Let's go to the bank right now."

He opened his door and slid out of the truck and turned back to her. Glory Rose did not move. "I don't want to go to the bank on our second date," she said.

Conrad huffed out a sigh and climbed back in. "This has to be taken care of, Glory Rose."

"Well, then I need a wealth manager to take care of it."

He blinked at her, his eyes searching hers. "One percent," he said. "And you have to let me know what that account is immediately. But I need time to get set up as a business in Texas, or we could both go to jail."

"Jail?" Glory Rose was sure he was joking now, and while his eyes continued to glitter like the stars, no teasing smile appeared to go with it.

"Yes," he said. "There are strict rules and regulations for wealth account managers."

"So you think your family would never accuse you of something."

"No," he said. "I don't think they would, but I did make them sign contracts. It helps a lot that there's no money being paid, though, but if I'm going to do yours, I'm going to have to get paid for it, and that means I have to set up a business, and that means I have to follow the rules and the regulations."

Glory Rose reached over and touched his hand. He turned his over and threaded his fingers through hers.

"You like rules and regulations, don't you, Conrad?"

"Yes, ma'am," he murmured. "I do."

"And you follow the rules and regulations."

He looked at her. "Almost all the time. I mean, I have a daughter and was never married, so sometimes, no." He swallowed, something nervous in his eyes now. "But I'm repenting of that, Glory Rose. You should know that I'm not gonna—I'm not—I'm not doing that again."

"No?" she asked.

He shook his head. "No, I won't be with another woman until I'm married to her."

She smiled and nodded. "Okay, Conrad."

Several beats of silence went by, and he tugged on her hand and said, "Come sit with me."

She did, her head almost touching the roof in the back of the truck.

"We really can't go to the bank today?" he asked, his voice a whisper as it sent shivers through her body.

"No," she insisted. "We're never going to the bank together on a date. That's not a date."

"So you'll get me everything I need," he said.

"Once you have your license and you're all set up, we can have a *business meeting* about it," she said. "And at that time, I will figure out what you need and get it for you."

She really liked the way this man's arms felt around her

waist and the warmth of his body seeping into hers. "And if we happen to then go on a date *after* that with dinner, and dancing, or a movie with my favorite candy, then that would be fine."

"A cowboy would need to know your favorite candy then," he whispered.

"I like those sour gummies," she said. "The grape ones, the peach ones, or the watermelon ones?"

"Sour watermelon gummies," he said. "How very you, sugar." He pressed his lips to the side of her neck, and Glory Rose turned to look at him.

"What are you doing on Friday?" he asked.

"That's tomorrow," she said, teasing him.

He didn't even blink. "What are you doing tomorrow night?"

"Oh, I don't know," she said. "I was thinking about making bagels with my cousins."

"Maybe after that, we can go out," he said.

Glory Rose leaned down and pressed her cheek to his, positioning her lips right at his ear. "I'll bring the bagel sandwiches," she whispered.

"It's a date," he whispered back, and better words had never been spoken to Glory Rose.

Chapter Seven

"It's just me," Conrad called as he pushed open JJ's front door. He still had a hard time calling out "us," as he was so used to going everywhere by himself, but he did carry Sarina in his arms that night because JJ and Ruby were going to babysit for him.

They'd been engaged for a couple of months now and weren't getting married until August.

JJ had had a particularly rough time in the longhorn pen that morning when Conrad had texted him to find out if he could babysit. JJ had said, *You'd be saving my life if I got to stay home tonight.*

That had spurred a back-and-forth exchange between Conrad and JJ, where Conrad didn't want to disrupt his plans, and JJ insisted that Ruby would be fine if they ordered pizza and laid on the couch and watched movies.

We have a lifetime to go out, JJ said. *If I want to stay in for one blasted night, I can stay in.*

He smiled just thinking about his cousin's grumpy demeanor and how Ruby, as bright and amazing as she was, had sunny-ed him up a little bit.

"Ooh, let me have her," Ruby said as she came into the living room from the kitchen at the back of the house. "Hi, Sarina-girl." She took the little girl who squealed and laughed to see Ruby, leaving Conrad with nothing to do with his hands.

"You're a little early, aren't you?" she asked.

"Yeah," he said. "I thought I'd check on JJ, see how he's doing."

Ruby sobered and rolled her eyes. "I sent him to the massage therapist."

"Oh," Conrad said. "I didn't know JJ would—"

"That's right," Ruby said. "He's totally hurt his right shoulder, and he insists it's fine. And then he hurts it again." She tsk'ed and turned to go into the kitchen. "I'm making chicken potstickers. You could come have some."

Conrad was taking Glory Rose out to dinner, but he wasn't going to argue about having an appetizer at JJ's house first. No, Ruby didn't live here with him, but she did come over to his house a lot, as she lived with her older brother, who was JJ's best friend.

"Where's Tate tonight?" Conrad asked as he followed Ruby into the kitchen.

"He and Clara Jean are in Amarillo," she said. "Clara Jean's getting shoes for the wedding."

Conrad wondered if they didn't have shoe stores here in Three Rivers, but he wasn't going to ask. "That sounds fun."

"Yeah, my parents are meeting them there," she said. "They're staying the whole weekend."

"That's nice. A fun little weekend getaway." He smiled at her and took one of the offered chicken potstickers. "You made these?"

"Sure did." She beamed with pride as she set Sarina on the counter and asked, "You want one?"

"Yes, pwease," Sarina said, and while Conrad hadn't heard the results of her speech assessment from yesterday, he sure loved hearing her voice.

"Good girl," he murmured, and he stroked her hair down the back.

"Who did your piggies?" Ruby asked. "They're so pretty."

"Daddy," she said.

Ruby looked at Conrad. "You do her hair?"

"Yes," Conrad said, not sure what to add to it. "If I don't pull it back, it's kind of crazy, and it gets all snagged in the chicken feathers and straw out on the farm."

Ruby smiled at him. "Who taught you how to do that?"

"Would you believe it if I said Elaine?" he asked. "She's always making me do things I don't want to do." Ruby laughed, and Conrad joined her in a chuckle. "She watches some videos or something, and then she comes and teaches me."

"That's awesome," Ruby said. "You're such a good dad."

Conrad nodded, but he wasn't so sure about that. "Well, anyway," he said. "If JJ's not here, just let him know if he needs anything to call me. I can come take care of those long-horns for a while."

"Yeah, he's gonna let you do that," Ruby said dryly. "I told him I could take care of the longhorns, and he said, and I quote: Over my dead body." She shook her head. "I don't know what he thinks I'm going to do once we're married and running this ranch together."

Conrad watched her fuss over Sarina, breaking off little bits of the meat mixture from inside the potsticker and feeding them to her. He knew exactly what JJ thought Ruby would do, and it would be to take care of the house and any kids they might have. He'd only call her out to the ranch if absolutely necessary, and to JJ, that would be never.

"Well, I'm literally ten minutes away," Conrad said. "I could come help with whatever he needs." He nodded and reached for another potsticker. "I'll text him."

"Yes, do that, and I'll tell him, and maybe the two of us can wear him down." She grinned at Conrad, and he moved into her and hugged her and Sarina at the same time.

"Thank you so much, Ruby," he said. "Sarina, you'll be good. You do exactly what Uncle JJ and Aunt Ruby tell you to do, okay? You go to bed right on time. No crying now."

"Okay, Daddy," she said, and she hugged his face as tight as she could in her little girl arms.

"Love you, sweets." He pressed a kiss to her chubby cheek, nodded at Ruby, and left the farmhouse.

He was early, about a half hour, to be exact. And since Glory Rose really was making bagels with her mother for that night's dinner, he didn't think he could show up early. He got behind the wheel of his luxury truck, and he connected his phone to the Bluetooth speaker.

He drew a deep breath, centered his thoughts, and murmured, "Where should I read, Lord?"

God didn't give him an answer for what book of scripture to start in, and Conrad figured the beginning was as good as anywhere. So he tapped to open his Bible app, and he went to Genesis chapter one.

The black triangle sat there waiting for him to tap, and he stared at it for an extra moment before he dropped his thumb onto it.

"Chapter One," a man's voice said in a deep rumble, and Conrad's soul soothed immediately.

If he didn't set an alarm, he'd simply drive around and lose track of time. So he set an alarm for fifteen minutes from now and set his truck in the direction of Shiloh Ridge.

With that done, he put the car in drive, made a wide arc, and left his cousin's property. Conrad heard the creation story with brand new ears, as if he'd never heard about the earth being formed and divided and beautified before. The story flowed through him as if it was one of his favorites, and his momma was telling it to him before he went to bed at night.

Before he knew it, his alarm went off, and he had to turn around and head back to Shiloh Ridge to get Glory Rose.

He'd just reached the sixth day, and he let the scriptures play as he continued to the ranch and turned onto the dirt road that would lead him up to the cabins where Glory Rose lived. He'd just passed under the arch, welcoming everyone to Shiloh Ridge at the top of the hill, though they had plenty of buildings and homes and fields down below, when he heard in the scriptures that God looked over his creations on the sixth day and called the work very good.

He reached out and turned down the volume on the scriptures as they continued to play.

"Did he say the other days were *very* good?" he asked himself. Or was it only the day that God had created man that was *very* good? And if so, what did that mean?

Conrad didn't have time to leaf through the wispy pages of his Bible, and he tapped to close the app before making the last turn that would take him down the road in front of Glory Rose's cabin.

He'd ordered himself a Bible online, and he expected it to be at the farmhouse in the next couple of days. He could look then at each of the proclamations that God had made after each of the creative days, and he'd find out if that was the only one where he'd said "very good" or not.

A sense of pride, for lack of a better word, filled him as he parked and got out of his truck. He'd done something that he'd been challenged to do. He'd read the scriptures, and while he didn't think he'd gotten the answer to whether he was forgiven or not, he sure felt good about himself.

That stinging, burning feeling in his chest came, and Conrad knew that the Lord felt good about him too. He reached out and put one hand against the corner of the hood of his truck, pausing to feel that pleasure from the Lord as deep as it would go.

"Thank you," he murmured. And then he set his sights on Glory Rose's front door and headed that way.

Before he got there, the door opened, and Fawn came out. "Hey, Conrad," she said in a rush, pulling the door closed behind her almost before she stood fully on the front porch. "So, you must not have gotten Glory Rose's texts."

"No," he said. "What's going on?"

"So she was down at her mom's making bagels this afternoon," she said. "And apparently there was a little boiling water mishap." Fawn hugged herself and added, "I mean, she's okay, she's okay. Everybody's okay."

"Oh," Conrad said. "Well, that's good."

"She just burned her hand a little bit," Fawn said. "But her momma insisted that she take her down to the emergency room, and they're on their way back right now."

"Okay," Conrad said. "Well, I can just wait or...or reschedule. I'll just go home."

"No, no," she said. "She doesn't want you to go home, but...." Fawn trailed off, and she wore a look of nervousness that didn't settle Conrad's stomach at all.

"But what?" he asked.

"She wants you to go to her parents' house and wait for her there, because her daddy's gonna want to see her hand, and all the bagels and everything are still there."

Conrad suddenly understood Fawn's nervousness, and his stomach vibrated with the force of four hives of angry hornets.

"All right," he said, his voice a bit more guarded than he would like Fawn to hear. "Uh, can you point me in the direction of which house is her parents'?"

"Oh, sure," Fawn said. "You go back out to the main road

101

and go back down past the barn. You know the road you come in on, where the arch is?"

"Yes, ma'am," he said.

"Right next to that is a great, big, giant homestead. That's where I grew up."

"Okay," Conrad said.

"Just keep going straight, right past the homestead. There's another house just a little bit down, right across from the big picnic area. That's where Glory Rose—that's where Uncle Ward and Aunt Dot live."

"Okay," he said. "And I should go right now?"

"She texted me when they left the hospital, and that was about a half-hour ago, so she might beat you there."

Conrad could pray for that on the four-minute drive down to her mama and daddy's house. "Thanks, Fawn," he said.

"Have fun tonight," she said. "Glory Rose is really good at making bagels."

Conrad waved and turned around to go back to his truck, thinking, *If she's really good at making bagels, why did she burn herself?*

But he would never say that out loud. He also couldn't believe he was going to meet her parents on their third date. "And she thought *you* were forward by asking her if she wanted kids on the second," he grumbled to himself as he got behind the wheel.

He drove as slowly as possible down the dirt roads to the house that Fawn had described, and it really only took him four minutes. He didn't see any other cars in the driveway, including Glory Rose's, and he didn't think that was a good sign. He wasn't sure if he should loiter in his truck or just go ring the doorbell.

Then he figured he'd never heard of a dead body up at Shiloh Ridge, so he got out of the truck and made his way to the front door. At least their porch sat back inside a little alcove, which blocked the wind.

Conrad rang the doorbell, tucked his hands in his pockets, and waited. Inside, he could hear someone playing the guitar —at least it sounded like it was someone, and not just the radio. But no one came to the door.

Conrad glanced over his shoulder, finding the peace and stillness at Shiloh Ridge absolute. He rang the doorbell again, this time adding five crisp knocks to it as well. The guitar playing inside ceased immediately, and someone yelled, "Coming!"

He wasn't sure if it was "coming" or "come in," but Conrad certainly wasn't going to walk into Glory Rose's parent's house while she wasn't there, unannounced.

He fell back a step just as the door opened and her daddy stood there. A frown formed on his face, and he said, "Conrad."

"Yeah, uh, hi," he said. "Um, Glory Rose told me to come —wait here?—we're going out tonight."

Ward Glover settled all of his weight on one foot and said, "Y'all are going out tonight," like he didn't believe it.

"I mean, maybe?" Conrad guessed. "If Glory Rose is all right, I'm just—Fawn told me to come wait here?" He hated how he was almost thirty years old and making everything he said into a question.

"All right." Ward backed up and allowed Conrad to enter the house. Conrad felt like a little child who'd done something wrong. To be honest, he'd felt the same way he had when he first told his parents about Sarina.

"Just go straight on back," Ward said. "Pick a couch. Silver's just polishing up his saddle stuff. He'll move it for you."

"Oh, hey, Conrad," the young man said, and he found a smile on his face. "Come on in. Glory says she's still about ten minutes out."

"Okay," Conrad said.

"She saw you on the camera."

Conrad nodded. He watched Silver work on his saddle for a bit, and the boy seemed to have a good air about him, but Ward moved around in the kitchen in a very obvious way as to let everyone know he was still there. Conrad glanced over his shoulder and found him doing absolutely nothing—but staring.

"You got a show coming up?" he asked.

"Yeah," Silver said. "In a couple weeks. I'm doing the dressage for the first time." He grinned like this was really great news. "So my tack's got to be perfect."

"He shines it every day," Ward said from the kitchen.

"Not every day," Silver protested. He rolled his eyes and looked at Conrad. "Not sure why he cares," he muttered under his breath. "He's not the one doing it."

Conrad smiled, but he said nothing. He knew when to hold his tongue, and a situation like this definitely called for silence.

"So you're going out with Glory?" Silver asked.

"Yeah," Conrad said. "It's only our third date, so I don't know—"

"How it's going?" Silver asked.

Conrad looked at him, this young man probably a decade younger than him, and he had no idea how to answer. "I don't know—I mean." He took a breath. "I made it to the third date, so I haven't messed up too badly yet." He chuckled, because he knew he would be the one to mess up and cause Glory Rose to break up with him.

Thankfully, Silver didn't push the issue, and Conrad pulled out his phone as a series of beeps sounded almost on top of each other.

"Ah, here's all of Glory Rose's texts," he said. "I was out on my cousin's, and he doesn't have great service there."

"He's got those new longhorns, though, right?" Silver asked, his face bright.

"Yeah, that's right," Conrad said. "They're giving him some trouble, though."

"They're really strong-willed," Silver said. "But the most beautiful animal in Texas."

Conrad matched his grin and quickly scrolled through Glory Rose's texts so that he could send her one of his own. *I'm sitting on your daddy's couch and he's staring a hole in the back of my head. Tell me you're almost here.*

He sent the message, and not ten seconds later, a door leading directly into the kitchen opened, and female voices came with it.

"You're staring a hole in the back of his head, Daddy?"

Glory Rose demanded, and Conrad got to his feet to face her. Sure enough, she wore her arm in a sling, and he knew they would not be going out that night. The look on her mother's face confirmed it.

He thought about taking her for a ride, and driving through somewhere, turning the chairs around, and having another in-cab picnic in his truck.

"How are you?" her daddy asked. "What happened? What's wrong with it?"

"Oh, she's fine," Dot said, as she brought up the rear and closed the door behind her. "It's only a third-degree burn on about one inch of the back of her forearm. Everything else wasn't even burnt that badly. They iced it and put a bunch of ointment on it. They said we have to come in next week just to check the regrowth of the skin."

"I'm fine, Daddy," Glory Rose said.

"Burns hurt," Ward insisted, and Conrad nodded, because he was right. Burns did hurt.

"They gave me some painkillers," Glory Rose said, and her mother held up a bag from the pharmacy.

"The sling is just a precaution. She couldn't hold still," Dot said. "She gets so nervous at the doctor."

"She's the only nurse I know who's a bad patient," Ward quipped, and they all smiled, even Glory Rose.

Her eyes switched to him, and Conrad lifted his hand in a wave. "Fawn told me to come down," he said. Her momma looked at him too, and her daddy turned and resumed his staring.

"Well, I got the bagels made," Glory Rose said as she moved past her parents and came into the living room.

"We should just reschedule," Conrad said.

"Absolutely not," Glory Rose said through clenched teeth as she arrived in front of him. "If I have to spend an evening with them picking over me, I'm going to die."

Conrad had no idea how he was going to get them out of there. These were *her* parents, and they clearly didn't approve of him going out with Glory Rose.

She'd not said that. Silver hadn't either, but the staring and the frowning were a dead giveaway.

Glory Rose looked up at him with something fierce and determined and utterly hopeful in her eyes as she whispered, "So, get us out of here."

Chapter Eight

Conrad wore pure panic on his face for one, two, three seconds, and then he blinked, and it all disappeared. "Well," he said in a loud voice, clearly meant for everyone in the house to hear. "We don't *have* to go to that symphony tonight, but they're only in town for one night."

"Oh, I want to go," Glory Rose said, playing right into his hand.

"What symphony?" Daddy asked.

Conrad looked past Glory Rose, and she caught the twinkle in his eye. "It's actually a quartet, sir," Conrad said in the same calm, gentle, firm way he said everything. "It's a buddy of mine from high school, and they play in really small venues. He plays the cello, and tonight they're at Terrible's."

"I've heard about them doing small stuff there," Momma said. "How many people does that seat?"

"I think sixty," Conrad said, and he reached out and took

her non-slinged hand. The sling was a joke, really. She didn't need it at all, but the moment they'd pinned her arm to her body, she had calmed down, and they'd been able to examine the skin that she'd injured. It really was nothing she couldn't have iced and put ointment on here at the house—and been on her date with Conrad by now.

"They sell out pretty fast when they do concerts there," he said. "I took the tickets from my grams."

"We *have* to go," Glory Rose said. "We can't take the tickets from your grandmother and then not use them." She turned and faced her parents. "I'm going out with Conrad," she said. "We'll literally be sitting at a table, maybe eating some pork nachos or something. My arm is fine."

Both of her parents wore a look that said she would be anything but fine if she went out with Conrad tonight. But it had nothing to do with her arm.

They're worried about you, she thought, and she wasn't sure where the words had come from, but she knew they were true.

"I'm going to be fine." She stepped away from Conrad and moved into the kitchen. "He's a really nice guy," she whispered to her parents. "I really like him. Can you not ruin this for me, please?"

"He has a three-year-old daughter," her mother whispered back, as if Glory Rose didn't know about Sarina's existence.

"Yes, he does," she hissed back fiercely. "And you know what? People who have three-year-old daughters are really great people."

"I'm not saying he's not a great person," Momma said.

"Then why don't you want me to go out with a great person?"

"Glory Rose," Daddy said in a tired voice.

"Can we please just talk about this later?" she asked. "Not that there's anything to talk about. I'm twenty-three years old, and I can go out with whoever I want."

Daddy's jaw clenched, but he nodded and said, "If you are in too much pain for even one second, you call me, and I will come get you."

"Okay, Daddy," Glory Rose smiled at him and hugged him as tight as she could with one arm.

"Ward, be careful," her momma said. "You're hugging her too hard. You're pressing her arm against her body."

"Well, I'm not gonna *not* hug my daughter," Daddy said. "She's fine. If she wasn't fine, she would've said so."

Glory Rose smiled, and her mom stepped in to hug her too. "Thanks for taking me to the hospital," she said. "Thanks for making the bagels with me."

"Are you really going to Terrible's?" Momma whispered. "If you were making bagels for bagel sandwiches, why would you be going to eat at Terrible's?"

Glory Rose stepped back and said, "Plans change all the time, Momma," and it wasn't a lie.

Plans *did* change all the time, just like she hadn't *planned* to have Conrad waiting on her parents' couch when she returned home from an ER visit. And just like she hadn't *planned* to spill the boiling water up her hand and arm, and she hadn't *planned* to go to Terrible's tonight to watch a concert.

She wasn't even sure if that was a real thing, but Daddy had a phone, and there was no way he wouldn't look that up before he let her out of the house, her age notwithstanding.

She glanced over to him as her mother released her, and sure enough, Daddy had his phone out. "Have fun at the quartet," he said, as he looked up. "Anything at all, Glory Rose, you call me."

"Conrad has a really nice truck," she said. "He can get me home just as easy as you can drive to town and pick me up."

Daddy looked over to where Conrad waited on the cusp of where the living room met the kitchen. "All right," he said gruffly. "You two behave tonight. Drive careful."

"Yes, sir," Conrad said, and he reached up and tipped his hat at her daddy. Glory Rose looked down at what she was wearing, and it was, for the second time in a row, not what she would have chosen to go out on a date with Conrad Walker.

But they were already late, and if they really were going to alter their plans to eat at Terrible's and attend a concert, she didn't have time to change her clothes.

"Ready?" he asked, and he had the good sense to keep his hands in his pockets. Too bad Glory Rose had no sense at all, and she looped her arm through his and said, "I'm ready, cowboy," in her usual flirtatious voice.

Her mother muttered, "Glory Rose," just loud enough for her to hear, and Daddy growled, "You be good, girl," as they headed for the front door.

Outside, Glory Rose kept her composure until she was seated and buckled in Conrad's truck. He slammed the door, and she started laughing. He got behind the wheel and said, "Yuck it up, girlfriend."

She reached for his hand, just so shiny-happy that he'd gotten her out of the house. "Is that what I am? Your girlfriend?"

He looked at her for a long moment and then pulled his seatbelt across his body and buckled it. "Well, it's date three," he said. "When do you become someone's girlfriend?"

"Oh, I don't know," she said. "Usually about the time I start kissing him."

Conrad cleared his throat, coughed, and said, "Well, we haven't done that." He flipped the truck into reverse and backed out of her parents' driveway.

"I'm really sorry," Glory Rose said. "The bagels are amazing. I'll bring you one tomorrow for breakfast."

"It's a long drive," he said.

"You and Sarina can gather the eggs," she said, as if he hadn't just rejected her. "And we'll make sandwiches."

He looked over at her as he went by the homestead and made the left turn to go down the road to the highway. "I'll text you if we have enough eggs for everyone," he said. "Grams will want a sandwich, too."

"I have to meet your grandmother?"

"I just suffered through an evening in your parents' house, *alone* with your daddy," he said. "You can meet Grams as my girlfriend, sugar."

"Hmm." Glory Rose shook her head, really enjoying this game. "Not your girlfriend unless there's a kiss."

Conrad chuckled too. "You're a pushy little thing, aren't you?"

"No," Glory Rose said. "I am not." She let a few seconds of silence go by. "I won't lie—I've thought about kissing you."

"You've thought about it?" he asked.

"You *haven't* thought about kissing me?" she asked, and even in the darkness, she caught the blush rising through his face.

"I've thought about it," he muttered.

"Yeah, that's what I thought," Glory Rose said.

"It's not a crime," he said.

"No," she said. "Kissing is not a crime."

"Neither is thinking about kissing."

"Well." She shook her hair over her shoulders. "Now that *that's* out of the way, and no one's committed any crimes, I find myself on a date wearing something I wish I wasn't wearing."

Conrad grinned at her. "We could stop and get you something else."

"Is there a concert at Terrible's tonight?"

"Yeah," he said. "But we don't have to go."

"Do you have tickets?"

He shrugged. "I mean, Grams does."

"Is she going?"

"Yeah." Conrad nodded. "She's goin' with my daddy."

"So who has Sarina?" she asked.

"JJ and Ruby."

"So we *don't* have a time constraint," Glory Rose said.

"No."

Her mind blitzed and whirred. "So what's your plan for date number three?"

"Well, my almost-girlfriend was going to make bagel sandwiches, and I was going to take her to the botanical gardens, where they have a display of a rare night orchid," he said. "But, we missed that window, and I couldn't really use that excuse to get this really beautiful woman away from her parents, because it's not one night only. So we can do that another night—maybe tomorrow?—I mean, if my kissing is acceptable at the end of the night—"

"Whoa, whoa," Glory Rose said. "Who says we have to wait till the end of the night to kiss?"

Conrad burst out laughing, and that made Glory Rose's heart so insanely happy. He reached over and took her hand, and she was so glad that it was not her left hand that had been burnt.

He lifted it to his lips and kissed the inside of her wrist, which was exactly like spilling boiling water up her arm, but this time, instead of yelping and dropping the pan and crying and then insisting she was all right as her mother drove her to the emergency room, Glory Rose let the delicious shivers skim through her body from the pleasurable touch of Conrad's lips.

"Maybe I won't kiss you at all," he said. "I think you've got to *earn* that kiss."

"Earn the kiss?" she asked. "How do you think I'm going to do that?"

"I don't know," Conrad said.

"What does it take to earn a kiss?"

"I don't know that either," Conrad said. "I'll know it when

it happens." He grinned over to her. "One, you have no dinner, so you're down a strike already. Two, we can't do what I planned—two strikes."

Glory Rose swallowed. "So we could...go to the mall," she said, an idea forming in her head as she spoke. "Go to the food court there, because they have *amazing* bagel bites at the Earthen Bakery. Don't be rolling your eyes like that either, Conrad Walker. I know you like bagel bites, because you told me in one of the text conversations that you grew up on them."

"I didn't *grow up* on them," he said calmly. "I ate a lot of them when my momma was pregnant with the triplets. That's all." He pointed a finger at her. "And don't let her hear you say that. She feels bad about the bagel bite year already."

Glory Rose giggled. "My lips are sealed."

"Also, I very nearly lied to your parents tonight," he said. "That's strike three. Had to meet your parents tonight as your non-boyfriend, when you *clearly* hadn't even told them we'd been out before. That's strike four and five."

"Whoa, whoa. Two strikes for that?" Glory Rose teased. "Come on. You're being excessive."

"You hadn't told your parents about us, though, right?"

"No," Glory Rose said, all of the teasing deflating right out of her as if someone had stabbed her balloon with a pin.

"They think I'm no good for you," he said.

"Did you hear what they said in the kitchen?" She looked over at him, her stomach tight.

"No," he said.

"They'll come around," she said.

"It's because of Sarina, right?"

"She has something to do with it, yeah."

"Did you tell them that I've already committed not to sleep with another woman until I'm married?"

"No," Glory Rose said. "I did not tell them that. When would I have had time to tell them that?"

"Strike six." He grinned at her, but it fell away quickly. "If I'm no good for you, Glory Rose, it's really okay."

"I think you're great for me," Glory Rose said in a small but powerful voice. "And just like I told them in the kitchen, *they* don't get to decide. I'm an adult, and I *really* like you. And if I want to go out with you, I will."

"What if I don't want to go out with you?" Conrad asked.

Glory Rose's heartbeat stopped. Positively, absolutely came to a complete standstill in her chest.

"You don't want to go out with me?" She didn't mean for her voice to come out quite so tinny and quite so tiny. But it had.

"I'm just teasin', sugar," he said. "Of course I want to go out with you. It's all I think about."

Every dark piece that had just entered her soul became bright. "Well, it can't be *all* you think about," she said. "Just five minutes ago, you admitted you'd thought about kissing me."

Conrad laughed, and Glory Rose forced herself not to jump right to the next conversation topic. She wanted this one to settle into her, where she could hear it later in her mind and analyze the real meaning behind the things they'd teased about—and the things they hadn't.

Because there was always some measure of truth beneath

the flirting too, and if Glory Rose gave space for silence, she could go over everything with a clear head and an open heart.

Not only that, but she'd found that if she let some quiet into a conversation, other people would speak up.

And today, she was blessed with Conrad's beautiful bass voice saying, "I sure like you too, Glory Rose," into the silence between them.

Chapter Nine

"Look at the size of that pretzel," Conrad said. "I've never seen anything like it." He'd also never felt anything like Glory Rose's hand in his, and while he definitely thought people kept glancing at them, it didn't seem to matter when she stood next to him.

"I can make pretzels too," Glory Rose said. "They're a lot like bagels in that you have to boil them first."

"Yeah, well, no more boiling for you for a while," Conrad said, smiling over to her. She'd removed the sling and left it in the truck, claiming she didn't need everyone in town asking her what had happened. She wore a long-sleeved sweater, and it covered up the bandage on her arm easily.

"So do you want pretzels or bagels?" Glory Rose asked. "I've never made a pretzel sandwich, though I suppose it could be done."

"Peanut butter and jelly on a pretzel?" Conrad thought

about it for a moment. "That sounds amazing, actually." But the menu didn't seem to have sandwich options, only dipping choices.

A group of teenagers moved past them, and one of the girls pushed a boy away as they all laughed. Conrad had no idea when he'd last come to the mall, but it wasn't somewhere he frequented very often—and those teenagers were why. He could get irritating conversations and loud laughter just by going to Seven Sons Ranch when the whole family was there for a Sabbath day meal.

"I don't want a pretzel," Conrad said, and he led Glory Rose over to the bagel shop in the food court. A quick glance around told him that plenty of people came to the mall on Friday night. Who knew?

"See, they've got breakfast sandwiches here," Glory Rose said.

"If we're going to have breakfast sandwiches in the morning," Conrad said. "I don't want one tonight."

Glory Rose turned around and surveyed the long row of food booths on the other wall. "Well, there's plenty of other places to eat."

Conrad turned too, not sure what he wanted—at least to eat. He knew he wanted to keep dating Glory Rose, but he worried about her parents' reaction to the news that they were going out. Her brother didn't seem to care, but Ward and Dot? They definitely cared.

Glory Rose had talked to them alone in the kitchen for a few seconds, and part of Conrad really wanted to know what they'd said, and the other part of him absolutely did not. The things he could make up inside his own mind already hurt enough.

And besides, Glory Rose stood at his side, her hand firmly in his, acting as a shield to anyone's judgment.

"Maybe pizza," he said.

"They have amazing spaghetti and meatballs at that place." Glory Rose started through the tables and chairs toward the Italian shop down on the end. "It's my momma's favorite place," she said. "We come here every year for her birthday."

"To an Italian shop in the mall?" Conrad asked. "I'm sure your aunt cooks better than that."

Glory Rose laughed, the sound of it only mixing in with the crowd around them. "Of course she does," she said. "But we get together a group of girls—cousins and aunts and my grandmother—and we come down here, get our nails done, go shopping, and eat pasta."

Conrad could admit he liked pasta, though he had not had experience with any of the rest of it. He panicked for a moment as he realized he was a girl-dad now, and he'd prob-ably have to deal with painting nails just like he did doing Sarina's hair. Maybe Elaine could help him with those things too.

They joined the cafeteria-style line, and Conrad asked, "Do you like zoos?"

Glory Rose looked at him like *he'd* turned into a zoo animal. "Zoos?" she asked. "Do I like *zoos*?"

He grinned at her. "Yeah. I was thinking of taking Sarina to the zoo in Amarillo in a couple of weeks." He swallowed as the line inched forward. He couldn't believe he was about to ask Glory Rose if she wanted to go on a date with him and his three-year-old daughter. But in addition to thinking about her, and thinking about kissing her, and planning their dates, he'd realized that she would need to spend time with him while he acted in the role of a father. She would have to spend time with Sarina too, and Sarina needed to spend time with her.

He had no idea how to explain complex family relationships to a toddler, and he didn't need to, but if he and Glory Rose were going to advance into dating and being boyfriend-girlfriend, she'd have to go on some dates with him and Sarina.

It would be great if she could go out with JJ and Ruby too, so that Conrad could get another opinion on her—not that he needed his cousin to like Glory Rose, but simply so Conrad could have an objective point of view on the relationship. He felt in so deep already, because he always fell fast for a pretty face.

She's more than a pretty face, he told himself. Glory Rose was the real deal. She'd gone to school and gotten her CNA. She worked with kids, and she helped around her family's ranch when she needed to. She spent time with her cousins and her parents, and even though she was six years younger than him, she had real adult conversations.

And best of all, she didn't judge Conrad.

"When were you thinking of going?" she asked.

Conrad studied the menu, though all the food sat out in front of him. He wasn't sure how to look at Glory Rose and talk to her about being an instant mother the moment they got married. Most couples had time—at least nine months—before they had to take their relationship from husband and wife to mother and father.

"I don't know," he said. "In a couple of weeks when the weather gets warmer." He glanced over to her, his eyes not truly landing on her face. "I'd ask JJ to come over and take care of the farm for a couple of days. We'll go stay in a hotel, go to the zoo. They have a big mall there, and I thought I'd take Sarina to that big candy store, and then the toy store."

He smiled at Glory Rose, finally letting himself look into her eyes. "When I was a kid, my momma and daddy would take me to Amarillo for an overnight trip, and we'd do all of those things. It was awesome because it was two days out of the year where the triplets stayed home, and I got my parents to myself."

"Sounds amazing," Glory Rose said.

"I don't mean to sound like I don't like the triplets." Conrad looked up to the man as he stepped to the counter, then he looked at Glory Rose. "What are you having, sugar?"

"I want the spaghetti and meatballs, please," she said, tipping up on her toes as if she needed to see over the glass instead of through it. "And I want an extra meatball and double the garlic bread."

Conrad chuckled. "Wow, double the garlic bread."

"Don't think I'm sharing with you, Mister." She hip-checked him. "That bread is all for me. It's *so* good."

"I'll get my own double order," he said, and he too looked at the man waiting for his preferences. "I'll take a slice of the all-meat pizza." He nodded down the counter. "And I want some of that Italian pasta salad down there, and I guess double the garlic bread."

"You got it," the man said, and Glory Rose pushed their tray down the shelf behind the people in front of them.

"Would you want me to go overnight to Amarillo?" Glory Rose asked.

Conrad's pulse sped and scattered through his veins. "I mean, I thought you could come for one of the days," he said. "I was thinking of going Friday to Saturday, and then if you came on Saturday, you wouldn't have to take work off. We could go to the zoo and get lunch and maybe hit the mall."

Glory Rose's eyes held something deep that Conrad couldn't decipher when she turned to look at him. "And you want me to come because...?"

"Well, Sarina's not going anywhere," he said. "And I figure in two or three weeks, we'll have been out a few more times, and you'll know if you want to keep seeing me or not."

"I thought we already went over that," Glory Rose said quietly. He could barely hear her, and he put their conversation on hold while they collected their food and then moved to the cash register to pay. He lifted the tray with all of their wares, and they both turned to face the seating area.

"We'll be lucky if we can find anywhere to sit," he said. "Why are so many people here?"

Glory Rose laughed. "Conrad, it's Friday night at the mall. You never came to the mall on the weekend?"

"Why would I come to the mall on the weekend?" he asked. "I only come to the mall during Christmas."

"Well, Three Rivers is a lot bigger than it used to be," Glory Rose said. "Look, there's a table over there." She led the way and Conrad wove through people, booths, tables, and chairs as she had somehow found the one place with two seats where they could sit.

He put their tray in the middle of the table and started unloading the food, because he didn't think this table could hold the tray as well as everything they'd gotten. He then took the tray over to the garbage can and set it on top and returned to Glory Rose.

"I was thinking that you might want to spend some time with Sarina." He kept his head ducked so his cowboy hat hid his face as he unwrapped the plastic spork he had gotten from the Italian place.

"And you want to see me interacting with her too." Somehow, he found the courage to look up. "There are a lot of different sides to a person," he said. "And being a dad is a big part of me, and I think you should get to see it, so you can decide if we should stay together."

She nodded as she twirled up a forkful of spaghetti. She lifted it, the end of the noodles hanging down, and she looked at him too. "You think a lot about things, don't you?"

"Yes," he said. "It's my numbers brain." He wasn't going to apologize for it. His momma had told him he didn't need to apologize for thinking analytically and critically and into the future. Those were good things that made him a very good wealth manager and very good at taking care of a farm—anticipating the needs and outlining steps to make sure that they were taken care of.

Now he just happened to be applying it to a relationship on the third date.

"I might be able to come," Glory Rose said. "The spring is a busy time on the ranch, as my daddy changes up a lot of the rotational ranching."

Conrad nodded. "Yep, spring is real busy on a ranch."

"We usually have one big branding day in March or April," she said. "As well as our spring breeding for winter calves."

"Sure, yeah," Conrad said. "Well, if it doesn't work out, that's fine. Like I said, Sarina's not going anywhere."

"Everyone helps on the ranch for big things like that," she said. "I would really call attention to myself if I wasn't there."

Conrad folded up his pizza and took a big bite, because he didn't want to say the first thing that had come into his mind. Glory Rose cut her meatball and stabbed a little piece of it on the end of her fork and put her bite of spaghetti in her mouth.

He wanted to enjoy dinner, and he wanted to enjoy his time with Glory Rose, and he *really* wanted to kiss her tonight so he could get the label of boyfriend. Then he could start introducing her around to his friends and family members as such.

But he couldn't do that if she was going to keep him in the shadows. He could barely taste the spicy pepperoni or the salty bacon as he swallowed. "So you don't want people to know that we're dating, is that it?"

She looked up, surprise in those pretty eyes. "Did I say that?"

"You said it would call attention to you if you weren't there, and that assumes that everyone will know you're out with me."

"I don't care if they know we're going out," she said, blinking at him faster than normal. "But that doesn't mean that I'm going to get up on top of True Blue and shout it into a megaphone either." She smiled at him and reached across the table to cover one of his hands with hers. "Conrad, I'm not embarrassed of you. I *want* to go out with you. I really like you."

"But your family—they don't feel the same way."

"I think they think a lot like you," she said slowly, a measure of carefulness in her voice. "They think about the future and the fact that you have a three-year-old and I'm only twenty-three. They think about the fact that if we do get married, I'll be a mom on day one, and not just a mom—a stepmom."

Conrad had thought about all of those things, yes, and he had no way to defend himself, so he said nothing.

"That doesn't mean they don't like you," she said. "And it doesn't mean that we should break up."

"What *does* it mean?" he asked.

"It means that we keep seeing each other," she said. "Because just like you, I have lots of different sides too. I'm the Glory Rose I am when I'm with you, and a different Glory Rose when I hang out with my cousins, and a different Glory Rose when I'm doing a family dinner with my mom and dad and siblings, and a different Glory Rose when we go across the street to the picnic area and every single Glover in the world comes. So yeah, I imagine I'll be a different Glory Rose for and to Sarina as well."

"Yeah, probably," he said.

"I really would like to come to Amarillo with you," she said. "Or even if we just hung out with Sarina at the farm or took her to the park here, because I think you're right. I think I have to see you with her, and you know what? You should be able to see me with her too."

"That's fair," he said.

"And you can decide when that time is," Glory Rose said. "I'll meet her in whatever capacity you want me to, when you're ready."

And that was why Glory Rose had more than a pretty face, and why Conrad felt himself falling in love with her, sitting there in the crowded mall food court eating a pretty good piece of pizza.

He didn't want to stay there for long, though, as Glory Rose needed to get a new outfit—one fit for her first kiss with him. Conrad also needed to figure out where that would happen, because he couldn't take her back to her parents' house and kiss her on the porch there.

They had a camera, and he was fairly certain that Ward was going to be sitting two feet from the front door, a shotgun across his lap, when Conrad brought Glory Rose home.

When they finished eating, he asked, "Where do you wanna go to get something to wear?"

"Oh, we don't really have to do that," she said. "You'll be so bored while I try on clothes."

"I don't mind." He stacked their plates and took them to the trashcan, and then led Glory Rose out of the food court and into the wider halls of the mall. They left behind some of the noise, and he took her hand in his. "I'm with you, Glory Rose. We can do whatever you want."

His eyes swept left and right, trying to figure out if he could kiss her here at the mall and how would he even do that —corner her in some sketchy alley? He shook himself out of his thoughts, because they were *ridiculous*.

"Can we go in the holiday shop?" Glory Rose asked, a hint of excitement in her voice. She took him to the left, over toward a large corner shop that was filled with only Christmas wares.

Conrad spotted at least six Christmas trees stretching up toward the ceiling, and the scent of cinnamon and clove hit him from ten feet away. "I guess," he said. "Why do you wanna go in there?"

"It's the best shop in the mall," Glory Rose said.

"There aren't even any clothes in here."

She laughed and picked up a snow globe at the front of the store. "I *love* Christmas," she said. "My family has this Angel Tree tradition, and we gather every year at the homestead for our annual ranch meeting, a huge dinner, and then we decorate a tree with all of my great-grandmother's ornaments."

"Then you don't need more ornaments," he said.

"That tree is at the homestead," Glory Rose said. "So at our house, my momma and daddy would take us kids out, and we'd chop down our own tree, and we'd each get a little section that we got to decorate ourselves." She beamed at him with all the brightness of the holy star on the night Christ was born.

"My momma and daddy fell in love over Christmas," she said. "My mom got snowed in at the house where they live now, and she got super sick, and Daddy took care of her."

"That's sweet," Conrad murmured, now seeing why Glory Rose loved all things Christmas.

"We decorate a lot at Christmas," she said. "We have some traditional things that we do every year, and then we get new stuff every year too." She smiled and moved deeper into the store, and Conrad went with her.

"I haven't had the same stocking in at least a decade," she said. "Momma either makes a new one, or she buys matching ones for all of us, or we come here, and we get to pick one out." She glanced over her shoulder, pure joy on her face.

Conrad couldn't help smiling, because she seemed so happy, and someone simply couldn't be in her presence without feeling that happiness too. He glanced around the store and realized that it was completely empty, except for a single employee standing behind the checkout counter, at least two-thirds of the way back.

Glory Rose went to the right where a twelve-foot Christmas tree stood. She gazed at it and said, "Wow, look at this tree."

It held only blue and silver ornaments, and they weren't the traditional sleighs and Santas and bells, but butterflies and hummingbirds and fireflies.

"They're clips," Glory Rose said, reaching out and pinching the clip together and removing it from the tree limb. *Click.* She quickly put it back. "I've never seen blue poinsettias before." She looked at him and paused. "What?"

"I've never seen a more beautiful woman," he said, his kissing opportunity opening right in front of him.

Glory Rose ducked her head and tucked her hair behind her ear as a pretty crimson flush filled her face. "Do you like Christmas, Conrad?"

"Sure," he said. "Who doesn't like Christmas?"

"There are people who don't like Christmas," she said.

He edged closer to her, moving her a little further behind the tree. If someone came into the store and deliberately looked over at them, they'd see them, but no one came in. The employee couldn't be seen past the tree, and Conrad lifted his hand and slid it along Glory Rose's face to the back of her neck.

"I'd like to kiss you now," he murmured.

"Right here?" she whispered.

"Have you forgotten that your momma and daddy have a camera on their front door?"

Alarm crossed her face, and then Glory Rose's mouth settled into a smile. Conrad couldn't look away from it, and when she didn't ask him another question, he pulled her close and lowered his head to kiss her.

One touch of his lips against hers, and Conrad fell. He didn't mind it, because he knew there'd be something there to catch him. He simply wanted to enjoy the sense of falling and kissing Glory Rose, and he allowed himself that one small pleasure as he stroked his mouth against hers.

He hadn't kissed a woman in a while, but he still remembered how to do it, and pure heat drove through him as Glory Rose decidedly kissed him back.

Chapter Ten

Glory Rose couldn't believe that Conrad had kissed her in the Christmas store. This had been her favorite place on earth before this kiss, and now it would be the most magical, delightful place she'd ever be able to visit. They could never move and never close, because Glory Rose was going to stop by the mall every day and stand in this very spot where Conrad Walker first kissed her.

He seemed to move slow in some ways and fast in others, and Glory Rose had never been kissed as completely, and as deeply, as Conrad kissed her standing next to that Christmas tree. He pulled away, but Glory Rose kept her eyes closed, because she needed this sensation and this moment to sink into every fiber of her being and fill her soul so that she could remember it forever.

"Okay?" he asked. "Your eyes are still closed."

Her eyelids fluttered open, and the world around her

seemed hazy. Now she suddenly felt too warm in her jacket, and a slip of embarrassment moved through her when she realized she had spaghetti-and-meatballs breath.

She looked at Conrad, who wore pure nerves and vulnerability in his expression. "It was bad, wasn't it?"

"No," she said a bit breathlessly. "It was the best kiss ever."

A smile exploded across Conrad's face. "So when you get the best kiss ever, you fall into a trance, is that it?"

Light and sound rushed back to Glory Rose, and she swatted at Conrad's chest. "I did not fall into a trance."

He chuckled and settled his cowboy hat back on his head. "You so did."

She didn't want him to get too far away from her, so she wrapped her arms around him and hugged him. "I think you're an incredible person, Conrad," she said into his chest.

"Thank you," he whispered into her hair. "I think you're an incredible person too."

She pulled back and looked up to him, really *feeling* that he thought she was incredible. She tipped up a little bit and touched her lips to his again in a sweeter, far more chaste kiss. "I definitely think you're my boyfriend now."

"Good news." He glanced toward the open area that led back into the mall. "Will you really bring bagels tomorrow morning for breakfast sandwiches?"

"I'd love to," Glory Rose said.

"Grams really isn't very scary," Conrad said. "I mean, even my ex-girlfriend and her aunt stayed with us when they brought Sarina."

He'd just opened a door, and Glory Rose wanted to know more about that, so she raised her eyebrows and stepped away from him. "Will you tell me how you found out about Sarina?"

"Yeah." He sighed. "I'm sure I'll tell you, but I don't really feel like it tonight." He looked over to her as they went through the store filled with holiday baubles and bits and ornaments and candies and confections. "Is that okay?"

"Of course it is," she said. "We have plenty of time to talk about it."

Back out in the main hallway of the mall, they simply walked slowly hand-in-hand until Conrad asked, "Who's the last guy you went out with?"

Every muscle in Glory Rose froze for a moment, which was quite awkward mid-step. She stumbled, and Conrad's hand in hers tightened.

"Oh, is this a sore subject?" He grinned at her, and Glory Rose found the muster to smile back.

"Not really a sore subject," she said. "I've dated here and there, but nothing ever serious—not that I didn't want to be serious with my last boyfriend."

"He didn't want to be serious with you?" Conrad asked.

"He said he did." Glory Rose shook her head, her own memories streaming through her mind. "But he really didn't. I think maybe our definitions of serious were just different."

"What was his?" Conrad asked.

"He just wanted to kiss me all the time," Glory Rose said. "He never came to the ranch. He always wanted me to go to his place, and we never went out."

"And your definition is?"

"I don't know," Glory Rose said thoughtfully. "Let me think about it for a minute." She did as they reached the end of the mall and the small department store there. Conrad simply turned and walked in front of it, and then turned and started walking back down the length of the mall again.

After a few minutes, Glory Rose snuggled in close to his side and brought her other hand over to hold his. "I think it's just what you said in the food court. *Serious* for me means that we get to see each other in all of our different ways. We get to see each other when we're stressed and know how to handle that. We get to see each other on birthdays and holidays, and you get to see me with my parents after I've burned my hand, and with my cousin-roommates, and up at Shiloh Ridge when we do cattle branding and breeding."

"Mm. I like that definition."

"We don't have to like every part of the other person, but we have to like enough of them that we can put up with the ones we don't like."

"What do you mean by that?" he asked.

"Well, for example, you might not like how I leave my clothes all over my bedroom," she said, a measure of teasing entering her voice now. "Or I might not like that you don't fold the laundry immediately after it's dry."

"Whoa, whoa," he said. "Who folds the laundry immediately after it's dry?" He laughed, a joyous, happy sound that made Glory Rose's heart beat faster.

"I think you might have an impossible definition of *serious*," he said. "Ain't no one folds their laundry immediately. Everyone lets it sit in the laundry basket for at least a week."

She laughed too because no, she didn't fold her laundry the moment the dryer buzzed. "You might really want to go skydiving," she said. "And I'm afraid of heights. So you'll have to decide if you can put up with that, and you'll be like, 'I'll go skydiving with my brothers and leave Glory Rose at home.'"

"I don't want to go skydiving," Conrad said.

"But you know what I mean," Glory Rose said. "Like, one of my aunts and uncles, they both love video games, and so they get along real well, and they have shared hobbies. But Aunt Willa really doesn't want six dogs, and Uncle Cactus has six dogs. It's part of him that she just allows him to do and to be. She puts up with it, because it's not really that big of a deal if there are six dogs sleeping out in the barn." Glory Rose looked over to him, a smile on her face. "Right? Willa says they're not sleeping in the house, so it's okay."

Conrad laughed again. He released her hand and put his arm around her waist and held her close. "I like your Aunt Willa and Uncle Cactus."

"I imagine it's like your Grams with the mini donkeys," Glory Rose said. "Surely she didn't imagine that when they moved here to be closer to all your uncles and their families that her husband would get fifty mini donkeys."

"It's only forty—well, after Gramps sold some."

"You see what I mean, though?"

Conrad chuckled and shook his head. "Yes, ma'am, I'm sure she didn't think she'd be living on a farm with mini donkeys."

"But there's more about your grandpa that she *did* love than what she didn't like about the mini donkeys, so it was okay."

"I see what you're saying, Glory Rose." He pressed a kiss to her temple and added, "I can't wait to see and get to know all the parts of you."

Conrad said the most beautiful, romantic things that Glory Rose had ever heard, and she decided on the drive back to Shiloh Ridge Ranch that she would kiss him for her momma and daddy's camera, and then she would go inside and talk to them about her very real and quickly deepening feelings for the cowboy who spoke such beautiful things in such a soft voice.

She didn't even have to go down the hall to her parents' bedroom and knock on the door. They both waited for her at the kitchen table when she entered their house after kissing Conrad and watching him drive off the ranch.

"Oh-ho," Daddy said. "You are in so much trouble." He stood up with a coffee cup in hand and turned toward the kitchen.

Glory Rose looked at her mother. "Why am I in trouble?"

Momma wore a frown between her eyes. "You didn't go to Terrible's. Ace and Holly Ann were there, and they said they didn't see you."

"You know who they did see?" Daddy asked from the kitchen, "Penny and Rhett Walker—using Penny's tickets."

"If you and Conrad want to date," Momma said. "Then just date. Don't lie about it."

Glory Rose glared at her parents and sat down at the end of the table. "I didn't lie about it," she said. "You knew I was going out with Conrad. I've never lied about that—and his grandmother *did* have tickets to Terrible's. We just decided not to use them." It wasn't exactly the truth, but it also wasn't a lie.

Daddy returned to the table with two mugs, and he put a steaming one in front of Glory Rose. "It's hot chocolate," he said gruffly, which was how Glory Rose knew she wasn't really in trouble.

She pulled the mug closer and wrapped her fingers around it, stealing the warmth from the ceramic. "I really like Conrad."

Momma flipped over her phone. "Yeah, we saw you kissing him on the porch. It did look like you two liked each other."

Glory Rose's face filled with heat. "You didn't have to watch."

"Glory."

She looked to her father, because when he spoke in that serious voice and didn't use the second half of her name, he really said so much more than just two syllables.

"I know you're worried about me," she said, the first prick of hot tears forming behind her eyes. "I want to believe that you would be worried no matter who I went out with, but I'm not sure that's true."

When neither Momma nor Daddy jumped in to say, "Of

course it's true," Glory Rose knew that this was Conrad-Walker-specific.

"He's a really good man," she said. "He owns his own farm that he takes care of all by himself. He helps his grandmother every single day, and he's a good dad to that little girl. He has a job outside the farm, and you know what?" She pointed one finger at her mom and then her dad. "He's a wealth manager, and he could really help us here at Shiloh Ridge. He says having my money in a bank account is the worst thing possible."

Daddy blinked. "You left your money in the bank account?"

"Ward," Momma said, and she shook her head.

"What else was I supposed to do with it?" Glory Rose asked. "You gave me no direction. I don't know what I'm doing."

She shook her head too. "That's neither here nor there. We're not talking about that right now, though Conrad *is* a wealth manager, and he's gone to school, and he helps his family with all of their money, and he manages all of his. And I don't know how much he has, but I know it's a heck of a lot more than what I have, so he's not going to take advantage of me for that the way Philip did. And he doesn't want to just hide me away the way Leo did. He came over here tonight *by himself*, even though Daddy glared a hole in the back of his head."

Glory Rose felt herself getting out of control, and she took a deep breath to pull on the reins. "I'm sorry," she murmured. "Give me a minute."

She sighed, so grateful to have such good parents that they did give her a minute. Neither one of them spoke or argued with her or tried to make their case for why Conrad wasn't good enough for her.

Because he was.

"I've liked him for a long time," she said. "Before any of us even knew about his daughter. At first, I thought it was just some silly crush." She picked at her fingernails and looked down at them. "But it's not. I have real feelings for him. He's funny and smart and charming, but he's quiet too, and he's strong and powerful without ever raising his voice, and we've been out three times, and I just kissed him for the first time tonight. And it's not like I'm going to get married next weekend."

She looked between her mother and her father, glad when she found Momma nodding in acceptance. "I know I have a long road to walk with him," she said. "But I want to do it. He's a good man, and he's trying to do the right thing, and he's repenting of the things he's done." She met her daddy's eyes. "Isn't that all we're expected to do?"

He reached out and covered her hand with his. "Yes, Glory Rose, you're right. That's all we're expected to do."

She gave a single nod and lifted her hot chocolate to her lips, hoping the action and the scalding liquid would keep her tears at bay. She should know better, and she set down her cup as the first tear fell.

"Oh, don't cry, Glory Rose," Momma said as she got up and came to hug Glory Rose.

"He's a really sweet man," Glory Rose said. "And I

promise as we get more serious, I'll bring him around, so that you guys can get to know him too."

Momma stepped back and sat down. Daddy squeezed Glory Rose's uninjured hand. "It's a good idea, Glory Rose. When you get more serious, of course we want to spend time to get to know him."

She nodded, her eyes and her nose filled with heat. "Can I stay here tonight?"

Momma quickly wiped at her own eyes and said, "Of course you can."

Glory Rose knew then that she didn't come home as often as she should, though she only lived five minutes down the road. She had a busy job, and she spent most evenings with Pearl Jo and Fawn. So she let the Lord gently chastise her that she needed to give more time to her family, and she got up and hugged Daddy and then Momma, and she let them accompany her into her old bedroom at the mouth of the hallway.

"I love you guys," she said as they headed for the door.

"Love you too, Glory Rose," Daddy said.

"And we love you," Momma said. She closed the door behind her, and Glory Rose rolled onto her side to face the window.

Blinds covered it, but she imagined that she could see through them and down the hill to Conrad's farm. "Bless him," she prayed. "With anything he needs to do or to feel whole and forgiven." She closed her eyes as if she'd fall asleep.

She quickly remembered that she needed to set an alarm, so she could get the bagels down to his farm for breakfast sandwiches in the morning. That done, she closed her eyes and whispered, "Thank you for such good parents, Lord. Please bless me to pay attention to the whisperings of the spirit whenever I'm with Conrad so that I can see him and know him for who he truly is."

She couldn't ask for more than that, and she believed that God would bless her with the discernment she needed to know every step of the way if she should stay with Conrad or not.

And she really hoped that she could.

Chapter Eleven

Penny Walker woke to the sound of the bell on the back door. Conrad had installed it so he could send Sarina back to the farmhouse while he stayed outside to do chores. He'd trained his beautiful daughter in the way to come to the house, and he always sent at least one dog with her.

Penny couldn't move as fast as she once had, so she wasn't surprised when she heard Conrad's low voice murmuring something to Sarina, and then the back door closed. Her bedroom sat closest to the kitchen and living room, and she always kept the door open, so she could hear Conrad and Sarina if they needed help in the night.

But she'd never gotten up to help them, because Conrad always took care of everything before she awakened. He was so much like Gideon in that way. Her husband had never been able to sleep much past dawn, and as they'd gotten older and Penny slept later, Gideon would get up, do his chores on the farm, and have breakfast made before Penny even realized that he wasn't in bed with her.

Her door opened further, and Penny blinked as little Sarina came into view. "Gams," she said, and Penny reached for her. Her great-granddaughter's face bloomed with a smile, and she ran toward her. "You wake. You wake."

"I'm awake, my beauty." Penny couldn't lift her up with one arm, so she pushed off her blanket and sat up. Sarina pressed right into her knees, and Penny patted her on the back in a sort of hug. "Have you gone out to the farm already?"

"Eggs," Sarina said. Then she babbled a long sentence with vowel and consonant sounds that Penny couldn't understand. She heard Conrad in the kitchen, opening the fridge and setting a pan on the stove. He'd get breakfast put together before long.

"How many eggs?" Penny asked as she bent over and picked up Sarina. Sarina held up both hands—all ten fingers—and said, "Eight."

"Eight eggs," Penny said, a smile filling her whole soul. "Our chickens are doing a good job."

"Chick, chick, chick," Sarina chirped.

Sometimes Penny simply pulled on a housecoat and went out to the kitchen to eat with Conrad and Sarina. But her old mind somehow remembered that Conrad had told her that Glory Rose would be coming for breakfast that day.

"You go out with your daddy now," she said. "Let Grams get dressed." She set Sarina on her feet, and the little girl ran out of the bedroom. Penny longed for the days when she had that much energy, but it took her much longer to get to her feet and walk to the door to close it. Her bedroom and Sarina's connected with a bathroom, and she hurried to brush her teeth and puff her hair and get on her clothes so that she could meet Conrad's new girlfriend.

She found him in the kitchen crisping bacon while coffee dripped into the pot. "Morning, Grams." He leaned into her as she kissed his cheek, and Penny was just so happy that she didn't have to wake up in this house alone, or make her own coffee, or wonder what the day was going to bring.

"How's the farm?" She moved over to the back door to check on the dogs. Conrad had three of them who went out onto the farm with him every day: a blue heeler, a yellow lab, and an Australian shepherd. He often used Boomerang to get Sarina back to the farmhouse because shepherds loved to herd, and it didn't matter if it was sheep, cattle, or children.

Sometimes Boomerang herded the chickens and turkeys, and Grams smiled at the three canines sitting in the shade on the back deck.

"Farm's great," he said. "Sari got eleven eggs today."

"She said eight," Grams said.

"We're working on the counting."

"Do they need to be fed?" she asked, indicating the dogs.

"Yep," Conrad said. "Sarina put water in the barn for them, but they haven't had breakfast yet."

"I'll do it," she said.

"Glory Rose just texted to say she left Shiloh Ridge," he said. "She should be here in about twenty-five minutes."

Penny nodded as she opened the garage door to fill the dogs' bowl with food. She paused, a thought in her mind, a question that she felt prompted to ask Conrad. "Are you nervous?"

"Yes," he said in a short, clipped tone. Conrad was what Penny would call even. He didn't get angry, and he didn't yell. He had frustrations and irritations, sure, but he usually coped with them by putting his head down and going to work. He reminded her very much of Gideon in that regard, as well as his daddy and Jeremiah, though Jeremiah tended to have more outbursts than Conrad or Rhett ever had.

"Why are you nervous?" Penny asked. "It's just me."

"And Sarina," he said.

"You think she won't like us?"

"I think she loves you already," Conrad said. "Glory Rose is...an optimist."

"You say that like it's a bad thing," Penny said.

Conrad grunted, and she took that as her hint to go get the dog food and give him a moment to think. So she did, taking her time on the three steps that led down to the main floor of the garage. Conrad had installed a railing there the very first week he'd moved into the farmhouse. He'd put handles in all of their bathrooms as well, because she and Gideon had definitely been getting up in age, even then.

She filled the dog bowl with food and went out the door that led directly into the backyard. She set it up on the deck and pushed it forward. "Here you go, hounds."

Stevie Nicks, the yellow lab, came over first because she was the pack leader and definitely the greediest of the dogs.

Penny drew in a deep breath of the crisp morning air, though the sun had already started to heat it. She loved early spring in the Texas Panhandle, and as she breathed out, she said, "I miss you, Gideon."

She took another breath, and this time as she exhaled, she said, "Thank you, Lord, for my time here on earth. Thank you for another morning with eleven eggs and a beautiful child and a new girlfriend."

She only wanted her sons, their wives, and all of her grandchildren to have nothing but happiness. She'd gotten married young, and she and Gideon had relied on each other for everything over many years and raising seven sons, watching them get married and have families of their own.

There had been some hard days and some very good ones. There had been a lot of laughter and yet a lot of tears as well. There had been times when everything went their way and times when there were accidents and mishaps and injuries.

Penny had learned to take the good with the bad, and in fact, she had learned that that was God's plan for His children. How would they even know the good from the bad if they didn't get to experience both?

So yes, she was grateful for the good times and the bad times and everything in between. She was grateful that Chloe had shown up in Three Rivers unannounced last summer with Sarina in tow, because the truth had finally come out. Conrad could finally heal and move forward.

And he had been doing that, and doing it really well.

"Bless him," she whispered, just like she did every morning, noon, and night. "Bless him to know how loved he is by me, by that little girl, by his family, and by Thee."

Penny knew the Glovers, of course. She'd lived in Three

Rivers for decades now, and the Glovers were old blood with the most successful ranch in town. She'd attended Ward and Dot's wedding, and she'd taken a gift at the birth of their oldest child, Glory Rose.

"Bless her," she prayed next. "To not be too nervous to come here. Bless her to be kind, and that if she is right for Conrad, that they will both grow to know it."

Satisfied with her morning prayer, Penny went back into the garage and up the steps and into the house. "All fed," she told Conrad.

"Thank you, Grams." He had the plate of bacon on the counter along with the container of orange juice, a plate of butter, a stack of Kraft singles, and Sarina's basket of eggs. "We're just waiting on Glory Rose to bring the bagels."

He hadn't put his daughter in her eating seat yet, probably because he wanted to introduce her to Glory Rose. Penny took another breath and asked, "Do you think we won't like her?"

Conrad looked at her, a hooded expression on his face. "I don't know, Grams," he said. "It's just weird for me, okay? I mean, I haven't had a girlfriend in a long time, and never since I bought this place and moved in here with you."

"So you used to be able to bring women home and not have to make it a big show?"

"Right," he said. "You know how I love the big show." A wry smile touched his lips.

Grams smiled too. "It doesn't have to be a big show," she said. "It's just me and Sarina, and we don't really care for a show either."

"I watch show," Sarina said, toddling over to Grams and tugging on the bottom of her shirt. "Watch show?"

"No, baby." Grams bent and picked up Sarina with a groan pulling through her back and coming out her mouth. "We're going to eat breakfast first, then maybe your daddy will let you watch a show."

Penny was always very careful not to promise Sarina anything from Conrad. She also tried very hard never to make any decisions for him, even something as simple as saying that Sarina could watch her cartoons after they ate breakfast.

She wanted to empower her grandson to make those decisions for himself, and for his daughter. He'd struggled with it in the beginning, but he'd grown into the role quite well over the past several months.

The doorbell rang, and that set Stormy off in the backyard. The blue heeler loved to bark at anything that moved or made a sound, but inside, all the humans looked toward the front door.

"Ding, dong, ding, ding, dong," Sarina sang, and Conrad wiped his hands on his jeans.

"That'll be Glory Rose," he said. "I'll get it. Will you just stay here?"

He didn't wait for Penny to confirm before he hurried out of the kitchen and down the short hallway to the front door. Penny wanted to migrate to the corner and watch Conrad's greeting for Glory Rose, but she didn't. She stayed where she stood and brushed Sarina's hair off her forehead. "Your daddy hasn't done your hair yet today."

"Daddy," Sarina said.

"Wow," a female voice mingled with Conrad's deeper one. Then he came around the corner, his hand in that of the prettiest brunette Penny had ever seen: Glory Rose Glover.

She'd had time to do her hair that day, and she'd clipped it back on both sides so that it sat out of her face. She wore a smile on her glossy lips, but no lipstick and very little makeup that Penny could see. Her dark eyes shone like welcome light in the middle of a stormy night, and she first glanced at Conrad and then back to Penny and Sarina.

"Let me take those bagels." He took the bag Glory Rose carried. "This is my grandmother," he said. "Penny Walker, and my daughter Sarina. Guys, this is Glory Rose." He grinned at her and then over to Penny. "My girlfriend."

Glory Rose moved forward as Conrad diverted into the kitchen. "It's so great to meet you," she said, her hand outstretched, but Penny required both arms to hold Sarina, and Glory Rose took the little girl easily into her own arms, settled her on her hip, and then hugged Penny with her free hand.

"It's lovely to meet you too," Penny said. "You're wearing a bandage, my dear. What happened?"

"Oh, just a tiny mishap with the boiling water when we were making the bagels," Glory Rose said as she lifted her wrapped hand. "It's nothing."

She smiled at Sarina. "Your daddy said he didn't have time to do your hair this morning, and that I could do it. Would that be okay?"

Sarina nodded, and Penny hoped that Glory Rose wouldn't feel too bad that she didn't say anything to her.

Sarina didn't speak a whole lot as it was, and while she was used to being passed around from person to person, she rarely went to someone that she didn't know.

"You can put her in her eating seat," Penny said. "Conrad does her hair there, and I'll help him with breakfast."

"I got it all out for you, Glory Rose," he said, and he nodded to the dining room table. "It's sitting right there."

"And this must be your seat," Glory Rose said, as she moved over to the pink plastic seat attached to a dining room chair, where the spray bottle, comb, and Sari's ponytail elastics waited.

"Seat," Sarina said, and Penny watched Conrad's face as he shone with absolute joy and wonder.

She joined him in the kitchen as he turned his back on the scene and started cracking the eggs that Sarina had collected that morning. Penny pressed in close to him and said, "I see why you were nervous."

"Yeah?" he asked. "Why's that?"

"Because she's wonderful," Penny said.

"She's been here for two minutes, Grams," he growled.

"A grandmother knows," she said. "She has a very good air about her, Conrad." Penny turned and looked at Glory Rose as she combed Sarina's hair, chitchatting a one-sided conversation with the child as she did.

Yes, Glory Rose had a very good way about her, and Penny smiled to herself, then prayed silently, *If it be Thy will, let me live long enough to see this through to a wedding.*

Chapter Twelve

Finn Ackerman reached up to open the door at the back of the farm supply store. "Right here, Bubba," he said as his almost three-year-old started to toddle off in a different direction. "Bubs, over here."

His son came his way, and Finn held the door while the little boy went sniffling inside. He didn't normally bring his kids to the small ranch owners' meetings that had started out with just a few people, including him and his brother-in-law. But Bubba was sick today, and Edith felt bad taking him over to Nikki's while she finished her book, so Finn had him. He bent and swooped his son into his arms, so he could get down the hall and into the meeting room that he'd rented for today's get-together.

He heard voices as he approached, so he wouldn't be the first one there. It didn't matter, though; most of the men and women who came to the meetings looked to him as their leader. He didn't intend to be, but he had started the meetings, and his friends and fellow small ranch owners seemed to respect him.

Of course, not everyone owned a small ranch, as Lincoln Glover had been coming to the meetings almost since the very beginning, and Shiloh Ridge was one of the biggest ranches in Texas. It was definitely the biggest one in the Panhandle.

Finn had bought a piece of land bordering the ranch where he'd grown up, and he and his wife ran it by themselves with their children. His younger half-sister had taken over Three Rivers Ranch where they'd both been raised, and Libby often came to the meetings with her husband, Rusty.

Today, though, Finn found only Rusty and Paul standing in the corner of the room closest to the beverage bar that he'd ordered from Sips. "Oh good, they brought the coffee, tea, and hot chocolate," he said.

Paul was his cousin—his daddy's sister's son—and he ran Courage Reins, which was an equine therapy unit housed at Three Rivers Ranch. Finn set Bubba in the middle of the table and said, "Stay right there, and Daddy will get you a drink."

He moved down the long row of tables to his friends and family. "How are you guys?" He saw Rusty and Paul often, but he still gave them a big three-way hug and then moved to get the hot chocolate for Bubba as promised.

"Things are going great," Paul said.

"No Libby today?" Finn asked.

"She's throwing up again," Rusty said. "I can't wait until she's out of the first trimester, if only so I don't have to see her crying every morning."

Finn's heart ached over that too, and he thanked the Good Lord Above that Edith had never been too sick during her three pregnancies. "I'm sorry," he said. "We can bring dinner by tonight."

"Your momma's cooking already," Rusty said with a smile. "So we should have enough for the next week. How about next weekend?" He chuckled and Finn joined him, because yes, his momma knew how to cook for a crowd.

She had to, because she had married Squire, Finn's step-daddy, when Finn was only five years old, and she became the matron at Three Rivers Ranch. They were a big cattle operation with over twenty cowboys who lived and worked on site. His momma knew how to feed them all, at any time of year, any type of food, for any meal.

"Maybe I should come over tonight then," Finn joked, and Paul said, "Brielle and I will definitely be by," with a large smile on his face.

"Howdy, boys."

Finn turned to find Lincoln Glover entering the room with his cousin, Wilder. Bear and Ranger Glover had run Shiloh Ridge for decades, but they were both now retired full-time from ranch work, and their oldest sons, Link and Wilder, ran the ranch together. From what Finn understood, their uncle Preacher still acted as their main foreman, and they were looking to fill the foreman position that Ward Glover had been doing in the agricultural department at Shiloh Ridge for many years.

They'd fill it from someone in the family, Finn knew that, but no announcements had been made yet.

"I've got invites for everyone here," Link said, and he threw a big pile of postcards on the table. "Misty and I are hosting a birthday party up at Shiloh Ridge in True Blue in the middle of March." He grinned around at those present. "We want everyone to come."

Finn took the small cup of hot chocolate down the table to his son and handed it to him. "Two hands, Bubba," he told him, and then he picked up one of the postcards. "You're gonna be thirty-three?" He grinned over at Link. "We'll be there, brother." He gave him a fist bump and then looked back at the invitation again.

True Blue was an event barn that Bishop Glover had conceptualized and restored many years ago. The Glover family held a lot of their parties there, including weddings, but they also offered it to the community for anyone else who needed a big event space.

With Link and Misty having their birthdays in the same month, just the Glover family required a big space. This invitation wasn't just for couples, either. At the bottom, it said *children are welcome*, and Finn couldn't wait to tell Edith about the party.

"You guys know Wilder, right?" Link asked. "He's gonna start coming to the meetings since he officially took over for his daddy this month." He smiled at his cousin, and Wilder raised his hand and waved to everyone there.

"This is everyone?" he asked. "I thought it would be a much bigger group."

"Oh, it's a much bigger group, all right," a grumpy voice said, and Finn tucked his postcard invitation away as Dawson

Rhinehart entered the room. He came with his younger brother Brandon, as they ran a lot of the operations on the Rhinehart Ranch, which was just south of Shiloh Ridge. Their older half-brother Duke had married a Glover, and they lived on and ran the ranch, but he didn't come to the meetings.

Duke was a generation older than Finn and the other men and women who attended these ranch meetings, though a small part of Finn wondered if he should personally extend an invite to this meeting. Perhaps he should simply let Dawson and Brandon take back the knowledge they learned here.

That thought rang true, and Finn stopped worrying about Duke Rhinehart and whether he might feel left out. Anyone could attend these meetings, and Dawson and Brandon certainly knew how to invite their older half-brother.

Laughter came down the hall as Dawson said, "There's plenty more people coming in. I just saw Henry and Angel parking when we got here." Sure enough, Henry and Angel entered the room next, as they ran her boarding stable, Lone Star, just outside of Amarillo. They lived halfway between Three Rivers and the boarding stable, and Henry was Paul's brother and Finn's cousin.

They had their first baby about eighteen months ago, and Finn wondered if they'd be making any announcements about having a second. Henry had a loud personality, and he stepped over to Brandon and hugged him, and then turned to Dawson and said, "So you just let that door slam in our faces, huh?" Then he laughed loudly and clapped Dawson into a hug also.

"Who are we missing?" Paul asked as he approached Finn

and handed him a cup of coffee. "I put cream and sugar in that."

"Thanks, brother," Finn said. He glanced around. "Link, is Mitch coming?"

Link shook his head. "He's got meetings with the construction crew all day today," he said. "He won't be here."

Mitch Glover wasn't really operating a ranch either, but he had bought a large piece of property on the southeastern highway where he was now building a deaf academy for students ages five to fifty-five.

From what Finn knew, Mitch had already hired an educational director and an administrative assistant to run the school, and now he just needed to build the facilities that would allow him to have students live on-site.

"The Walkers aren't here either," Rusty said. "I don't see JJ or Conrad."

There'd been a bit of hurt feelings surrounding Conrad when he first found out that he had a daughter, and he'd skipped meetings for a couple of months. He'd since returned, and Finn added, "Alex isn't here either, and I didn't hear that he wasn't coming today."

"I'm right here," Alex said as he rounded the corner. "And JJ and Conrad and Tate are right behind me."

Oh yes, Tate Reynolds. He'd been living at Seven Sons for almost a year now, and he'd worked there for a few summers before that. He wanted to buy his own place here in Three Rivers, and he and Clara Jean Walker were getting married in a couple of months.

Finn almost expected him to take over all of the farmland

that fed Wilde & Organic, as Clara Jean had been working there for years, and her mother owned the grocery store.

"All right," he said. "Everyone take seats. The Walkers are on their way in."

"Oh, you got a coffee bar," Brandon said. "Bless you."

Finn pulled out the chair right in front of Bubba and sat down with his coffee. "Yes, there's a hot bar," he said. "Coffee, tea, hot chocolate. Get a drink, get your announcements ready, and then we'll go over our plans for breeding season."

He tried to set a topic each month, and he asked for suggestions all the time. Not all of them ran a cattle ranch, but springtime was an incredibly busy time and the best time to bring new livestock to a farm or ranch. There was often an explosion of growth in March and April, leading into the summer months as all sorts of animals produced young or owners brought on new animals.

"Sorry we're late," JJ said as he led the Walker clan into the room. "Oh, it smells good in here."

"I told you they'd have coffee," Conrad said. "We didn't need to go through that drive-through." He didn't seem terribly upset about it, and all of the Walkers skipped the coffee bar, because they carried in to-go cups with them.

Only a few empty seats remained, and Finn grinned around at all of his friends and fellow ranchers. "How is everyone?" he asked.

"Doing great," and "Good," and "Hanging in there," came from everyone, and then all eyes looked at him again.

Link reached into the middle of the table and lifted his postcards. "Misty and I are having a big party next month," he said. "We want everyone to come. Please take these so I don't have to take them home to my wife and tell her I didn't hand them out." He grinned around, and everyone took a postcard until they all had one.

"We can bring kids?" Henry asked.

"Yep," Link said. "The more the merrier. We're gonna have some games and activities for them up at the ranch." He picked up the leftover cards. "I'll make sure I take one to Ollie and Mitch." He glanced down the row. "Is there anyone else who needs one?"

Finn wasn't sure who else he would invite, so he kept quiet. No one else made any suggestions either, and Link tucked away the extra invitations.

"Personal news or announcements?" Finn asked. He smiled at his son, who could make a toy out of a paper cup. "I had to bring Bubba with me today, because he's not feeling good, and we didn't want to take him over to Alex's and get the twins sick."

He looked at his brother-in-law, who had sat next to him. "You're up, brother."

"Has anyone looked at the forecast?" he asked. "Because it looks like there's gonna be a lot of rain in the next couple of weeks, and I'm worried about my place getting sinkholes again."

He exchanged a glance with Finn, and Finn well remembered the sinkholes that had been on Alex's ranch. He and Edith had been dating at the time, and Finn had single-handedly figured out how to deal with the sinkholes, and he and Alex had fixed them.

"If that happens, we'll come help," Finn said.

"I've got some news," Rusty said. "Some of you know already, but Libby's pregnant. She's due in September, and she's real worried about it, because it's right during harvest time."

"We'll come help," Finn said again, because he would and he knew every man and woman sitting at the table, though they had their own harvest to bring in every autumn, would leave their ranch or farm and come help Libby as well.

"That's great news," Angel said. "I didn't know she was pregnant." She beamed at Rusty and then picked up her phone. "I'll text her congratulations right now."

"One of our master horsemen is leaving," Henry said. "And we need to replace him. If any of you know someone who's exceptional with horses, will you please send him my way? I need him at Lone Star."

Finn nodded and made a mental note of the personnel that Henry needed.

"I'm seeing someone new," Brandon said.

"When *aren't* you seeing someone new?" Dawson asked him. He wore his grumpy cowboy expression, but Brandon simply waved his hand at him, a huge smile on his face.

"Who is it?" Wilder asked.

Finn chuckled and shook his head. "Oh, Brandon never tells."

"I tell," Brandon said. "When I make it to date ten. And just because I haven't ever made it there doesn't mean I wouldn't tell."

JJ lifted his coffee cup to his mouth, took a sip, and said, "Conrad's seeing someone new too."

"That's not your news to tell," Tate said. "Leave the man alone."

"Oh, he's gonna tell," JJ said, and he smiled over to his cousin. "Right, Conrad?"

Conrad looked at Link and then Wilder, his eyes bouncing between the two of them, and Finn sensed something in the air that had not been there a moment ago. Conrad swallowed and cleared his throat. "Yeah," he said. "I'm seeing someone new, and it's not like we can keep it a secret in this town."

"You're dating a Glover," JJ said. "I don't know what you thought would happen."

"You're dating a Glover?" Link asked. "Who?"

"I know who," Wilder said with a wildly wide smile on his face.

Conrad gestured to him, and Wilder glanced around the group and said, "It's Glory Rose."

"It could've been your sister," Link said, and they laughed.

"Fawn's pretty too," Conrad said, and he ducked his cowboy hat so Finn couldn't see his eyes.

"How long has that been going on?" Finn asked. "Are you getting serious?"

Conrad raised his eyes again, and he looked boldly at Finn. "I have a three-year-old daughter, so everything I do is serious."

"It's been a couple weeks," JJ said. "They're going real slow, because yes, Conrad takes everything way too seriously."

"I take everything way too seriously? Have you met your-self?" Conrad tipped his head back and laughed, and Finn sure did like it when JJ joined him. He added his own chuckles to those in the group, and he looked at the next person in line.

Tate had a really bright personality, a quick laugh, and a big smile. "Clara Jean is talking to her uncle about taking over the farmland that produces for the grocery store," he said. "If she can do that, we're gonna buy it from him, build a house on it, and live there." He grinned and grinned and grinned. "I might just have my own piece of land sooner than I thought."

JJ clapped him on the shoulder and nodded, his smile firmly in place. "You will, brother."

Finn nodded and said, "Let us know if we can come help. We can get a house built lickety-split. You guys can be moved in before long."

"Probably not before you get married," Paul said. "But faster than a contractor."

"Yeah, talk to Mitch about that," Link said.

Dawson passed on his news, saying things were fine with their new baby who had just been born in December. "She's a real cute little thing," Dawson said with a smile. "I fear she's going to be my downfall."

"Daughters always are."

Finn turned to look over his shoulder at the new voice that had entered the conversation. Oliver Walker stood there, and he raised his hand. "Hello, sorry I'm late," he said. He glanced around. "And I'm really the only one who has a daughter besides Dawson?"

Finn looked around the table as well, and he realized that yes, none of them had girls. Link and Misty had two sons. He and Edith had three. Alex and Nikki had their twin boys, and Henry had a son. Dawson's oldest was a boy, and Paul and Brielle didn't have children yet. Libby and Rusty were pregnant with their first. Tate, Wilder, and JJ weren't married yet.

Then his eyes landed on Conrad, whose face had turned a deep maroon red. "I have a daughter." He glanced down the table to Dawson. "And yes, they turn your life upside down."

"Any news, Wilder?" Finn asked, hoping to keep the conversation moving so that Conrad wouldn't feel too awkward. "We always do a little bit of personal news at the beginning," he explained. "You can pass. You can say something about a job need or something you're worried about, like Alex, or you can say that you're seeing someone, or that you're engaged, or that you're pregnant."

"Well, I'm not pregnant," Wilder said. Another round of laughter moved through the room, and he added, "And I'm not drowning; that's about as good as it gets."

And for taking over at a huge operation like Shiloh Ridge, Finn was pretty proud of him for not drowning. "All right," he said. "We're gonna be talking about breeding this month and any other animal care needs that you have."

He looked to the man on his left side, because he asked him to lead out and get the conversation started. "Link?"

"We're doing pretty good with breeding cattle," he said. "We've got a schedule, and it goes pretty well. What I'm wondering about is if any of you have any experience with guineafowl."

"Guineafowl?" Conrad asked. "They're like game birds. You can house them with turkeys and chickens, right?"

"That's what I'm asking," Link said. "We do a lot of animal work on our fields, but we've never had guineafowl."

"They're really good at getting rid of pests," JJ said. "I knew a guy in school who used them in Missouri to get rid of ticks."

"That's interesting. We do always have a big problem with grasshoppers." He typed something into his phone, and then Rusty asked a question about Link's schedule with breeding.

Finn didn't run a cattle operation the way they did at Shiloh Ridge, Seven Sons, or Three Rivers, so he went to get his son another cup of hot chocolate, and he quickly texted Edith a picture of the invitation to Link and Misty's party.

He didn't expect her to respond, because she was on a deadline and needed to get her writing done, but she texted back almost immediately with, *I'm clearing our schedule now and adding that to the calendar.*

Finn turned around and looked at all the good men and women he had the privilege of working with and being friends with, and as he returned to his seat, he'd never felt so loved by those around him in the room—and by God above.

For he knew that the Lord had directed his feet to Three Rivers, to the land that he and his wife owned and worked, and to these people.

And not only had God done that for Finn, He'd done it for every single person in the room as well. They were all here together at this time for a reason, and Finn was so grateful for a loving Heavenly Father who guided His children in such a way.

Chapter Thirteen

M itchell Glover hated with his whole soul that he had to use Lacy as an interpreter. But he did, because he couldn't talk to the construction manager with his hands, and the construction manager didn't seem to understand that he had to look straight at Mitch before he spoke.

He kept glancing around and throwing his hand up, or wiping his mouth, or taking a drink, and Mitch couldn't read lips if he couldn't see the man's mouth.

Thankfully, he'd learned that early on, and Lacy had been in town for the past couple of months. She had grown up hearing, with a deaf brother, and was exceptionally skilled in sign language and interpreting. In fact, she had gone to college and studied interpreting and had been interpreting for the state of Texas for five years before Mitch poached her away to be his educational director.

He did not want her to be his interpreter, but he saw no

other way to communicate when the construction team called meetings. He'd used Link a time or two, but Link was extremely busy at Shiloh Ridge and married with two kids. Lacy already lived on the property that Mitch had purchased, and she knew everything he had planned in intimate detail.

In fact he'd planned most of it with her.

He had a few secret hidden plans that every time they came up, he squashed them right back down. Mitch had never struggled to get a date or go out with a woman, hearing or otherwise, and he'd really like to go out with Lacy Hayes. But he'd hired her after several online video interviews, and he had no idea just how powerful and beautiful she'd be in person.

He had too much on his plate to be dating anyway, and he certainly couldn't start a relationship with the woman on which his entire deaf academy hinged. What if they broke up?

Mitch had no evidence that he could sustain a relationship for longer than a few months, for he had never done that, and he certainly needed Lacy in his life for a lot longer than a few months.

So he pushed away the feelings he had for her and focused on being professional. They worked together on building a deaf curriculum, starting in kindergarten and going all the way through adulthood.

Right now, they sat at a triangular table that Mitch had built specifically for meeting with hearing people. That way, he could see them, and he could see Lacy almost at the same time.

Dealing with hearing people irritated Mitch, though he

tried not to let it. Everyone in his family was hearing. Heck, everyone in Three Rivers was hearing, and hearing people simply didn't understand, well, that deaf people couldn't hear.

Sure, intellectually, they knew it, but they didn't *understand* what it really meant to be hearing. Mitch could be in a room, and someone could call his name, and he wouldn't know.

They didn't have to look at one another to communicate, and they talked over each other incessantly. Mitch hated that the most—that hearing people interrupted each other. In the deaf community, they didn't do that. He got to say what he wanted to say, and the person he was talking to waited until he finished, and then they responded. Hearing people didn't do that.

Lacy wore her luxurious blonde hair completely down and perfectly straight. She signed as she spoke with the construction manager, a man named William, who insisted they call him Bill. So Mitch and Lacy had made up a sign like the bill of a baseball hat for his name.

Right now, Lacy explained to him the layout of the dormitories that Mitch wanted—a design that he'd gotten from an architect and paid quite a lot of money for. "They'll be five floors each," she said, but Bill was already shaking his head.

"You don't have the permit to build a five-story building on your land," he said. "If you want a building taller than three stories, you have to get a special permit from the Three Rivers Planning and Zoning Commission."

Lacy finished signing and then picked up her pen to write down the information. Mitch signed something to her, but he didn't wait long enough. Bill's mouth was already moving, and Lacy held up one hand to silence him.

Pure satisfaction drove through Mitch as she said, "Wait just a minute, Bill. Mitch has something to say," and she waited for him to sign to her.

Is it just the residential buildings that can't be more than three stories? Mitch asked. *Or is it our academy as well?*

She repeated the question to Bill, who said, "All buildings."

I thought I bought a commercial piece of property, Mitch said.

"You did," Bill said. "But that doesn't mean that you can build anything you want on it without approval. And the permits you got are standard. They only allow a three-story building."

There were definitely taller buildings in Three Rivers, and Mitch would simply have to get the permit he needed. *How long does it take to get a permit?* he asked.

"You have to submit and wait for the Planning and Zoning Commission to meet," Bill said. "They do that once a month; I think on the third Wednesday."

The calendar had just turned over to March, so the third Wednesday wouldn't be for another couple of weeks. Mitch nodded to Lacy, and she would make sure that they got that filed on time.

How far will this put us back then? he asked. *Can you pour the foundations for the buildings before we have the permit?*

Bill frowned, and if Mitch could assign a sound to him, he

would say he was growling. "I can," Bill said, but then he didn't go on.

Mitch waved at Lacy, and she said, "And?"

"Technically I'm not supposed to," Bill said. "Because I have to get the plans approved before we build. And you're trying to build a five-story building, which will not be approved. But I can pour the foundations, and we can get started on at least the first three levels."

Mitch nodded. *I want to do that. I can't afford to lose any time.* He'd been warned by his momma and daddy, as well as Uncle Bishop and Aunt Montana, that construction always took much longer than predicted.

"Add another half of what they told you," Aunt Montana had told him. "So if they're telling you a year, Mitch, it'll be eighteen months."

Mitch was planning on eighteen months because he'd been told twelve, but he still didn't want to wait to pour the foundations for the dormitories. Eighteen months would put him in summertime next year, and that would allow him to open the academy in the fall, and he really wanted to open the academy in time for the new school year.

The meeting with Bill ended, and the construction manager left the room. Mitch sighed, and though he couldn't hear himself, he knew he made noise. Lacy tapped the table in front of him, and he glanced up. "What was that?" she asked.

I don't like dealing with the construction, he said.

"We could hire someone," Lacy said. She was always very good not to start sentences with "you should" as Mitch had learned that he didn't like being told what to do. He had a vision, and he wanted people around him to help him adjust or change his vision, but he didn't want them to tell him what it should be.

"There are plenty of people who could deal with the construction and the coming together of the physical facilities," Lacy said. "They're called a physical facilities manager, and you know you're going to need one once the academy opens anyway."

He jotted down "physical facilities manager" and looked up again. *What do you mean? What does the physical facilities manager do?*

"They make sure the air-conditioning works in the summer and the heat works in the winter," she said. "If a student spills something on the carpet and it needs to be cleaned or replaced, your physical facilities manager will do it. They'll determine which rooms get new dressers, new beds, new appliances—all of that. Anything to do with your physical facilities and the maintaining of the dormitories and the buildings—the roofing, the windows—a physical facilities manager will handle that."

So I need a physical facilities manager, Mitch said. *And it will be a full-time position?*

"Absolutely," Lacy said.

Mitch needed teachers too, and he needed resident assistants to help with the underage students. He needed groundskeepers and housekeepers and extracurricular activity directors.

He knew he'd bitten off a huge chunk of life when he'd

decided to open this deaf academy, but he didn't regret it for a single second.

Let's add the physical facilities manager to our list of jobs that we're going to put up next week, he said. *You'll help me with the interviews?*

She smiled at him, and it was seriously the most beautiful sight Mitch had ever seen. His heart pounded wildly in his chest, and he wanted to reach out and cover her hand with his and then ask her to dinner, signing with only one hand.

"I love doing interviews," she said, and she gathered together her papers and closed her folder. She stood, and Mitch took the half-second before she looked at him to admire the curve of her hip and the color of her blouse. Then he jumped to his feet too and said, *We really can't afford to lose any time on this build.*

"We won't," she said, her face determined. "Let's go back to your office and get everything in line for the jobs." She raised her eyebrows, and Mitch nodded. He followed her out of the general meeting room that he'd put on the main floor of the big farmhouse he'd bought. He lived on the second floor, and Lacy lived on the third.

He'd converted those areas into separate apartments after purchasing the property and house last autumn. They both had offices on this level, and Mitch was planning to build an administration building specifically for the academy, where all of the classes and other faculty offices would be located.

Do we need to provide housing for any of these positions? Mitch asked as he settled behind his desk. Lacy, ever the professional that she was, waited until he was settled and looked at her before she answered.

"I don't think so, Mitch. Maybe your Dean of Students. It might be nice if he had a place on campus since he'll be so involved in their lives."

And the resident assistants, he said. *But we're planning on them having their own floor.*

"Right," she said. "But your teachers, your physical facilities manager, your groundskeepers, your housekeepers—they can live in town and come out to the academy to do their jobs. They don't need to be on-site."

I'll do some more research, Mitch told her, and he woke his computer by jostling the mouse. *I want parents to feel like we have enough adult supervision here, or they won't want to let their kids live here during the school year.*

He glanced over to her and found her signing—*might be requirements*—and he nodded.

Yes, there very well might be state requirements for the number of adults I have to have on-site at all times compared to the number of full-time students I house.

Mitch had spent the last several years at the first deaf college in the country, and he'd learned more than he'd ever thought possible about sign language and teaching sign language to someone else. But now that he was back in Three Rivers, he once again felt like he was drinking from a fire hose and learning so many things that he didn't even know he hadn't known.

He typed up his notes and then turned to look at Lacy.

Thank you so much, he said. *For interpreting for me, for being here with me, for taking on this project.*

She waved her hand as if to say, *It's no problem, Mitch.*

She smiled with her straight white teeth, framed by those pretty pink lips, and Mitch lost his mind for a moment. *Would you go out with me?*

Her smile disappeared in the blink of an eye, and what Mitch cataloged as pure panic paraded across her face. He started to wave his hands, saying, *Never mind. Forget it,* but she jumped to her feet, her hands already flying.

Her mouth moved too. "I don't think that would be very smart," and then she turned on her heel and marched out of his office.

Mitch once again sighed, this time bigger than the last, though he couldn't hear it. *Great,* he thought to himself. *You've made a mess of things now.*

Chapter Fourteen

"Wait just a minute," Conrad said, trying to keep the irritation out of his voice. Sarina wanted to run before he even got her all the way out of the truck. He set her on her feet and slammed the door, saying, "All right, go on now."

She ran off yelling, "Rube, Rube, Rube," over and over again at the top of her lungs.

Conrad chuckled to himself, glad that his daughter liked Ruby Reynolds. This wasn't her house, but Sarina obviously associated JJ's farmhouse with Ruby, and why shouldn't she? She'd barely reached the bottom step when the front door of the farmhouse opened, and Ruby came outside.

"Sari." She waited patiently at the top of the steps for Sari to do her two-step shuffle up to the porch. Ruby giggled as she wrapped her up in a hug and picked her up. She looked down to Conrad, who'd only moved to the front of his pickup truck. "JJ and Tate are with the longhorns," she called.

He waved and said, "Thank you, Ruby," before he headed to the left to go around the house and into the backyard. JJ had a pretty nice operation beyond that, with a couple of brand-new barns and stables that he'd put in since he bought this place last year, and pastures and fields that already seemed to be thriving with emerald green grass.

What wasn't thriving was JJ's shoulder. He'd gotten a massage and some arnica ointment for it, but he still struggled with pain—so much so that he'd finally gone to the doctor and they'd done an MRI and an X-ray and couldn't find anything that was torn, broken, or otherwise fixable—at least with surgery.

JJ had been given some painkillers and the instruction to "rest as much as possible." Thus, Conrad had come over to help with the longhorns, but he wasn't surprised at all that JJ was outside already.

He *was* surprised to find his cousin merely leaning against the fence while Tate worked inside the paddock with the longhorns. Most cattle simply grazed, and ranchers used them to maintain their pastures and fields. They may sell them for slaughter or use them as milk cows, or even raise them to be sold to other farms and ranches. Sometimes they were raised for show.

JJ wanted to raise longhorn cattle as a herd, because he wanted them here at Seven Sons. He also wanted to be able to sell starter animals for other ranchers and farmers who wanted longhorn herds on their ranches.

And those buyers expected cattle who knew how to go down a chute, knew how to stand still for vaccinations, knew how to follow the herd to get from pasture to pasture, and were generally accustomed to being around humans.

Unfortunately, none of the longhorns that JJ had purchased knew how to do any of those things. Thus, he wanted to work with them on a daily basis to teach and train them in all the things cattle were expected to do on a ranch.

Today, Tate had a trailer backed up to the other side of the paddock, and none of the longhorns seemed keen on getting inside. They all clustered over by the fence in the corner near JJ, which caused Conrad to smile as he approached.

"Doesn't look like it's going well," he said.

JJ turned and looked over his shoulder at him. "Definitely not," he said. "I think longhorns might be more stubborn than beef cattle."

"No one likes getting on a trailer," Conrad said. "Even the mini donkeys bray about it incessantly." He joined his cousin at the fence, actually proud of him for being on this side of it.

"Can we try it with Boomerang?" JJ asked.

"That's why I brought him," Conrad said. He vaulted the fence and whistled for his Australian Shepherd to join him in the paddock. Boomerang didn't have a lot of practice herding cattle, especially not cattle with horns that spanned five feet across their heads.

Conrad whistled and walked toward the trailer, pulling Boomerang along with him by saying, "Come on, bud. We gotta get them in here, at the trailer." He turned around and looked at Tate on his left now, and all the cattle over in the right corner. He started edging right, and he called, "Round 'em up, round 'em up."

Boomerang took off like a shot, and he ran straight toward the cattle as if he'd been bowled down a lane toward ten pins.

"He's gonna drive them your way," Conrad called to Tate, who lifted the construction-orange flag and waved it.

Conrad kept walking closer to the fence on his right side because he didn't want to be taken out by the horns on any of those cows. Boomerang barked once just before he veered sharply to the right as well and got the cattle moving exactly where Conrad had predicted— toward Tate. The ground shook as they lumbered, and several of them lowed as Tate raised the flag and his other arm as well, making himself as big as possible.

The cattle wouldn't want to go that direction either, and now Conrad had them hemmed in on the right. Boomerang hung over on Conrad's side for a moment, barked once, and then ran behind the cattle over to Tate, keeping them in one group moving steadily toward the trailer—their only option of escape.

It had an extra wide opening for their horns, and Conrad figured only four or five of them would fit inside. Behind him, JJ yelled something and started running toward the fence. He got to the trailer about the same time as the first longhorn had no choice but to go up and into it. It clanked, the sound of hoof on metal almost deafening in the Texas country silence.

Conrad whistled, and Boomerang turned to him, cutting away from the massive cattle. He didn't know how to tell

Boomerang to count out five longhorns and then separate the rest.

Turned out, it didn't matter. When the trailer filled with the four longhorns it would hold, Tate swung open the other half of the gate, and the rest of the longhorns simply paraded through that and into the adjoining pasture.

JJ whooped, and Tate left the gate open while Conrad arrived at the back of the trailer.

"He's gonna want your dog," Tate said with a giant smile. "Heck, *I* want your dog. He's incredible."

"Australian Shepherds love to herd," Conrad said. He crouched down and gave his dog some love, because Boomerang was an excellent herding canine.

"Now we've got to figure out how to get them off the trailer," JJ called, and Conrad straightened as his cousin beamed at him from the back of the trailer.

"You got them here," Conrad said. "How did you get them off the trailer?"

Longhorns required a lot of knowledge and patience and special equipment because they weren't like regular cows. They had *enormous* horns. Conrad understood the allure of the animal, though, and why JJ loved them so much. They really were spectacular with those giant racks and their pretty brown and white coats.

"I'm gonna drive them around a bit," JJ said. "Then we have doors that lead right out of each chute." He grinned and clapped Conrad on the shoulder. "Can I borrow your dog?"

Conrad smiled at him at well. "Yeah, you can borrow him

until you get your own. You're gonna need one with all these longhorns you've got." He glanced over into the other pasture, where another eight cattle had found the furthest place from the trailer, and the gate, and the men.

"It's a nice herd," Conrad said. "You definitely need a dog to go with it."

"Yep," JJ said. "Let's go for a drive." Tate closed the back of the trailer, and all three of them went around to get in the cab of JJ's truck.

He drove down the service road that led along his pastures and farmland, and which connected to the main body of Seven Sons.

"Text my daddy, would you?" JJ asked, and he really was far happier than Conrad had ever seen him. "He'll want to see the longhorns on the trailer."

"Maybe he'll get you a dog for your birthday," Conrad said as he sent the text to Uncle Jeremiah. He said it happily too because after this, he had a date up at Shiloh Ridge with Sarina and Boomerang to check out Link's new addition to his livestock.

"Did you hear Link got guineafowl?" he asked.

"He put it on the text," JJ said. "You goin' up there?"

"Yeah, after this," Conrad said. "Glory Rose is gonna make me dinner at her cabin."

"Oh, I see how it is." JJ grinned over to Conrad, who rode in the passenger seat with Tate in the back. "You and Glory Rose are getting along real well?"

Conrad appreciated that JJ had formed it as a question.

He nodded and glanced out the side window. "Yeah, real well," he said. "I really like her."

He looked over to JJ. "Have you seen Ruby with Sarina? I know you guys said you aren't going to have kids right away, but she's amazing with her."

JJ's face broke into a wide grin. "I know, right? We talked about it the other night, and even she's surprised that Sarina likes her so much."

Conrad wasn't sure why Sarina had taken such a shine to Ruby either. She didn't look like Chloe, and she'd left town for a few months to do an interior design internship, and Sarina hadn't seen her once.

He twisted and looked at Tate in the backseat. "You and Clara Jean are going to be married in only another month."

Tate grinned with all the wattage of the sun. "Sure are." He sighed and said, "Man, being in love is the best, isn't it?"

"It's not bad," JJ said.

"I can't comment on that," Conrad said, and he once again looked away.

"You've never been in love?" JJ asked. "Even with Chloe?"

A sting pierced Conrad's chest. "I was in love with Chloe," he murmured. He drew a deep breath and looked forward out the windshield, the barn with the big American flag that he had grown up working in and admiring coming into view. "She just wasn't in love with me."

"I'm sorry, brother," JJ said.

"But hey, Glory Rose seems to like you," Tate said.

"How is she with Sarina?"

Conrad found a small smile coming to his face and his spirits lifting as he replaced the thoughts of his bad relationship with Chloe with everything Glory Rose.

"You know," he said. "She's really good with her and really likes her." Then he tried to play things cool with a half-shrug. "I mean, they've only done a few things together, and she's not yelling Glory Rose's name as she runs toward the house." He grinned over to JJ. "But I think they're getting along real nice."

"That's great." JJ came to a stop several yards from the barn. "Did my daddy answer?"

Conrad looked at his phone and said, "Nope, but he's read it." Only a moment later, not only did Uncle Jeremiah come out of the barn, but so did Uncle Liam and Uncle Skyler.

JJ dropped from the truck, already laughing, and he spread his arms wide as he said, "Come see the longhorns I got in the trailer." Conrad got out of the truck too, and he opened the back door so Boomerang could get down.

"You go tell him it was you who got those longhorns in the trailer," he told his dog. Boomerang didn't need to be told twice to run toward Uncle Jeremiah. The man loved dogs, and dogs loved him, and Boomerang ran straight to him and sat down, his tongue hanging out.

Conrad hoped this wouldn't take too long as he still had to get back to JJ's ranch, get his daughter, and get over to Shiloh Ridge—and the woman he was fast falling in love with.

* * *

Conrad shielded Sarina as much as he could as she whimpered into his chest. "Are they this loud all the time?" he yelled over the squawking of the guineafowl.

Link grinned at them like their feathers came coated in gold. "Yep," he said. "They're like a live alarm system. Something comes too close, they go nuts."

Conrad was going to go nuts if he stood here for much longer. "It's a great enclosure," he said. "Don't you need them out in the fields, though?"

He turned toward Link, who radiated pure joy. Their eyes met, and Link laughed out loud. "Yeah, the goal is to get them into the rotation with the other birds," he said. "But I'm using them in this field for pest control right now."

Conrad looked up into the sky. "What about owls and hawks?"

"That's another reason we're keeping them in here for now." Link reached out and checked the gate in front of him, which stood as tall as him. It was securely locked, of course, and the best wire mesh stretched in every direction—even up over the top of the guineafowl's enclosure.

Link had built it in a series of trees on the edge of a pasture, as guineafowl like to roost up high. They then had free range to roam—well, as far as the chicken wire would allow them to—out into the field.

"Once we let them out during the day," Link said. "They'll be in fields where we have hawk deterrents."

"Oh, sure," Conrad said. "What are you using for that? Decoy owls?" It was pretty common to put statues of owls in the middle of fields to prevent hawks from coming down. He even found some of his Gramps's shiny object deterrents, which were merely broken CDs and long ropes of tinfoil that Gramps had hung on a wire hanger.

Hawks weren't crows, and they didn't like shiny objects, and reflective CDs would keep them out of the fields and away from the chickens, turkeys, and guineafowl during the day.

"So you have to round them up at the end of every day and put them back in their enclosures, right?" Conrad yelled.

"Dad." Sarina lifted her head and put her hands on the sides of Conrad's face. She got really close. He looked at her, but he couldn't focus. She whined and cried and covered her ears with her hands.

"I know, baby," he said. "It's loud. Stay against my chest." He tucked her back into his chest and covered her other ear with his hand too.

"We can go," Link said. "You've seen them. This is what they do." He turned and walked away from the enclosure, and Conrad went with him. With every step they took, the guineafowl got quieter, not only because they were getting further away, but because they were calming down.

"Those are great," Conrad said. "It's a good addition to Shiloh Ridge."

"We got fifty of them," Link said with a smile. "I think I'm gonna have to hire a cowboy just to take care of the guineafowl." He laughed, but Conrad didn't think he was joking.

"Well, I'll let you get over to Glory Rose's," Link said.

"Misty and the kids want me to get back so we can go to town for dinner." He grinned at Conrad, who nodded.

"I'm sure I'm not late," he said. "I've only been here for a half-hour."

Link chuckled and shook his head. "Well, I'm not going to cross Glory Rose. I'll tell you that much."

Conrad smiled at him too. "What do you mean? Did she say something?"

"Oh, she said something all right," he said. "She said if I made you even one minute late because we were looking at *my birds*, she'd leave one in my bed." He tipped his head back and laughed up into the sky, but Conrad blinked, not sure what to make of that.

"She was *joking*," Link said. "I don't think Glory Rose has ever slaughtered anything."

Conrad wasn't sure how he felt about that either, because he did live on a farm, and he did kill his chickens and turkeys for food. "She said she wants to live on a homestead," he said. "But she hasn't learned how to slaughter a chicken?"

"Oh, Glory Rose can say whatever she wants," Link said. "But no, she doesn't know how to do any of that stuff." He grinned at Conrad and opened the door of his truck. "Good to see you, man. Hope you have fun with Glory Rose." He got behind the wheel of his truck, and Conrad waved to him as he drove away from their livestock enclosures. Conrad put Sarina in her car seat and checked his phone, and he wasn't late, but he wasn't super early either.

He tapped to call Glory Rose, and she answered with, "Do not tell me you're going to be late, because this food has five more minutes and then it's coming out of the oven and it's going to be amazing."

"I'm not going to be late, sugar," he said. "I was just checking to see if I could come early."

"Of course," she said. "Are you all done with the guineafowl?"

"Yep, I'm on my way."

"All right, see you soon," she trilled, and the call ended.

Conrad had to go back in front of the cowboy cabins he'd already been by, and then past the great big homestead where he knew Bear Glover lived. He went past Glory Rose's aunt Etta's homestead, and then her uncle Judge's, and around the corner, where he drove past Glory Rose's parents' house, and then the main homestead and a lot of their stables and barns.

Glory Rose had drawn him a map, and she'd labeled it with her aunts' and uncles' names, which made him smile in this moment.

He continued past True Blue, the family barn where Link's party would be later this month. He finally made the turn onto Glory Rose's lane, where four more cabins sat among the trees.

Her car sat in the driveway along with another SUV, and he pulled up in front of the house but stayed on the road. A single car or truck could get by him easily, and he quickly got Sarina out of the back and said, "Let's go see Glory Rose."

"Rose, Rose," Sari said, and she flapped her arms and legs in excitement. She babbled something else that Conrad couldn't decipher, but he grinned at her all the same. "Yeah, you like Glory Rose, don't you?"

Sari did like Glory Rose, and Conrad sure was happy about that. He went up onto her small front porch and knocked before he simply opened the door and stepped inside. "It's just us," he said, and he found Glory Rose standing in the kitchen with an apron tied around her waist.

Her dark hair spilled over her shoulders freely tonight, and she wore a pair of jean shorts and a sleeveless shirt the color of bright, ripe, red strawberries.

He didn't see either of her roommate-cousins, and she started toward him with a smile and a "Hey, cowboy," as he moved further into the house to get closer to her.

It almost felt like he'd been turned to steel, and she was the strongest magnet on the planet. He was drawn to her, and he easily shifted Sari to his hip and held her securely while he wrapped his other hand around Glory Rose's back and pulled her into him. "It's so good to see you," he said just before he leaned down and kissed her.

He hadn't even anticipated the feelings running through him, but a *needful* feeling to be with her and to let her know how much he liked her crashed through him with the force of water going over a cliff.

Of course, he missed her during the day, but he'd never felt like this before, and he hadn't even realized that he felt like it until he'd walked into her house and saw her.

Something shifted between them as she kissed him back, and Conrad told himself to slow down and be good. Sari wiggled at his side and that got him to pull away to set her down. He cleared his throat and looked around Glory Rose's cabin, suddenly nervous to be there.

When he finally looked at her, she gave him a peaceful smile and said, "There you are."

He didn't know what she meant, but she reached up with one delicate hand and slid it along his jaw to cup his face in her palm. "Are you okay?"

"Yeah." He breathed out, the nerves going with the air. "Now that I'm here with you, I'm great."

Chapter Fifteen

Something had shifted inside Conrad, but Glory Rose couldn't tell what. He said he was fine, and she told herself not to needle him with questions.

"Great," she said. "Did you like the new enclosure?"

"Yeah, it's great." He followed her into the kitchen, where Glory Rose saw that the timer on the oven only had four seconds left. She reached out to silence it before it went off and picked up the hot pads to get their dinner out of the oven.

"The guineafowl are real loud, though," he said. "It's a good thing you live way up here, or you'd go nuts."

She laughed, because he wasn't wrong. "You should see Link and Wilder with those guineafowl," she said dryly. "They're like little boys on Christmas morning." She bent and pulled out the chicken cordon bleu casserole that she'd made for their dinner that night.

The breadcrumb topping looked brown and crisp, just the

way her mother said it should, but worry still ran through Glory Rose. "Okay," she said as she tossed the potholders onto the counter. "I don't cook a whole lot, just so you know, and if this is gross, then we don't have to eat it."

"It's not going to be gross, Rose." Conrad's arm snaked around her waist again, and he pulled her into his side.

"Just Rose, huh?" she asked.

"Does anyone ever call you just Glory?" he asked.

"No."

"No nickname at all?"

Glory Rose snuggled into his side and put her arm around him too. "When my daddy's real mad at me, he goes *Glory*, and usually there's a lot of disgust or weariness or, you know, that parental disappointment in the syllables."

Conrad chuckled. "I understand the parental disappointment."

She looked up at him. "Do you have a nickname?"

"No, ma'am," he said. "It's always Conrad."

Behind them, something crashed, and Conrad spun away from her. "Sari, what are you doing?"

Glory Rose couldn't believe it, but she'd *forgotten* about Conrad's daughter. She had no idea what that said about her, but embarrassment filled her, and she quickly used the potholders to get the casserole over onto the small island in the kitchen. She'd already laid three plates there, along with a couple of forks and a spoon, and she had the salad out and ready to mix. She did that while Conrad told Sari that she couldn't touch anything she wanted and that she needed to come over and get ready for dinner.

Glory Rose nodded to the small table she, Fawn, and Pearl Jo used whenever they sat down to meals. One of the long sides of the table had been pushed against the wall, leaving enough room for four spots—two on each end and two on the open side.

She nodded to it as she opened a drawer to pull out a pair of scissors to cut open the bag of salad. "I got her a seat," she said.

Conrad held his daughter in his arms, looked at the seat, then back to Glory Rose, and then at the seat again. She sliced open the top of the bag of salad while he stood like a statue in her cabin.

Her heart pounded. "Is it the wrong kind?"

"No." His voice came out growly and gruff, and he turned his back on her and started putting his daughter in the high-chair seat—one that Glory Rose had bought specifically for this dinner.

She dumped the lettuce into the bowl and then sliced open the top of the sunflower seeds, the bacon bits, and the croutons, quickly adding them. "Are we still going over to Elaine's tomorrow?"

"Yes," Conrad said.

Another single word answer, Glory Rose thought. She wasn't sure what was going on with him. She sure had enjoyed kissing him when he arrived, and there'd been something different in his touch. He'd looked at her differently when he pulled away, and then he seemed nervous, and he wouldn't look at her at all.

And now he wouldn't talk to her.

"I just have everything set up here on the bar," she said, wondering how long she would play this off as nothing. "We can get our food here and take it over to the table. There's not much room there."

Conrad didn't answer at all other than to turn and take the few steps over to the island and Glory Rose.

"Are you sure you're okay?" she asked him quietly. "If you're too tired or don't want to be here, you can just go—"

"I'm fine," Conrad said.

Glory Rose pressed her lips together and abandoned mixing up the salad. She looked at him and bravely said, "You're not fine. There's something going on."

His dark eyes landed on hers, and Glory Rose felt sure that the world could be devoured by fire, and she would not look away from Conrad Walker. "You bought my daughter a seat for your table," he said. "And I don't know. There's this feeling inside of me that's just rushing around, and I can't grab onto it, and I can't tell what it is."

Glory Rose reached out and took his hand in hers, hoping to steady him. "Is it a good feeling?"

He nodded, a swallow moving down the sexy column of his neck.

"All right," Glory Rose said as casually as she could. "As long as there's nothing wrong and you're not upset with me."

"There's nothing wrong, Rose." He moved closer and gathered her into his broad chest, where he held her within the safety of his arms. "I'm not upset with you." He tightened his grip, and Glory Rose put her arms around him too. She could fall in love with this man standing here like this, especially when he said, "I think I'm falling in love with you."

She tried to pull away so that she could see his face, but he held her fast. "I don't want you to look at me," he whispered. "I don't want to talk about it."

Glory Rose sure did, but she found she didn't have the words.

"Can we just sit with it?" Conrad asked. "Just let me feel it for a while longer, and then maybe I'll know what it is."

She nodded against his chest, and she really wanted him to know that she was falling in love with him too. *The way you kiss him tells him that*, she told herself, and she forced her voice to stay silent.

They stood in the kitchen for several long moments, and then Sari slapped her hands on her tray and yelled, "Dad-Daddy! Eat-eat!"

Glory Rose started to giggle and couldn't stop. Conrad released her, turning immediately to his daughter while he grumbled, "*She* always knows exactly what *she* wants."

The wind nearly blew Glory Rose off her feet as she hurried up the sidewalk toward a pretty blue house with a stark white door, bearing a bright green wreath for St. Patrick's Day. She'd never been here before, but she'd had no reason to come to Elaine Walker's house.

Until today.

Thankfully, Conrad's truck already sat in the driveway, as

Glory Rose had gotten off work a little bit late. That meant she'd been caught in the worst of traffic, and her stomach growled in a way that made her hope that the dinner Elaine had promised had already been served.

The blue house sported a porch that ran from corner to corner, and Glory Rose loved it. She took a moment to admire the swing down on the end, where Elaine had piled some very festive green pillows, and she wondered if the other woman had time to simply sit out here and sip sweet tea in the evenings.

"Focus," Glory Rose muttered to herself, and she reached to ring the doorbell. She heard it ding and dong throughout the house and then Sari singing along with it the way she had at Conrad's house. Her heart swelled with love for the little girl, and she wore a huge smile when Elaine pulled open the front door and appeared in front of her.

"I'm so sorry I'm late," Glory Rose said. "We had two extra appointments this afternoon, and neither one of them went very fast."

"It's fine," Elaine said at the same time Conrad's deeper voice joined hers, echoing the same words.

"I said I got it," Elaine said, glaring at her brother.

"And I said *I* wanted to get it," Conrad fired right back. "She's *my* girlfriend."

"Maybe I wanted to meet her without you hovering two inches away." Elaine gave him a spicy look, smiled almost sarcastically at Glory Rose, and turned to go back into the house. "Hurry up and kiss her, Conrad. Dinner is on the table."

Conrad wore the stormiest expression Glory Rose had ever seen when he looked at her. "I'm not going kiss you now."

Glory Rose laughed and pressed into his chest. "Then can I kiss you?" She had no idea what he'd been feeling last night, but she knew a certain kind of emptiness now that she'd never known before. When she was with Conrad, anything seemed possible, and the world was bright and full of goodness. Without him, she had to endure long appointments, stormy weather, and days filled with hopelessness.

Yes, she was definitely falling too fast for Conrad. He didn't seem to mind, though, as she took his face in her hands and kissed him. She didn't linger very long, and yet when she pulled away, her lungs cried for air.

She took a deep breath and stepped past him into the house. "What can I help with?" she asked Elaine as she walked along the back of the couch, through the front living room, and into the kitchen at the rear.

"Oh, everything's ready." Elaine gave Glory Rose a smile that had a touch of sheepishness to it. "I'm sorry about saying that stuff about kissing at the door," she said. "I really am a nice person."

"Elaine is the best," Conrad said. He closed the door and followed Glory Rose into the kitchen. "She made one of our favorite things tonight, isn't that right, Sari?"

"Mac-mac-cheese! Mac-mac-cheese!" Sari chanted, and Elaine smiled over to her with such love that Glory Rose knew she was a good person.

She detoured over to the table where Sari had already

been strapped in, and she picked up the pink plastic bowl in front of her. "I'll get it for you, okay, baby?"

"Rose, mac-mac-cheese. Rose, Rose."

"She's really on one tonight," Conrad said with a chuckle. He peered at Elaine. "Are you sure you didn't give her any candy or cookies this afternoon?"

"I told her she had to wait until after dinner," Elaine said with a hint of coolness in her voice. "After the third one." She turned her back on her brother and took the pink bowl from Glory Rose with a quick smile. "She's impossible to say no to. You'll learn that fast enough."

Glory Rose laughed with Elaine, and she took her bowl of mac and cheese with fried spam in it back to the table. Once they had food, Elaine said, "You can tell I'm a master in the kitchen."

"I like mac and cheese," Glory Rose said. "My daddy used to put hotdogs in it."

"Ours too," Elaine said, a brightness entering her face. "I like the fried spam, though. It's a little crispier."

Glory Rose took a bite, and the saltiness and the crispy spam with the creamy mac and cheese made her moan. She nodded. "Yeah, this is good."

"There you go, Connie," she said, and she slapped his chest. "You've got a low bar for cooking."

"Don't call me Connie," he said.

"You said you didn't have any nicknames," Glory Rose teased.

He glared at her. "I don't." He switched his lasers over to his sister. "Laney knows not to call me Connie."

"You call me Laney."

"You like it." He shook his head and ate another bite of mac and cheese. "So listen, before we get to the nail painting and that new hairstyle you've got for me tonight, I wanted to run a few names by you."

Glory Rose continued to eat in silence because she wasn't sure what they were talking about.

Elaine drew in a big breath, boxed up her shoulders, and then blew it all out. She set down her fork and shook her hands like she was about to enter a boxing ring. "All right," she said. "Lay them on me."

Conrad chuckled. "It wouldn't kill you to be nice to some of these guys."

"I'm nice to everyone I go out with," Elaine said. She looked over to Glory Rose. "Heaven help me, I've told Conrad that he can set me up with some of his friends."

"Oh, do you have friends?" Glory Rose asked.

"Ha ha, very funny," Conrad said. "Of course I have friends."

"*Non-married* friends?" Glory Rose asked. "And JJ and Tate don't count. They're engaged."

"I thought you'd be on my side," Conrad said. "In fact, I was counting on it, because you know some of these guys."

Glory Rose could not think of a single person that she and Conrad were both friends with. "Okay," she said. "Who?"

"For example, my first offering for you tonight, Laney, is Wilder."

"Like Wilder Glover?" Elaine asked, and she didn't sound fond of Glory Rose's cousin.

Glory Rose's eyebrows rose in surprise. "You want to set her up with one of my cousins?"

"Well, your brother is too young," he said.

Glory Rose blinked several times in rapid succession. Then she started to laugh. "You're right," she said between giggles. "Flint's a little bit too young for Elaine, but Silver's twenty. Elaine's only twenty-three." She glanced over to Elaine. "Right? You're twenty-three?"

"I am twenty-three," Elaine said. "But I don't want anyone younger than me."

"She has a lot of rules," Conrad said. "We probably should've led with those." He glanced at his sister. "Wilder is older than you."

Glory Rose nodded, because Wilder was older than her, so he was definitely older than Elaine.

"So is Robbie Glover," Conrad said. "And Finn's half-brothers Michael and Sam are both older than you."

"Three Rivers Ranch is so far away," Elaine complained.

"You did not give me a radius that I had to stick within," Conrad said without missing a beat. "Henry's brother, Rich, is also twenty-five, and that's two years older than you." He glanced down at his phone, and Glory Rose suspected that he had notes typed up there.

Notes for cowboys that Elaine could go out with.

She found the whole thing comical, but she stuffed her mouth with more spam-mac and cheese, so she wouldn't laugh. After all, neither of the Walkers were laughing. Elaine also had not outright rejected Rich.

"The other boys in our family," she said. "Are Smiles, Gun, and Johnny, but I think they're all younger than you."

Elaine looked over to her. "Johnny is my age, and you guys have some really weird names in your family. Smiles? Gun?"

Glory Rose laughed fully now because Elaine certainly wasn't wrong.

"Garth Ahlstrom also has a couple of boys who aren't married yet," Conrad said. "His son Jake is my same age. I think he'll be thirty next month, and Carson is twenty-six or twenty-seven." He flipped over his phone, his list clearly exhausted.

Elaine took a bite of mac and cheese, and when she looked up, she narrowed her eyes at her brother. "It really feels like you just went through everyone at Three Rivers Ranch."

"And Shiloh Ridge," he said, his smile growing by the moment.

"I've been out with Carson," Elaine said. "He didn't like me very much, and that means that he's poisoned Jake against me."

"Are you hearing yourself?" Conrad asked. "*Poisoned Jake against me?*" He shook his head and took another big bite of mac and cheese.

"I might try Rich," she said. She cut a glance over to Glory Rose. "And even Wilder. He's really handsome."

Her face turned a deep shade of red that only made Glory Rose's laughter rise up higher inside her. "We Glovers have good genes," she said as coolly as she could, but when she looked at Conrad, she couldn't hold it in, and they both started to laugh.

"What?" she asked around her laughter. "We do."

"Yeah, you sure are pretty," he said.

"Oh, gag," Elaine said. "I already have to put up with so much from Clara Jean. I'm not going to sit in my own home while you two have a flirt-fest."

"*You* invited *me* to dinner," Conrad said.

"You said you needed more hairstyles," Elaine shot back. "And that you might want me to show you how to paint Sari's nails because that's what girls do, and you need help with girls." She pointed her spoon at him. "I'm just trying to help you out, brother."

"And I'm trying to help you out with a date," he said. "What's wrong with Michael or Sam?"

Elaine clenched her jaw. "I might try Michael, but he's third."

"You just want someone who's ten years older than you," Conrad teased. "Don't deny it. You like an older man."

Elaine shook her hair over her shoulders and held her head high as she said, "I'm not going to deny it."

That caused another round of giggles to spill out of Glory Rose's mouth. She sure did like the dynamic between Elaine and Conrad, and she enjoyed watching him be an older brother, a single girl-dad, and her boyfriend all at the same time.

Once the conversation all quieted, she looked at Elaine. "What kind of hair are we doing tonight?"

Elaine smiled at her. Glory Rose sure hoped that she liked her because Conrad's sister's opinion would matter to him.

"Conrad really liked the French braids you did on Sari's hair, and he wanted to learn how to do it."

Glory Rose switched her gaze over to Conrad. "I could've shown you how to do that," she said, not really quite sure why the air in her lungs suddenly pinched.

"So he'll ask you next time," Elaine said. "I think it was just habit that he asked me." She looked over to her brother. "Right, Conrad?"

"Right," he mumbled. "It was just a habit."

Glory Rose wasn't sure if he spoke the truth or not, but she also didn't want to let it bother her too much. He was used to relying on Elaine for how to do Sari's hair, and she didn't need to be jealous of his sister.

Yes, she wanted him to come to her for any girl-things he might need to know because she wanted to spend time with him and his daughter. At the same time, she knew it wasn't reasonable for him to cut off all contact with his family, as they were his biggest support system.

So she nodded and said, "I can put in a good word for you with Wilder, Laney. He's real busy at the ranch right now, but I'm sure he'd be interested in going out with you."

She smiled and noted that Elaine's face once again took on a pinkish hue. "Thanks, Glory Rose," she said. "Now Conrad says you two are going to Amarillo for a zoo weekend, and I'd love to hear more about that."

"Laney," Conrad warned, but Glory Rose only smiled because she had no problem talking about the weekend trip she and Conrad had been planning.

"She can know about it, right?" she asked, and Conrad gave a grudging nod. "Good," Glory Rose said. "Because I've got something that is going to take you out of your comfort zone too."

"Oh, do tell," Elaine said, and she clapped her hands and rubbed them together.

Conrad's eyebrows went up, and Glory Rose grinned sweetly at him as she said, "My parents have invited you to our family picnic following the Easter services, and I think you should come."

His eyebrows bunched down. "When's Easter?"

"It's late this year," Glory Rose said. "It's not until the third week of April. But they know how busy people can be, and Daddy's planning a big cookout, and they want to meet you properly."

"They want to skewer me and roast me like a pig, you mean," he grumbled.

"No," she said. "When I told them about the trip to Amarillo, they thought that sounded pretty serious, and I told them we *were* serious." So many more words flowed between them, because they'd had this conversation before. "That was when Momma and Daddy said I should start bringing you around Shiloh Ridge more."

"Your whole family will be there, right?" he asked.

"Yes, sir."

He looked at Elaine, whose eyebrows went up, and then he looked at Glory Rose again. "All right, sugar. I'd love to go to your family picnic after Easter services—and meet every Glover under the sun."

Chapter Sixteen

Conrad glanced in the rearview mirror and found his precious daughter's eyelids had started to grow heavy. She fought sleep and jerked her head up again. Conrad smiled to himself and looked out the windshield.

"We're almost there, baby," he said. He'd done all of his morning chores, stocked the house with food for Grams, and double-checked with JJ, Tate, Austin, and Easton to make sure that his farm—and his grandmother—would be taken care of until Sunday afternoon, when he'd return.

He and Sari were only about twenty minutes away from Amarillo, and after they checked in at the hotel, he planned to take her to the indoor pool for a little swimming. Then they'd go get pizza and pasta for dinner.

Glory Rose was joining them tomorrow morning for their visit to the zoo. They'd go to lunch and then to the mall to the giant toy store and the big candy shop. Glory Rose would return home that night, and Conrad and Sari would stay until Sunday and then make the drive back to Three Rivers.

"Should we listen to some scriptures?" he asked, and when he looked in the rearview mirror this time, he found that Sari had fallen asleep. He picked up his phone, as the road between Three Rivers and Amarillo was straight and long and not very populated at two-thirty in the afternoon.

He tapped on his Bible app, and since he was driving, he didn't have time to sit and think about what he might listen to today.

He'd been following his gut and simply tapping in the app wherever it felt good. This time, he simply dropped his thumb, and the rich bass voice that had been reading to him all this time said, "Isaiah, chapter one."

Conrad groaned. Isaiah spoke in a lot of parables, with a lot of symbolism, and that wasn't Conrad's strong suit. He figured he could listen for twenty minutes, and then he could choose a different book of scripture and come back to Isaiah later.

He learned he had to focus on the words, really push everything else out of his mind, and pay attention to the doctrines and stories in the scriptures, or else it could be on, and he wouldn't even know what was being said.

In this chapter, it sure seemed like God was mad that His children weren't obedient, and honestly, Conrad felt like that about a lot of the Bible.

There was a pause in the dictation, and then the narrator said, "Wash you, make you clean; put away the evil of your doings from before mine eyes; cease to do evil."

He quickly picked up his phone and paused it, for he felt the stinging in his chest that he had described to Pastor Glover. "Cease to do evil," he murmured to himself. He had done that.

"Wash yourself; make you clean."

He didn't know how to do that. He needed the cleansing fire of the Holy Spirit, and he felt like he'd been trying to find it.

He glanced down at the app and pressed the play button. "Learn to do well; seek judgment, relieve the oppressed, judge the fatherless, plead for the widow."

He paused the scripture app again, for this was not a jealous God rebuking His children. This was God telling Conrad what he needed to do to feel clean and forgiven.

"Cease to do evil, make yourself clean, seek judgment, do well, relieve the oppressed, plead for the widow." Conrad knew he'd missed some, but he repeated the ones that he could remember.

He tried to do good. He helped others when he could. He prayed, though he could admit that his pleadings were mostly for himself, his daughter, Grams, and his family. Perhaps he could do a better job of seeking out those who needed help.

Still, his chest felt like someone had turned it into a washing machine and then turned it on. It hummed and vibrated, and he knew with certainty that this was God speaking to him through the scriptures.

Pastor Glover had been right, and Conrad couldn't believe it.

He tapped again, and the narrator said, "Come now, and

let us reason together, saith the Lord: though your sins be as scarlet, they shall be as white as snow; though they be red like crimson, they shall be as wool."

All of the air in his lungs whooshed out of his mouth, and he paused the app again. Goosebumps ran up his arms, across his shoulders to the the back of his neck, and he *knew* in that singular moment on the highway between Three Rivers and Amarillo that he had been forgiven.

He had reasoned together with the pastor, with his parents, and with his grandmother. He had tried to make as many things right as possible between him and Chloe, and him and everyone around him who may have been hurt, and him and his daughter.

And now God had just spoken to him through a scripture recorded thousands of years ago that said *though his sins be as scarlet, they shall be as white as snow.*

He was forgiven.

Through the atoning sacrifice of Jesus Christ, Conrad personally was forgiven.

He wept in the silence in his truck, and he wasn't sure how many verses he listened to, but it didn't matter. Pastor Glover had told him to simply read something every day, and the answer would come.

"Thank you for giving me the hope that what she said would be true," he whispered. The road blurred in front of him, and he wiped his eyes. "Thank you for giving me the exact scripture I needed to hear to hear Your voice."

He didn't turn on the app again, and he didn't turn on the

radio. He simply finished his drive into Amarillo with the burning of the Spirit in his soul, cleansing him.

He pulled into the parking lot of the hotel that he'd booked, but he didn't get out. He simply turned and looked at Sari, his beautiful, precious, sleeping angel. He felt inadequate in so many ways to be her father, but that heavy burden didn't rest solely on his shoulders anymore.

He looked down at his phone and woke it so that he could see the words that he had heard in his ears. "Let us reason together; though they be red like crimson, they shall be as wool."

He looked up. "I'm pure again."

A fresh round of tears spilled down his face, and the very first person that Conrad wanted to talk to was his father. He had reasoned together with his momma and daddy so many times over so many things, and they'd stood by him, and supported him, and loved him, even in his bad decisions.

Even in his sins.

Conrad had never felt as loved as he did in that moment by his parents, by his grandmother, by his sweet daughter, and most of all, by God.

He wiped his face again and opened the glove box to pull out a napkin. He blew his nose and dried his eyes, because he didn't want to walk into the hotel with a three-year-old and look like he'd been sobbing.

The next person he wanted to talk to was Glory Rose, but he'd learned from her that sometimes he just needed to sit with what had been said, and what had been felt, and let it sink deep into him so that it became a part of him.

She did that, and Conrad really admired her ability to do so.

So he didn't pick up the phone and call his daddy, and he didn't call Glory Rose. Instead, he sent her a text that said, *I can't wait until you get here tomorrow. Text me when you're leaving so I know when to expect you.*

He followed that up with, *Something amazing happened today that I want to tell you about.*

One more text: *Do you think we could start going to church together—me, you, and Sari? It's okay if you don't want to, but maybe something to start thinking about.*

He saw Glory Rose every day, whether they had a planned date or not. Sometimes he stopped by her office and dropped off lunch, and she almost always came by the farmhouse on her way back up to Shiloh Ridge.

Sometimes he did plan structured dates where he'd go pick her up and take her to dinner or a movie. They'd only been seeing each other for about four weeks now, but they'd had a lot of really great conversations, and they'd started moving into more serious things—like this trip to Amarillo.

Going to church together would be another step in that direction. Meeting her family would be a third. She'd already invited him to the all-Glover picnic next month, and Conrad found that he wanted to do something smaller with just her parents and perhaps her brothers.

She'd been over to JJ's house with him and Ruby, and Conrad had taken her to Elaine's as well, but his brothers didn't know Glory Rose at all, and Conrad thought that maybe they should plan a cousin night where Glory Rose, JJ and Ruby, and Tate and Clara Jean could come along.

He could host it at his house, because Grams loved that kind of stuff.

His phone buzzed, and he looked at it. Glory Rose had said, *I can't wait to see you and hear all about it.* She'd included a unicorn emoji, and then another text came in that said, *I would love to sit with you and Sari at church.* For this text, she used the hallelujah hands emoji, and Conrad smiled, even as he sniffled.

"Lord, I'm really falling in love with her," he said. "Tell me if it's the right thing or not."

Conrad didn't often get messages from the Lord or promptings or super strong feelings, and as he sat in the silence of his truck, he wasn't sure if that meant he should continue and do whatever he needed to do with Glory Rose or if he should pull back.

"God will tell you," he told himself because that was something his momma had taught him. "God expects us to act," she'd said. "So act, make a decision, do something. If it's wrong, God will tell you."

He looked at his phone again and quickly scrolled down to the string that had both his momma and his daddy in it. He didn't often message them together, but they'd had a few joint conversations over the past several months since Sari had come into all of their lives.

I just want you both to know how much I love you, Conrad typed out. *You have been amazing parents who have always loved and supported me, and I'm so grateful for all of your counsel over the years.*

The words blurred, and he quickly wiped his eyes again to send the text.

Something amazing happened today, and I finally feel forgiven.

Before he could send that text, his phone rang, and *Daddy* sat on the screen. Conrad pulled in a breath to control his emotions. He wasn't sure if he wanted to talk to his father or not, but in the end, he figured he didn't have to tell him the whole story.

So he swiped on the call and said, "Hey."

"Where are you?" Daddy asked.

"Sari and I just got to Amarillo." Conrad sniffled, which was a dead giveaway. His daddy didn't launch right into the next question or statement, and Conrad fought his emotions, so he didn't want to speak either.

"Your mother is giving me her worried eyes," Daddy finally said.

A half-laugh, half-sob burst out of Conrad's mouth. "I didn't get to send my second text," he said, his voice definitely too nasally and filled with tears. "I'll tell you guys all about it when we get back, but something amazing happened on the way here, and I just wanted you to know that I finally feel forgiven."

"Oh." The word sounded like Daddy had just let it out without thought. He didn't continue, and Conrad took a deep breath and wiped his face for hopefully the final time. "I love you guys," he said. "And I really appreciate your examples of faith and all the things you taught me."

"I can't wait to hear the story," Daddy said. "We love you, Conrad."

"We love you so much," Momma said. "You and Sari have fun in Amarillo."

"We will," he said. "Glory Rose is coming to the zoo tomorrow. It's going to be a blast." And with a heart finally not carrying the burdens of his past, Conrad ended the call and got out of his truck.

He opened the passenger door and said, "Come on, Sari-girl. It's time to wake up." She whimpered as he unbuckled her, and he picked her up and cradled her against his chest as she woke slowly. "We're here," he said. "Don't you want to go swimming?"

"Swim," she said, her voice still a little bit groggy. He pressed a kiss to her forehead, grabbed his bag in which he had packed both of their things, and closed the door before he headed inside. He tipped his head back and looked up into the brilliant spring sky and said, "Thank you for my daughter."

For Sari was a miracle, and how she'd come into his life was a miracle, and the fact that a person could be forgiven was a miracle. Conrad felt all of them way down deep inside his soul as he went to check in to the hotel.

"Rose?" Sari asked.

"Yep," Conrad said. "Glory Rose is coming tomorrow."

And he couldn't wait to see her, kiss her, and tell her everything.

Chapter Seventeen

"Glory Rose," Pearl Jo said, and she stomped her foot. "You have got to stop this. They have stores in Amarillo."

"Yeah, aren't you going to the mall?" Fawn asked.

Glory Rose looked between her two cousins, who both stood in the kitchen. "Maybe I should take a sweatshirt."

Pearl Jo moved to block the hallway. "You're not taking a sweatshirt," she said. "You're not even staying overnight, and you packed an extra set of clothes and a toothbrush."

Glory Rose looked at her, pure nerves assaulting her. "I'm so nervous," she said. "Why am I so nervous?"

"I don't know," Fawn said. "It's not like you're even taking the road trip together. You're driving there on your own, staying for a few hours, and driving home."

Pearl Jo pointed at Fawn and nodded. "All you need is your phone charger. Have you got that?"

Glory Rose had a phone charger in her purse and in her car. She nodded and said, "Yes. Okay, I'm ready." She looked over at Fawn. "I'm ready, right?"

Fawn grinned at her. "You're so ready, Glory Rose, and you're going to be late if you don't leave in the next thirty seconds."

"Okay, give me a hug," she said, feeling very near tears. She rushed to Pearl Jo, who held her firmly, while Fawn came in on the side. Glory Rose hugged them both and said, "Thank you so much. I don't know why I'm acting so crazy."

"Try to get it out before you get there," Pearl Jo said with a grin as Glory Rose stepped back. "And drive safe. There's no timeline for today. When you get there, you get there."

Glory Rose nodded. "Okay, yes. Okay, I'm going to go now." She turned, picked up her purse, and headed for the door. She really did need to get herself together, because Fawn was right. She was driving to Amarillo by herself, not with Conrad and Sari. She'd meet them, they'd go to the zoo and the mall, and get some food. She'd done that a bunch of times with Conrad already, right here in Three Rivers.

She'd hosted him and Sari at her house, and they'd eaten dinner together at Elaine's too. The only difference about this trip was she had to drive an hour to get there. Thankfully, by the time she arrived at the hotel address that Conrad had given her, her nerves had settled, and her phone had charged back to one hundred percent.

She quickly texted Pearl Jo and Fawn that she had arrived and that she'd text them when she was leaving later.

Then she texted Conrad that she had just parked next to

his truck in the lot. He texted back with, *We'll be down in a few minutes. Do you want to come up or just wait down there?*

She saw no reason to go upstairs only to have to come back down, so she said, *I'll wait here.*

It only took about five minutes for Conrad to exit the hotel and walk toward her, at which time all of her nerves were completely and utterly gone. She knew this man, and he was her handsome, flirty boyfriend, and a single dad to Sari.

"Rose!" Sari called. "Look!"

Glory Rose didn't know what she was supposed to look at, but she figured Conrad could give her some help once they weren't fifteen yards apart.

"Wait till I get there," Conrad said, but Sari had already started to dive for Glory Rose.

She thrust her arms out and caught the little girl, thankfully hauling her up to her chest as she giggled. "You've got to wait for your daddy to give you to me," she said. "I might've dropped you."

"Look," Sari said again, and this time she puffed out her chest. She said several words, only one of which Glory Rose understood—*shirt.*

"Did you get a new shirt?" she asked.

"Shirt," Sari repeated. She pointed to the heart on it. "Heart," she said. She pointed to the flower and said, "Fowr."

Glory Rose grinned at her and let her go through every object on her shirt, and then she looked at Conrad. He wore pure, unadulterated love on his face, and Glory Rose knew exactly how he felt.

"You are so smart," she said, her emotions wavering. She hugged the little girl tight and said, "I love you so much."

"Should we go, baby?" Conrad asked. "It's time to go see the animals."

"A-imals, a-imals." Sari tried to kill herself again by diving out of Glory Rose's arms, but she managed to get the little girl on her feet and not her head.

"She's really wild today," Glory Rose said.

Conrad chuckled. "We had some sugary cereal for breakfast, and we never do that."

"No eggs to gather here." Glory Rose stepped into his arms and looked up at him. "I was so nervous to come this morning for some reason, and now that I'm here looking at you, I don't even know why."

He smiled down at her and gently pressed a kiss to her lips while Sari pulled on his hand. "I was a little nervous for you to come too," he said.

"Then I reminded myself it's just a zoo and the mall and lunch, and we've done all of that in Three Rivers."

"Yeah, the farm is basically a zoo." He chuckled and stepped back so he could pick up his daughter. "Let me just put her in her seat." He moved over to the truck and got her buckled in. He slammed the door and pushed a button twice on his key fob, the truck's engine roaring to life, but Conrad came right back to Glory Rose. "You got everything you need, sugar?"

"I didn't really like that kiss," she teased.

Conrad's eyes sparkled with that male desire that she liked. "No? You didn't like that kiss?"

"It was a little too short," Glory Rose said.

"Hmm. Well, let's see what I can do about that." Conrad slid one hand along the side of her face and touched his mouth to hers in the same sweet, chaste kiss as a moment ago. He stroked his lips against hers, deepening the kiss, and Glory Rose sank into the beauty and warmth and goodness of Conrad.

Since they stood out in the parking lot, he didn't go too fast or too far or stay for too long, but it was definitely an A-plus kiss.

"Better?" he asked.

"So much better." Glory Rose opened her eyes and looked at him. He seemed the same on the outside, but at the same time, something had definitely changed. He *glowed* now, and Glory Rose could barely stand to be in his presence for how shiny and smiley he was.

"So something amazing happened yesterday, huh?" She moved down the side of the truck to the passenger door, Conrad hot on her heels. He opened the door for her and said, "Yeah, something amazing."

She faced him instead of getting straight in the truck. "You seem different."

"A good different or a bad different?" he asked.

"Good different."

"Well, as long as it's good," he said, repeating part of a conversation they'd had before. "I'll tell you about it later," he said. "Let's get to the zoo while it's still cool."

Cool was such a relative term in Texas, but Glory Rose got in the truck, and while Conrad walked around to get behind the wheel, she turned and looked at Sari. "What are you hoping to see at the zoo?"

"Gwen," Sari said.

"A—what?"

"Gwen," Sari said again, her face full of happiness.

"Penguin?" Glory Rose asked. She glanced over at Conrad as he climbed in the truck. "Are there penguins at the Amarillo zoo?"

"Oh, is that what she's been saying?" Conrad asked. "I couldn't quite figure out what she wanted to see. A penguin." He grinned at his little girl and then over to Glory Rose. "I don't know if there's penguins there. I guess we'll find out."

The next week, Glory Rose's feet hurt more than usual. She'd been in and out of patient rooms all day long, taking temperatures, weighing babies and children, making notes on charts, and running around.

Spring had definitely hit Three Rivers, and as more people left their homes to interact with one another, a fresh round of germs had made itself known in town. They'd had six emergency appointments today, and Glory Rose still had to update patient files and change out the paper in rooms four and five, as well as disinfect them.

She loved her job, but some days simply felt like existing inside a tornado, and today was one of those days. Aunt Willa had asked her to sing in the choir for Easter, and they had rehearsal that night. She needed to hurry to finish the charts, wipe down countertops and patient beds, and get out of here. Even if she did all of that in the next ten minutes, she knew she'd be showing up at the church in her scrubs, dinnerless.

Conrad only lived ten minutes from the church, but she didn't want to text him and ask him to bring her something to eat. She'd already text-complained to him during the fifteen minutes she'd found to sit down and eat lunch.

He had his own problems too, as it had been raining a lot in the past week since they'd returned from Amarillo, and he'd sent her a picture of what used to be a dry field and was now a pond on his farm.

Everyone in the Glover family had been praying that the sun would come out and the water would dry up, so that Lincoln and Misty could have their birthday party as planned. It wasn't until next weekend, but Glory Rose had been enlisted to help with the little kids.

They'd rented a bounce house as well as several lawn games that they were planning to put out in the grass behind True Blue. The barn would be filled with food, a go-fish game, face painting, and tables for the adults to sit and chat or play cards. Glory Rose had gone through her parents' game closet and pulled out everything that could be played in a few minutes with a big group.

That was when she had discovered that they had two boxes of *Scrabble*, one of her daddy's favorite games.

She'd pulled her hair back into a ponytail today, and she'd been wearing it so long that her head ached. She finished cleaning up in the rooms so that they would be ready in the morning, and then she sat down in front of the patient tablet to get all of the notes typed in.

Fifteen minutes, she coached herself. *You can do anything for fifteen minutes.*

Then, even though she might be late to choir practice, she'd drive through Sips and get the biggest Diet Coke she could and down that with some painkillers. She might even have a granola bar at the bottom of her purse, as she'd started putting snacks in her bag whenever she left the house and was planning to see Sari that day. Then, if the girl was ever hungry, Glory Rose had the solution.

A couple of other nurses were still in the office completing their evening tasks, but the front desk reception had cleared out, and all of the doctors had left. Glory Rose kept her head down and her fingers moving, and she didn't pay attention to anything going on around her.

Until she heard one of the other CNAs say, "It's just so hard being a stepmom. I don't know where the boundary is, and Thad is the worst at telling me. He just gets mad."

Glory Rose looked up and over to the two women standing at the end of the counter. Jackie wore a sympathetic smile and nodded. "It's hard enough being a parent when the child is biological."

"Tell me about it," Katie said. "Did you see that mom in here earlier with her daughter? I'm really glad that Doctor Morgan told her that she needed to go get a child psychologist evaluation."

Glory Rose's heart pounded in her chest. She'd been in the office all day, and yes, she'd been there for the seven-year-old's screaming session that had happened a few hours ago. The little girl's mother couldn't get her to do anything—not even stand on the scale to get her weight or sit still so that someone could take her temperature.

On days like today, Glory Rose's patience ran all the way out before the hours at work did. She put her head down, but Katie's words wouldn't leave her mind.

It's so hard being a stepmom.

It's so hard being a stepmom.

It's so hard being a stepmom.

Irritation combined with her exhaustion, and Glory Rose tapped out the last of the notes, shut down the tablet, and turned her back on her friends. She usually got along really well with everyone, and she hadn't been able to attend Katie's wedding last spring, as it had happened on the same weekend as the breeding at Shiloh Ridge.

She honestly hadn't remembered that Katie was a step-mom. She didn't know how old the stepchild was, and she only knew of Katie's husband in passing.

So don't judge, she told herself as she grabbed her purse and then went into the faculty room to grab her lunchbox out of the fridge.

Every step she took got faster and faster, until she practically ran from the doctor's office. By the time she reached her car, she'd started crying. She quickly got behind the wheel, tossing her purse onto the passenger seat carelessly, in full sobs now.

She wasn't even sure why.

"It's just a bad day," she said out loud, tears streaming

down her face. "Everybody has bad days and long hours at work."

But she couldn't stop crying, and she certainly couldn't show up at the church and sing praises for the Savior in her current condition.

She saw Jackie and Katie come out of the doctor's office, and the need to get out of the parking lot clawed at her. Glory Rose quickly put her car in reverse and got out of there.

Several minutes later, she pulled up to Conrad's farmhouse, no idea what roads she'd taken to get there, if she'd stopped at the sign at the end of the block, or if the lights she'd gone through were red or green.

All she knew was she wanted to see Conrad in this, one of her lowest moments in months, and she hurried up to the porch and rang the doorbell.

She hadn't even checked if his truck sat in the driveway, and she hugged herself as she wept and turned to do that. Sure enough, his big black truck sat there, and she'd parked right behind it.

She was hungry and hot and tired, and she had no idea what to say when the door creaked open and Conrad asked, "Glory Rose, are you okay?"

She simply cried harder.

Chapter Eighteen

"Okay," he said quietly and patiently the way he had several times already. Glory Rose was still crying hard, and Conrad still wasn't sure why.

"Let's just go lay down for a minute." He led her into Sari's room, glad Grams had taken her over to his parents that afternoon. He expected them back at any time, though, and he told himself he wasn't doing anything wrong by taking care of Glory Rose.

Sari had a small toddler bed, and he wouldn't be able to fit into it with Glory Rose anyway. He did pull back Sari's pink pony comforter, and Glory Rose curled herself onto the little mattress.

"I'm sorry," she sobbed. "I don't even know what's wrong with me."

He'd asked her if she was hurt, and she'd said no. He'd checked her hands and elbows and knees, and she wasn't bleeding anywhere. He'd managed to get her in the house and close the door so the air-conditioning wouldn't leak out, and now he knelt beside his daughter's bed and smoothed Glory Rose's hair back over her shoulder.

"My ponytail is so tight," she said, and Conrad reached back to work the elastic out of it. He ran his fingers through her hair and caught the faint grumble of her stomach behind her tears. "Are you hungry, sugar?"

"Yes," she said in one of the most pathetic voices he'd ever heard.

"Will you be okay if I run and get you something to eat?"

She nodded, her dark, beautiful eyes filled with water that he wanted to brush away and then kiss away and then protect her from whatever had caused her to hurt like this. He swiped at her eyes and kissed her cheek. "Give me two minutes, okay? You call me if you need me."

She sniffled and nodded, and Conrad hurried into the kitchen, where he quickly grabbed a cup of noodles, filled the water up to the line, and stuck it in the microwave. In the meantime, he returned to the pantry and pulled out a package of peanut butter crackers. Sari loved these things, but he happened to know that Glory Rose did as well.

He jogged around the corner and back into Sari's room, ripping open the package of crackers as he went. "Start with this, sugar." He knelt in front of Glory Rose again and handed her a single cracker as if she couldn't hold the whole package. He pushed her hair back and found that she'd stopped crying, though she was still sniffling and hiccupping.

She stuck the whole cracker in her mouth, and Conrad

handed her the package. "I'm making noodles," he said. "I'll be right back." This time, in the kitchen, Conrad paced along the counter in front of the stove while he waited for the microwave to finish counting down. "Dear Lord," he prayed. "I don't know what to do here. Did something happen to her family?"

She still wore her scrubs, and Conrad figured she'd probably just gotten off work. "Did something happen at work?" he wondered aloud. "I thought she was going to choir practice tonight."

He couldn't riddle it out, and finally, the microwave beeped, and he yanked open the door and pulled out the noodles. He grabbed a spoon and a fork, leaving the utensil drawer open, and headed back to Sari's room.

Glory Rose had only eaten three of the crackers, and she'd put the others on the little table next to Sari's bed. She sat up as he entered the room. "I'm so embarrassed," she said. "I have no idea what I'm doing here."

"You showed up and rang the doorbell," he said. He held out the cup of noodles. "Do you want to come eat?" She nodded, and he extended his hand to help her stand, since the toddler bed squatted quite low to the ground.

They went out into the living room, where Glory Rose sat in the corner of the couch, and Conrad pressed in close beside her. They'd had a great weekend in Amarillo last week, though the zoo didn't have any penguins. They'd loaded up on candy that he loved as a boy and enough to keep Sari happy for the next six months.

She had brand new pajamas and slippers with her favorite

cartoon characters from the toy store and three new plastic ponies to play with as well. He'd seen Glory Rose every day since, but they hadn't had a chance to sit together at church yet, because he'd been driving home from Amarillo on Sunday morning.

Glory Rose ate several bites of noodles and then handed him the cup. "These are really good," she said, as if he'd hand-rolled them himself. "I need to text my aunt." She looked around. "I'm not quite sure where my phone is."

"Maybe you didn't bring it in with you," he said. He hadn't patted her down, and no, he hadn't seen her phone. He pulled his out. "I can text her." He looked over to Glory Rose. "Which aunt, and what am I telling them?"

Glory Rose curled into his side, and he put his arm around her because he didn't want to miss the opportunity to hold her close when she needed him. He could certainly text one-handed.

"Aunt Willa," she whispered. "Tell her that I can't make it to choir practice tonight, and I'm really sorry, but I can come out to the Edge Cabin, and she can rehearse with me there."

It took Conrad several seconds using only a few fingers to get the text typed and sent, and then he set his phone down on the couch beside him and pulled Glory Rose closer. "I'm worried about you," he said. "What's going on?"

"I had a really bad day at work," Glory Rose said. "And when I get really stressed and really hungry and really over-whelmed, the only way I know how to get rid of all that energy is to cry."

Conrad rubbed his hand up and down her arm. "Okay," he said. "I'm sorry you had a bad day at work."

She gave a short little nod against his chest.

"What do you need from me?" he asked. "Whatever it is, I'll do it. Do you want some tea?"

She sat up slightly and looked up at him. "You know what my momma used to make me when I had really bad days?"

He smiled at her and pushed her hair behind her ear. "Did she tell you that you're the most beautiful woman in the world?"

A small smile appeared on Glory Rose's face. "No," she whispered. "She'd make me broth, and Daddy would play the guitar, and once I'd calmed down, we'd talk through it all."

"Is that what you want to do tonight?"

"I'd love some broth," she said. "Then maybe we can just go see the mini donkeys. I don't really want to talk about it yet."

Conrad nodded, though something seethed in his stomach. He knew how to boil water, and he could drop in a bouillon cube, and they could walk along the fence where the mini donkeys pastured.

"JJ still has Boomerang," he said as he moved into the kitchen and got down a mug. "But Stevie Nicks and Stormy are here, and they love it when people are sad. Stevie Nicks will climb right into your lap."

He chuckled. Glory Rose didn't, and he filled the mug and set it in the microwave. He wondered if there was more to her bad day at work, especially since she said she didn't want to talk about it. That usually meant that it was something with him, and she needed time to think through what she wanted to say.

He decided he would ask when she was ready to talk, and he moved over to the kitchen sink and looked out the window at the farm beyond. "It's a real pretty evening," he said. "The sunset is going to be beautiful."

The microwave beeped then, and he turned to get out the mug. He couldn't get his thick fingers to unwrap the bouillon cube very quickly, and he struggled for several long moments before he finally got it. He dropped in the yellow cube and started to stir until the broth came together.

"I hope chicken is okay," he said as he moved back into the living room. Glory Rose had laid down on the couch, and Conrad realized she'd fallen asleep.

He could gaze at her beautiful face forever and always find something new to admire. He turned and set the broth on the dining room table, his protective instinct dictating his every action. He eased Glory Rose into his arms, noting that she only stirred slightly, similar to the way Sari did when she was very tired.

He took her down the hall past Sari's room and past Grams's room, and into his. Somehow, he managed to pull back the covers on the side of the bed where he didn't sleep, so the sheets at least had a chance of being clean. He laid Glory Rose in his bed, and she snuggled in deep against the pillow, a soft sigh coming out of her mouth.

He covered her up and tiptoed out of his bedroom, gently pulling the door closed behind him. "Lord, I just want to take care of that woman," he said. "But she won't be able to sleep here, so please help me to know how long I should let her rest."

"Daddy," Sari called.

"We're back." Grams's voice followed. "You've got both dogs with their noses pressed against the back door," she said as Conrad hurried down the hall. She moved over to the sliding glass door and started to open it. "What's wrong with you guys?"

"I've got Glory Rose in the bedroom," he said, panic streaming through him.

Grams turned toward him, surprise etched in every line on her face. "Glory Rose is in your bedroom?"

"She just came over," he said, his hands wrapping around each other as Sari came over to him, babbling about something they'd done at his parents' house. "She was sobbing, so upset. I fed her a little bit of food. I got her calmed down, and she fell asleep on the couch while I was making her broth." He pointed out all of the pieces of evidence as he spoke, his hands flying wildly left and right.

Grams came to stand in front of him. "Okay, Conrad," she said, taking his hands in hers. "It's okay." She peered past him down the hall. "We'll let her sleep for an hour or so, and then I'll go check on her, okay?"

Conrad nodded and then turned his attention to Sari. She held out her hand as pleased as punch, and Conrad knelt down in front of her. "Look at that," he said. "You've got a ladybug on your hand."

He smiled at Sari and pressed a kiss to her forehead. Both dogs came over toward him, almost knocking him back. "Hey, guys," he said. "Yeah, Glory Rose is upset, but she's okay. She's going to be okay."

"Rose?" Sari asked, and Conrad shook his head. "No, baby, she's sleeping. Let's get you in the tub. Then you'll be all clean and fresh when Glory Rose wakes up."

Conrad suspected that Glory Rose would be humiliated and embarrassed when she found herself awakening in Conrad's bed, and he prayed that those feelings wouldn't stay for very long. He *wanted* her to come to him when she needed comfort and help. He wanted to see her when she had a bad day at work and came home sobbing. He wanted to take care of her and get her dinner and broth and a couple of caring dogs and many braying mini donkeys.

Whatever she needed, Conrad would do or get for her.

He wasn't sure if that meant he was in love with Glory Rose, and while she would be upset by what had happened tonight, he certainly wasn't. He had exposed a new layer of Glory Rose that he had never seen before.

He continued to pray for her as he went down the hall with Sari and helped her get in the bathtub. She brought her plastic ponies in and splashed around with them while he sat on the stool she used to wash her hands at the sink. He still hadn't started potty training yet, because the time he'd thought he might be able to dedicate to that had gone to Glory Rose instead.

But it didn't matter. He didn't have to have Sari potty trained on her third birthday. He tapped and opened his scripture app. "Should we read tonight?"

He thought it would calm him, and he liked reading to

Sari as she sometimes repeated the words and phrases in the scriptures that he said.

"Jesus," Sari said, and Conrad grinned at her.

"Yeah, let's read something about Jesus." He tapped to go to the New Testament in the Bible. He started to read the story of the Savior's birth, and he hadn't even finished a chapter before Glory Rose appeared in the doorway.

He didn't pause but instead gestured for her to come in, which she did. He tapped the closed toilet, and she sat down, crowding in close to him as he continued to read about how there was no room at the inn for Joseph and Mary.

Glory Rose put her arm around his shoulders, her fingers brushing through his hair every so often as he read. He finished the story and set his phone on the counter behind him.

"Baby Jesus," Sari said, and she finally looked up from her splashing ponies, her face bright, and when she saw Glory Rose, she said, "Rose." She held up both ponies, one clutched in each fist. "Ponies."

Glory Rose flowed from the closed toilet onto her knees in front of the tub. "Yeah, you got your ponies," she said quietly. "Is it time to wash your hair?"

She had to be exhausted still, but Conrad simply sat on the stepping stool and watched his gorgeous girlfriend help his daughter with her hair. When she was shampooed and conditioned, Conrad got up and un-stopped the tub and held out a towel for her. He wrapped her up, snuggled her close, kissed her while she giggled, and said, "Go find Grams. I'll be right out with your PJs."

His little girl did what he'd said, and Glory Rose continued to clean up around the tub with a hand towel. "You don't have to do that," he said.

She handed him the towel, her eyes finally coming up to meet his. "Thank you for taking care of me," she said, and Conrad recognized that she'd moved past her embarrassment and had not apologized. Warmth filled him from head to toe, and he reached out and let his fingers brush hers. "What are boyfriends for, if not to take care of their girlfriends?"

She smiled, and Conrad leaned down and matched his to hers in a soft kiss. "Do you still want to go see the donkeys?" he asked.

She nodded, and he took her hand and led her out into the hall. "Let me grab some PJs for Sari." He ducked into his daughter's bedroom to do that, and then they paused in the living room, where Conrad handed them to Grams, leaned down and kissed her, and said, "I'm gonna go out on the farm with Glory Rose for a few minutes. Are you okay in here with her?"

"We're totally fine." She reached out with her warm, papery hand and squeezed Glory Rose's, and then they left the farmhouse to go see the mini donkeys.

Chapter Nineteen

"It's kind of muddy right there," Conrad said, and he guided her closer to the fence line so that she wouldn't have to step in it. He did, and Glory Rose noticed the way that he took the worst of everything and helped her find the drier, safer parts of the path.

Stevie Nicks, his yellow lab, walked right at her side and looked up at her seemingly every other step, like a mother hen. Glory Rose reached down on her next step and stroked the dog's head, trying to reassure her that she was okay. She'd at least stopped crying, and that was a huge win.

They went past the chicken and turkey coops, as Conrad had three of them right next to each other. The birds were divided up, but Glory Rose couldn't tell how, as there seemed to be chickens and turkeys in all three of the pens.

His goat enclosure and milking shed came next. Glory

Rose smiled at the craftsmanship of it. "Did you build that?" she asked.

"Sure did," Conrad spoke softly, the way he sometimes did, and right now, Glory Rose appreciated the low volume of their conversation.

A big barn stood next to that, and Glory Rose wondered if the stargazing there would be as magnificent as it had been at the Kingman's ranch.

The dirt road they walked on separated his buildings from his pastures, and as they walked, Glory Rose became aware that his horses had joined them. She paused and moved closer to the fence to meet the magnificent animals. Stevie Nicks laid down right on her feet, and a rush of appreciation filled her for the gentle canine.

"What are their names?" she asked as she held out her hand for his tall, tawny horse to sniff. She moved down to Conrad, who stood on Glory Rose's left side, not really interested in Glory Rose at all.

"This here's Madonna," he said, and he carried a smile in his voice that Glory Rose also found on his face. "She's a good cutting horse, and I use her when I have to go help at Seven Sons."

"Mm," Glory Rose hummed. "She's really pretty."

"She doesn't get to work as much as she used to," Conrad said. "But I think she's got a pretty good life here."

The sound of the braying mini donkeys made Glory Rose turn and look down toward the sound. They'd gathered one hundred yards down at the fence, keeping them in their paddock and the horses over here. "Oh, they're jealous," she said.

Conrad chuckled. "Donkeys are really social animals," he said. "Most people don't know that, and yes, when they see me, they want me to be down by them."

"It's not too muddy here," she said.

"I've got my pump working." Conrad turned around and leaned his back against the fence. "It's not quite a homestead, but I do have solar panels to power the barn."

He looked down toward the mini donkey pasture. "There's a well out there, and when it rains a lot, like it has been, I can pump the water out of the field and into the well."

Glory Rose stepped to his side, glad when he put his arm around her and held her close. "Most people pump water *out* of the well."

"Well, we've got city water at the house," he said. "And I fill the well up in the spring and then pump it back out all summer long."

"So it's like half a homestead." Glory Rose started to feel more like herself, and she heard it in her voice.

She wondered if Conrad could too. He looked at her and pressed a kiss to her temple. "Sure, it's like half a homestead."

One of his horses huffed, and he turned around and said, "Oh, I didn't forget about you, Cyndi."

Glory Rose watched him stroke down the chestnut's neck. "So you name all your horses and dogs after famous female rock stars?" she asked.

He grinned at the horse and then her. "Just some of them."

"Do the mini donkeys have rock star names?"

"Gramps named all the mini donkeys," Conrad said with a shake of his head. "No rock stars."

"How do you even keep track of forty mini donkey names?"

Conrad laughed, the joy of it filling the evening sky around them. The last thing she remembered before she fell asleep was Conrad telling her that the sunset tonight would be beautiful—and it would be.

"Come on, sugar." Conrad took her hand, and they continued down the road at a leisurely pace.

The mini donkeys got louder as they approached, and Conrad whistled and held up his free hand. "All right, all right," he called. "We're here. Calm down."

He opened the gate and moved into the horse paddock, pushing them back and using his body to provide a safe space for Glory Rose to enter the pasture as well. "We just have to go down to that gate there," he said. "I need two levels of barrier with them." She smiled as she moved down a few feet to the next gate, opened it herself, and walked into the mini donkey herd.

They came up to about her waist, some with their heads angling up a little bit higher. She could stroke them easily, which she did, and she loved their big, tall ears and their long noses.

"Oh, you guys are the cutest things in the world, aren't you?" she said, as even smaller donkeys crowded in around her.

"Let's move away from the fence," Conrad said. "They'll

come with us." He moved through the multicolored donkeys. He had everything from a mottled gray and white, to a solid tan, to a dark gray, to a brighter tan, to a darker brown donkey with white legs.

Some of them stood no taller than a child, and some, like the first that had greeted her, had to be close to the maximum height for mini donkeys. He touched each one he went by, but he didn't say anything to them.

Glory Rose felt her happiness increase by degrees with every donkey that came over to say hello. Some of them actually sounded like they were saying hello, and she crouched down in front of one of the shorter donkeys and stroked her hands down his neck.

"She's a micro mini donkey," Conrad said. "Her name is Fruity Pebbles, because sometimes her spots look a little bit colored."

Glory Rose smiled at the miniature donkey and then straightened and joined Conrad again. She took his hand, gratitude flowing freely through her now. She'd already thanked him, and she didn't want to do so again, so she simply enjoyed the evening air and the scent of donkeys and mud and spring flowers as they walked around the pasture for a little bit longer.

When they finally walked back to the farmhouse, their view was the beautiful gold, red, orange, and navy of the sunset, and Glory Rose, despite her awful day and complete breakdown, sighed at the sight. "God is good," she murmured, resting her head against Conrad's arm.

"He sure is."

By the time Glory Rose got in her SUV, and Conrad closed the door behind her, full dark had claimed the day. She'd stayed for dinner, and she'd helped put Sari to bed, and she'd double-checked with Conrad that he would be up at Shiloh Ridge the following day to kick off their breeding season.

It certainly lasted longer than a day, but starting in March, as they did, they would start to have new calves on the ranch in December. Glory Rose well-remembered calving season, because Daddy always had to take overnight shifts to sit with cattle or go out when they went into labor. Cows didn't seem to care if their babies came in the middle of the night, or bright and early in the morning, or right when it was time to go to bed.

Her family always did a breeding weekend to kick off the season, and they'd provide meals for lunch and dinner tomorrow, as well as breakfast on Sunday, before they'd leave a skeleton crew on the ranch, and almost everyone else would go to church.

Then, after church, they had a big party, because the Glovers used any opportunity they could to have a big party.

And Glory Rose loved it. She'd loved growing up a Glover, and she could only hope and pray they wouldn't eat Conrad alive.

"He'll be able to hold his own," she whispered, because while he was quiet, that didn't mean he was weak.

* * *

Glory Rose felt like her old self when she woke the following morning. She showered and dressed in her ranch clothes, braided her hair back, and hurried to eat a bowl of instant oatmeal before she went over to her aunt's house to help with the food. When she and Fawn got to the homestead, all the parking spots had been filled.

Uncle Ranger stood outside, and he leaned in the window Fawn had rolled down. "We could use you guys down at True Blue instead of here. There's already a lot of people here."

"Sure," Fawn said, and she leaned out the window to give her daddy a quick and awkward hug. "How's Momma? Is she okay?"

Her father smiled and said, "She's moving pretty slow this morning, but she has plenty of help here. Misty and Sammy are up at True Blue, and they need help with tables and chairs and tents."

"We'll go," Fawn said, and they continued past the road that led off the ranch, and then the family cemetery. True Blue sat on the right side of the road, and another hundred yards up the lane sat Uncle Ace's house. He'd planted a lot of trees after he'd built their house, and Glory Rose couldn't see it until she drove right in front of it.

Uncle Bishop lived back behind True Blue, his driveway long and his front yard melting into the big grassy area behind the barn. That was where they found Misty, Link, Uncle Bear, and Aunt Sammy laying out tent poles.

They'd have tables and chairs inside too, and all of the food would be indoors as well. But containing dozens of teenagers and children and cowboys required more than the big banquet hall inside the barn.

Glory Rose moved over to her aunt and said, "Hey, Aunt Sammy," as she gave her a hug.

"Oh, how are you, Glory Rose?" she asked. "We just sent your cowboy over to Bishop's."

Glory Rose blinked in surprise. "Conrad is here already?"

Aunt Sammy smiled prettily. "Yep, he got here just a few minutes ago."

Glory Rose looked over to Uncle Bishop's house. "Why'd you send him over to Uncle Bishop's?"

"They're going to set up the volleyball net," Uncle Bear said. "Robbie and Ollie are bringing over more tents."

Glory Rose wasn't the greatest at setting up the big, heavy canvas tent, but she could sort poles and thread canvas, and then she'd let the taller, stronger men step in to raise the walls and roof.

Pearl Jo had left the cabin before Fawn and Glory Rose, and she figured she was at the homestead with her momma, who still ran her catering company. Aunt Holly Ann had been feeding all of the Glovers for many years, as had Uncle Bishop and Aunt Etta, so she wasn't sure why Bishop wasn't helping with the food this morning.

Glory Rose decided she didn't care. Families grew and changed all the time, and there was no better uncle for Conrad to work with than Uncle Bishop. He was kind and accepting and funny, and he didn't say embarrassing things.

She helped move poles around for a few minutes, and

when Robbie arrived with another bag, she unzipped it and kept going.

She glanced over to Uncle Bishop's house seemingly every minute, but she didn't see Conrad. "What's going on over there?" she asked Robbie.

"Oh, they found a huge nest of mice in the storage shed," Robbie said. "I've never heard my dad scream like that." He chuckled and pulled on the canvas as he backed up to lay it out flat. "I don't think we're going to be playing volleyball today."

"They chewed a hole in the net," Ollie added.

"Oh, nope. No volleyball today," Glory Rose said, and a moment later, Conrad and Bishop came around the side of the house.

Sure enough, they did not carry the volleyball net poles or the net. Uncle Bishop was smiling, though, and he looked at Conrad as they talked. Conrad wore a grin as well, and Glory Rose simply loved the sight of him.

He wore a pair of gloves, and his eyes latched on to Glory Rose's from one hundred yards away. She left the poles behind and went to meet him, as she wanted to introduce him around to everyone.

"You found mice, huh?" she called.

Uncle Bishop shook his head like it was the saddest thing ever. "We're not going to be able to play volleyball today unless someone drives to town and gets a new net."

"It's not worth that," Uncle Bear called. "We can put out the horseshoes, and the croquet."

Uncle Bishop nodded. "There's tons of lawn games in the barn."

"Did you play mouse exterminator this morning?" Glory Rose asked as she neared Conrad.

He chuckled, finally reached her, and drew her into a hug. "I love seeing you in the morning," he murmured, his mouth right at her ear.

"You were early," she whispered. "I would have been here to introduce you around."

"Nervous energy," he said back. "Grams is gonna bring Sari up for lunch, and I expect that'll be a whole circus too."

Glory Rose stepped back and beamed up at him. "We're the Glovers. Circuses are what we do best."

Chapter Twenty

Conrad enjoyed the feel of Glory Rose's hand in his as she led him over to the group of men and women working to put up tents. "Everyone," she called. "This is my boyfriend, Conrad Walker. I know, I know. A lot of you know him." She looked at him, her smile as bright as the springtime sunshine. "But yeah, he's going to be here working with us today. And he's got a great pair of hands, so don't be afraid to give him a job."

Heat filled his face, because he did know most of the people already there and working. He'd already shaken hands with Bear and Bishop and Link, who he spent quite a bit of time with, actually. A few more people had arrived, and Conrad was pretty sure they belonged to Ace and Holly Ann Glover.

Sammy came over to him, though she'd already greeted him and said, "It's great to meet you as Glory Rose's boyfriend." She glanced over her shoulder. "Now I could use your muscles over here on the corner of the tent."

"Yes, ma'am," he said, and he dropped Glory Rose's hand to go with her aunt.

"I'm sure you know Gunnison," Link said. "He's Ace's oldest."

"Yeah, sure," Conrad said, and he shook the young man's hand. "Glory Rose lives with Pearl Jo, and she's your sister."

"That's right," Gun said. "Aunt Sammy, Daddy had to go down to town to get a bunch more bread because the stuff that Momma had in the freezer was moldy."

"Okay," Sammy said, and she turned around to find Bishop. "Bishop, Ace had to go to town."

"I'm already talking to him," Bishop called, and he did have his phone up to his ear as he walked away from the group.

"Okay, boys," Bear called. "Let's see if we can get this first tent up."

He stood on one of the corners, and Conrad bent to pick up the other front corner. Gunnison moved down to the middle pole, and everybody fanned out around the tent.

"We pull them straight out," Bear called. "On three: One, two, three!"

Conrad pulled the pole up and out, and it really strained his muscles, but the tent came up quite nicely. Sammy, Misty, and Glory Rose hurried inside with the center poles that would anchor the roof and hold the tent while they staked it.

"We're here," a couple of people called, and Conrad looked to see who had arrived. More young people like him and Glory Rose, and it was obvious that Ranger was sending everyone down here.

He figured it was a good move, since they had plenty of physical things to set up, and there would be too many hands in the kitchen with all of them.

He dusted his gloves together, and then pulled the rope out tight and pressed in the stake as far as he could without any tools.

Link came over with a hammer. "I'll finish it up."

He did while Conrad watched as the two people who had arrived, a man and a woman, bumped knuckles with Gun and hugged Misty.

"That's Johnny and Judy," Link said. "They're Ida's oldest. Twins."

"Oh, sure," Conrad said. They had to be close to Glory Rose's age, though he wasn't for-certain.

She'd gone inside the tent and hadn't come out yet, and Conrad told himself he didn't need to stick to her side like glue. He was a grown man, and he could look around and find tasks to do, so he moved over to the other tent and started threading the pole through the corner canvas.

A few minutes later, the others working on the tent had everything ready, and they pulled that tent up as well. Some people worked on tying back the flaps so that the air would flow through, and a half-hour later, four huge tents took up the grassy area behind the blue barn.

Someone had gotten out the lawn games, and Conrad used the pair of gloves that Bishop had given him to wipe the sweat from his brow.

"Conrad, hey."

"Ollie." He shook the other man's hand, and nodded to Aurora, his wife. They'd brought their four kids, and his oldest, Jewel, who had just turned twelve, stuck close to him and Rory, while the others ran over to the croquet set and started setting up the pickets.

"How are you guys doing?" he asked.

"Great," Ollie said. "You guys got the tents up early. What time did you get here?"

"Oh, I don't know," Conrad said. "I left my place at seven-thirty."

Ollie nodded. "They're whipping tables and chairs up inside, but it didn't look like they needed more help."

"Sounds good," Conrad said, because he could just stand and chat if they didn't need him inside. "How are things at your place? Have you flooded?"

"Yes," Rory said as Jewel went to meet a couple of other teenagers. "We managed to get everything up on tables that we'd already planted, but we lost some of our early starts."

Conrad nodded. "Grams hadn't had me plant the garden yet, so I'm just ankle-deep in mud."

He grinned at them while Ollie shook his head. "Hey, I was gonna ask you," he said. "I know you're busy with your own place and all, but I have to go out of town for a couple weeks at the beginning of May for a big project at work."

"Okay," Conrad said, looking between him and Rory.

"I could use some help on the farm," Rory said. "I mean, it's not really a farm, but—"

Ollie leaned closer. "She's pregnant again," he said. "And

the heat really bothers her, so I don't want her cutting the grass or working in the garden. Could you come over and just make sure the basics are taken care of while I'm gone?"

"Yeah, of course," Conrad said, and he grinned over at Rory. "Congratulations."

She rested one hand on her still-flat stomach. "Tell Ollie. He's not happy about it."

"I am too happy about it," Ollie said, but Rory had already turned and said, "I'm going back inside," over her shoulder.

"I'm happy about it," Ollie called after her, but he blew out an exasperated breath as he faced the tents again.

Conrad had no idea what to say, and Oliver wore unhappiness etched in the lines around and between his eyes.

"When I first met Sarina," he said. "I knew instantly that she was mine. I didn't question it for a moment, and I loved her instantly."

Ollie looked at him. The weight of his eyes on the side of Conrad's face sat heavily. He said nothing, but he seemed to hang on every word.

"I can't say that I was happy about having her," he said. "I had no idea what I was doing. I didn't know how I would tell everyone. I didn't even know what little girls needed. I didn't know what they ate. I didn't know what time she should go to bed." He looked down at the ground and scuffed the dirt with the toe of his cowboy boot.

"So yeah, I wasn't really happy about it in the beginning." He looked up and met Ollie's eyes. "So I know you'll love that baby," he said. "Because I loved Sarina with my whole soul the moment I saw her." He nodded and swallowed. "But it took some time before I was happy about being her dad. And you know what? That's okay."

Ollie reached up and brushed at his eyes as he looked away. "Thanks, Conrad," he said. "Of course, I'm going to love that baby. I just thought we were done having kids."

"How old is Lennon?" Conrad asked.

"He's almost five," Ollie said. "He's going to kindergarten in the fall, and Rory has really been looking forward to starting up her sewing business again."

"Yeah," Conrad said, though he knew that Ollie and Rory were just like him and Glory Rose—they didn't need the money.

"So she's pretending to be really jazzed about the pregnancy," Ollie said. "But I know she's not as happy as she says she is."

"Maybe she just needs some time too," Conrad said.

Ollie nodded, his jaw clenched hard.

Robbie approached with his younger sister, Georgia, and Conrad wasn't sure of the gap between them, but it was several years as Georgia had just graduated from high school recently, and Robbie had already been to college and back and been working on the ranch for a couple of years.

"We haven't told anyone," Ollie muttered under his breath.

"I won't say anything," Conrad said.

The others arrived, and they brought with them a few more young adults that Conrad wasn't sure he knew.

"This is Bell," Ollie said. "He's Libby and Mister's oldest.

He just graduated from high school last year." He smiled at the young man as Conrad shook his hand.

"His younger sister, Marley. They've got two more, but I don't know where they are." Ollie looked around. "And Hank," he said, stepping back to make room for another cowboy. "He's Preacher and Charlie's. He's your same age, right, Bell?"

"Yep, we're the same age," Bell said. He reached out and tapped Conrad's knuckles in greeting.

"And I think you probably know Smiles and Rock," Ollie said, as he moved in and gave a double hug to two more young men. "They're Bear and Sammy's oldest boys—besides Link."

Conrad shook hands all around, though he was probably several years older than everyone who had just arrived. Oliver was older than him by several years, and he fit right in with all of these Glovers, so Conrad could too.

"All right." Smiles stepped forward and leaned in as if he had a great secret to tell. "Mitch is on his way here, and I want to surprise him with that new dog his daddy got him."

"Did you bring it with you?" Johnny asked.

"Uncle Cactus is coming right now," Smiles said. "He's asked us to keep Mitch busy for a few minutes and then bring him outside." He looked around the group. "So we need a plan."

Conrad had no idea what that meant. Couldn't they just keep Mitch inside and talk to him for a few minutes? Why did there need to be a plan? None of the cowboys in the circle said anything.

Ollie started to chuckle. "If you need some elaborate plan," he said. "We need to get a woman in this huddle."

"What's going on over here?" Conrad stepped back and made room for Glory Rose between him and Ollie. "You boys look like you're up to trouble."

Conrad started to chuckle, and Smiles told Glory Rose what he wanted.

She said, "Oh, okay, where's Uncle Cactus going to put the puppy?"

"He's riding over with his horse and all of his other dogs," Smiles said. "So I think he just wants to make sure that Mitch isn't out here and can't see him coming."

Glory Rose nodded, a determined glint in her eye. "All right, boys," she said, and she leaned in too. Conrad moved with her, noting that all of the other Glovers did as well. "Here's what we're going to do."

Conrad liked seeing her in this way, and watching how everyone, from multiple aunts and uncles to her cousins, listened to her and took on their roles.

"All right," she said with a clap of her hands. "Everyone know what they're going to be doing?"

Conrad had no idea, because he'd zoned out a little bit while Glory Rose issued instructions. He still had no idea what was so hard about keeping someone inside and talking to them.

She nodded to Smiles and Rock. "All right, you two are our first line of defense, because you know sign language the best. See if you can recruit Link and Misty, but I think Misty ran down to the homestead to start bringing food up."

"I can do that too," Conrad said. "I've got my truck."

Glory Rose linked her arm through his as the Glovers broke up and headed inside True Blue.

She turned him in that direction, and they walked that way at a much slower clip. "Oh no, cowboy," she said with plenty of her usual flirtation in her voice. "You and I are the last defense, and we have to make sure that Uncle Cactus is ready with the puppy before we let Mitch come outside."

Conrad chuckled. "What are we going to do—stand at the door and bounce him if he tries to get outside?"

"Yes," Glory Rose said as she followed the others in the back door and the blissful air conditioning. "That's exactly what we're going to do. And I gave us the best job, because we get to stand in the air conditioning, but we don't really have to do anything."

He pulled her close and chuckled as he pressed his lips to her hairline. "Smart and beautiful. It's a dangerous combination."

They had plenty of day left, and Conrad still had plenty of other Glovers to interact with, but everyone so far had been kind and accepting, and he felt like he could belong here at Shiloh Ridge just as easily as he did at Seven Sons, and he thanked the Lord for that great blessing.

He prayed that when he brought Glory Rose to one of his huge family functions, she would feel the same way.

Chapter Twenty-One

L incoln Glover groaned as he rolled over and sat up. His alarm hadn't gone off yet, and nine times out of ten, he woke before it did.

Behind him, he heard the deep, even breathing of his wife, and he padded quietly into the bathroom to take care of his needs. When he returned to the bedroom, he first silenced the alarm on his phone and then climbed back into bed with Misty. He drew her into his arms, and she started to wake. "We should've just done our birthday celebration last weekend when we had breeding weekend."

Misty moaned but didn't say anything else. They'd set up tents and tables and chairs, and they'd fed almost one hundred people as they'd kicked off breeding season. They'd continued all week, and breeding would continue for another couple of weeks as well. Link was in charge of that side of the ranch, while Wilder worked with Uncle Preacher and Uncle Ward to learn the rotational ranching and all of the agricultural needs at Shiloh Ridge.

Link really liked working with Wilder, and he'd spent four years doing a Range and Ranch Management degree at Texas A&M. He knew a lot, and now he just had to put that knowledge into practice with real animals and real land, real fences, real men, and real weather conditions in the Texas Panhandle.

Today, they'd have to set up all those tables and chairs and tents again, but instead of his aunts and uncles spending hours cooking and serving three meals over the course of twenty-four hours, Link and Misty had decided to cater their birthday party.

He still had work to do on the ranch that day, as the party wasn't until evening, but he couldn't make himself get out of bed. Their youngest son acted as an alarm for Misty, as he usually woke and fussed for her to come get him out of his crib.

When Scout's cries came down the hall and met his ears, Link rolled away from his wife and said, "I'll get him."

The boy could walk now, and Link wasn't surprised to find him standing at his crib, both hands gripping the top of it like he might climb out at any moment.

When Lincoln stepped into the room, he grinned at how his son's face brightened, and he said, "Daddy."

Mom and *dad* were about all that Scout could say right now, and Link lifted his fifteen-month-old out of the crib. "Morning, my boy." He pressed a kiss to the boy's chubby cheek. "Are you hungry?"

Before he took Scout out into the kitchen, he changed his

diaper and then crept out of the room, which he shared with his four-year-old brother, Diesel. The Top Cottage, where he and Misty lived, wasn't a big house like some of the others that had been built at Shiloh Ridge.

As Link put Scout on the couch and turned on the TV so that he could start breakfast and coffee, he wondered how much longer he and Misty could stay in the cottage.

She wasn't pregnant again yet, but they wanted more children. In particular, she wanted a girl, and that meant at least one more child, if they were lucky. The Top Cottage had three bedrooms and two bathrooms, and if they only had three kids, Link could probably live here his whole life. But if they had more, he'd definitely need somewhere else to live.

The ranch had plenty of space and wide open fields, and he'd already started talking to his daddy, Uncle Ward, Uncle Preacher, and Uncle Ranger about a possible location for a house. But Uncle Bishop and Aunt Montana certainly couldn't work at the clip that they'd once had.

Bishop had turned fifty last year, and Montana was older than him, and while they still worked and filled a lot of the construction needs around the ranch, he didn't want to ask them to build a house for him.

He put together breakfast and fed himself and Scout before Misty and Diesel got up. He did a second round for them, enjoying his small family in this quaint cottage before he had to go out onto the ranch. "Your phone was buzzing a lot," she said. "You left it in the bedroom."

"Shoot." Link jogged down the hall and picked up his phone from the nightstand. Sure enough, he'd missed over twenty texts, which, in the Glover family, wasn't that hard to do.

Smiles had started a thread off of the main ranch string, and he'd said, *Happy Birthday, brother. We're going to take over your chores today so you have the whole day off.*

He blinked as he looked at the next text, where Smiles had then assigned out everything that Link usually did to various cousins and siblings.

Rock was going to take care of the horses.

Birch and Willow, who were June and Judge's two oldest, had agreed to do the morning ride of the fence line.

Betty, Hank, and Daisy—Uncle Preacher's kids—had taken over all of the animal feeding that Link usually did.

Duke and Arizona's kids, Shiloh, April, Dwayne, and Dallas, were going to head up checking on the feed supply levels, which Link did once a week on Saturdays.

Everyone else had said that they would set up the tables and chairs and tents for the party that night. And Hailey, who had joined the Glover family when Aunt Etta had married her husband, August, said she would drive down to town and get all of the food. Johnny and Judy lived in town, and they said they'd meet her there, because everyone knew there would be a lot to transport.

Once everyone had confirmed their job for the day, messages started saying, *He can't still be asleep, can he?*

Smiles texted: *Link, are you there? Are you getting this message?*

Gunnison had texted, *I'll go check the barn to see if he's there already.*

And a few seconds later, Silver had said, *I'm in the stable and he's not here.*

Glory Rose: *It's his birthday. Maybe he's sleeping in. Give him a minute to answer.*

Link grinned at his phone, so grateful to be a Glover. He quickly tapped out a message, *I'm here. Sorry, I left my phone in the bedroom while I made breakfast. You guys really don't have to do all my chores today.*

That got an immediate backlash from a dozen people who said, *Yes, we do.*

It's your birthday.

You never take a day off.

Enjoy your time with your wife and kids.

In fact, Sunnie, his youngest sister said: *Heather and I are going to be there at eleven-thirty to babysit the kids so you and Misty can go to lunch by yourselves.*

Pure joy and gratitude gathered in Link's soul, and he turned around and hurried back into the kitchen. "Everyone's taking care of everything on the ranch for me today," he said. "I have the whole day off."

Misty blinked at him. "The whole day off?"

He grinned and nodded. "And the girls are coming to babysit at eleven-thirty, so we can go to lunch together."

Misty stood up, pure hope on her face. "A real lunch date."

He pulled her close and kissed her gently. "A real lunch date," he murmured against her lips. "And maybe I can have them bring the kids down, and we can take them to the park or a movie."

"But we have to get ready for the party," Misty said.

"They're handling the party too," Link said. "Everything, all day long. We don't have to do anything."

She smiled at him. "You have a really great family."

"They're your family too," he said, and they were, because the Glovers folded in anyone who came to Shiloh Ridge, and they loved them and served them.

"All right, boys," Misty said, "Diesel, take Scout into your room and you guys get some clothes on. Daddy has the whole day off." She looked at him and beamed. "And we're gonna go horseback riding, just for fun."

Diesel cheered and scrambled down from the chair. Link moved over and helped Scout get out of his seat that they still strapped him in, and he toddled after his brother, yelling something that sounded dangerously close to, "Horse. Horse. Horse!"

Link kissed his wife again, whose birthday was actually in a couple of days. "I love you," he said.

"I love you too, Link."

"I know I work a lot," he said.

"It's not too much," she said.

"You'll tell me if it is?"

She nodded. "I'll tell you if it is." She looked up at him, and he could get lost in her pretty eyes, even all these years later. "I actually really love our life here," she said. "It feels simple and slow, even though I know you're busy."

He nodded and searched her face. "Are you thinking about having another baby?"

She shrugged and curled into his chest. "I wouldn't say no."

Link tended to follow his wife's lead on these things, and they didn't need to have baby after baby the way his daddy did, because he hadn't gotten married when he was forty-five.

"Well, we'll just see what God gives us," he said.

Yelling came down the hall, and Misty said, "He's already given us two amazing boys who *never* fight."

Crying started, and Link grinned in that direction. "That's my cue."

"I don't even know what they could possibly be fighting about," she said. "It's not like Scout can wear Diesel's clothes."

"Oh, I'm sure he stepped on him or something," Link said, and he took a step away from his wife, and then turned back to her. He cradled her face in his hands and kissed her deeper than before. "What do you want to do on our day off?"

"I think we've got the whole thing planned already," she said. "Horseback riding, a lunch date, and a movie with the kids. Then we'll get to see all of our friends and family for the party tonight."

"Sounds like the perfect day," Link said.

"It's going to be the perfect day," Misty agreed, and Link hurried down the hall as a scream filled the rafters at the Top Cottage.

Chapter Twenty-Two

S miles Glover pulled up to the homestead and leaned on the horn. Wilder came out only a moment later, and he jogged down the steps, then the sidewalk, and in between the fence posts that marked the barrier between the parking gravel and the front yard.

Smiles was actually six months older than Wilder, but he'd lived for a couple of years on the ranch after high school, when Wilder had gone straight to college, so Smiles still had two years of school left.

He honestly didn't know what he would do at that time, because his older brother Link ran the ranch, and Wilder had just returned to do the same thing.

They'll need you, he thought, because it had taken his daddy and Wilder's daddy and all of the Glovers to run Shiloh Ridge for the past several years.

"Howdy," Wilder said, as he catapulted into the truck. "You ready for this?"

Smiles smiled. "Of course. I'm so ready. I love a good party." He'd orchestrated today so that Link could have the whole day off, something he knew his brother absolutely never got.

He'd grown up watching his daddy do the same thing—work and work and work and work some more. It had taken Smiles a couple of weeks to talk to everyone at Shiloh Ridge and figure out what Link did on Saturdays, and then assign people to take those jobs so that the man could have his birthday to himself and his wife. He hoped that Link and Misty had had an amazing day.

They'd put together a big party that evening for friends and family, and Smiles wanted to get there early so that he wouldn't have to fight for parking. Plus, he and Wilder needed to get the tables and chairs set up.

Betty had organized the decorating committee, and she had a whole mess of people who wanted to help already at the barn.

Smiles was a lot like his momma in that he loved people, and he had gone around with her to take birthday gifts and cupcakes whenever there was something to celebrate on the ranch. Rock seemed to have inherited all of daddy's grumpy qualities, and he'd rather die than go around and talk to people unannounced.

Momma had told Smiles that he would probably have to be the one to continue that at Shiloh Ridge. So when he walked in and found a plethora of balloons being made into arches and streamers hanging from rafters, he clapped loudly and yelled, "This is great!"

Since he'd also inherited his daddy's big, deep, grizzly-bear voice—as well as his broad chest and shoulders—everyone heard him. His family beamed back at him, and Smiles went to pull out the racks of tables and chairs that the Glover family owned for occasions just like this.

There were so many of them, and Smiles had organized well, so it didn't take long to get the room set up for eating and socializing.

Hailey, Johnny, and Judy should be here with the food soon, and Smiles took a moment to sit down with his cousins and best friends.

"I missed Shiloh Ridge," he said, and Wilder lifted his bottle of water to his lips and nodded.

"I missed it when I was gone too," he said.

"I didn't think I would," Smiles said. "Since I stayed for a couple of years, but I do."

Birch pulled out a chair and sat down. He reached over and knocked knuckles with Smiles and then Wilder. "I'm going to Amarillo State in the fall."

"Oh, that's great," Smiles said. "I didn't know you'd got accepted."

"I just got the letter," he said. "But it's pretty late in the year, so we've got to figure out housing."

"I'm sure there will be something," Wilder said.

"What are you going to study?" Smiles asked.

Birch shrugged his shoulders and looked over as another cousin joined them. Gun sighed as he sat down. He'd gone to college for a couple of years, but he hadn't finished before coming back to the ranch.

"I don't know," Birch said. "Maybe you guys could give me some ideas of what would be useful around the ranch."

"Are you talking about college?" Gun asked.

"Yep."

Smiles had no advice, but Gun said, "Well, you shouldn't choose based on what'll be beneficial for the ranch."

Birch looked at him and raised his eyebrows. "No?"

Gun shook his head. "No. You'll just end up quitting because you'll be too unhappy." He gave them a dry look. "Ask me how I know."

Smiles's smile faltered. "I didn't know you didn't like what you were doing," he said.

"I'm glad Wilder got the ranch management degree," Gun said. "I hated it. I don't think I'm cut out for business."

"What do you want to do?" Wilder asked.

"I actually think I'd be way happier if I could build something or fix something," Gun said. "So right now, I'm just living my year at the ranch, but I'm going to talk to Aunt Sammy about being a ranch mechanic, and Uncle Bishop and Aunt Montana about construction. I think both of those fit my personality way better."

"Those are both solid," Smiles said.

"Do you like what you're doing?" Birch asked, and everyone looked at him.

"I don't know," he said. "I haven't ever really thought about what I would like to do."

"That's just because you're so positive," Wilder said, and he rolled his eyes.

Gun gave a dry laugh. "He's not wrong. Some people can just do whatever and be happy."

Smiles's heart ached for Gun, because he did want his cousin to be happy and feel productive at the ranch.

"Not everyone has to come back to the ranch, you know?" he said. "Mitch didn't. Heck, none of Cactus's boys did."

"Chaz will," Wilder said. "Eventually."

"Yeah," Gun said. "Chaz will."

Smiles supposed they were right about that, but before he could agree, an alarm went off on his phone. "Oh, it's time to get started," he said. "Let's get the music playing."

He got to his feet and went to get the sound system going. By the time he came out of the control room, the food had arrived, and that meant guests would be here any moment.

Smiles had staged Link and Misty to be the last to arrive. But it wasn't a surprise party. They'd planned it, and he'd simply taken over this morning.

He tried not to hear his sister's voice, who told him he took over everything, whether people wanted him to or not. He did have a tendency to do that, and his momma had told him that it could be a good quality if he channeled it correctly.

Smiles thought providing a day of rest and birthday fun for Link seemed like a good idea, so he'd texted them about an hour ago to say that they were running behind at True Blue and asked them if they would please come down at six-thirty instead of six.

The time had not changed for anyone else, and Smiles turned into his Smiley-Mister-Politician Personality, as Heather called him, as the guests started to arrive. Link was about eight years older than Smiles, but he knew a lot of the cowboys around town simply by working with his daddy on the ranch over the years.

So he said hello to Finn and Edith and told the boys there was a bounce house behind the barn. That nearly caused a riot when Edith said they had to eat first, and Smiles decided to keep the bounce house to himself for the next little bit.

He welcomed Henry and Angel Marshall to the ranch. They had a cute little boy who toddled in with them carrying a gift way too big for him.

Smiles grinned, because he'd grown up with a lot of children around, and he loved them as much as he loved anyone.

Uncle Duke and Aunt Arizona arrived with Brandon, and Smiles clapped his hand with the older cowboy. "I thought you were bringing a date," he said.

Brandon wore a smile too, but something edgy appeared in his eyes as he said, "Nah. Didn't work out."

"Okay." He watched the man migrate over to his brother, not sure if he should ask another question or simply pray for Brandon.

Aunt June and Uncle Judge arrived with a whole laundry basket of brightly colored birthday gifts, followed closely by the rest of Link's aunts and uncles. Aunt Ida joined her twins and started serving dinner according to Smiles's plan.

He knew Link liked having his cake first on his birthday, and he wanted to sing "Happy Birthday" and light the candles when Link and Misty walked in. He went around to all the tables and thanked everyone for coming, explained why Misty and Link and their boys weren't there yet, and what would happen when they arrived.

And then, in true Glover fashion, Link entered True Blue five minutes before six-thirty, almost catching Smiles unaware.

He didn't stand at the front of the barn the way he should have, but he nodded to Wilder, who grabbed the mic and said, "Happy Birthday, Link and Misty!"

And since Smiles had made it around to everyone and they knew the cue, the crowd that had gathered in True Blue launched into an off-key, incredibly loud rendition of *Happy Birthday*.

Link picked up his youngest son and held his wife's hand as the crowd sang to them, all of them smiling out at everyone who'd come.

Smiles grinned and grinned and grinned, though his emotions definitely teetered on the edge of tears. When the song ended, Wilder stepped over to Link and offered him the mic.

He took it and said, "Wow."

Smiles expected him to go on, but he didn't, and he watched as his older brother's chin shook and he swallowed several times. Link finally shook his head and gave the mic to Misty, who said, "That was amazing. We love you all so much, and we know who's behind organizing this."

She found Smiles and gestured to him. "Everyone give it up for Smiles, who always knows how to throw the best parties."

The crowd erupted into cowboy whooping and cheering, which made Smiles glad he stood at the back of the room, because he wouldn't have to give a speech. He'd find himself just like Link, choked up and unable to say anything.

"There's cake!" Daddy bellowed, and sure enough, Momma and Uncle Bishop wheeled out a cake—legit wheeled it out on a cart. Aunt Ida and Aunt Holly Ann had worked on it together, and it stood five tiers tall and had been decorated with cowboy items like boots, hats, cacti, horses, dogs, and chickens. It had been done in bright frostings and fondant, and it absolutely screamed Shiloh Ridge and Link and Misty.

Smiles loved his family so much in that moment.

Cake started getting served, and Smiles stayed at the back, hugging and laughing and accepting the praise of his friends and family members. He expected Wilder to come to his side, because he'd done a lot for this party too, but he didn't.

After Squire and Kelly Ackerman had told him, "Great job on the party, Smiles," and gone to get their piece of cake, he saw Wilder had already gotten his treat and was sitting at a table with none other than Elaine Walker. His face shone, and he laughed in a way that Smiles only saw Wilder do with women he was interested in.

Well, that's interesting, Smiles thought to himself, and then Link and Misty arrived and pulled him into a hug. "Thank you so much," Link said, his voice catching on the last word. "You made it an incredible birthday for both of us."

"I hope so," Smiles said. "You guys do so much for the ranch." He pulled back and grinned at both of them. "I hope there's a place for me here when I'm done with school in a couple of years."

Link took him by the shoulders and said, "Smiles, there will always be a place for you at Shiloh Ridge."

Chapter Twenty-Three

Tate Reynolds squeezed his fiancée's hand as they pulled up to a beautiful house on the east side of Three Rivers. Clara Jean was a few years younger than him, but she was a powerhouse to be reckoned with.

He loved her more and more every single day, and he borrowed from her well of courage as she got out of her own car. He joined her, because Tate didn't actually own a car. The differences between him and Clara Jean were astronomical. She was a billionaire, and when he'd come to Seven Sons, he'd had two-hundred-fifty dollars in his bank account saved from his part-time job at Amarillo State.

He'd been injured within an hour of arriving at his best friend's ranch to work for the summer, and Clara Jean never seemed to stop moving or working. She still lived at home, helped her momma and daddy around the house, on the ranch, with her siblings, and she worked full-time at Wilde & Organic, the grocery store her family had owned for decades.

Her momma's sister had run it for a while, but she only had two kids, and neither of them wanted to take over the store. Clara Jean's uncle had been working for the family grocery store since he was a teenager, just like her.

He'd managed and cultivated and grown and produced all of their fruits and vegetables for the past almost fifty years. He'd gotten divorced a few years ago, and currently, none of his children or ex-wife lived in the Texas Panhandle.

Clara Jean had gone to her uncle Mike and asked him about taking over the farmland—the one hundred fifty acres of farmland that fed Wilde & Organic.

Mike had employees. He had to deal with workers in the fields. He had to understand how agriculture worked, when to plant things so that they would be ripe at the right season, and a multitude of other things. And Clara Jean wanted it all.

When she'd shared her hopes and dreams of obtaining the farmland and ultimately taking over Wilde & Organic, Tate had never felt the level of peace and serenity that he did in that moment.

He'd been saving for about a year now to buy his own piece of land in the Three Rivers area. He thought it would be more like a one-man operation, like what Finn Ackerman or Alex Baxter did.

They had a good, sizable chunk of land, with some animals, that they cultivated with their wife and kids. That was the kind of life Tate wanted, and he wanted it with Clara Jean.

Today, two days before their wedding, they were going to sign the paperwork that would transfer ownership of the farmland to Tate and Clara Jean—really just Clara Jean, as their estate lawyer had advised that it would be far easier to have a single name on the deed in case of death or divorce, though Tate wasn't planning on experiencing either.

"Are you ready?" Clara Jean asked.

Tate took her hand again and faced the house. "I'm ready," he said, because he'd already been over his insecurities with his almost-wife. She didn't need to hear them again. She'd assured him and reassured him that she loved him, but Tate could admit that he felt a massive imbalance between him and Clara Jean.

She had so much money, so much wealth, so much beauty, so much goodness, and so many opportunities. He felt like the cowboy from the wrong side of the tracks, sneaking his way in and using the small-town billionaire to get what he wanted. He'd asked her if she wanted him to sign a prenup before they got married, and she'd laughed bitterly and left him sitting at her momma's dining room table.

She'd actually slammed the door as she'd left, and Tate had looked over to her parents with a frown etched between his eyes.

Whitney had stood up and said, "She loves you, Tate. You better figure out how to accept it." She'd taken her coffee cup and left the kitchen as well, leaving Tate with Clara Jean's daddy.

"I don't know how to feel like a man with her," he'd told Jeremiah. "Men are supposed to provide and protect, and I can't do either. *She* provides everything for *me*, and when she does, she gives me the protection I want to give to her."

Jeremiah had done him the great favor of simply nodding as if he agreed, though he'd been nothing but kind and accepting of Tate since that first summer he'd come to Seven Sons with JJ to work the ranch.

"You're a good man, Tate," he'd said. "She does love you, and she needs a man like you at her side, because wealth and land—they don't mean anything if you don't have someone to share them with."

Since then, Tate had been trying to find his new role, and that was at Clara Jean's side, not behind her. They went up the stairs together, and her uncle opened the door with a smile on his face.

"There you are. I was beginning to worry if that road closure had forced you around the top of town."

"Oh, there's a road closure?" Tate asked. "We must have missed it."

"Yeah, there was a car fire on the highway," he said. "They've got it contained, though it did ignite some of the grass on the side of the road."

"Oh, no," Clara Jean said. "Where is it?"

"I guess a big construction truck was dragging a chain on the highway," he said. "Going out to where Mitch is building that deaf academy. It sparked and the car behind him caught on fire. The driver went off the road, and that started the grass ablaze as well. I think they have it contained now." He looked down at his phone as if to check, and Tate and Clara Jean squeezed by him to go inside the house.

"I can't believe there's been a wildfire already," Clara Jean said. "We usually don't have to worry about that until July or August."

"That's why it didn't get too far," Mike said. "It's still really wet from that rain we had last month."

"You didn't have to get lunch," Tate said when he spied everything laid out on the dining room table, including the contract and a pen next to Clara Jean's spot. "We told you it was fine."

In fact, he had planned a celebratory lunch with Clara Jean at their favorite place where they'd had their first date. He told himself he could take her there for dinner or lunch tomorrow, or when they got back from their honeymoon, which JJ had given them as a wedding gift.

Tate had grown up on a farm an hour away from where he went to college, which was an hour away from where he lived now and where he wanted to build his life. He'd never really been bitten by the travel bug, but JJ had booked a cruise around the Caribbean for him and Clara Jean for their honeymoon.

"Uh, yeah, but you knew I'd get lunch." Mike laughed, and he led them over to the table. "Clara Jean, let's just sign this and get it done."

"Sure," she said, and Tate moved to pull her chair out for her.

"I had Walter look this over. And he said he texted you that he thought everything looked amazing and was ready to go."

Clara Jean nodded as she sat down. Tate pushed her chair

in and sat kitty-corner from her, with her uncle sitting across from him.

"Yes," she said. "He said everything was in order, and that when I signed it, I could take it to him, and he would get everything notarized and transferred." She picked up the pen and looked at the pages. "You're not planning on leaving until the end of the year, right?" She scanned down the page. "He said he put that in, and I just want to make sure."

Despite her maturity and how well she ran everything in her life, Clara Jean had wanted Mike to stay on and help her through the transition. She wanted him to stay for a full year, but he'd agreed to stay until December thirty-first, and she'd worried that she would have no idea how to fill the shelves at Wilde & Organic from January to April. Tate had assured her over and over that they would figure it out, and that he was willing to do whatever it took to run the farmland and help her at the store.

And he was.

"Yep," Mike said. "It's right there at the top of the second page."

Clara Jean initialed the first one and flipped to the second one. She saw it, smiled, initialed the second page, and then signed on the third. "All right." She turned the whole packet over and pushed the pen closer to her uncle. "We really appreciate this, Uncle Mike. You're making a lot of dreams come true today."

She nodded, as sober as ever, and got up and went to hug her uncle. Tate's own emotions quivered when he heard her sniffling, and she smiled at him with wet eyes as she returned to her seat.

He just wanted to leave now, so that they could go have their own private celebration. But he picked up his fork and said, "This looks amazing. Where did you get it?"

"Stone's Throw," Mike said, "And you two are going to do amazing things with that farmland. I trust you both." He smiled at Tate and then Clara Jean. "I'm just glad it gets to stay in the family. I was worried there for a year or two."

Tate was glad that he got to be part of the Walker family, and that Clara Jean would soon bear his last name. He felt like he'd been waiting to start his life for years, and he'd had no idea why he'd needed to go to college for four years to earn a degree in Agricultural Science, but now he knew why.

God had a bigger plan for him than Tate had known. While getting hit by a bull and breaking and bruising ribs had not been at the top of Tate's Amazing Things To Do List, it was the exact thing that he'd needed in his life.

As he looked back, even as young as he was, he could clearly see God's hand leading him every step of the way—first to Amarillo State, for a degree that Tate believed he didn't need. He'd only gone because he'd earned a scholarship, and he was the first person in his family to have ever done so.

Once there, on the very first day, his roommate was JJ Walker.

They'd become instant friends, and Tate and JJ had been inseparable all through college, supporting one another in hard classes and watching out for one another when no one else did.

Now Tate was going to marry JJ's sister and cultivate family land with her.

Yes, God had been very good to him, and he'd carefully led Tate along the path he should be on.

With the paperwork signed, Tate couldn't wait to say, "I do," and hear Clara Jean say it back to him, so they could start this journey together as man and wife.

Chapter Twenty-Four

For once, Conrad enjoyed everyone looking his way when he walked into the North Hampton House for Tate and Clara Jean's wedding. Glory Rose wore a bright red dress that made her look like a celebrity. She'd painted that dark makeup around her eyes and put a hint of redness in her cheeks and on her lips, and Conrad had stood on her front porch, totally speechless when he'd picked her up.

"Now I know I don't get dressed up enough when we go out," she'd teased him. He'd snapped his jaw closed and taken her hand and driven back down to town.

He was good friends with Tate, but the man had family to walk in the wedding party, so Conrad simply got to sit in the audience and enjoy the festivities. He knew JJ and Ruby would be walking in the wedding party and sitting in the front row, and he paused to say hello to Aunt Marcy and Uncle Wyatt as he headed in that direction. They had three of their four kids with them, but none of them lived in Three Rivers anymore.

Warren and Cole both rode the rodeo circuit, and Harry had just finished his junior year of college. Rachel, their youngest, had graduated from high school last year and gone to Amarillo State, where she was studying ranch management and business.

Warren and Cole trained in Montana, and apparently Cole couldn't get away to come for the wedding, but Warren had.

Conrad brought Glory Rose to his side and tucked her close. "Guys, this is Glory Rose. Rose, this is Warren and Harry and Rachel. They're my Uncle Wyatt and Aunt Marcy's kids."

"Oh, you're the Walkers who don't live here," she said.

"Well, we do," Uncle Wyatt said with his Rodeo King smile on his face.

"Sometimes," Aunt Marcy said with a smile. "Wyatt travels a lot with the boys, and I find myself staying in our apartment in Amarillo more often than not."

"She likes to come have lunch with me," Rachel said, grinning.

Out of all of Conrad's uncles, Uncle Wyatt had the most money because he'd become a billionaire on his own as a bull rider, and that didn't even take into account the money he had inherited from Gramps and Grams.

"Aunt Marcy owns Payne's Pest-Free," Conrad said with a hint of pride in his voice. "She keeps all of our crops healthy and thriving."

"Well, I used to," Aunt Marcy said with a grin. "I've flown over Shiloh Ridge many times. Your Uncle Bear sure was a beast."

Glory Rose giggled, "I bet you have, ma'am," she said. "Uncle Bear can be a grizzly."

Someone else caught Glory Rose's hand, and she turned toward them. Of course, the whole town had come for Tate and Clara Jean's wedding because Clara Jean was a Walker, and everyone knew the Walkers.

Glory Rose stepped back, and Conrad moved to her side.

"I'm sure you know the Bellamores," she said, smiling at them. "My mother has done a bunch of work with them."

"Absolutely." Conrad grinned and shook Britt's hand, then leaned in a brushed his lips along Gabi's cheek. Then, slowly, they moved down another row. He felt like he was the star of the show, because everyone kept looking at Glory Rose, and while Tate was probably the luckiest man on the planet that day, because he was marrying the love of his life, Conrad felt like it was him—because he had Glory Rose on his arm.

They finally made it to the second row, and Glory Rose moved down about halfway and sat next to her cousin, Gun, who had come with Pearl Jo and Ashton, his siblings.

They chit-chatted for a moment, and then Glory turned into him, tucked her arm through his, and curled her fingers between his. He leaned over and kissed her as she said, "Oh, Sari wants to come over."

Conrad turned and found his momma and daddy on the other side of the aisle, with Daddy wrestling with Sari as she tried to get off his lap. He finally set her down, and she ran toward Conrad, saying, "Dad-Daddy, Dad-Daddy!"

"Howdy, little lady." He swept her up into his arms and settled her on his lap. "I thought you were gonna sit with Grandma and Grandpa for the wedding."

"Gampa," she said. "I go to iveh with Gampa." She reached up and tugged on the knot on Conrad's tie. He gently pushed her hand down and looked over to his father. "Yeah," he said, though he didn't know what Sari had said and where Daddy wanted to take her. "You can go with Grandpa."

"Hi, Sari," Glory Rose said, leaning in to give her a kiss.

"Rose, you come, Gampa."

She grinned at her while Conrad marveled that his little girl had started to speak in sentences. "Oh, I'm probably not going to come to the river, Sari; it's just for you."

"I go iveh," she said. "You we go iveh—fish."

Glory Rose nodded, the brightness in her face so beautiful. "Yes, I'll take you fishing again."

Sari seemed satisfied by this conversation, and she wiggled to get down and go back to his parents. Conrad smiled at her and leaned against Glory Rose. "You took her fishing?"

"Yeah, at Link's birthday party," she said. "Remember, you boys were doing something up on the roof? I called to you."

"Oh, right," he said. "I didn't know you actually took a fishing pole or anything."

"We didn't," Glory Rose said.

"You know, when I got her," he said. "I had no idea how much joy she would bring me."

Glory Rose stayed silent at his side.

"I'd gone to the grocery store, and I joined a checkout lane right behind a blonde woman wearing a sweater."

Glory Rose's hand in his tightened, her way of saying, *Keep talking, cowboy.*

Conrad wasn't even sure where this conversation had come from, or why he'd started it. "I thought it was weird, because we don't really wear sweaters in the summer here, but whatever. Then the woman turned around, and it was Chloe. She was alone, but she freaked out. She started sobbing, and she ran into the bathroom. The clerks had to help me put the rest of our stuff on the belt, and I'm pretty sure I threw my wallet at Rhonda and I ran into the women's bathroom after her."

"You went into the women's bathroom, huh?" Glory Rose whispered.

"Yep. She told me there about Sari. We got all our stuff loaded up, and I drove her to the hotel where they were staying, and I met her, and everything in my life felt like it had been put in a blender. All the things that I'd been doing to try to reintroduce light in my life got snuffed out, and everything was dark. And I remember just thinking, *get home to Grams, take your daughter and get home to Grams, and everything will be okay.*"

"Yeah."

"Of course, there's a lot more that I needed to do than that, but that was the first thing I did, and Grams has helped me every day since, and everything in my life is so bright now, and I just didn't know that Sari would bring me so much joy."

He ducked his head, getting his mouth closer to Glory Rose. "Does any of that make sense?"

"Yes," she said. "Of course it does."

She looked up at him, her eyes serious. "You are a beautiful, beautiful man, Conrad."

He touched his lips to hers quickly and whispered, "I'm terrified of losing Grams."

Glory Rose nodded. "I'm sure you are," she whispered back. "I've lost my grandmother, and it will be very difficult." She reached up and cradled his face in one hand, the pocket between them intimate and private. "But I'll be right here to help you," she said. "If you want me to be."

"I do," he whispered, recognizing the power of such small words.

The music changed, and the moment broke, and Conrad let the momentum of the day carry him to his feet. The rest of the crowd did too, and he turned to watch the wedding party walk down the aisle to the altar.

The North Hampton House was a beautiful wedding venue with deep, rich hardwood floors and a whole wall of stained-glass windows with petals and ivy woven through them. Loads of sunlight came in and showered over the altar, which Clara Jean had dressed with fruits and vegetables, like the photography that her mother was known for.

She'd also just signed a contract to take over the grocery store and all of the farmland that produced the organic fruits and vegetables she loved, so the edible altar sure fit.

Tate appeared at the end of the aisle, and he shone like freshly polished silver. He wore a smile as wide as the sky, and he looked to his right as JJ came to his side. They wore matching black tuxedos with matching black cowboy hats, but they were the epitome of opposites. JJ refused to crack a smile, though Conrad could tell he had to fight hard to keep it off his face.

The pair of them walked down the aisle together with the wedding party behind them, consisting of Tate's younger brother, Jason, his mother and father, and then all the brides-maids—Clara Jean's younger sisters, Emily and Hattie, as well as Tate's two younger sisters.

Everyone gathered around Tate and hugged him and shook his hand, and Conrad watched as Jeremiah hurried back out of the room.

Elaine came down the aisle next, and Conrad's heart swelled with love for her, because he knew how very hard it was for her to be the only person in the aisle, carrying an enor-mous bouquet made from fruits and vegetables.

A cabbage sat in the middle, with the leaves peeled back and sculpted to look like a flower, and lettuces and cut straw-berries and tomatoes and chunks of watermelon that poked out. Murmurs moved through the crowd as Elaine bore the beautiful bouquet down the aisle. She stood next to Tate, and they faced the top of the aisle where Clara Jean and Uncle Jeremiah now stood arm-in-arm.

She wore a dress that seemed to billow around her like moving water. As they stepped slowly, the fabric rippled, and she wore a cape that fastened to the front straps of her dress and went over her shoulders in a long train. She'd done her hair up in dark curls and fastened a crown of diamonds there.

For all intents and purposes, Conrad really believed she was a queen.

He'd never been married, but he'd attended several weddings for his friends, and now this first one in the Walker family. Clara Jean leaned in and kissed both of Elaine's cheeks. She turned to her father and gripped him in a tight hug, and then she took her giant vegetable bouquet and let Tate put one arm around her and use the other to help her support the weight of the bouquet.

They faced the man who would marry them on the other side of the altar, who happened to be Judge Glover.

Conrad leaned down and whispered, "Would you want your uncle to marry us?"

Glory Rose pulled in a breath. "Wow, Mister Walker, you're bringing up marriage, and we haven't even been dating for two months?"

He chuckled and then silenced himself because Judge had just said, "One of my absolute favorite things to do is marry two people in love," and Conrad didn't want to miss a moment of his cousin's wedding.

He hadn't truly thought about marrying Glory Rose until that very moment, and he had to keep pushing the fantasies away so that he could focus on what Judge said.

He noted that Glory Rose had not answered his question, but it didn't worry him. He had plenty of time to get the answers he needed—as long as he could keep the radiant Glory Rose at his side.

Chapter Twenty-Five

Brandon Rhinehart pulled up to Romanescos, where he and Grace Shelby had agreed to meet for their second date. She'd wanted to meet him at the mall for their first, and Brandon was growing tired of starting new relationships, getting three or four dates in, and losing them.

Sometimes, he didn't want to keep seeing the woman, and sometimes, they didn't want to keep seeing him. He longed for the kind of relationship that he saw Dawson and Caroline cultivating, and he'd been spending more and more time with his oldest brother, Duke, and his wife, Arizona.

They'd been married for a long time now, and they loved and served one another relentlessly. He wanted someone like that, someone that he was frantic to see at the end of every day and desperate to hear from.

He wanted someone who knew him so well that she would set out the buttermilk syrup just for him when everybody else wanted maple. And he wanted to bring home fresh flowers to her, because he knew she liked them sitting on the living room table, even though no one ever came to visit.

He also very much felt his age, as he was about to turn thirty-six next month.

His daddy had told him he wasn't getting any younger, and if he wanted to find a woman and have a family, he better get started. Brandon could admit that he'd always been a little bit of a flirt, and he'd never had a problem getting a date, but keeping one was another story.

A sigh pulled through his body as he got out of his truck and started for the front doors of the Greek restaurant.

Grace had agreed to another date, but she didn't want to give Brandon her address so that he could come pick her up. That was a red flag for him, telling him that she wasn't that into him, and yet he opened the door, and when he saw her, he grinned and said, "Wow, you look amazing."

Again, Brandon knew how to act on a date. He wanted to be able to act like himself. He wanted to be able to have bad days and talk about more than what he did on the ranch, and what she did for work, and how many brothers and sisters they had. He was tired of the surface details, but he had no idea how to find someone that he could have a deeper, more long-lasting relationship with.

He talked to women everywhere he went, including grocery stores, convenience stores, and drive-through restaurants. He flirted on TwoCents, the small-town recommendation app that had since expanded to include a social feature that allowed people to talk and set meetups. In fact, each of his last four first dates had originated by him initiating contact with someone on TwoCents.

And yes, he was painfully aware that he usually initiated contact on that app. Three Rivers didn't have a dating app otherwise, and long-distance dating didn't appeal to him.

Grace rose from where she waited on the padded bench, and she stood probably a good foot shorter than Brandon. He still leaned down and gave her a quick kiss on each cheek. "Did you put our names on the list?"

"I thought you were going to call in," she said, a hint of exasperation in her voice.

"They don't have a call-in line anymore," he said. "You have to do it online."

"Well, then you should have done that." She sighed mightily and turned to walk away to the hostess station. Brandon didn't want to pay for a meal for a woman who clearly didn't want to spend time with him, and he glanced to the couple waiting down on the end of the bench.

"How long did they say for you guys?" he asked.

"Thirty minutes," she said.

He prayed with everything inside him that Grace wouldn't want to wait that long. And sure enough, she returned and said, "It's an hour."

"Okay," he said, as jovially as possible. "Let's just go somewhere else."

He turned around and walked out, part of him hoping that Grace would say she didn't want to go somewhere else, then he could end things out on the sidewalk with a little bit more privacy.

She followed him. "Where do you want to go?"

He honestly just wanted to go home, but it was a forty-minute drive back up to the Rhinehart Ranch, where he lived in a cabin by himself since Dawson had married Caroline. They'd built a house around the corner and down the street, still on the ranch but near the border of their property.

"You tell me what you're craving," he said. "I can follow you there, or we can go in my truck."

She eyed the big blue truck like it might roar to life and run her over. "The pizza places are pretty fast."

Brandon's first instinct was to go along and go open her door for her. His momma had raised him to be a Texas gentleman, after all, but the part of him that had started to believe that he would never find someone right for him raged in his chest.

"If you're just looking to get this meal over with as fast as possible," he said. "We don't have to go at all."

She brought her eyes back to his, and Brandon raised his eyebrows in challenge. "You don't seem like you want to go out with me, and that's fine. We don't have to go out."

She swallowed and clutched her purse a little tighter. "Okay," she said. "I'm just really busy at work right now."

"Sure," Brandon said, sarcastically. "You're not at work right now. It's fine. I get it." He stepped over to his door and opened it.

"Brandon," she said.

"No." He turned back to her. "You don't have to explain. In fact, it's better if you don't, but it would have been nice if you would have just texted me and canceled, so I didn't have to drive forty minutes down out of the hills just to be told that you want to get this date over with as fast as possible."

She had the decency to look ashamed, and she ducked her head and nodded. "You're right," she said, "I should have texted."

"Yes, you should have." With that, he turned around and got in his truck, slamming the door a little bit too loudly behind him. His heart yelled at him that he should roll down his window and apologize.

But he couldn't make himself do it.

He waited until Grace had walked away, and then he pulled out of the parking lot so that she didn't think he wanted to see what kind of vehicle she drove and stalk her.

"That's the last thing I need," he muttered to himself.

He'd been out with at least two dozen women in the past few years, and he honestly wondered how many more Three Rivers would have who didn't know about him. Women had a network, he knew, and they talked to one another, and he could only guess at what the women in this town said about him.

He'd never really gotten any negative feedback, like *he's creepy*, or *he comes on too strong*, or anything like that. He felt like he was personable. He could carry a conversation. He liked to joke and laugh, and he had a good sense of humor. There was just something about him that didn't appeal to women looking for something long-term.

No one would know that he'd left and come back with only a ten-minute gap in between, but Brandon still drove over to his favorite hamburger joint and pulled into one of the drive-in spaces. *Maybe you're not marriage material,* he thought.

The waitress roller-skated over to his window, and he rolled it down and put in his order for a bacon cheeseburger and French fries.

"I want one of those Oreo shakes too," he said. "With chocolate ice cream."

"You got it," she said, and she skated away.

Brandon sighed as he waited for his food. Maybe he could talk to Arizona about what he needed to do when it came to women. Dawson had never dated a whole lot, and yet he'd managed to find the perfect complement to himself. He and Caroline hadn't liked each other much at first, but the spark and attraction between them had been wildly hot.

Brandon had never felt like that around anyone.

"It's maybe-definitely you," he said, but he didn't know what needed to change in order to become the man that a woman would want.

Maybe he needed to adjust his expectations for his life. Not everyone had to get married and have a family, right? Just because everyone around him did that didn't mean it was the only way to live a good life.

"What should I be doing, Lord?" He realized that he'd left his window down, and he hurried to roll it up so no one could hear his pathetic pleas. "I don't know what to do with my life."

He'd grown up on the family ranch, and it was simply expected that he would stay and help to run it. But Duke had a big family now, and Dawson's was growing. They could run the ranch without him, but Brandon had never wanted to leave.

Maybe I could get my own place, he thought, his mind flying through the other men and women who attended the small ranch owners' meetings in town. Finn Ackerman had a one-man operation, and so did Alex Baxter. Mitch had found a big piece of land to build his dream, while JJ, Paul, and Libby had taken over operations for their fathers. Angel and Henry ran an enormous boarding stable, also passed down through the family.

Perhaps that simply wasn't in the cards for Brandon. And while he continued to wait for his food, he picked up his phone and started looking at real estate listings around Three Rivers. Within thirty seconds, he realized he would never be able to afford anything like what he had now, or even anything like what Finn and Alex owned.

Disgusted, he tossed his phone onto the passenger seat. "Those places cost three-quarters of a million dollars," he said. "I can't believe that."

But the numbers had been right there on his phone.

He'd been working his family ranch since he was old enough to walk, and yes, he had a little bit of savings, but not enough to buy his own place. His tongue felt too thick in his mouth, and he felt absolutely and utterly lost.

It was the worst feeling he'd ever had.

Brandon closed his eyes, and he'd always been one to see life as more from the perspective of a glass half-full instead of empty, but in this moment, he couldn't do it.

When he tried to picture his future, all he saw was darkness. Deep, depressing darkness. God was being entirely unfair or cruel, because He refused to shine a light on even a single step that Brandon could take.

Tapping sounded on his window, and he jerked his eyes open and hurried to roll it down so that he could receive his dinner.

"Sorry," he said.

"You're fine," the woman drawled, and she hooked the tray to his door. "Just push the buzzer if you need anything."

Brandon ate off the tray now secured to the side of his truck, knowing that something needed to change.

And change drastically, and change quickly.

He simply didn't know what.

Chapter Twenty-Six

G lory Rose pulled her belt around her waist a little bit further so that the buckle sat right in the middle.

Traditionally, she and her siblings got new clothes for Easter, and this year was no different just because they'd become adults. Silver and Flint had already sent her pictures of their matching ties, of which Daddy had gotten a new one as well. She loved the bright pink with white paisley flowers, and she'd told them all so.

Glory Rose didn't have the same style as her mother, but she knew Momma would show up at church today wearing a new dress, and Glory Rose had stopped by the house last night to pick up hers.

She looked at herself in the mirror on the back of her closet door and tucked her hair behind her ears. With her dark hair and eyes and slightly tan skin that came from Momma, she definitely looked better in bold, bright colors.

Unlike her mother, she wasn't afraid to wear them. Conrad had gushed and drooled over the red dress she'd worn to Clara Jean's wedding, and she couldn't wait to see his reaction for this bright blue Easter dress. White, watercolor flowers splashed across it, and Glory Rose felt very much like springtime. She turned from her reflection just as the doorbell rang.

"Glory Rose," Fawn called.

"I'm coming!" She quickly grabbed her purse, because she hadn't put on her lip gloss yet, and she headed out to greet Conrad. They weren't going to prom, and he was a decade out of high school, but she'd told him the color of her dress, and hey, if he felt like getting an Easter tie to match, he could.

But Conrad was still not used to the bright colors that Glory Rose wore, obviously, for his tie looked like more of a muted royal blue—nowhere near the color of her dress.

"Look at you, sugar." He came toward her, his face brightening to make up for the lack of blue in his tie. "When you said *blue*, I saw a completely different color." He took her in his arms and then twirled her away from him while she giggled. "Happy Easter."

"Happy Easter to you too, cowboy." She tipped up and kissed him and then turned to Fawn. "Are you riding with us?"

"Yep." Fawn downed the last of her protein drink and tossed the bottle in the trashcan. "Pearl Jo texted and said she's going to come down with Gun and Robbie."

"All right." Glory Rose took Conrad's hand and headed for the front door. She didn't mind sharing him with her cousins and her family, and he'd been up to Shiloh Ridge several times since breeding weekend.

Now that they had been dating for a full two months, Glory Rose had started to feel settled and serious with him. *Two months isn't a very long time,* her mind whispered at her, and she could acknowledge that.

She did, and then she argued with herself while Conrad opened her door: *I've known him for longer than two months.*

It wasn't like they had gone from stranger to serious in sixty days. She'd known him for a couple of years, and she'd texted back and forth with him since last summer, even if they'd never been able to set up a date.

He leaned into the open doorway of the truck once she'd climbed into the passenger seat. "You are gorgeous, Glory Rose. How did I get you to go out with me?" He didn't wait for her to answer before he backed up and closed the door. He opened Fawn's door too, and she climbed into the back seat.

"Will you ask him if Austin or Easton are dating?" Fawn whispered.

Glory Rose turned and looked at her cousin. "What?"

"He's *so* handsome." Fawn straightened up as Conrad opened his door and sat behind the wheel.

"We ready, ladies?"

Glory Rose grinned at Fawn and then Conrad. "We're ready." She faced the front again as Conrad went down to the end of the lane and swung around in a wide arc to go back past the house.

He adjusted the radio and took Glory Rose's hand in his. "Grams is bringing Sari, but I told her that I just wanted it to be us three." He glanced in the rearview mirror and quickly over to Glory Rose. "Is that okay?"

"Yeah, it's totally fine," Glory Rose said. "Fawn is going sit with Pearl Jo anyway."

"Yeah," Fawn said. "Don't worry, I won't sit by you."

"It's not that I don't want you to," Conrad said.

"Yes, it's exactly that you don't want me to." Fawn grinned. "It's totally fine, Conrad. This is your first Sunday sitting together at church. I get it."

Glory Rose looked out the passenger window, because though Conrad had asked her to sit with him and Sari at church about a month ago, their Sundays hadn't lined up until now.

Glory Rose had grown up on a ranch, and she understood that sometimes things happened that prevented someone from doing what they wanted to do. They only had a few minutes until they reached the church, and she looked over to Conrad. "So do your brothers date?"

Fawn sucked in an audible breath in the back seat, and Conrad looked at Glory Rose. "Do my brothers date?"

"Yeah." Glory Rose grinned at him. "I've got an awful lot of single female cousins, and it sure seems to me that there's a lot of you Walker men who are not attached."

Conrad laughed. "Austin dates a lot, but Easton is a little squirrely. He's the smartest of us all," he said. "He just sort of lives in his own world."

Glory Rose caught Fawn shaking her head out of the corner of her eye, and she said, "Maybe Jason."

"Jason doesn't even live here," Fawn said. "Glory Rose, you are the worst at this."

They all laughed, even Glory Rose, because, no, she was not a matchmaker.

"My momma can help you find someone," Conrad said, once again glancing in the rearview mirror at Fawn. "She's really good at setting people up."

"Would she do it for her own son?" Fawn asked.

"Are you really sweet on Austin?"

"I mean, I don't really know him," Fawn said.

"She thinks you're handsome," Glory Rose said. "You can own it. I always tell Conrad that we Glovers have really good genes, and that's why I'm so pretty."

"Oh, my word," Fawn said. "You do not say that."

Conrad laughed. "She so does."

"He knows he's good looking."

Conrad looked over to her again, "I do?"

She stared at him, surprised, "You don't—"

He slammed on the brakes, his attention returning out the windshield. "I guess I should pay attention to what's going on around me."

His face turned that shade of brick red that Glory Rose loved so much while he found them a parking spot. A lot of cars poured into the parking lot, as Easter was one of the most attended Sundays of the year.

Both Aunt Willa and Uncle Patrick would be speaking today, and there would be a lot of musical numbers in the program. Glory Rose waited for Conrad to come around and open her door, and he took her hand as they walked toward the little white chapel.

Inside, the noise level grew, and Conrad gripped her hand and expertly kept her with him as he navigated the crowd into the chapel. His grandmother had already arrived, and he stopped about two-thirds back and lifted his daughter into his arms. "Thank you, Grams."

"You're welcome, my boy."

Then Conrad led her further down and slid into a bench on the side. Glory Rose joined him, feeling very exposed and open on the end. She suddenly knew what he'd meant when he said it felt like everyone watched him.

She felt like that right now, and her skin prickled as she imagined everyone examining her, making judgments about what she wore and who she was with. She'd curled her hair that morning, but she didn't think she wore too much makeup. She glanced over to Conrad and leaned into his bicep. "Could you switch me? I don't like sitting on the end."

"Sure." He stood up, and Glory Rose scooted over. "I've got to grab her bag," he said. "I'll be right back." He left, and Glory Rose looked at Sari. Two warring emotions flowed through her: pure panic that she had just been left with this little girl who wasn't hers, and pure love that Conrad trusted her enough to leave her with his daughter, even if only for a few seconds.

It took more than a few seconds, though, because everyone in town knew Conrad, and it took him a few minutes to get back to his grandmother, get the bag, and return because everyone kept stopping him to chat.

He sat down and blew out his breath. "I feel like I just ran a marathon."

Glory Rose giggled and took the diaper bag from her boyfriend. She assumed it had been packed with books and snacks and quiet toys, so Sari could make it through the sermon.

They had arrived early, and it took several minutes until the organist sat down and began to play. A pianist joined her, and Glory Rose basked in the warmth of the music.

She loved music as it always calmed her and chased away her fears, even when she didn't know what she was afraid of. Conrad took her hand, and Glory Rose unzipped the diaper bag mere moments before the choir started down the aisle singing.

Glory Rose realized in that moment that she would have to crawl over Conrad every time she had to go sing. But thankfully, she was only doing two songs in today's services.

Still, she felt certain that having him stand so that she could get out of the pew would only call more attention to her —and to him, and Conrad hated being in the spotlight.

"Glow-Roe," Sarina said, and Glory Rose turned her attention to the little girl. "I sit you?"

"Yes, of course," she whispered, and she uncrossed her legs to pull the little girl onto her lap. Then, because it felt natural, she reached into the bag and pulled out a board book. She held it in front of Sari while she watched the choir members climb the steps up to the stage.

Aunt Willa stood behind the mic first this morning and

said, "Brothers and sisters, we just listened to 'Easter Hosanna.' Do you know what Hosanna means?"

Glory Rose thought of Hosanna as a praising word, something she would sing or say to bring praise to Jesus.

Willa smiled around at the congregation. "It comes from a Hebrew word that is often understood to mean 'save us' or 'save, please.' And the crowds used it when Jesus entered Jerusalem on Palm Sunday. Have you ever thought that when you are shouting Hosannas to the Lord that you are quite literally asking Him to save you?

"The term has evolved over time," Aunt Willa continued. "And now it is an expression of gratitude and worship as well, and most people think of it that way."

Glory Rose nodded because that had been the first thought that had come to her mind.

"But I wonder if we should think of it as a plea for salvation at the same time that we're expressing our gratitude for our Lord and Savior, Jesus Christ.

"His view is eternal, and he doesn't care what's going on in politics right now, or on social media, or in our society. He wants to save us *eternally*, so as we go through our Easter worship today, and you think of Jesus Christ and His sacrifice for you, there will be times when you'll be singing 'Hosanna, Hosanna, Sing Hosannas to the Lord,' just like our choir did as they came in.

"I've been thinking a lot about what it means when I sing that. Are you asking God to save you from something right now? Sometimes we need His help in that exact moment.

When you need saving, I testify that the Savior will be there for you.

"Perhaps you can remember to *sing hosanna* when you find yourself looking at or watching something that you know you shouldn't. Perhaps you can *cry hosanna* when you are hurt or ill. Or when we're called upon to serve others, we can say a prayer of hosanna, asking the Lord to save us and the person we're meant to help, all through the grace and power of God."

She paused for a moment and surveyed the congregation again. Glory Rose always liked the things she said, as Aunt Willa knew how to speak to a person's soul.

"Pastor Knowlton and I are not going to talk a lot today, but we're going to let you feel the spirit of Easter through a musical program with some narration. I've asked my son to narrate for us, and he has asked a friend of his to interpret for all of you so that you can hear the program."

She opened her arm, and Mitch walked up the steps, a grumbly, growly look on his face. A beautiful blonde woman followed him, and she didn't look super happy to be there either. They both wore Easter pastels, so they'd gotten that memo, and Mitch stood to the side while the woman positioned herself between him and his mother.

"After the program," Willa said into the mic. "Pastor Knowlton will say a few words and we'll release you to spend this Sabbath day with your thoughts, with the Savior, and with your loved ones." She looked at the blonde woman, her grin on megawatt. "Lacy."

Lacy stepped up to the mic, and Aunt Willa gestured the crowd forward.

Glory Rose stood up, and Conrad did as well. She moved past him and started going down the aisle when she realized she still carried Sari in her arms. "Oh," she said right out loud, which only drew more attention to her.

She turned around and hurried back up the aisle and passed Sari to Conrad, and then with her face flaming, she turned around and continued the trek to her place in the soprano section of the choir.

Glory Rose's embarrassment didn't stay long, because the beautiful music and melody chased it away. She loved God, and she loved her Savior, and as she sang for Them—and Conrad—she wondered if she was in love with him too. She wasn't sure, as Glory Rose had never been in love before, but she knew how to trust her instincts, and she knew God would lead her where she needed to go.

Still, she found herself praying that the post-Easter services picnic would go off without a hitch, and that every Glover would be on their very best behavior when Conrad came up to the ranch for his second big family gathering.

Chapter Twenty-Seven

Conrad felt the weight and heat of the sun as he got out of his truck at Shiloh Ridge Ranch. A parking area had been set up almost directly across the street from Ward and Dot Glover's house. It looked like fresh gravel, and someone had roped off the area with pink ribbon, of all things.

The moment Conrad had seen Glory Rose's dress, he'd realized how very seriously she took holidays and special occasions. He now had two pieces of proof that every time he came to her house to pick her up for something even as mundane as church, she would be dressed like a rock star.

Her brothers and father had been wearing matching ties, and her mother had worn a new dress as well. Conrad was used to this kind of behavior, because money could buy a lot of things, including clothing, to make a person stand out.

The problem was, Conrad didn't want to stand out. And yet, as far as he knew, he was the only person showing up for

309

the Glovers' Easter picnic today who didn't actually have the last name of Glover.

Glory Rose put her hand in his, and that anchored Conrad enough for him to take the first step. And then after that, all he had to do was take another one and then another one, and before he knew it, he'd gone past the barn where a graveled picnic area opened up.

A row of three fire pits stretched in front of him, with gray rock around them and permanent seats in the form of stumps and carved rocks.

"Wow," Conrad said. "This is incredible."

"It's my daddy's brainchild," Glory Rose said with pride obvious in her voice. "He wanted a place outdoors where the family could gather, just like we have True Blue for indoor celebrations."

Conrad wasn't sure what the difference was between an indoor and an outdoor celebration, other than one was inside and one wasn't. But he nodded.

"We do a lot of marshmallow roasts," she said. "And tin foil dinner nights and cobbler parties."

"I could get behind a cobbler party."

Glory Rose laughed, but Conrad's attention got diverted as a few of her uncles emerged from the back of the barn carrying folding tables.

"I'll go help," he said, and he moved away from Glory Rose to help her uncle set up a table.

The man seemed startled when Conrad pulled out the legs and slid down the metal piece to keep it in place. "Hey," he said with a smile. "I'm Conrad Walker."

"Oh," the man said. "You're Glory Rose's new boyfriend."

"Yes," he said. "I know you're a cop in town—or you were."

The man smiled too, finally. "I still am. I'm Ida's husband, Brady."

Conrad wondered if he ever got tired of introducing himself as *Ida's husband*, but it hadn't bothered him that he'd been given the label of *Glory Rose's boyfriend*. So probably not.

"I know your twins," Conrad said. "And I think you have a couple of other kids as well."

"Yep," Brady said "Riggs will graduate from high school this year, but Sonora has got another couple of years to go."

"Thank you, baby," a woman said, and Conrad glanced over to her. Ida carried a huge metal bowl covered with several sheets of plastic wrap. She tipped up and kissed her husband on the cheek, and then looked at Conrad. "There are more tables, Conrad."

"Sure," he said, and he went with Brady to get them. By the time they had the tables set up in a square horseshoe shape, people had arrived with food, and it just kept coming. Potato salad, pea salad, frog eye salad—a whole table of salads.

Conrad stood next to Johnny and his dad as Bishop arrived carrying a huge tray of barbecue ribs. Then Bear carried in a roasting pan with a turkey that had to weigh twenty pounds, with Cactus right behind him with a candied ham shank, which he then proceeded to carve right out in the open.

"This is incredible," Conrad said. "I've never seen this much food outside before."

"We learned to move things outside pretty early on," Brady said with a chuckle. "The noise this lot makes indoors is enough to deafen a person."

Johnny laughed. "He's not wrong."

Conrad realized then how very small his family was compared to the Glovers. His daddy had six brothers. There were twelve Glovers between two families, seven in one and five in another. They were almost *double* the size of the Walkers.

He felt very small and insignificant as Ace came to stand next to Brady. "Howdy, Conrad," he said.

"Hey." Conrad reached out and shook Ace's hand quickly. He realized he'd lost sight of Glory Rose and Sari, and panic flowed through him as he searched the burgeoning crowd for them.

He felt like everyone was looking back at him, but he still couldn't find Glory Rose and her bright blue dress. "What's your daughter's name?" Brady asked.

Conrad pulled himself back into the tight group of men. "Sarina."

The circle widened as Ranger joined them, along with Wilder, and a measure of relief flowed through Conrad. They'd had two more ranch owners' meetings, and he'd said more than a few words to Wilder.

Gunnison joined the group, saying, "The word is that Hazel dropped a cake right outside the car. There's crying in the parking lot."

"We best stay here, then," Ranger said, and he cast a smile around the group.

"How old is your daughter?" Brady asked.

All eyes came back to him, and Conrad really didn't want to be the subject of Twenty Questions. "She's three."

"And you didn't know about her till last summer?" The man definitely put off a cop vibe, and he spoke in short, clipped words.

"Nope," Conrad said, because he really didn't think he had to repeat this story over and over again.

"Conrad."

He turned as Glory Rose came up behind him. She carried Sari in her arms, and he'd never been so glad to see the pair of them. "I have to go help my cousin with something." She passed Sari to Conrad and hurried away again.

"This is her," he said, smiling at her. "Sari, say hi to all the cowboys."

"Hi," she said.

"Say *howdy, cowboys*."

She looked at Conrad and placed one hand on either side of his face and squeezed. "Daddy cowboy."

He chuckled. "Yep, Daddy's a cowboy. Say *howdy, cowboys*." She looked around at all of them, but she did not say what he wanted her to.

"She's doing a speech program," he said, as if he had to explain anything to these men. "When I first got her, she could't say hardly anything at all."

"That's great," Ranger said.

"She's got different colored eyes," Brady said. "Those must come from her mother."

Conrad's heart seized in his chest. "Yes," he managed to say. "Chloe has blonde hair and hazel eyes, and Sari gets her eyes from her mother."

"She looks enough like you and Glory Rose though," Brady said, and Conrad turned his attention to him, his heart dropping down into his stomach.

"Dad," Johnny said. "Don't say stuff like that."

"What?" Brady looked from his son back to Sari, and Conrad wanted to shield his daughter from his prying eyes. "She does. She's got dark hair."

He looked at Conrad again as if he needed to in order to determine the color of his hair. "But you've got dark eyes, and so does Glory Rose. So everyone will wonder where those light eyes came from."

Wilder met Conrad's eyes, and he wore a look of sympathy but said nothing.

"Well," Conrad said. "I'm not really trying to pass Sari off as Glory Rose's daughter." He looked at the cop, and he probably only stood an inch taller than Conrad, but he felt like a child. "In fact, everyone knows Sari is not Glory Rose's, and I'm not going to lie to my daughter about who her mother is."

"I didn't say you were going to lie about it," Brady said.

"Brady," Ranger said. "Leave the boy alone."

Conrad whipped his attention to Ranger, a sudden fire raging through his veins. "I'm not a boy."

"No, I know you're not," Ranger said. "That's not what I meant."

Conrad didn't mean to snap, and he dropped his head and hid his face with his cowboy hat. "I'm sorry," he said softly. "I didn't mean to get upset by that."

"How old are you?" Ace asked.

"Should we go get something to drink?" Johnny asked in a really loud voice, clearly trying to end the conversation.

Ace frowned at him, and then his son. "What did I say wrong?"

"I don't know," Gun said. "Would you like it if someone asked you how old you were?"

"It's a common question," Ace asked. "I'm not asking to be rude."

"Maybe we could ask someone else some questions," Wilder said, and his voice came out mild, like Conrad's.

"It's fine," Conrad said, though everything inside him quaked, and he felt dangerously close to breaking down. He swallowed. "I'll be thirty in the fall."

"Wow," Ace said. "That's quite a bit older than Glory Rose, isn't it?" He looked over to Ranger, who simply shook his head.

"Glory Rose is twenty-four, Daddy," Gun said. "It's not that big of a deal." He looked over to Conrad with apology in his eyes too.

"So does her mother live around here?" Brady asked, and Johnny audibly groaned.

"I'm going to get something to drink. Conrad?"

He waved at him, and Johnny walked away from the conversation.

Conrad wanted to do the same thing, but Sari wiggled,

and he put her down and said, "Stay here, baby. We have to wait for everyone to be ready to eat lunch."

He didn't want to stand with this group of men anymore, though he knew they weren't really trying to hurt him. Brady just had a blunt, brusque way about him, and he actually thought it made sense that Glory Rose's family would want to know more about him.

He took a couple of steps away as Sari did, but it certainly wasn't enough distance where he couldn't hear Brady as he said, "I don't get what the big deal is. If the boy can't answer some questions, he's never going to survive in this family."

"He's answering your questions just fine," Ranger said in a pointed voice. "Maybe he doesn't need fifteen questions being fired at him on all sides. He's been up here before."

"If he's going to marry Glory Rose, we should know a little bit about him," Ace said. "I didn't mean anything by it."

"I know you didn't," Ranger said, "But we don't have to like Conrad. *Glory Rose* likes Conrad, and that's good enough."

"Dad, he can hear you," Wilder said.

Conrad bent and picked up his daughter, a snake moving through his stomach. He had no idea where he was going, but he stepped away from all the Glovers.

He simply knew he couldn't stay there.

"Conrad," Wilder said, but he lifted his hand and kept going.

We don't have to like Conrad.

They didn't like him. With every crunching step he took

against the gravel, he wondered what he'd done to make them dislike him.

He treated Glory Rose like a queen. He took good care of his farm and his grandmother and his daughter. He had money and an education.

So why don't they like you? The thought gnawed at him and gnawed at him as he put Sari in her car seat and got behind the wheel.

He watched a couple of late Glovers hurry down the gravel path along the barn and back to the picnic area.

It didn't matter.

He had to get out of there, and he started his truck and flipped the gear shift into reverse to do exactly that.

Chapter Twenty-Eight

"Glory Rose." Fawn nodded toward the barn. "Your boyfriend just left."

Glory Rose spun away from the table where all the potato chips had been set out. She'd been sneaking a few every couple of minutes because she needed to eat, and not everyone had arrived yet.

"What? He left?"

"He took Sari," Fawn said. "And I can't really tell what Wilder is trying to tell me, but it doesn't look good." She hooked her thumb over to where her brother stood with his dad, Uncle Ace, Uncle Brady, and Gunnison.

"Conrad was with them?"

"Yep," Fawn said. "I got that much."

"What did they say to him?" she asked.

"I don't know," Fawn said. "But he's leaving. You should go after him."

Indecision raged through Glory Rose. Could she really just run off during the family Easter picnic? She took another look at Fawn, and then something shouted in her mind that she better go after Conrad, and she better go now.

So she did, hurrying across the gravel in her sandals and past the barn. Conrad had already started backing out of his parking space, and she waved her arms and ran toward him.

"Conrad!" She hated that her voice carried through the ranch stillness out here, and she hoped no one could hear her back at the picnic area. "Conrad, wait!"

Glory Rose did not spend a lot of time running, especially not in wedged footwear. But she managed to make it to his spot and hurry down the length of the truck parked there, before he put the truck in drive and left.

He caught sight of her right as he started forward, and he jammed on the brakes and stopped the truck. She tried to read the expression on his face through the glass and couldn't do it. So she hurried over to the passenger door and yanked on the handle to open it.

It wouldn't budge, and to her horror and surprise, Conrad *rolled down the window* instead of unlocking the truck.

"I have to go," he said, in a horribly terse voice.

"Why?" Glory Rose stepped up onto the runner of the truck. "Where are you going?"

"They don't want me here," he said. "They don't even like me."

Worlds collided in Glory Rose's brain because she could not understand what a couple of her uncles could have possibly said to Conrad in the ten minutes she hadn't been at his side. "Can you let me in?"

"I just have to go," he said. "You're not going to come. Just get down. I'll call you later."

"No," she said, surprised at the strength of her own voice. "No, you're not just going to call me later. We're going to talk about this right now."

Conrad glared at her, and Glory Rose gave his attitude right back. "We've put off a lot of conversations if we don't want to have them right then, but we're having this one, Conrad. I can't go back there without you. Everyone's expecting you."

"I don't care what anyone expects of me," he said. "And that's the problem, Rose. You *do* care, you do what everyone expects you to do. You're little Miss Perfect. Well, I'm not."

Glory Rose fell back as if he had struck her. "I am not perfect," she said.

"Yeah, well, you're too good for me." He spoke in his quiet, powerful voice, the edge of anger already fading away. "And everyone back there knows it," he said. "I know it."

He looked away and out the driver's side window, a sigh slipping from his mouth. "Glory Rose, we're all just waiting for you to know it."

"I don't think that," she said. "And whatever my stupid uncle said to you doesn't matter. They don't think that either."

"They do, though," he said. "And it's fine. I know who I am, and I also know what it looks like on the outside. But I don't want to be here. I don't want everyone looking at me and judging me that my tie is the wrong color."

"Your tie is not the wrong color," Glory Rose practically yelled.

"And that Sari's eyes aren't mine, and we won't be able to pass her off as our daughter."

Glory Rose's chest filled with ice. "Who said that?"

"It doesn't matter." He took a deep breath and slowly blew it out. "I know not everyone feels that way. I know not everyone is judging me. Your cousins were actually really nice, but I'm just not up to this today. Glory Rose, please. Can I just go home?"

She climbed up on the runner again. "Unlock the door. I'll go with you."

He looked at her, a fiercely determined edge in his eyes. "I'm not going to take you from your family, Rose. I know they're really important to you, as they should be."

"Glow-Roe, we go," Sari yelled from the back seat.

"Sari, hush," Conrad said, and it was the first time that she'd seen him speak to his daughter in anything but the kindest, most adoring voice ever.

"Dad-Daddy," Sari said, kicking her feet. "We go. We go."

"Yeah, we're gonna go in a minute," he said. He lifted his eyes to Glory Rose's again. "Tell your mom and dad I'm really sorry."

"Glory Rose?"

She turned around at the sound of her mother's voice, and she felt caught between two things she really wanted—all the beauty and safety of Conrad Walker...and her family.

She held up her hand to her mother, who she desperately loved. "Just a minute, Momma."

Glory Rose turned back to her boyfriend. "Conrad, please don't go." She wasn't above begging, because she didn't want this to be a two-month relationship that ended, because one of her uncles had said something stupid.

"It's a huge picnic area," she said. "Please just come back. We'll sit way on the other side from anyone that you've talked to."

"I don't know, Glory Rose."

"Daddy, I eat," Sari said, and Glory Rose employed all of her bravery. She reached inside the truck and unlocked it, then dropped to the ground and opened the door. She climbed into the passenger seat and looked at him. "Let's go for a drive, if you want. Your daughter is hungry."

"Don't tell me what my daughter needs," he said. "I know what my daughter needs."

"Glory Rose," Momma called again.

Glory Rose leaned out the window, wishing she could explain everything right now. "We'll be right back, Momma." Then she rolled up her window and looked at Conrad again. "I didn't mean to tell you what your daughter needed."

He reached over and took her hand. "I didn't mean to snap at you. I just...." He shook his head, pulled his hand away, and put the truck in drive. He didn't peel out, spraying gravel everywhere, but drove slowly past the homestead and then under the arch and off the ranch.

"I guess I was just hoping that with enough time, I wouldn't have to answer questions I've answered before," he said. "I wouldn't have to revisit that place where all I feel is stupid and inadequate and not good enough." He glanced over to her, and Glory Rose's heart ached for him.

"I'm sorry my family did that to you," she said. "I know they didn't mean it."

"It doesn't matter what they meant, Glory Rose. It matters how I take it, and I know they can't control that either. So I know this is a me-problem. But guess what? I get to have problems too."

"I know you do," she said, but he didn't seem to be listening to much of what she said.

"Remember that day you showed up at my house, sobbing? Well, that's how I feel right now. And I just want to be in a place where everybody loves me even though I'm not perfect, and no one's judging me even though I've made a lot of mistakes. And you know what? It's really hard to do that with your family, because they *are* seemingly perfect, even though I know they're not. I know you're not too, but you sure *seem* like you are."

He turned before he got to the road that led to Seven Sons, and went down the highway running east. "I don't want to be there," he said. "So I'm not going to go back." He gripped the steering wheel, and he sounded so final.

"This is just how it is," he said. "This is how I am."

Glory Rose nodded. "Okay, Conrad."

"Dawson said some stuff once at one of our ranch owner meetings several months ago. And I have a lot thicker skin now, but it hurt my feelings, and it made me feel like even my own friends had never made mistakes in their life, and certainly not a mistake big enough that the whole town knows about."

Glory Rose didn't want to try to interrupt him and give any excuses or reasons for why her uncles had said what they did. She didn't even know what they had said.

"And you know what? I left the meeting, and I didn't go back for a couple of months, even though Dawson apologized and came to the farm and we worked it out." He refused to look at her, and Glory Rose realized Conrad ranted the way she cried, and once he got everything out, he'd go back to his calm, quiet self.

"It's fine, but I don't want all their eyes on me, and I don't want anyone whispering about me, and I don't want anyone tiptoeing around in their cowboy boots around me either. That's even worse."

"I'm really sorry," she said quietly.

"It's not your fault, Rose. It's my fault, and I know it's my fault."

"You've been forgiven," she said, her words quivering.

"I know," he said softly. "But internal wounds are really hard to see."

She didn't know what to say, because she didn't want to lose Conrad, but she also didn't want to lose her family.

Now, every big event that she invited him to, they would both show up and walk around like the gravel had turned into eggshells.

"I'm sorry I reacted the way I did," he said. "There were just so many questions, and Brady made it sound like we were going to pretend like Sari was ours." He looked over to Glory

Rose, pure fire in his eyes. "Never once have I thought that we were going to pretend like Sari was your daughter."

"I didn't think that either," Glory Rose said.

"I still call and text Chloe all the time." He gripped the steering wheel. "I don't know if I've told you that, but I do. I send her pictures of Sari all the time, and we call on important days. We already have a call set up for Mother's Day. I'm not going to deny Chloe that just because we made a mistake. Sari is still her daughter."

"I know that, Conrad."

"Okay." Several seconds of silence went by, and his shoulders deflated again. "Okay," he said. "I'm going to stop talking now before I say something I don't want to say."

"You should be able to say whatever you want," she said.

"And I have." He nodded like that was that. He reached the T-junction where the eastern highway went north and south, and he did a U-turn and started back down the highway they'd just traveled.

"I'm going to take you back to the ranch," he said.

"Please just come have something to eat," Glory Rose said, tears pressing behind her eyes. "I'll go get plates for all of us, and we can go up to my cabin."

Her phone vibrated, and she looked down at it in her lap. She hadn't even realized that she'd brought it with her. Relief rushed through her at the sight of the text from her mother.

"Momma says she's getting food for us and putting it at the house." She looked over to Conrad. "Will you *please* come if we can eat in privacy at my parents' house?"

Conrad's jaw tightened, but he nodded.

"They have a really nice back deck," she said, feeling a little rambly now. "And they're on the hill, so we'll have a really good view of Three Rivers."

Conrad reached over and covered her hands and her phone with his. "I'm sorry, Glory Rose," he said. "I've made a mess of everything again."

"No, you haven't," she said. "It's fine."

He pulled his hand away, and she quickly texted her mother that they would be back in a few minutes and that, yes, they would like the food at the house.

Then she turned away from Conrad, knowing she was going to cry and hating herself for it. As the first tears slithered out of the corners of her eyes, she said, "I'm not crying because I'm upset, okay?"

Conrad didn't answer, and Glory Rose reached into the glove box to get out a napkin to wipe her nose and eyes. By the time he turned back onto the ranch, she'd stopped weeping, and she turned around and looked at Sari. "Are you hungry, baby?"

"Eat," Sari said. "I hungry. We eat, Glow-Roe?"

Glory Rose grinned at her, a fresh round of tears streaming down her face, because she could not imagine her life without this little girl and her handsome father in it.

"That's right," she said. "We're going to eat in just a few minutes." She settled back in her seat and looked out the windshield as Conrad went up the hill and under the sign that welcomed them to Shiloh Ridge.

Glory Rose had always loved being a Glover, but right now it didn't feel very good or very shiny, and she prayed that

Conrad would be able to find a way to feel good about himself, to feel like her equal, to feel like he belonged.

Because to her, he did.

And she wanted to belong to him too, and right now, she simply hoped he wouldn't break up with her over their Easter lunch.

Chapter Twenty-Nine

C onrad reached over and put another chunk of cheese on Sari's plate.

Somehow, Dot had a seat for Sari to sit in just like the one at Glory Rose's house, and he suspected that someone had gone up the lane to get it, so that his daughter would have somewhere to eat.

She reached for the chunk, lifted it up, and said, "Cheese, Dad."

"Yeah," he murmured, and he picked out another chunk from his pasta salad to put on her plate.

There had been enough food at the house to feed him and Sari at least ten times, and guilt continued to needle through his stomach and lungs as he finished up his roast turkey. When Sari started throwing her food, he pulled her plate away from her.

"I'll go get something to clean her up," he said.

Glory Rose got to her feet first. "I'll get it." She slid open the back door and went inside the house.

Conrad sighed and pushed his hands through his hair, effectively dislodging his cowboy hat. "I've made a real mess of things, Sari," he said.

"Mess?" Sari asked. She looked over to him, and Conrad couldn't imagine a day where he wouldn't love her, or a situation that would happen where he wouldn't want to be there for her. She'd been part of his life now for ten months, and he loved her so, so much.

He lifted his phone. "Smile for Momma."

Sari did, really cheesing it up so that her eyes practically squished closed. Conrad took the picture anyway, though she had remnants of lunch on her face. He started a text to Chloe as Glory Rose came outside with a washcloth.

"Here you go, Sari-girl." She wiped up his daughter and unbuckled her from the seat. She held her on her hip and gave her a kiss and a smile and then set her on the grass. "Go play."

She stood on the edge of the deck that was only one step up from the lawn and watched his daughter. Conrad watched her, and when she turned to face him, he had no idea what to say.

She wore a hint of hesitation in her expression. Conrad got to his feet too and wiped his hands on the washcloth. Then he moved over to the bench built into the back of the house.

"Will you sit with me?" he asked, and he sat down right in

the middle of it, so that Glory Rose's only choice was to sit on his lap.

She eyed him warily and folded her arms. Conrad grinned at her, but the action only stayed on his face for a single second before it fell away. "I'm really sorry," he said. "I know I ruined today."

She sighed, shook her head, and stepped over to him. She curled herself into his arms, and she looked at his hair as she ran her fingers through it. Conrad simply closed his eyes and tried to memorize the sensations moving through his body as Glory Rose touched him.

"You didn't ruin anything," she said.

"Everyone's going to make a big deal over me now," he said. "That's the last thing I want."

She laid her head in the hollow of his neck, and it made him feel so strong and so capable. "I'll threaten them within an inch of their lives that if they put a spotlight on you at all next time you come to anything, I'll...."

Conrad chuckled. "You'll what?" he teased. "What will you do to them, sugar?"

"Stop it." She pushed against his chest, and he kneaded her closer.

"I'm thinking about quitting my job," she said.

Conrad opened his eyes as Sari laughed out in the yard. He found her crouched down at the edge of the bark that housed a play set, and he could just imagine Glory Rose swinging there as a little girl.

"You are?" he asked.

"Yeah." She exhaled a long breath. "I'm so tired at the end of every day. I saw an opening come up at a preschool," she said. "And it's only part-time. I can help around the ranch if I'm bored."

She sure could, and he simply nodded. Sari straightened and looked back to them, "Glow-Roe. Glow-Roe," she yelled. "Bug."

"She's found a bug," Conrad said. "She loves bugs."

"I've noticed that about her," Glory Rose said, and she slid off Conrad's lap and walked across the deck toward his daughter.

Glory Rose crouched down when she reached Sari, and Conrad loved watching the two of them interact. After only a few seconds, she straightened, picked Sari up, and put her in the swing. Sari wore pure joy on her face as Glory Rose pushed her, and Conrad felt for the first time like he had an equal partner in parenting Sari.

He didn't have to get up and do everything. He didn't have to look at every bug. He didn't have to get the washcloth to clean up her face. He didn't have to bend to Sari's whims, and though he had definitely made a big mess between himself and Glory Rose's uncles today, he sure didn't want to lose her.

His phone buzzed, and he looked over to the picnic table where he'd left it. One more smile in Glory Rose and Sari's direction, and he got up to look at his phone.

Chloe had texted, *She is the best girl ever.*

There was no emoji the way there was when Glory Rose texted him, but Conrad smiled all the same. Sari *was* the best girl ever, and he loved being her dad.

Another message came in. *I miss both of you.*

Conrad dropped his phone, and he felt like he'd taken a giant breath of liquid nitrogen. Everything, starting with his tongue and moving down his throat and into his lungs, froze. He heard someone say his name, but he couldn't look away from that message.

I miss both of you. What did that mean? Chloe hadn't wanted anything to do with him for a long time. He'd moved past her. He'd moved on. Heck, he'd been taking care of Sari single-handedly for almost a year, when he'd once offered to have Chloe stay in town and co-parent with him. He would have *married* her four years ago, and she missed him now?

A fire ignited in his stomach, thawing out his lungs, his throat, his tongue, and he looked up to find Glory Rose helping Sari make the step up to the deck. "Conrad," she said. "My momma asked you a question."

Conrad looked over his shoulder and found Dot standing there. She wore a peculiar look on her face, and Conrad hadn't even heard her. He fumbled to grab his phone and shove it in his back pocket.

"Hey," he said. "I'm really sorry." He cleared his throat. "Thanks for the food."

"Of course," Dot said. "That's all I asked—if you'd gotten enough to eat."

"Yeah," he said as Glory Rose came to his side. He put his arm around her as Sari continued over toward Dot.

"Gams," she said.

"No, baby," Conrad said. "That's not Grams."

"Gamma?" she tried next.

Conrad looked at Dot, who wore a look of pure adoration on her face as she bent down and picked up Sari. "Hey girl," she said.

Glory Rose stared at Conrad, but he couldn't look away from Dot holding his daughter.

Glory Rose moved away from him and crowded in close to Sari. "Sari, this is my momma. Her name is Dot." She reached out and booped Sari's nose with her finger. "Can you say Dot?"

Conrad flew into action and joined them. "Say hi, Dot," he said.

"Hi, Dot," Sari said, and Dot looked like Sari had roped the moon and brought it down just for her.

"Oh, she's adorable." She giggled and snuggled her close. "Can I take her?" She turned to go back in the house, and Conrad exchanged a look with Glory Rose.

"Where are you going to take her, Momma?"

"Just in here." Dot moved back into the house. "I'm tired, so I left Daddy and the boys at the picnic and came home."

Glory followed her. "Momma, you're tired? Did you check your blood sugar?"

"I just did," she said. "It's low." She sank onto the couch with a groan. "Could you put a movie on for me, Glory Rose? I just want to sleep."

"Did you take your glucose tablets?" she asked.

"Yes," Dot said, and her gaze sharpened. "I don't need you to mother me, Glory Rose."

Conrad entered the house and closed the door behind

them to seal in the air conditioning and keep the heat out. "Sari needs a nap too," he said. "I can just go on home."

Glory Rose spun back toward him, and he saw the same indecision on her face now that he'd seen as she stood in the parking lot looking between him and her mother.

"Maybe we can put her down here." Her eyebrows rose up high, hope etched in both her eyes.

Conrad didn't want to leave yet, so he nodded and looked past Glory Rose to her mother. She'd already laid down on the couch, and Sari had curled against her chest, perfectly content in the arms of the older woman.

"Wow," he whispered. "Look at that."

Glory Rose faced her mother too, and then she moved to pull a blanket out of an ottoman, and she covered both her mother and Sari. She kissed them both and picked up the remote control. "What do you want to watch, Momma?"

"Just put on something for Sari," Dot said, without opening her eyes. "We just want to rest. Isn't that right, baby?"

Sari said nothing, and Conrad didn't know how to feel. Sari was used to spending time with his mother, as well as Grams, and perhaps Dot simply reminded her of them.

Glory Rose put on a cartoon and set the remote on the table in front of her mother. "It's right here, Momma. We won't go very far."

"Okay," her momma said. "I have my phone, and if you keep yours on, I can call you if I need anything."

Glory Rose bent down and pressed a kiss to her mother's head and then whispered something to Sari before she turned and faced Conrad. She approached and took his hand. "We can just go sit on the backyard again," she said. "Or we can go for a walk around the ranch."

Conrad wasn't sure what he wanted to do, but his phone in his back pocket felt like it might burn a hole in his jeans, so he took it out and handed it to Glory Rose. "Let's go for a walk."

Chapter Thirty

Glory Rose wasn't sure what Conrad wanted her to say. They'd left the house and walked down the road toward the Ranch House. The sun beat down on Texas today, and Glory Rose didn't want to be outside for very long, at least not moving and without shade.

Uncle Judge and Aunt June had built a gazebo on the edge of their property, and it offered the very best view of Three Rivers from anywhere at Shiloh Ridge. She wanted to go there, and she could sneak into the garage and get something cold to drink too.

"I don't like that text," she said.

"Join the club." Conrad sounded like he'd just been told that there would be no Christmas. He caught her hand on his next step and said, "I'm totally over Chloe. You know that, right?"

"I'm not jealous," Glory Rose said. "I'm surprised about that, but I'm not jealous."

"What *are* you feeling?"

"I don't know," she said, but the words sounded false. "Actually, I do know. I'm feeling very protective of you right now, and I don't want her sending you texts like that, because I don't think they're good for you."

Conrad tugged her off the road and over toward the side of the stables.

"Where are you going?" she asked as she stumbled to keep up with him. To her knowledge, he'd only been on the ranch a few times, and most of that had been at True Blue or her house. He'd gone to see the guineafowl enclosure one time, and that was nowhere near this stable.

He didn't answer but towed her over to the side of the stable and into the shade. He turned to face her. "You're feeling very protective of me right now?"

"Yes." Glory Rose reached up and fiddled with his collar. He'd taken off the blue tie in his truck, but he still wore his white shirt, now unbuttoned a couple of times. "That's okay, right?"

Conrad breathed in through his nose, and Glory Rose barely had time to look up before he kissed her.

Oh, how she loved the taste of this man. He broke away almost violently. "I'm so sorry," he said, before he kissed her again.

"I wish I could rewind time."

Another kiss with a deep stroke that left Glory Rose hanging on to Conrad's shoulders for dear life.

"I hate that I made today a bad day." He slid his lips across her jaw and down her neck.

"I hate that Chloe texted me that." He pressed a kiss to her neck and then up behind her ear. "What am I supposed to say?"

Glory Rose could barely get her mind to think, and Conrad lifted his head and gazed at her. Though she had her eyes closed and couldn't see him, she knew because the weight of his gaze carried something that no one else's did.

"You're keeping your eyes closed again," he teased.

She smiled and refused to open them. "I don't have any of the answers for you."

Conrad pulled her into his chest, and Glory Rose opened her eyes and found herself looking toward the Ranch House. "My uncle Preacher got in a car accident once," she said. "Out on the Eastern Highway. It was before I was born, and it was really bad."

Conrad didn't say anything, but she knew he'd heard her. "He lived in that house with my uncle Judge, and every day, my daddy would go get him and make him walk from the house to the stables right here where we stand."

She gave a light laugh that almost sounded like a sob. Thankfully, no tears came out of her eyes. "You should hear the two of them tell the same story," she said. "Daddy has one version, where he used his exceptional skill of discipline to help his best friend and cousin. Uncle Preacher tells a totally different story." She laughed, and it did sound happy now. "He says it was torture, and that Daddy just showed up every day to make him hurt."

"He probably needed to walk though, right?" Conrad asked.

"Doctor's orders," Glory Rose said. "Uncle Preacher had a lot of surgeries over a lot of years after that car accident, and he can still walk, but he's had a limp my whole life."

She had no idea why she'd brought that up. Just looking at the house and seeing the distance from the front door to the stables had reminded her of it.

"They have a gazebo in their backyard," she said. "It's shady, and we'll be able to see the whole town."

She pushed away from him and looked up at him, his dark eyes meeting hers. "I have a secret."

"You do?" Delight filled his expression. "Will you tell me?"

She nodded and started toward the Ranch House. "I used to come sit in this gazebo all the time," Glory Rose said. "I've texted you from the bench there several times, because when I sit in the gazebo, I can see your farm."

"So you've been stalking me," he teased.

Glory Rose smiled at the ground. "I like to think of it as being persistent," she said. "But yes, I've liked you for a long time, Conrad, and I would come to my aunt and uncle's house and look at your farm and wonder what you were doing. I fantasized that I might be able to see you doing your chores or mowing your lawn. And I used to sit there and wonder how I could get you to ask me out."

"I'm real sorry, sugar." He didn't give an excuse or a reason for why he hadn't asked her out, and Glory Rose didn't really need one.

They walked to the gazebo and sat down. Conrad sighed and gazed out toward the town of Three Rivers. "Look at that. You *can* see my farm." He put his arm around her, and she tucked herself into his side. "This is a great view."

"Yeah," she said. "It's the best."

A couple of minutes went by where the silence between them sounded beautiful and kind. Then Conrad asked, "Would you be there with me when I call Chloe for Mother's Day?"

"Yes," Glory Rose said without hesitation.

"I'm going to have to talk to her," he said. "I can't cut her out of our lives completely."

"I know that," Glory Rose said. "What are you going to say about her text?"

"I'm going to tell her that she can't send me stuff like that," Conrad said. "That it's not fair to her or me or Sari."

Glory Rose nodded, "All right."

"Would you go out with me this weekend?" he asked.

Glory Rose smiled to herself, because he hadn't asked her out in several weeks. They saw each other every day, and their dates were implied. "Yes."

"Will you just come down to the farm on Friday?" he asked. "That's where it will be."

"All right," she said, a pinch of worry in her chest. "Does this mean I won't see you until Friday?"

"No," he murmured. He placed a kiss on her hairline. "I just want to have a special date on Friday at my place."

"I'll come by around six," she said. "Okay?"

"All right."

* * *

Glory Rose didn't see Conrad as often that week, despite what he'd said in the gazebo, so when she pulled up to the farmhouse on Friday night, her heart pounded in her chest in a strange way.

He'd dropped lunch off at the office on Tuesday, but she hadn't seen him, and she'd stopped by the farmhouse on Wednesday, and she'd taken Sari out to gather the eggs, as Conrad was already milking the goats.

But he didn't come up to Shiloh Ridge the way he usually did, and he didn't ask her to come to the farm or invite her to stop by at-will.

So things between them had definitely shifted, and Glory Rose wasn't sure she liked the change.

She got out of her SUV and surveyed the front of the farmhouse. Something had been taped to the front door, and she walked in that direction. When she gained the porch, she saw a sign had been printed that said: *Glory Rose—go around the garage* with an arrow pointing to the right.

Excitement built inside her as she turned around and skipped down the steps to do as the sign had said. At the corner of the garage, a bright pink arrow pointed the way. She went past the sign and through the gate into the backyard.

She expected to see Conrad's dogs, but she didn't. Another arrow had been nailed to a fence post in front of her, and she cut across the lawn to go in the direction that it pointed.

She passed the chickens and the turkeys, each enclosure

with an arrow pointing her along the way. A horse snuffled at her, and Glory Rose smiled over to Cyndi Lauper, but she didn't slow her step.

Conrad had hammered five pink arrows pointing to the barn in the middle of the road, and she laughed when she saw that they had been taped to the end of yardsticks. She went into the barn, expecting to find her handsome boyfriend there.

Something didn't smell quite right. It wasn't as barny as she expected. Something else mingled with the straw and the leather and the dirt, but she couldn't place what it was. She looked around, but no arrows pointed the way.

Then Conrad descended from the loft, wearing his dark-wash jeans, cowboy boots, and that delicious hat. "You made it."

"I feel like I'm on a scavenger hunt," she said.

He smiled as he faced her. "Sadly, no, unless I'm your prize."

She grinned at him and leaned into his chest. "I can think of worse things to win."

He drew her into him and kissed her, if only for a moment. "I hope you're hungry."

"I'm always hungry," she said.

He chuckled, and he led her over to the ladder and nodded up it. Glory Rose climbed, and he came up after her, joining her as she stood staring at a picnic table that had been built out of hay bales. He'd laid a tablecloth across it, and a picnic basket rested on the end.

"What is this?" she asked.

"Dinner," he said, and the extra scent she'd detected

below suddenly made sense. "I'm hoping you can stay late enough for stargazing." He nodded over to the window, which wasn't open right now, where he had set some pillows and blankets.

She turned toward him, tears pricking her eyes.

"You're crying," he said. "I thought this would be romantic."

"Happy tears." She took his face in her hands and kissed him. "These are happy tears, Conrad. I've been worried all week that we're broken. You said nothing would change, but it changed." She pulled away and searched his face. "*We've* changed. We're different. Can't you feel it?"

"Yes," he murmured. "Sometimes change isn't bad, though."

It didn't feel great to Glory Rose, but she nodded. He led her over to the picnic hay-table, and she scooted onto a bale, and he sat down on the other half of it.

"This might also be a little bit of a bribe," he admitted.

"A bribe?"

He opened the picnic basket and started unloading food. "I told my parents that we're pretty serious," he said, as he set a piece of chocolate cake in front of her. "That hasn't changed for me, Glory Rose." He looked at her from under the brim of that dark, sexy cowboy hat. "Has that changed for you?"

"No," she murmured.

"They want you to come over for dinner," he said. "Me and you and them."

"What about Sari?" she asked.

"My momma said it's up to me if I want to bring her or

not. I'm thinking I might leave her with Grams. I love her, but she is a distraction."

Glory Rose nodded and took the fork that he handed her. "So you're bribing me with chocolate cake to eat with your parents?"

He nodded to it. "It's my momma's chocolate cake, and she promised to make it if you'll come for dinner."

Glory Rose would have said yes without the chocolate cake, but she made a big show of forking off the tip and studying it. "This better be the most amazing chocolate cake ever," she teased.

When she put the bite in her mouth, the groan of happiness and satisfaction that came out of her mouth was no tease. "Okay, yes," she said, already forking off another bite. "Absolutely yes."

Conrad laughed and set out real food. "My momma made all of this for us," he said. "And she also told me something really wise."

Glory Rose looked at the fried chicken, the mashed potatoes and gravy, and the coleslaw. "What was that?" she asked.

"She told me that I'm a Walker and you're a Glover, and we both have really big families with a lot of different personalities." He put a biscuit on her plate and then gave her a heaping spoonful of mashed potatoes. He did the same for himself while Glory Rose enjoyed her chocolate cake.

"But she said when we get married, we won't be Walkers or Glovers, we'll be *us*. We'll have to build our own family, me and you. And of course, you're going to still want to do things with your family, and I'm still going to want to do things with my family, but that neither one of them will be as important as *our* family."

Glory Rose nodded, though she hadn't really realized where he was going until he'd finished.

"Do you think that's true?" he asked.

"I think it's something that people should work on, yes." She ducked her head. "I know I need to work on it."

"I know your family will accept me eventually," he said. "And that my family will love you no matter what. But I think my momma is right. Even if we get married and our last name is Walker, we still have to build our own family, and it will be the most important thing we work on."

"I agree," Glory Rose said.

Conrad reached out with his own fork and took one of the last bites of her chocolate cake. He grinned as he pulled the fork out of his mouth. "Now that's good."

He sobered and met her eyes in all seriousness. "I would choose you first over anyone else," he said. "I think that's what my momma was saying. You have to choose me over anyone else, and I have to choose you over anyone else."

Glory Rose swallowed, a little bit nervous about that for some reason. "Even Sari?" she asked.

Something shuttered over Conrad's eyes. "I think we both have something to work on," he said. "Because I don't know if I'm supposed to choose you over Sari or not."

He lifted his piece of fried chicken. "But I do know I'm supposed to choose you over my momma and daddy, and I guess I'm just hoping that you believe that too, and that you'll actually be able to do it."

He took a bite of his chicken and then put a wing on her plate. "Let's just enjoy dinner now—and stars later."

She smiled at him. "Yes, I can't wait for the stars later." Maybe they'd be able to reveal the secrets of the universe to her—or at least help her learn how to put Conrad first in all things—so she wouldn't lose him.

Chapter Thirty-One

"N o, I'm not going to come today," Conrad told Grams over breakfast on Mother's Day. "Sari and I are talking to Chloe at ten."

Grams took another sip of her English breakfast tea and nodded. "I thought maybe you'd go down to Dallas to see her."

Conrad shook his head. He hadn't told Grams about the weird text from Chloe, nor how he'd told her not to send him stuff like that anymore. Thankfully, she'd backtracked quickly, and they'd resumed their normal, *Here's a picture of your daughter—Thanks for sending this, Conrad. She's so cute,* rhythm of messages.

Conrad wasn't entirely sure what his responsibility was. He had his daughter's birth certificate, and it listed Chloe as well as himself. He'd gone to the courthouse here in Three Rivers to make sure that he had legal and full custody of

Sarina, so that Chloe couldn't show up out of nowhere and take Sarina home with her without Conrad getting a say in it.

She'd signed all the papers, and never once in the last ten months had she asked for Conrad to bring Sari to Dallas, or even hinted that she might want to take care of her someday.

Conrad pushed those things out of his mind as his phone alerted with his security camera app telling him someone had arrived at the farmhouse.

"Glory Rose is here." He pushed away from the table and took his dishes to the kitchen sink. "I'll be right back."

"Glow-Roe," Sari said.

Conrad grinned at her and dropped a kiss on her forehead. "Yep, Glory Rose is here," he said. "And then we're gonna call your momma. Okay?"

He met Grams's eyes, and while she didn't say anything, he could tell she sure had something on her mind.

"I don't know where I would be without you, Grams," he said. "You've helped me so much this year." He moved over to her and hugged her tight. "Are you going to the homestead after church?"

"Yep," Grams said. "Are you and Glory Rose coming?"

"I don't know," Conrad muttered. He felt like he needed more time with just him and Glory Rose before he started bringing her around to the entire Walker clan. That was one thing where he felt like they'd made a mistake in the past couple of months. He didn't need to be involved in everything Glory Rose had going on with her massive family. They still needed time to build who they were together, and he simply didn't know if he was going to even mention the

Mother's Day feast happening at Uncle Jeremiah's house today.

He left the kitchen and went down the short hallway to the front door. "Of course you're going to tell her about it," he muttered. "Because you're going."

He simply had no idea how he could tell her he didn't want her to come—and it wasn't even that he didn't want her to come. His feelings mished-and-mashed together, and Conrad had no idea what was the right thing, so he simply opened the door and went out onto the porch, where he found Glory Rose bent over into the back of her SUV.

She straightened, and she wore the prettiest orange dress in the world.

"Well, well," Conrad said as he went down the front steps. "Don't you look nice?" He knew how to flirt with Glory Rose, and they had plenty of serious conversations too. What Conrad really needed was more *time*.

"Howdy, cowboy," Glory Rose said with a smile. She now carried three gift bags in her hand.

Conrad eyed them. "What are those?"

"Just a few little things," she said. "Something for your momma, something for Grams." She lifted her hand that carried two of the bags, and Conrad could admit that they weren't very big. "And something for Sari, just because she's cute." Glory Rose giggled, and Conrad took the gift bags from her and pressed his mouth to hers.

"Mm, you smell good," he said as he pulled back. "Listen... I have to drive Grams to church, and then we'll come back here and do the phone call. Okay?"

"All right," Glory Rose said. "I can stay here with Sari if you want."

Conrad searched her face. "Yeah, okay," he said. "There's another thing." He looked down at the ground and ran the toe of his boot along the edge where the cement met the grass. "My family is having a big luncheon for Mother's Day today," he said. "I didn't tell you about it because I wasn't sure if—" He cut off, still not sure of anything.

"It's all right," Glory Rose said. "We're having a big thing up at Shiloh Ridge too, and I'm just going to go to that." She put her hand under his chin and lifted his head up. "It's okay, Conrad."

"I just feel like maybe we're a little fractured," he said. "Like we could go to Uncle Jeremiah's, say hello to everyone, and then go to Shiloh Ridge."

Her eyebrows went up. "Is that what you want to do?"

He sighed, frustration coating the sound, "I don't know, Glory Rose. What do you think?"

She thought for a moment, looked past him to the farmhouse, and then brought her eyes back to his. "I think, Conrad, that if we do keep dating, and let's just say we get married, we're going to have to figure this out for everything."

"I know," he said miserably.

"You're welcome to come with me today," she said. "And I'm happy to go with you."

"Then maybe we should just do both," he said. "Uncle Jeremiah is serving lunch at twelve-thirty."

Glory Rose gave him a pretty smile, which reached all the

way to her eyes. "I can't wait to taste your uncle's cooking," she said. "You and JJ have been bragging about it for months."

Conrad laughed, glad when the tension between them shattered and dissipated. He took her hand and led her toward the porch. "What time are you guys eating?"

"After church," she said somewhat evasively. "We can just show up anytime, Conrad. There will be food if we want it, and if we're full from your luncheon, then we'll just eat cake."

"Everything is cake with you, isn't it?" he teased.

"There's always room for more cake," Glory Rose said in a very serious voice.

He took her inside, where he found Grams ready to go, her purse looped over her arm and her hat fixed firmly in place. "Ready, Grams?"

"I'm ready."

"Sari." Conrad moved over to his daughter and swooped her up, causing her to giggle. He grinned at her and settled her on his hip. "Glory Rose is gonna stay here with you while I drive Grams to church."

"Glow-Roe." Sari wiggled to get down, and the moment Conrad set her on her feet, she ran and launched herself into Glory Rose's arms.

Conrad chuckled and put all of the gifts on the dining room table. "Grams, one of these is for you. It's from Glory Rose."

"Oh, you sweet thing." Grams moved over to Glory Rose and gave her a kiss on each cheek. "You didn't have to get me a gift."

"Well, you're a mother, aren't you?" Glory Rose said. "Happy Mother's Day."

Grams beamed with all the shininess of a new penny, and she led the way outside to Conrad's truck.

He expected a lecture on the way to church, or at least for Grams to say what was on her mind, but she stayed silent. He dropped her off right at the front door, where she said, "Well, maybe I'll see you at Jeremiah's."

"Yeah," he said. "Maybe." Because while he'd talked with Glory Rose about it, he still wasn't sure what to do. He knew how to get home, and he knew how to call Chloe at ten a.m., and he knew how to say, "Hey, Chloe, Happy Mother's Day."

"Mom," Sari yelled, and Conrad tipped the phone so that it showed mostly her.

"Hey, Sarina, my baby doll."

Sari put her hands on both sides of the phone and pulled it closer. "Mom, go—fish—iveh—flor—bee—bug!"

Conrad chuckled, and Chloe downright laughed.

"My Daddy took her fishing," Conrad said. "And she's obsessed with bugs."

"Bug," Sari said. "They be ant and bee, bee and boy, crawl on your face." She threw her arms up and then touched her face, and Conrad pulled the phone back.

"Baby, we've got to keep the phone back here, okay? Your momma can't see you."

Chloe started talking and asking Sari questions, and Conrad marveled that she spoke so much better now. After several minutes, Chloe said, "Okay, Sari, give your momma a kiss."

Sari put her mouth right on the phone and said, "Mwah!" as she kissed the screen.

"I love you too, Sari," Chloe said, and Conrad nodded to Glory Rose.

She got up from where she'd been sitting at the end of the table, and she gathered Sari from his lap. "Let's go out with the dogs."

"Dog go bark, bark," Sari said. "Some they go—" She howled as Glory Rose opened the sliding door and herded Sari outside.

Conrad waited until they'd left, and then he looked at Chloe. "So that was Glory Rose," he said. "I'm seeing her."

"Oh." Chloe's eyebrows went up. "So that's why you chewed me out about saying I missed you."

Conrad ducked his head. "That wasn't the entire reason, Chloe," he said. "You can't be saying that stuff, regardless of if I have a girlfriend or not. It's—"

"I know," she interrupted. "I don't need you to tell me again. I was just missing you and Sari, that's all. I won't tell you when I am."

"All right." He looked at her and smiled. "Isn't she doing so great with her speech?"

Chloe looked away and sniffled. "Yeah," she said. "I'm so glad she has you to take her to those appointments and get her the help she needs."

"Me too," Conrad whispered.

"I didn't even know she wasn't talking normally." Chloe looked the other direction, and Conrad recognized the tactic not to look at him.

"Chloe," he said. "It's not your fault."

"I know," she said, but her voice pitched up. "It feels like it though."

"I didn't know either," he said. "The only reason I took her in was because Grams mentioned that she didn't think she was talking as much as she should've been."

Chloe nodded, and thoughts flew from one side of Conrad's mind to the other. "You said you were going to see a therapist," he said. "You don't have to tell me, but did you?"

She looked at him then, and she nodded.

"Do you need me to pay for it?" he asked.

Tears streamed down her face, and she said, "I want to say no, but it's kind of expensive, and she wants me to come in once a week, but I can't afford that."

"All right," Conrad said easily. "I'll send you some money."

"It's a hundred dollars an appointment," she said. "She doesn't take insurance."

"Okay," Conrad said. "It's no problem."

"Maybe just for a few months," Chloe said. "Then I can cut back."

"Chloe," he said. "You had to do something incredibly difficult, and you need help. And I'm more than happy to contribute however I can."

She nodded again, sniffled, and wiped her eyes. "You're doing an amazing job with her, Conrad, and I'm really glad that you're dating again."

He nodded, his voice tied in a knot. He still managed to say, "Me too, Chloe. You take care now."

"You too."

The call ended, and Conrad set his phone down on the table in front of him.

Four hundred dollars per month for therapy was nothing to him. The calls usually drained him, but today he didn't feel quite as numb or like he needed to hide in his office behind charts and numbers for the rest of the day. He got up, took his phone with him, and went to find Glory Rose and Sari on the farm.

In fact, Conrad felt better than he had in a long time, and if he could just figure out how to balance his family with the Glover family, with Glory Rose and then Sari and Grams too, he'd be living the high life.

* * *

Conrad looked up from his desk when someone knocked on his office door. He didn't close it because neither Grams nor Sari could climb the steps to the second floor, and he wanted to be able to hear either one of them if they called out.

Glory Rose leaned in the doorway, a sexy smile on her face. He rose to his feet. "So you found the place."

"Yeah," she said, looking around. "It looks real nice."

He looked from the filing cabinet, which housed his printer, to the bare wall without any photos, to the window, back to his desk. "You're lying."

Glory Rose giggled. "It could use some sprucing up."

"I don't even have any chairs in here," he said, just now realizing it. "It's not like I have meetings."

Glory Rose entered the office, and she wasn't wearing her usual scrubs.

"Did you not go to work today?" Conrad asked.

She shook her head. "I put in my two weeks' notice, and I have so much vacation time built up that I'm going to take vacation days until next Friday. Then I'm done."

Conrad blinked at her. "Wow," he said. "But you didn't get that preschool job."

She shook her head. "Nope. I need to figure out what I really want to do."

"You love kids." He went around his desk and pulled her into his arms. "Will you be happy without something to do?"

"I'm going to find something," she said. "And yes, it will probably involve kids."

"Besides the homestead dream," he asked. "Have you ever had any other big things that you wish you could have? You know, like how Mitch is opening a deaf academy—something like that."

Glory Rose stepped out of his arms and tipped up on her toes to kiss him. He went with her for as long as she wanted, missing her when she pulled away. "I don't know," she said. "The preschool job sounded really good, and they felt bad they couldn't hire me."

"Maybe you could run a preschool of your own," he said. "I'm sure we can find a building in town to rent."

Glory Rose nodded. "So you got your business license," she said, clearly changing the subject.

A certain giddiness moved through Conrad. "Let me get you a chair. Just a second." He dashed out into the hall and opened the closet where a couple of folding chairs waited. He grabbed one and went back into his office and set it up in front of his desk.

"I got my business license, yes," he said. "And while I'm not taking on any clients, at least I can do your wealth management legally." He rounded the desk and tapped a folder. "I've printed out all the paperwork I need you to fill out, and I can email it to you too, because sometimes it's easier to fill it out on a computer than it is by hand."

He sat down and pushed a folder toward her that had her name on the front scrawled in his cowboy handwriting. She looked at it and then him, wonder and awe in her expression.

"What?" he asked.

"This is a purple folder." She held it up as if he hadn't seen it before.

He grinned at her. "I know. Your favorite color is purple."

Glory Rose stood up and brought the folder with her as she rounded the desk. He had a big executive desk chair with plenty of padding and armrests, and he leaned back and opened his arms when it became apparent she was going to sit on his lap.

"Could you email me the paperwork?" she asked.

"This is a *business meeting*, Miss Glover." He grinned at her, his arms around her waist nice and firm. "I don't think this is appropriate for business."

"Hm." She pressed a kiss to his cheek, which he leaned into heavily. "What else do you need to know, Mister Walker?"

"Everything's in the paperwork," he growled. He moved

his hand up her back and into her hair. "As soon as you get it back to me, I can make a plan for what I'd like to do with your money. We'll have several more of these meetings so that you can tell me what you want, and then I just...do it."

"I expect there to be a chair for me to sit in next time, Mister Walker, if you don't want me to sit on your lap."

Conrad grinned at her. "And what if I do?"

"Oh, I think that would be *highly inappropriate*," she teased.

Conrad couldn't stop smiling, and he matched his mouth to Glory Rose's, beyond thrilled when she sat in his lap and kissed him for as long as he wanted. Finally, she laid her head against his shoulder, and he simply held her in his arms.

"We're still on this weekend with my parents?" he asked.

"Yes," she said. "And I was thinking—you were right about Mother's Day. I'm glad that we didn't go to either of our family's big luncheons."

"Me too," Conrad said.

They'd spent some time out on the farm, and when Glory Rose needed to leave to get to her luncheon, Conrad had kissed her and watched her drive away. He hadn't gone to his either, but instead, he'd taken Glory Rose's gift and one of his own over to his mother's house later that evening. She'd saved him some of Uncle Jeremiah's chicken pot pie, and Sari had gotten her beloved mac and cheese—which actually Grams's recipe.

But he and Glory Rose would be attending dinner with his parents this weekend, just the two of them, and Conrad couldn't wait to see a side of Glory Rose that he hadn't yet.

She'd see a side of him she hadn't either, and Conrad really hoped the pieces of him added up to more good than bad.

Chapter Thirty-Two

G lory Rose sat at her mother's vanity and let her momma braid back her hair. She had dinner plans tonight with Conrad's parents, but she hadn't told anyone about them. In fact, since Easter, she hadn't talked about Conrad much with anyone—not Fawn, not Pearl Jo, not her parents.

She wanted her voice to have weight when she did choose to say something, and no one had said anything negative about the two of them leaving on Easter. With how many Glovers existed, most people probably didn't even know Glory Rose hadn't been there.

"I'm surprised you can get here and get changed so quickly after work," Momma said, her fingers moving deftly through Glory Rose's hair as she braided in ribbons.

Glory Rose's heart beat a little bit faster. "I didn't go to work today," she said.

Momma met her eyes in the mirror. "You didn't go yesterday either, did you?"

"No," Glory Rose said, and she looked down at the vanity. She'd already done her makeup, so her kit sat there, zipped together and ready to go back in her bag. "I quit my job."

Momma's hands stilled completely. "You quit your job?"

Glory Rose nodded slightly so as not to disturb the braiding. "It was too much."

"You loved that job," Momma said. "You were so happy when you got it."

"It was ten hours a day, Momma, plus travel time."

Her mother resumed the braiding. "So you couldn't see Conrad enough?"

"Conrad had nothing to do with it," Glory Rose said. "But yes, I have more time to see him now."

But she didn't actually see him more than she had before. He had a very busy life taking care of a farm, his grandmother, and a three-year-old daughter. Glory Rose had seen him more in the past few weeks than she had the week after Easter, and she was glad for that.

"How are things going with him?" Momma asked. "You don't say much."

Glory Rose shook her head. "No," she said. "I don't."

"Why is that?" Momma asked. "I know you guys had some problems around Easter, but you're still seeing him, right?"

"Yeah, we're still together," Glory Rose said. "I like him as much as I always have." She met her mother's eyes in the mirror, deciding to be brave and bold. "Did you and Daddy ever just...feel smothered by being Glovers?"

Momma burst out laughing, but Glory Rose hadn't meant to be funny.

"All the time," Momma said as she quieted. "Here's what you have to know about being a Glover." She paused, her eyes on her work. "It's wonderful. It's the most wonderful thing in the world. Any of the people here at this ranch would drop everything if you needed help, and they'd be there."

Glory Rose nodded, because that was a wonderful blessing, and she had witnessed it several times in her life.

"But you also have to understand," Momma said. "That if you don't put boundaries on how far you'll go for the Glovers, they'll take everything you have."

Wow, Glory Rose thought. That sounded so...bad.

"So of course Daddy and I have felt smothered before." She reached for another ribbon and tied it into Glory Rose's hair before she continued. "We chose not to go to certain things, or we'd go for ten minutes. Sometimes we would plan things with Uncle Tyson in town, specifically so that we would have somewhere else to be during a big family function here on the ranch." She looked up and met Glory Rose's eyes. "I'm surprised you didn't realize that."

"I didn't," Glory Rose said.

"Conrad's got a big family too," Momma said easily, leading her in the conversation.

But Glory Rose didn't want to have it, so she simply said, "Yeah, he does."

Momma didn't press the issue, and she braided to the

end of Glory Rose's hair and put an elastic band there. She rested both hands on her shoulders and looked at her in the mirror again. "You are a beautiful young woman, Glory Rose."

"Thank you, Momma." Her emotions quivered, and then a horrible banging noise rang through the house, startling them both. Momma jumped to her feet and spun toward the open bedroom door.

"What is—?"

A scream filled the house, making Glory Rose's blood run cold.

Momma ran out of the bedroom, and Glory Rose followed. She heard Daddy talking in the kitchen, his voice low and gruff and speaking fast. Silver paced along the front of the island, sobbing. Positively *sobbing*.

"What is going on?" Momma asked.

"Oh, Glory Rose is here?" Silver ran toward her and latched onto her with tight fingers along both of her biceps. "You have to come with me."

"Come with you where?" Glory Rose asked.

"His horse had an accident," Daddy said, and Glory Rose's heart fell to the soles of her shoes.

"Lucky Charms?"

"We have to go back to the boarding stable right now," Silver said.

"Son, they're going to take care of him."

"Glory Rose, you *have* to come with me," Silver said. "You have a vet tech degree."

"No, no," Glory Rose said, trying to stop as Silver pulled

her toward the garage door exit. "No, I don't! I went for one year."

"They can't get a vet out until tomorrow," he said. "And I called Uncle Cactus, but he has the flu." He looked at Daddy, and then Glory Rose. "Fawn's in Omaha at that conference. There isn't anyone else. You have to come."

He was frantic and scared, and Glory Rose told herself that the boarding stable was down in town and she could check on Silver's horse and still make it in time for dinner with Conrad's parents.

"I don't know what you think I'm going to do," she said, though something shouted in her head that she could call Fawn and have her cousin walk her through it.

"You're going to come look at his leg," Silver said.

"Can he walk?"

"Silver," Daddy warned. "He's at a stable. The vet will be there in the morning."

"There are a million vets in this town," Glory Rose said, confused as she looked over to her father. "There are a hundred ranches and farms. You're telling me you can't find someone to look at him tonight?"

"I can," Silver said. "And it's you."

"Well, who else have you called?" Momma asked.

"I don't have time for this." Silver started to cry again. "I'm already out of the shows for the rest of the year," he said. "I can't find another horse in time."

He looked at Glory Rose, his dark eyes full of pleading. "Please, Glory Rose. He knows you, he's already scared, and they've put him in a stall that's not his."

"I don't know why you left," Daddy said.

"They told me I was too hysterical," Silver growled. "But I'm calmed down now."

Glory Rose wanted to challenge that, as his scream still echoed through her soul, but she said nothing. As far as anyone knew, she was going to dinner with Conrad, and she did that almost every night, so she could cancel.

She looked at her brother, indecision raging through her. Momma's words haunted her from only minutes ago: *any of the Glovers would drop everything to help you if you needed it.*

She'd been raised with that service mentality. She glared at her brother. "I will come look, but you get ten minutes and I'm driving my own car."

"Fine, fine," Silver said, and he turned around and walked out.

Glory Rose had been planning to go all the way to Conrad's farm, though he lived fifteen minutes past his parents' house, and they were planning to drive together to meet his parents for dinner.

She grabbed her purse and stomped out of the house without a word to her parents. She didn't take the time to text Conrad anything, because she was not planning on being late or missing dinner, and he didn't need to know anything right now.

She drove to the boarding stable on the west side of town, out past Momma's landscaping company, and followed her brother through the office and out onto the grounds. He could have housed Lucky Charms at Shiloh Ridge, but he wasn't a working horse; he was a show horse. And while

Silver owned him, he also rented him out to other riders for lessons.

"Were you riding him?" Glory Rose asked as she jogged to keep up with her long-legged brother.

"No," he bit out. "Clancy was." He scoffed. "He pushed him too hard, and Lucky stumbled. What a fool."

They walked forever, but that was probably only Glory Rose's opinion, as she wore unfit footwear for a boarding stable.

"Silver, I really can't stay long," she said.

"It won't take long." He led her down to the last stall in a pretty blue stable. "There's no one even here," he complained. "They told me they wouldn't leave him unattended."

The horse had definitely been left unattended, and Silver opened the top half of the stall door.

Lucky Charm stood in the tiny space, and Silver said, "He can't be in here. Look how small it is."

"Actually," Glory Rose said. "This is a great place for him. We don't want him to have a big open area so that he can try to walk around." She spied a door on the side of the stall. "Are there lights in this place?"

It took Silver a few minutes to find the lights, and then the stable flooded with fluorescents. Glory Rose entered the stall from the side, being careful not to get too far behind Lucky Charms. The last thing she needed was to get kicked or injured tonight.

"Oh, I see," she said. "It's this front one."

Lucky Charm's front right leg definitely had some swelling around the ankle, and he'd been biting at it a little bit.

"Did they give him any pain medication?" Glory Rose asked, and while she had not continued her studies in veterinary science, she had done a year of vet tech school. "He's tied, right?"

"He's tied," Silver said. "I'm going to call them, but I'll be right here."

"All right," Glory Rose said, and she knelt down to look closer at Lucky Charm's leg. "Is it a sprain or a break?" she wondered, and she reached out and touched the horse's body up where his leg connected to it. His flesh rippled, and he snorted softly, but he let her do it.

"I think...I think this just might be a pretty bad sprain," she said. "If we can get this wrapped up and get you some pain meds, maybe put a cold compress on it, you'll be all right until the vet comes."

"No pain meds!" Silver roared into the night, which caused his horse to startle.

Glory Rose shot to her feet. "I am in the stall with your horse!"

"Sorry," Silver said. "They didn't even give him any pain meds. They stuffed him in this closet and left him."

"Call Uncle Cactus and ask him what to give a horse who has a sprained leg."

"Aunt Willa wouldn't even put him on the phone," Silver said, his voice hovering near tears.

"Call again," Glory Rose said firmly. "And explain the situation. Tell him we don't want him to come down. We just need to know how much pain medication to give him. Do you know how much Lucky Charms weighs?"

"Yes," Silver said.

"Call Uncle Cactus." She left the stall, surprised at her brother's inability to take control of this situation. He was so good with Lucky Charms—and all horses—otherwise.

He started to make the call, and Glory Rose went further into the stable to try to find the medical supplies. She did not work here, nor had she ever been here, and it took her several long minutes to find the medical supply closet and get the bandages and padding that she needed.

She spied a fridge and she stepped over to it, opened it, and prayed there would be ice packs inside. To her great relief, there were, and she grabbed one that would surround Lucky Charms's ankle and hopefully, *hopefully* bring down the swelling and ease his pain.

Silver arrived in the supply room. "Cactus said to find some bute and give him two-point-five mils."

"All right," Glory Rose said. "Let's see if we can find it."

She had a terrible feeling that she was going to get arrested for rummaging through this medical supply closet unauthorized. After all, people couldn't just take horse tranquilizers whenever they wanted.

It's not a tranquilizer, she told herself. *It's an authorized equine pain medication. And Lucky Charms needs it.*

"I called Babs too," Silver grumbled. "She said they're short-staffed, and they don't have anyone to sit with Lucky Charm, so I'm going to stay the night."

"Okay," Glory Rose said.

"I want you to stay with me."

"I can't, Silver," Glory Rose said.

"I won't know what to do if something happens."

"Yes, you will," she said. "I don't understand why you can't get Boone out here."

"Boone is down in the Hill Country," he said. "He's not even in town."

Glory Rose really couldn't stay with Silver and his injured horse all night long. "Here it is," she said, and she reached for the bottle.

They took all of the supplies with them and returned to Lucky Charm's stall. Glory Rose fell into a rhythm, her mind remembering how to dress an animal's leg, because this was pretty simple, and she was surprised that the boarding stable owner hadn't done the most basic things.

When she said so, Silver said, "Babs is just their daughter. They're on vacation in Africa."

"So this simply happened at the worst time possible," Glory Rose said, with Boone out of town, Fawn at a conference, Uncle Cactus ill, the stable short-staffed, and the owner not even here.

"Yes," Silver said miserably. He sniffled, and Glory Rose got to her feet and hugged him.

"Silver, it's going to be okay."

"He will not be able to show on that leg," Silver said as he gripped her tightly. "Please, Glory Rose, can't you stay?"

She had not looked at a clock in a long time, but she knew she was already late for dinner.

"I can't," she said. "I have something I'm doing tonight, but then maybe I can come back."

Silver nodded and released her, and she knelt down to

resume her work. "This ice pack can't stay on all night, okay?" she said. "I'd say about an hour, and then you need to take it off and check his leg."

"Okay," Silver said.

"You know what to do with horses," she said. "You've been around them your whole life, and you've been showing for years."

"I know," Silver said. "I just lost my head."

"If you're going to stay all night, put the ice pack on again in a couple of hours. And did Uncle Cactus say anything about when to give more medicine?"

"He said it should last all night," he said. "And then we don't want Lucky Charms to have too much medicine before the vet comes anyway."

"Okay," Glory Rose said.

She finished up with the bandaging, and then she looked at Silver. "Okay, he just needs the meds."

Her brother stared steadily back at her. "Yep, he just needs the meds."

"I'm not going to give them to him," she said.

"You know how way better than me. You're a CNA. You give shots."

"To *humans*," she said.

They stood off in a battle of wills for a few more seconds, and Glory Rose knew she was not going to win. She rolled her eyes, sighed, and said, "Fine, I'll do it."

She prepared the syringe because she did know how to do that. She had worked with Uncle Cactus for a whole summer.

Ten years ago, whispered through her mind, but she

ignored it. She had given cattle vaccinations during that summer, and she had a year of vet tech training. She could give a horse a shot.

Can you though? she wondered, and it took her a couple of minutes to psych herself up to doing it.

Finally, she got the job done, and she breathed out as the horse just shuffled his feet a little bit. "He's not trying to put weight on the front leg," she said. "That's a good thing, but he's going to get tired. You should try to get him to lay down."

"How am I supposed to get him to lay down?"

"The same way you get him to trot funny," Glory Rose snapped. "I have to go."

"Thank you, Glory Rose," Silver called after her, and Glory Rose waved to him as she hurried away.

It took her another ten minutes to get to her car, and when she got there, panting, out of breath, and sweating with the sun going down, she also felt like crying.

Her phone rang, and Conrad's name sat there. Right below it in teeny, tiny words, it said that she'd missed a call from him only three minutes ago, and she cursed herself for being in such a hurry that she'd left her phone behind.

She swiped on the call. "Hey, I'm so sorry. I'm going—"

"It's fine, Glory Rose." He cut her off in a tight shotgun-round-burst of a voice. "Dinner's canceled. I hope whatever you're doing is worth it."

And with that, he hung up.

Chapter Thirty-Three

"Ignore it," Conrad said as the doorbell rang. "It's Glory Rose, and I don't want to talk to her."

Sarina looked up at him from where she played on the floor with her ponies. "Ding dong. Ding dong," she sang, but Conrad didn't smile.

"Conrad," Grams whispered. "She won't just leave, will she?"

No, Glory Rose would not. The fact that she'd come to the farmhouse after he'd hung up on her told him that.

He heaved himself off the couch and stomped out of the room. He yanked open the front door and kept going, nearly barreling into Glory Rose, who stood on the front porch.

"I told you dinner was canceled," he said.

"You didn't let me say anything," she shot back.

"You were an hour late, and we couldn't find you," he said.

"Do you know that I called your momma to find out where you were, and she said that you'd gone with Silver to the boarding stable?"

"Yeah, his horse got injured." Glory Rose wore fire in her face. "I was coming to dinner."

"You know it's standard practice that if you're going to be late that you call or text," he said. "Or at least, you know, have your phone with you."

"I left it in the car on accident," she said. "I was only supposed to be at the stable for ten minutes."

Conrad went down the steps away from her, but she followed. At the end of the sidewalk, he turned right as his farm ran for about a mile on this road.

"I don't know what to say to you," he said.

"I'm really sorry," Glory Rose said. "It was an emergency."

"Not according to your daddy," Conrad said. "He said that horse was stabilized and fine and that the vet was going to be there first thing in the morning."

"Silver was frantic," she said.

Conrad nodded, because he did admire Glory Rose for wanting to help her brother. Could he really fault her for that? Was he really going to break up with her because she didn't answer her phone?

"I sure like you, Glory Rose," he said. "I think we're real good together."

"I do too," she said.

"But right now, I don't see a future with you."

He heard the air wisp out of her mouth. "What?"

"It's gone dark," he said. "Or at least...there's just the future according to Glory Rose, whatever works for her."

"That is not true."

"I know we have a lot of balancing that we'll have to do," he said. "This dinner was really important to me, and I thought it was important to you too."

"It was," she said. "It *is*."

"It took us weeks to schedule it."

"I know," Glory Rose said.

He let the silence sit, and he heard his parents giving him counsel as he'd stayed for *an hour* at their house waiting for Glory Rose. He'd called her *nine* times and texted her twice as much before he'd finally called her parents.

A rush of emotion moved through him, because that had been a terrible hour for him. His imagination had come up with all kinds of horrible scenarios, some of which left Glory Rose on the side of the road, unable to answer her phone.

"You taught me something," he said. "And I think we should do it."

His voice hurt coming out of his mouth, but when his momma had said the words he was about to say to Glory Rose, he'd felt that stinging in his chest, and he knew she was right.

"What's that?" Glory Rose asked.

"We just need some time to sit with it," he said.

"Sit with what? Me missing dinner?"

"No," he said. "Sit with us being...." He sighed. "Not together."

She stopped walking, and he took another couple of steps and then stopped too. "You're breaking up with me?"

"I don't want to," he said to the night sky. "I think maybe we should just think about it as a little break, not a break*up*." He turned around and faced her. "Time to just sit with our own thoughts and figure out what we really want from the other."

"I told him ten times I had to go," Glory Rose said.

"Yeah, but you didn't go, did you? And I'm not saying that I'm going to be perfect. I told Grams I'd be off the ranch today by two to take Sari to her appointment, but I didn't make it. My momma came to get her to her speech lesson. So I get it. Things happen. But you know what? I texted her ten times in that hour and kept her updated."

"So you're mad I didn't communicate."

"I'm mad about all of it," Conrad said. "Truth be told, Glory Rose." He drew a deep breath as nothing but pure exhaustion moved through him. "There's been some part of me that's been mad about your family since Easter, and I'm requesting a little bit of time for it to sit with me. That's all."

She was so pretty, what with the way the last of the sunlight barely glinted off her hair. She'd woven ribbons into the braid tonight, and Conrad would have been impressed with those a couple of hours ago.

He knew, on some level, he loved her, but he also knew that he didn't want to be second when he didn't have to be. That was another thing his momma had taught him: *You're worth being first.*

"Sometimes," Daddy had said. "You do have to come second, and you will be once Glory Rose starts having babies of her own, but you shouldn't be second to her momma or her family or her dreams. Her dreams should be yours too."

While Conrad knew Glory wasn't off living her dreams tonight instead of having dinner with him and his parents, it didn't make the knife in his chest any less real. He'd felt abandoned, and then he'd worried that she'd been hurt.

Those feelings had spiraled into anger when she wouldn't answer her phone, and then he'd been assaulted by guilt, because he shouldn't be mad when she might be hurt.

Honestly, how a person could feel all of this in a single evening, Conrad didn't understand.

Exhaustion ran through him anew, and Glory Rose finally nodded. "Let's take some time to sit with it then."

He nodded too, and they started back toward the farmhouse. He didn't have anything else to say, and Glory Rose simply sniffled along the way.

He shoved his hands in his pockets when he got to the driveway. "It's a weird time of night, and I know you don't like driving in twilight. Will you text me when you get home?"

She nodded, and then she got behind the wheel of her car and left. Conrad stared down the street long after her brake lights had disappeared, wondering if he'd done the right thing. He didn't dare ask God, in case the answer that he got only made him feel more foolish.

Eventually, he went in the farmhouse and collapsed on the end of the couch where he'd been sitting before. Grams said nothing, and when it was time to put Sari to bed, Conrad got up and did it. He'd been in this place before, where he walked around the house like a zombie, numb, doing whatever needed to be done without allowing himself to think or feel too much.

He returned to the living room and helped Grams off the couch.

"Do you need help in the bathroom?" he asked when he reached her bedroom doorway.

"Not tonight, dear," she said. "What happened with you and Glory Rose?"

"We're just taking a little break right now," Conrad said.

"I'm really sorry, my boy." Grams shuffled back over to him and cradled his face in her hand. "You seemed very happy with her."

"I was—I am," Conrad said. "There's just some things to figure out, that's all."

Grams nodded. "I love you."

He nodded too, and he waited in the hall, just in case she called for help. He'd installed handles in the bathroom to help her get up and down, but she still sometimes needed extra support, especially lately.

She didn't call, and when he heard her shuffling and getting into bed, he gently brought the door almost all the way closed.

Then he had to face his empty farmhouse. He'd spent several evenings in this exact situation with Sari and Grams in bed with his whole night open. So he and Glory Rose would hang out on the couch, play cards, talk, or just watch TV.

Crushing loneliness accompanied him into the living room, but he couldn't stay there for long. The TV held nothing that would entertain him, and it was too dark to go out on the farm.

So Conrad did what always soothed him: He went upstairs to his office and lost himself inside numbers and charts and figures.

At least then he wouldn't have to think about the fact that he and Glory Rose were on a "little break" that felt like his heart shattering.

Chapter Thirty-Four

Wilder Glover left the homestead where he'd grown up, glad neither of his parents had intercepted him on the way out the door. "You've really got to get your own place," he muttered to himself, and he thought of the empty cowboy cabins they had over in Cabin Row.

Link had lived in one for a while before he and Misty had gotten married and moved into the Top Cottage. Wilder could have one at any time; he just had to say something, and saying something would require him to tell his momma and daddy that he didn't want to live under their roof anymore.

Fawn had already moved out, and the main offices for the ranch were in the homestead—on the second floor, east wing. It simply didn't make a whole lot of sense for Wilder to move out.

He got in his truck and got off the ranch without having to see anyone and tell them where he was going. He'd been flirting with Elaine Walker since Link and Misty's birthday party in March. And finally, he'd gotten Glory Rose to give him her number.

He told no one about their forthcoming date, and he wasn't sure why. "Maybe because you hardly ever date," he said, as he drove down the dirt road toward the highway. He'd dated a little bit in high school and college, and whenever the subject came up, Wilder did what he did best. He stayed quiet.

No one needed to know that he'd had his heart broken by a pretty brunette named Kayla.

He'd been in love with her through his whole junior year of college, but she was a year older than him, and she'd graduated and...left.

She'd said if their paths ever crossed again, it would be God bringing them back together. Wilder had grown tired of waiting on the Lord, and over Christmas break of his senior year, after stalking her online, he'd shown up at her office in New Mexico.

She'd been dating someone else. Turned out her words were just words, and they were not backed up by any feelings —certainly not the same kind of feelings that Wilder had.

Humiliation streamed through him now as loudly as it had a few years ago. No, Wilder had not told anyone about that. And in fact, he'd told his momma a little white lie about what he'd done that Christmas. After all, he couldn't tell her he'd laid in bed and cried while he watched reruns of his favorite sci-fi show, nor could he tell her about the trip to Albu-querque.

Thankfully, he'd already been twenty-one, and he didn't have to get anybody to sign off on giving him money from his trust for the trip.

Elaine lived in a cute, blue one-story house in Monkeytown, and Wilder's pulse beat hard at him as he walked up to her front door. She had decorated it with a wreath made of wildflowers, and as he got closer, he could tell they weren't real. He didn't know what they were made of, so he reached out and touched one.

"Oh, it's wood," he said, and he knew immediately that those were not cheap. He also knew the Walkers had plenty of money, just like the Glovers.

He hesitated to ring the doorbell as he thought about Glory Rose and Conrad. Apparently, they'd broken up a couple of weeks ago, though Wilder had just found out from Fawn. When he'd asked why, Fawn had said, "It's complicated when you have a big family."

And now here was Wilder, a Glover, trying to do something with Elaine, a Walker. *Hey*, he told himself silently. *At least you don't have a three-year-old daughter.*

He had no idea how much that would complicate things, but he figured quite a lot. Glory Rose had never said anything about Conrad's daughter being a problem, and Fawn hadn't made it seem like she was the issue either.

Wilder knew relationships were more complicated than they ever seemed on the surface, and that some people could keep really, really good secrets—because he was one of those people.

Her doorbell camera beeped, and Elaine's pretty Texas

twang came over the speaker. "Are you just gonna stand on my front porch and talk to yourself, or are you going to ring the doorbell?"

Wilder grinned and reached out and rang the doorbell. The door opened only a half a second later, and Elaine in all her curvy glory stood on the other side. She put one hand on her delicious hip and said, "You were talking to yourself, and you touched my flower arrangement." She narrowed her eyes at him, as if he had done something scandalous.

"I couldn't tell what it was made of," he said. "And I was just thinking about Conrad and Glory Rose."

Elaine nodded soberly and reached for something inside the door that he could not see. She came up with a purse. "Yeah, Conrad is...." and then she trailed off. "Well, it's not my place to say," she said. "But it's really sad about him and Glory Rose."

"Yeah," Wilder said. He smiled at her and glanced down to her cute ankle boots. "You look really nice."

A smile bloomed on her face. "Thank you. This is a new sweater."

He reached out and touched it too, and only when he looked up to meet Elaine's gaze again did he realize what he'd done. He quickly pulled his hand back. "Sorry," he mumbled. "I'm sort of tactile."

"I can see that," she said.

"It's a really soft sweater," he offered.

Elaine stepped down onto the porch and pulled her front door closed. Wilder went with her down the front steps to the sidewalk. "So you said you like Japanese food," he said.

"Did I?" Elaine asked.

"Yes," Wilder said. "I'm almost sure you did, and there's a new place on the north side of town that Henry says is really good."

"All right, I'll roll with it," Elaine said. While relief rang through Wilder, he wanted to pull up the texts that they'd exchanged in the past couple of weeks and show her that she'd said she liked Japanese food, but he didn't.

The weekend traffic was insane the moment they pulled off of Elaine's street, and he looked at the clock. "I don't think we're going to make our reservation," he said.

"You have to have a reservation at this place?"

"The website said it was recommended," Wilder said. "I'm going to call them and see if we can push it back a half-hour."

Since traffic barely inched forward, he felt safe doing so, and thankfully, the restaurant said that they'd keep a table for them.

"You know, reservations don't really mean anything," Elaine said.

Wilder looked over to her. "What do you mean?"

"I mean, we'll get there, and you'll say, 'I have a reservation,' and they'll say, 'Okay, it'll be a half hour.'"

"I don't think so," he said with a chuckle. "The reservation holds the table for you."

"And how many busy restaurants have you been to where there's empty tables?"

Wilder blinked and edged forward on Main Street.

"Exactly," Elaine said.

"Well, then I guess we'll just see when we get there," he said. "So, you're an artist?"

"No," Elaine said.

Frustration built beneath his tongue. "I'm almost sure you told me you were an artist." He looked over to Elaine. "I haven't been texting a bunch of other women—just you—and I have a pretty good memory."

She gave him a smile. "I do some art, I suppose, but I wouldn't call myself an artist."

"Well, you did." He laughed. "I know I didn't make that up."

"Oh, it was probably just the mood I was in that day," she said.

"You get to be what you want based on the mood you're in?" he asked.

"Yeah," she said. "I do." And she offered no further explanation.

Wilder looked over to her. "I can't figure you out."

She grinned at him. "You should stop trying. I'm an enigma." She laughed, and he did too.

Traffic opened up, and they only arrived about ten minutes late for their reservation. When Wilder stepped up to the podium and said, "Wilder Glover, for two. I had a reservation," he glanced around the restaurant as the woman studied her seating chart.

Then she said, "Yes, Mister Glover, right this way."

He smirked at Elaine and gestured for her to follow the hostess first. She rolled her eyes and then giggled. Wilder sure liked the sound of that.

They sat down with menus, and as Wilder tried to figure out how to order, he asked "So if you're not an artist today, what are you?"

"Today I was an errand girl," she said. "I helped my aunt finish up her jewelry orders, and then I took them all to the post office."

Wilder nodded and pointed to the menu. "Do you understand what any of this is?"

Elaine laughed again, and instead of reaching across the table and pointing things out, she got up and slid onto the same side of the bench as him. His heart flopped wildly in his chest as she leaned in close and pointed. "You can get sushi rolls here," she said. "But I wish to remind you that we live in the Texas Panhandle, and I don't know if I can go out with a man who eats sushi."

Wilder chuckled. "Noted."

"Over here are the main noodle dishes. This whole side is à la carte, and the dinners are back here." She turned his menu over, and Wilder finally found what he was looking for.

"What are you going to get?" he asked.

Elaine's hair sat in soft curls around her face, and he had half a mind to move one back about the same time she did it. He had no idea if her hair was naturally curly or if she'd done that with an appliance. She blinked, breaking the spell between them, and slid out of the booth. "I'm going to get ramen," she said.

He nodded. The waiter appeared, they put in their orders, and as Elaine lifted her glass of water to her lips, she asked, "So you run the ranch?"

"Oh, no, ma'am," he said, shaking his head with a laugh. "I'm a junior foreman right now. Link and Preacher are our main foremen. I'm taking Ward's place."

"So you're the only one doing what you do," she said.

"Well, Uncle Ward is helping a lot still," he said. "Of course, we have a lot of men working there. A lot of my uncles still do lots of work around the ranch, and a lot of my cousins."

Elaine nodded. "Yeah. Most of my uncle's kids still work at Seven Sons too," she said.

"JJ runs that place now, though, right?"

She nodded. "Yeah, he took over at the beginning of this year, but Uncle Skyler and Uncle Micah and Uncle Liam still do a whole lot." She set her water glass down. "And they have men that live and work there too."

"Of course," Wilder said.

He enjoyed his conversation with Elaine, and she flirted with him several times. He did his best to keep up with her, and as they walked out of the restaurant an hour and a half later, he wondered if he could hold her hand. She seemed like the kind of woman who would make the move or let him know if she wanted him to, and he didn't get that vibe from her. So he kept his hands to himself and opened the passenger door of his truck so that she could climb up.

"We could go over to the creamery," he said. "To get dessert."

Elaine looked at him, and he smiled at her. "I've had a real great time tonight. Maybe we could go out again."

She smiled too and said, "I don't know, Wilder."

His heart dropped all the way to the soles of his feet. "Oh
—oh-kay."

He told himself not to say "oh" again, and with nothing
more in his mind, he stepped back and slammed the door. He
walked around the front of the truck, cursing himself for
picking a restaurant so far away from her house. Hopefully,
the traffic would be thinned by now.

He got behind the wheel, and she said, "I had a good time
too."

"But you don't want to go out again," he said.

"I mean, I don't know," she said for the second time.

"No man wants to hear 'I don't know if I want to go out
with you.'" He looked over at her. "If there's no spark, just say
there's no spark." There were whole fireworks shows for him,
but he'd rather know now than later if she didn't feel the same.

"I think you're really handsome." She looked away and
clutched her purse in her lap. "It's probably not you, Wilder.
In all honesty."

He pulled out of the parking lot of the restaurant and
started to drive back toward her house. He didn't know what
to say, and she seemed like she had more on her mind. She
didn't say anything until they got to her house, and Wilder did
the Texas gentleman thing—he got down, opened her door,
and walked her up to the front door.

"Well, thanks for giving it a try," he said. "Sorry there was
nothing there for you."

"Me too," she said sincerely. "You're a really great guy,
Wilder."

He took a micro step toward her. "And you don't want a great guy?"

"I want someone who makes my heart sing every time I see him," she said. "And you're handsome and you're kind and you're a good man."

Wilder didn't need to torture himself anymore. He gave her a sad smile and said, "But no singing."

She shook her head, and he nodded his acceptance. "Okay," he said. "Let's still be friends. You can text me, and if we run into each other at the grocery store, it won't be awkward, okay?"

Wilder had to see too many people in town for that.

"Yeah. Okay," Elaine said. She opened her door and stepped up into her house. "Have a good night."

"You too." He made the lonely trek back to his truck.

"No singing," he said thoughtfully, as he left Monkeytown and got on the highway to get back to Shiloh Ridge.

He wasn't sure what that meant for Elaine, but as he drove, he could acknowledge that he wanted someone that made his heart sing every time he saw them too. And maybe if he didn't quit trying, he would find that woman.

Chapter Thirty-Five

Mitch kept his office door closed. Number one, that would force Lacy to knock, and number two, she might walk on by if she thought she would be bothering him.

She never bothered him.

But since his blunder a few months ago in asking her to dinner, their relationship had definitely cooled slightly—not that it had been warming up at all—but she'd been more playful with him. She'd told him personal things, and they'd become friends.

Now, everything felt clinical, and she only texted and spoke to him with the utmost of professionalism.

As she should, he thought.

He pushed away from his desk, stood up, and turned around to look out the window. His office sat at the back of the house, and it overlooked the farm beyond. He did not have the mental bandwidth or the green thumb to plant a garden or cultivate the crops. Heck, it was all Mitch could do to keep up with keeping the grass cut and watered.

He hadn't lived in a place that he had to take care of physically the way he did here in a very long time, if ever. He paid a couple of his cousins, Birch and Hank, to come down and mow the lawn, put down weed treatments, and take care of the property. They'd both graduated from high school about three weeks ago and claimed that they wanted the money before they left for college.

Mitch wasn't sure who he would get to come do his yard work then, but he'd figure it out just like he did everything else.

Even Lacy? he wondered.

He turned around when Champ put his paw on his leg and then trotted to the door. He couldn't yell *come in* because Mitch did not speak.

He could have Champ open the door by giving him a hand signal, but he wasn't surprised to see the door open and Lacy peek her head in before he could prompt his hearing dog. His heartbeat leapfrogged over itself, and he gestured for her to enter.

She left the door open as she signed and said, "I'm sorry, sir, I just need you to sign these invoices. And I brought the mail." She had it tucked under her arm, which meant she didn't sign as usual, but Mitch still got the message.

Thank you, he said, and he took the mail from her. She then placed a manila folder on his desk, and they both sat down—her in a nice plush wing-back chair in front of his desk, and him in his rolling desk chair behind it. He ignored the invoices for a moment, because he held an invitation in his hand.

He ripped it open and found an announcement for his Uncle Bear's birthday the following month. He handed it to Lacy, because it had her name at the top as well as his. He watched her face closely, not even daring to blink for fear that the *Mitch and Lacy* that he'd seen scrawled in black marker at the top of the invitation would be imprinted on the back of his eyelids.

Mitch and Lacy had such a nice ring to it, at least in his own ears.

She looked up, surprised. "I'm invited?" she asked.

He shrugged. *Seems like it.*

She set the invitation down and watched it as if it might come to life and attack her. "I don't need to go," she said. "Isn't he your uncle?"

Mitch nodded. *You should come. It's a good time.*

He looked away, and since he didn't speak, he never needed to clear his throat, but he did it anyway. Then he reached for the huge water bottle that he kept next to his laptop, and he picked it up. He took a drink, and in his haste to cover up the clearing of his throat, he started to cough. Humiliation ran through him again, and he wondered if he'd ever regain his status with the woman in front of him.

She gave him a small smile as he stopped coughing, and he shook his head and took another big drink. *That just went down the wrong pipe*, he said, grinning.

"I nearly choked on a mini cucumber this morning," Lacy said.

Mitch laughed, glad when she did too. He nodded to the invitation and waited until she looked at him.

You should come and be my interpreter, he said. *I only have a couple of cousins who I can really talk with, and sometimes the big parties are really hard for me.*

Lacy picked up the invitation again, and then she lifted her phone from her lap and typed into it. "I just put it on my calendar," she said. "Is there a dress code?"

Mitch grinned, sure it was too wide for something as simple as her question. No, he was smiling because she'd agreed to come to a family birthday party with him.

As your interpreter, his mind whispered at him. *You should be ashamed of yourself.*

And he was for about five seconds, and then he realized that the gorgeous blonde was going to be his interpreter-slash-date, and he could work on getting that first word out of the equation.

No dress code, he signed. *It'll probably be at True Blue, my family's barn, and there will be a lot of barbecue and a lot of kids, though I guess most of them are grown up now.*

"Is there anyone as old as you?" she asked, and Mitch couldn't tell if she was flirting or not, because he could not hear the pitch of her voice. He had to rely solely on her hands and her facial expressions, and Lacy was a master and gave nothing away.

I'm the oldest, he said. *And Cactus is my stepdad, remember?*

"Yes," Lacy said. "I remember."

Link was my best friend growing up, he said. *And he knows sign language the best, maybe even as good as you.*

Lacy pressed one palm to her heart in mock surprise. "As good as me?" She smiled and shook her head. "I don't think so."

Mitch laughed again, and then he looked down at the folder in front of him. He flipped it open to see what invoices she needed signed. *Did the permit get submitted to the construction company?*

"Yes, sir," she said. "That top one is for the cement company. The second one is half of the deposit for the plumbing, and the third one is everything we need for HVAC and roofing."

Mitch looked back at the first invoice. He signed it where necessary, trying not to worry about how much money things cost. He'd inherited a lot of money from his stepdad when he turned twenty-one, and he could afford this build.

He signed the second one, but on the third, he raised his eyes again and signed, *The HVAC company is doing roofing as well?*

Lacy nodded. "It's the same company; two brothers. One brother does roofing, the other does the HVAC. They give you a deal when you do both. So you can see at the bottom there, we're getting twenty-percent off, which is quite a huge deal for the buildings that we have going in."

Mitch checked the discount, and it was a good deal. He signed the invoice and passed the folder back to her. He expected her to stand and leave the room with a curt nod the way she had before, but she didn't. She set the folder in her lap with her phone, and Mitch raised his eyebrows at her. She didn't look at him, though, which was her way of saying she wasn't ready to talk yet.

Mitch could gaze at her beauty all day, so he simply waited, and when she finally looked at him, he asked, *Is there anything else?*

"Yes." He watched her swallow, and an alarm went off in his head, screaming, *she's nervous.*

He didn't like that. Lacy had never been nervous in front of him—not during their video interviews, not the first day she'd shown up on this property—where she would live with him alone until their academy opened. Never.

"I wanted to ask you about my brother," she said.

Mitch gestured for her to go on, for he knew that her brother was deaf, and that she'd grown up as his interpreter, and that he was the reason that she had gone into Deaf Studies and become an interpreter.

"I think he would be an amazing faculty member here," she said.

Mitch frowned. *I thought we had decided not to hire him.*

They'd had this conversation before, and Lacy had said she *didn't* want Jacob to work at the same place she did.

"He's going through a hard time right now," Lacy said. "I think it would be good for him to be here."

Surprise ran through Mitch. *Oh, you want him to come right now?*

"He could work with me on the educational programming," she said. "Or he could be a groundskeeper, that physical facilities assistant that we talked about, or any other thing that you need. I know you work twelve hours a day, and I'm putting in long hours too, and we could use another person."

Mitch watched her, trying to figure out what she was really saying. He hated not being able to hear voices at times like these, and he cocked his head. At which point Lacy smiled and said, "There's nothing to figure out, Mitch. My brother just needs help right now, and so do we. And I think it would be a good fit."

What kind of salary are we talking? he asked, because while he was a billionaire, that didn't mean he wanted to throw his money around willy-nilly.

"I told him for being an administrative assistant, which is basically what he would be to both me and you, that you could probably pay him sixty-thousand per year." She swallowed hard. "But if I overstepped, I can take another figure to him."

Mitch let another moment go by. *And you're sure you want him here?*

Lacy nodded without hesitation.

All right, I'll get the paperwork ready for him. Is he going to live with you?

He'd converted the second floor of this house into his apartment, and it consisted of a long hall down the middle, with rooms off each side—two bedrooms, a bathroom, and a third bedroom he used as a living room, as it held a couch and a TV.

They shared the kitchen on the first floor, and they both had offices here as well. Lacy's apartment on the third floor was identical to his, but her ceilings were lower as the A-frame of the roof came down on each side.

"No," she said. "I'm going to get him set up with some housing in town."

Mitch knew Lacy and her brother had some history, as most siblings did, but her love and devotion for him also stood out to Mitch. *All right*, he said.

Lacy nodded too, and she stood up. "Thank you, Mitch," she said—and it was the first time in a long time that she had not called him sir.

Mitch smiled at her, and she turned to leave. He couldn't call after her, and even if he signed, she wouldn't see it. So he got to his feet, which made the chair make noise on the floor, not that he could hear it. But she could, and she turned back to him, her eyebrows raised.

You might want to wear dancing shoes for my uncle's party, he said. *Uncle Bear loves to dance.*

A mild look of horror crossed her face, and then she nodded again. "Noted," she said before she left his office.

Mitch turned back to the window, this time his heart much lighter, and everything in his life much brighter. Lacy might not be counting his uncle's birthday party as a date, but Mitch certainly was.

Chapter Thirty-Six

L acy Hayes could not believe the nerves running through her. "This is just a job," she told herself, even as she paused in front of the mirror above her dresser one more time. Not a hair sat out of place, and in fact, her long, blonde hair had fallen in perfect waves today, just like she'd hoped it would.

She put makeup on, because she was going out to a birthday party, and she always dressed professionally for a job anyway. This job just happened to be with her extremely good-looking cowboy billionaire boss.

Would you go to dinner with me?

The words rang in her mind, though Mitch had not said them out loud. Lacy had been surprised, to be sure, because she had not picked up on any hints that Mitch was interested in her romantically.

Since then, she'd seen all kinds of signs—little ones, sure—

like how he washed her coffee cup every day for her and set it to dry in the dish drainer.

He always beat her downstairs in the morning and made the coffee. She'd made one comment about liking maple cream, and the next day, a carton of it sat in the fridge.

When they ordered lunch in during a working session, he always let her choose the restaurant. He always put the order in.

He did not treat her like a secretary or an assistant, and Lacy had admired him for that from the beginning.

She knew he didn't really need an interpreter for his uncle's birthday party. He had several cousins who could communicate well with him via sign language, one of which was extremely fluent.

Lacy pulled the collar on her blouse over a titch, so that it sat straight. She'd met some of Mitch's family members before, of course—his parents and Link and one cousin named Smiles. She had not met Bear, though Mitch spoke of him often. He was the oldest and grumpiest of the Glovers, and Mitch's daddy was second oldest and sometimes the grumpiest.

Mitch had been off the property several times in the last few weeks as his daddy had been sick with a spring flu. He'd gone to help his momma take care of him and other things around their house that sat at Shiloh Ridge.

Lacy had been on the ranch a couple of times, fleetingly, to drop something off or pick something up, but she spent the majority of her time here on this property on the east side of town, where she and Mitch were building their dreams.

"It's his dream," she whispered to herself, her eyes locked onto her reflection. In truth, it was her dream too, and when she'd seen the job come up, it was as if God had opened heaven and beckoned for her to apply.

This job and this academy were made for her, and she for them, and she would not do anything to jeopardize it. "Which is why you can't go out with him," she said. "Even if he's charming, even if he's funny, even if you like him. There are hundreds of charming, funny men that you could be with."

If she didn't work twelve hours a day in a small Texas town, she could probably find them.

While this job and this place were her dream, the truth was, she'd needed a fresh start. She'd had no problem leaving San Antonio and her job with the state interpreting office there to come to this small Texas town in the Panhandle.

Sometimes she missed the roar of the sea, but she didn't miss the way her friends looked at her, or the way her momma stopped by after work just to make sure she'd fed herself. She didn't miss the house that she and her husband had purchased, or the rose bushes that Landon had planted just for her. She *couldn't* miss those things, or she'd miss out on living life in the present.

She turned away from her reflection, because it was almost time to leave to go to the birthday party. Mitch had quipped about how the Glovers were never late. In fact, if someone showed up fifteen minutes early, they were fifteen minutes late.

So Lacy left her third-floor apartment and went down the steps, only glancing at Mitch's closed door that led to his apartment as she went by. She found him in the living room reading something on his phone, and of course, he couldn't hear her coming.

She paused and simply watched him. He wore a cowboy hat, which made her heart beat faster, and a denim shirt that she could only see the top two or three inches of.

Mitch had studied at Whispering Paws, and he was an excellent sign language teacher and dog trainer. She couldn't think of a more capable man to open a deaf academy. She swallowed hard as her emotions rose through her, because he was also the exact type of man that Lacy wanted in her personal life.

He was strong. He worked hard. He solved problems. He thought on his feet. He could be a little bit intense and passionate about the things he cared about, and Lacy had once been on the receiving end of that, and she loved the passion and intensity with which her husband had loved her.

But Landon was a reminder of why she shouldn't date Mitch. If she did, she would have to tell him about her husband. And Lacy had really enjoyed the past several months here where no one knew about Landon's passing, and she didn't have to talk about him or catch anyone watching her and know exactly what they were thinking.

She'd enjoyed being a ghost, a stranger, a blank canvas that only she got to paint on, and if she opened the door to a more personal relationship, she would have to illustrate the story of her past.

"Champ," she said. "Tell Mitch I'm here." She stepped into the living room, and Champ alerted for Mitch. He looked up immediately and twisted to look over his shoulder. His grin appeared on his face, and oh, Lacy sure liked it.

He had straight white teeth, and he got to his feet and held his arms out to the sides as he turned in a full circle. He shoved his phone in his back pocket and said, *I'm wearing denim from head to toe*, as if she were blind.

She grinned at him. "You sure are," she said, her hands moving naturally with the words. Most hearing people didn't know that sign language wasn't an exact mirror of English, and she had to say something in English that didn't exactly match her hands.

It was hard work, and she'd studied interpreting for six years and had a master's degree, though she'd been signing since she was eight years old. That was when her brother Jacob had been born. Her mother had made an attempt to learn American Sign Language, but her brother had really grown up communicating with exact signed English, which wasn't a language, and made it very difficult for deaf people to communicate with others.

Lacy had been his interpreter for a long time, and she'd done the best she could until she could take formal ASL classes.

You look really nice too, Mitch said, and Lacy gestured to her dress.

"Do you like it? It's new." Lacy knew she looked good in blue, and she always felt comfortable in the color, so she'd bought herself a new dress that was blue from head to toe. "It's not denim, but we're about the same color."

She moved closer to him and pushed her hip almost

against his. "Look." She watched his face, but his eyes had dropped to her body, so he did not see her last sign, and it didn't matter, because he was already looking.

He lifted his eyes to meet hers. In interpretation, there was so much eye contact, so Lacy rarely felt self-conscious about it. She saw so many things swimming in Mitch's eyes—from pure desire to hope, to determination, to irritation. He reached out and put his hand lightly on the back of her elbow.

He signed with only one hand as he said, *You sure are pretty*, and then he stepped back and put an appropriate distance between them.

Are you ready to meet the wild and crazy Glover family?

Lacy's pulse romped through her body, and she nodded. "Yes, sir."

Mitch smiled again, checked his back pocket for his phone, and then swiped his keys off the coffee table. He jangled them in front of Champ's face, and the dog moved toward the front door.

Mitch had replaced all the doorknobs in the house from the round kind that required a hand to turn, to the lever kind that a dog could push down with his paw. Champ opened the front door, nosing it all the way open, and turned to look over his shoulder at Mitch and Lacy.

"I love that dog," she said as she signed to Mitch.

Me too, he said before he led the way out the door.

Lacy followed, and one good thing about working with a deaf man was that he couldn't hear her when she muttered to herself, "Just because he thinks you're pretty doesn't mean you should date him."

They had another year of construction on this academy, and Mitch wanted to open before next fall. Lacy would do everything she could to help him realize that dream—because it had become her dream too.

So even though he moved to the passenger door and opened it for her, Lacy strengthened her resolve and told herself for the fiftieth time that her job and her dreams were more important than her heart.

Maybe once he gets the academy open, she thought as she watched Mitch walk around the front of the truck. *Then you can go out with him.*

That single word—*maybe*—had been the bane of Lacy's existence for years now.

Maybe this medication will work.

Maybe that surgery will take care of the problem.

Maybe tomorrow will be a better day, and maybe in a year when the academy opened, she could go out to dinner with Mitch as more than friends.

Maybe.

Maybe.

Maybe.

Chapter Thirty-Seven

G lory Rose walked back to her cabin with Pearl Jo. She had not found another job off the ranch, and in fact, she hadn't even been looking. She'd been working this summer with Pearl Jo and Wilder on their field maintenance, livestock rotation, and small animal care.

She basically did the job of a three-year-old and fed the chickens every day.

As she and Pearl Jo reached the trees, and thus the shade, the temperature went down a couple of degrees. Relief moved through Glory Rose, and Pearl Jo looked over to her.

"You told me today was the deadline for your decision on whether you would go to Finn's party or not." Pearl Jo held up both hands and wouldn't meet Glory Rose's eyes. "I'm not going to sway you one way or the other, but Fawn is going to ask when she gets home tonight, because you told us today was the deadline."

Glory Rose's good feelings about that day, and the relief from the relentless sun, disappeared. She groaned in an exaggerated way. "I don't want to go to the party."

"You don't even know if Conrad will be there."

Glory Rose gave a mirthless laugh. "He'll be there."

She hadn't specifically asked Wilder or Link to give her updates on the ranch owners' meetings and whether Conrad attended. She *knew* he attended every month. She *knew* he was friends with her cousins and Finn Ackerman, who ran the group.

Of course Conrad would attend his birthday party. They'd both gone last year, and Glory Rose had asked Joelle Stockton to talk to Conrad and see if he would dance with her. She'd gotten his number at that very party, and she'd been flirting with him every day since—well, not for the past couple of months, since he'd said he needed a "little break" to think through things.

"How much time does a person need to think anyway?" she asked. Her voice came out angry, but what really ran through her was hurt. "I thought he would have called me by now."

Pearl Jo linked her arm through Glory Rose's. "I know, sweetie. I still think he's going to, and I think you should go to the party. Yes, he's going to be there, and he's going to take one look at you and realize that the past couple of months were the biggest mistake of his life."

Glory Rose appreciated the words, but she didn't believe them. She also couldn't wallow—as her momma called it—for much longer. She drew in a deep breath, which lifted her shoulders up tall and strong.

"I'm going to go to the party." She met Pearl Jo's eyes as she slowly exhaled. "Maybe I'll meet someone else there."

Pearl Jo laughed this time. "Right," she said. "Who are we going to meet that we don't already know?"

"You never know," Glory Rose said. "Wilder's been out with two or three women that we didn't know existed."

"Too bad about him and Elaine," Pearl Jo said. "They'd be really cute together."

Glory Rose shrugged one shoulder, their cabin coming into view. "Elaine wants someone older than her," she said. "And I heard she started dating someone else."

"Who?" Pearl Jo asked.

"A new cowboy who came to work for Mason Wisenhouer."

"Oh, they have a nice operation," Pearl Jo said.

"Yeah, and he was new in town, so you never know."

She went up the steps to the small back deck, where she and her cousins kept a few chairs so they could sit outside at night. Nothing felt as good as the air conditioning inside, and Glory Rose detoured over to the fridge to get something cold to drink while Pearl Jo went down the hall.

"I'm going to shower real quick," she said. "If Gun and Ashton get here before I'm ready, tell them I'll only be a few minutes."

"Okay," Glory Rose called after her.

She'd forgotten that Pearl Jo was having a sibling night, and within twenty minutes, she'd left, leaving Glory Rose in the cabin alone. Fawn would be home from work in another hour, but Glory Rose couldn't stand the silence.

She checked her phone just to make sure Conrad hadn't called or texted. He hadn't, and she muttered to herself, "You have to give up the delusion that he's going to get back together with you."

She simply didn't know how. She did know how to get in her car and drive on the dirt roads at Shiloh Ridge Ranch until she parked at the Ranch House. She did know how to walk across the lawn to the gazebo, and she did know how to sit on the bench there watching the wind blow the clouds through the sky, and the tall trees sway back and forth, and Conrad's farm down below.

She'd fantasized so many times about life in that farmhouse with him, on that ranch with Sarina, and she let her imagination run wild again that afternoon.

So today wasn't going to be the day that she got over Conrad Walker. That was fine. There was always tomorrow.

* * *

Glory Rose leaned against the fence and watched as Silver led Lucky Charms through his exercises. His riding coach stood beside her, and she called out instructions, which Silver executed flawlessly.

"He's looking really good," Glory Rose said, pride riding in her voice.

Silver had practically been living at the barn since Lucky Charms' accident. "He's worked really hard to rehabilitate that horse," Joanne said. She moved down the fence and called something else about keeping Lucky Charms' head up. Silver made a tiny adjustment, and the horse's head came up the way Joanne wanted.

Silver had told Glory Rose that he was going to try for the fall shows, and watching her brother work with his beloved horse, Glory Rose believed he would make it—*and he'll probably win*, she thought, because Silver was very good at what he did.

She wished she knew what to do with her life. She wished she had half the passion Silver had for training and showing horses. She knew there'd always be a place for her at Shiloh Ridge, and she did love her family and wanted to be able to see them often. But she wasn't passionate about agriculture the way Wilder was, or animal science the way Pearl Jo was, or maintaining the family legacy the way Link and Misty were.

She thought of Aunt Sammy and how she'd started her own mechanic shop in her twenties. Then Aunt Oakley, who'd been a Formula One racecar driver, retired and opened a huge motor sports complex in Three Rivers.

Aunt Montana had built her construction firm from ground zero, and Aunt Holly Ann still ran her own catering company, doing events all over town. Glory Rose had helped her aunt a couple of times since she'd quit her job at the doctor's office, but she wasn't passionate about cooking either.

Judy and Hailey, Aunt Ida and Etta's daughters, had started doing a lot of their community outreach at Shiloh

Ridge that their mothers had done for years. Glory Rose did love the ranch, and she supposed she could join their team.

And she could always find a homestead, leave the ranch, and try to make it on her own. Her heart did love the idea of homesteading, but seeing as how she could barely function as a human being right now, Glory Rose didn't think homesteading was a viable option.

Silver finished his lesson, and Glory Rose went with him to brush down his horse and put away his tack. He spoke to Lucky Charms in a low, soothing voice as he worked on the horse. Glory Rose sat on a nearby bench, alone with her own thoughts, which was the worst place to be.

Aunt Charlie had owned a unique ice cream company before she'd become Preacher's wife, and even Glory Rose's own momma still owned From the Ground Up, a premier landscaping company in Three Rivers. She hadn't been the one driving the big dump truck for a while now, and she did a lot of the administrative work that needed to be done from the home office that she shared with Daddy.

Every aunt or uncle that Glory Rose could think of had something they were passionate about. Why couldn't she find one thing?

Please, Lord, she prayed silently. *I need something to become. I need my life to have meaning.*

God didn't immediately tell her what she should be doing, and Glory Rose thought of something that Conrad had told her a while ago: *Just act,* he'd said.

My momma told me I needed to act, and God would let me know if what I was doing was wrong or not.

Glory Rose had not been acting. She'd barely been existing, and even that felt hard.

"Are you ready?" Silver asked, interrupting her thoughts.

She looked up. "Yes." She got to her feet, her heartbeat feeling like a tremor as it moved through her body. She and Silver would drive back to the ranch, where they'd get cleaned up and get ready to go to Finn's party.

She'd need to become suddenly allergic to bees or force herself to throw up to get out of going now, as her brother left her alone with her thoughts again. Glory Rose decided that her first action would be to attend this party with as much enthusiasm as she could muster.

What do you think of that, Lord? she thought, but she got no answer.

Chapter Thirty-Eight

Conrad hurried up the steps and across the deck to the farmhouse. He rushed inside, barely feeling the cool kiss of air conditioning against his skin.

"There's a broken water pipe out there," he said. "But I got it fixed for now."

Grams looked over from where she sat on the couch with Sari in her lap. "You're covered in mud," she said, as if Conrad didn't know. He wanted to reach up and wipe his hand through his hair, which had grown long in the past couple of months.

"Yeah." He gave a chuckle. "I'm gonna go shower real quick, and then JJ is going to be here to go to the party."

"Good luck," Grams said, as Conrad kicked off his boots by the door and hoped he wouldn't drip too much mud on the way to the bathroom.

He'd warred with himself for hours, days, a full month,

about going to Finn's birthday party tonight. He didn't see a way out without saying, *I just can't face Glory Rose*—which wasn't even true. He *could* face Glory Rose, and in fact, he *wanted* to see her.

As he scrubbed the day's work from his skin and hair, a quiet kind of excitement built inside him. He'd been praying to know what to do about Glory Rose since he'd gotten Finn's invitation to his birthday party. Sometimes he found himself standing at the fence with his horses the way he and Glory Rose had several times. He'd spoken to them about her, and he'd looked up into the hills, imagining that he could see the gazebo at the Ranch House. He couldn't, but his mind could conjure up beautiful pictures and perfect scenarios.

As he pulled on his best pair of clean jeans, he prayed, "Please just let it go well tonight." He wasn't even sure what that entailed. Did that mean he wanted to get back together with Glory Rose, or did that mean he would simply have peace when he saw her?

His heart cried because he wanted to be with her.

He left the bedroom and heard his cousin chatting with Grams. He arrived in the kitchen and stopped, taking in JJ and Ruby in their casual finest clothes.

"I need a plan," he said.

JJ turned toward him. "A plan?"

Conrad thought about the plan that Glory Rose had come up with to keep Mitch inside when his father had wanted to surprise him with a new dog. It had turned out that that dog, while a good canine, had not been able to learn the things Mitch needed it to learn to be a hearing dog. Conrad understood that Cactus had simply added it to his pack, so not every pairing was a match.

He smiled at his cousin and his fiancée. "My therapist challenged me to do something I'm uncomfortable with every day," he said. "I'll admit I haven't really done it, though life seems to challenge me on a daily basis."

"Yeah, Grams told me about the broken water pipe," JJ said. "I can bring the excavator over."

"That would be great," Conrad said as he moved over to the fridge and got out a bottle of sparkling water.

"So what do you need a plan for?" Ruby asked.

He met JJ's eyes and grinned. JJ chuckled and shook his head. "He wants to get back together with Glory Rose."

Ruby's eyes widened slightly, and then she smiled. "Of course, he does. He's been in love with her forever."

"Not forever," Conrad said.

"I don't think you need a plan, brother." JJ clapped him on the shoulder and took his sparkling water from him. "I don't know how you drink this stuff."

"I like the burn," Conrad said, taking the bottle back. "I'm not asking you to drink it." He glanced over to Ruby. "And I definitely need a plan."

"I think you just walk up to her at the party and ask her to dance with you." Ruby said.

"You don't need a plan, brother."

"Okay, you had a whole plan for moving to San Antonio with Ruby," he said. "And it took you *three weeks* to plan your proposal." He twisted the cap on his water bottle, the hiss of the carbonation release bringing him such satisfaction. "I can't just walk up to her at a party and ask her to dance."

"Why not?" JJ asked.

"What if she says no?" Fear bolted through Conrad, and he tried to push it away. "Doctor Larson says if I have a plan, then I won't be afraid."

"She might still say no to your whole plan," JJ said. "And then you've wasted all that time *making* a plan."

Ruby giggled and shook her head. "Can we discuss the plan on the way to the party? We're going to be late." She moved into the living room and bent down to collect Sari. "Come with me, baby girl, we're going to the birthday party."

"Birfday parry, happy birfday, happy birfday!" Sari sang, and Conrad loved that she had started putting together so many words. She hadn't asked about Glory Rose, but Conrad didn't expect his three-year-old to do that.

Ruby led the way out of the farmhouse, and Conrad hung back while JJ followed her. "You're okay, Grams?" he asked. "You have everything you need for tonight?"

He sank down on the couch next to her because Grams had turned eighty-two last month, and she was moving slower than ever.

"I'm fine, my boy," she said with a smile.

"I'm going to be out late," he said. "I'll check on you when I get home."

She nodded and took his hand in both of her papery ones. "Conrad, are you in love with that woman?"

He thought about the question, something he'd done several times since he'd initiated a "little break" between him and Glory Rose. "Yes," he said, and he waited for God to tell him that he was wrong, but He didn't.

"Yes," he said in a stronger voice. "I'm in love with Glory Rose, and I want her back in my life. I want her here at the farmhouse. I want her to help me raise Sari." He ducked his head, though he'd never had to hide anything from Grams. "I want to build a family with her, and if she wants to turn this place into more of a homestead, I would do it for her. If she wants to open a daycare, I want to help her." He looked up at his grandmother. "My life seems empty without her, and it kind of hurts that I can't talk to her."

"You can," she whispered.

"So what do you think I should do?" he asked.

She waited a moment, her expression thoughtful. "I think a man like you, Conrad, does need a plan, and it's smart of you to make one. You and Glory Rose attended this party last year together, and I'm pretty sure you started talking to her then."

"Yeah." Conrad nodded, his memories flowing thick and fast through his mind. "Yeah, she sent Jo Stockton over to talk to me."

An idea bloomed and took root in his soul. "She said she did it because she was nervous, and I first danced with Jo, and then Glory Rose, and I got her number." He drew in a breath as his emotions hitched in his chest. "I don't want to ever dance with anyone but Glory Rose again."

"Then maybe you do simply plan to walk up to her and ask her to dance," Grams said, but Conrad had a better idea, so he simply smiled at Grams, leaned over, and kissed her cheek.

"I love you so much. Call me if you need anything."

"I will," Grams said, but Conrad knew she wouldn't. She'd probably call Uncle Jeremiah or Daddy, as they lived closer than where Conrad would be for tonight's party. He hurried to get in the back seat of JJ's truck, ignoring his cousin's raised eyebrows.

"I have a plan," he said. "But I don't want to talk about it."

JJ was the best person ever because he never made Conrad talk when he didn't want to. He simply chatted with Ruby, and they sang along to the radio as he drove them almost an hour out to Three Rivers. Conrad's heart flopped wildly in his chest because he wasn't even sure if Jo Stockton would be at the party tonight. He figured she would be as she still lived on the ranch with her parents, and she'd known Finn her whole life.

As they approached the barn where the music and festivities poured out, JJ stepped closer to him. "Tell me what we're doing, brother."

"I need to find Jo Stockton," Conrad said.

"Jo Stockton?" JJ didn't even ask why. He simply reached over and took Sari from Conrad as he said, "We'll find Jo Stockton then."

They entered the barn, their steps strong and sure. Conrad stalled and ducked out of the doorway so he could take in the scene. As usual, it seemed like the entire town had shown up for Finn's birthday party, as the Ackermans were well-known and ran a generational cattle ranch.

Finn stood about two-thirds of the way back in the barn with his sister, brother-in-law, wife, and his youngest son in his arms. They talked and laughed, as many other groups of people did around the barn. The food had been set up at the back, and the dance floor took up the right half of the barn, directly across from where Conrad hid in the shadows.

Three Rivers held summer dances every weekend from May to October, and they put a dance floor down right over the grass so that everyone could line dance and swing and mingle with each other. Finn's daddy had bought the old dance floor squares when the town had decided to buy new ones, and they put them down every year for Finn's birthday and, assumedly, for other family events as well.

Someone approached on the left, and Conrad looked over, his pulse pounding against the back of his tongue.

"Word on the street is that you're looking for me," Jo said. She wore her cowgirl hat low over her eyes, and she looked at Conrad like perhaps they would do an illicit deal here in the dark.

He grinned as happiness burst through him. "I am, yeah," he said.

"What can I do for you?"

"Is Glory Rose here?" he asked.

"Yep." Jo simply stared out into the barn. "She got here about ten minutes ago. She's back by the refreshment table, glued to Fawn and Pearl Jo."

"That's not going to be good," Conrad said.

"It's a tough wall to get through," Jo acknowledged.

"Will you talk to her for me?" Conrad asked, feeling slightly silly. He'd be thirty next month. He should be able to talk to a woman, especially one he was in love with. "Find out if she'll dance with me," he said.

"Do I have to dance with anyone?" Jo looked at him, her smile starting small and growing bigger and bigger. "And do you have a message for me to give her?"

Conrad swallowed, because there was a lot he wanted to say to Glory Rose that he didn't want to say to Jo. "No message," he said, the words barely croaking out of his throat.

"The dancing is going to start soon," Jo said, and in fact, the song that had been playing ended, and Finn's momma stepped up onto a table.

"Welcome, everyone," she said into a mic. "There's lots of food back here, as well as cake, and we don't really have any big presents for Finn this year, so he's going to open them in a little bit, and we're going to go ahead and open the dance floor now."

Loud music blared through the barn, a popular line dance song that caused dozens of cowboys to whoop and flood the dance floor. Conrad was not one of them, and in the commotion, he turned toward Jo, his eyebrows raised.

"Will you do it?"

She pushed away from the wall. "I'm on my way right now."

Conrad let her get a few steps away, because that was the plan he'd formulated in his mind. Then he followed her, intending to stop by the cake table and get as much as he could carry, because while Glory Rose might tell him no, he'd never known her to turn down chocolate cake.

Chapter Thirty-Nine

Glory Rose shifted to the right, making room for Jo Stockton as she arrived in their little huddle.

"Hey, Jo," she said, because she'd been friends with the other cowgirl for a long time. Jo had definitely embraced the country lifestyle more than Glory Rose had, if her plaid shirt and jeans and big belt buckle told anyone anything.

"Hey," Jo said. "What are you girls doing tonight?"

Glory Rose exchanged a glance with Fawn. "Just hanging out," Fawn said. The country music blared at them as the line dancing around them continued. Glory Rose loved to dance, but she wasn't feeling particularly social tonight.

She hadn't seen Conrad yet, and she'd started to wonder if he was going to come at all, and what she would do if he didn't. She worried just as much about what her reaction would be when she saw him, and she really just wanted to get it over with, so that she wouldn't have to stew on it anymore.

"Well, it seems I've been tasked as the matchmaker tonight," Jo said dryly. "Just from walking from one side of the barn to the other, I've had all kinds of cowboys ask me about you guys."

"Oh, you're just making that up," Fawn said.

Jo's stoic demeanor didn't crack. "Oh, I can assure you, I'm not," she said. "It's really all quite boring."

Glory Rose grinned at her. "Says the woman who's dated more than all of us put together."

Pearl Jo nodded and drained the last of her punch. "Probably just Fawn and Glory Rose," she said. "No one ever asks me to dance."

Jo trained her eyes on Pearl Jo. "Actually," she said. "There's a fine young man by the name of Joseph who would like to be your dance partner for the first slow dance."

"Oh, I can't date a Joseph," Pearl Jo said. "Can you imagine Joe and Pearl Jo?" She laughed.

"We don't know any Josephs anyway," Glory Rose said. "That sounds made up."

Jo shrugged, obviously not going to try to convince them of anything. "Your loss," she said. "Joseph is a great farrier, and Henry and Angel keep trying to recruit him for Lone Star, but he's got his own business and makes really great money working the farms and ranches around Three Rivers."

"Wait," Fawn said. "Are you talking about Joe Nylon?"

"Yeah," Jo said. "He's great."

"He's, like, thirty-five years old," Fawn said.

"You should set him up with Elaine," Glory Rose said, a big smile on her face.

"Elaine is dating Jace Farren," Jo said.

"Right," Glory Rose said.

Jo turned around and surveyed the barn. "Yeah, they're here somewhere," she said. "She brought him tonight."

"Wow," Glory Rose said, and a sting of missing moved through her, because she'd liked Elaine, and she would have liked to meet her new boyfriend.

Then Jo said, "Rich stopped me just a minute ago and asked if you're seeing anyone, Fawn."

"Rich Marshall?" Fawn asked, her voice pitching up comically.

Glory Rose stifled a giggle and had to look away from her cousin's stunned face.

"The one and the same," Jo said. "Seems he finds himself entranced with your beauty."

Fawn scoffed, and Pearl Jo laughed right out loud. "She tried working with him all last year," Pearl Jo said. "He told her he was dating someone when he wasn't."

"Well, apparently they've broken up," Jo said, her voice almost bored. She looked at Glory Rose, whose heart started to wail. She'd mentioned she would try to find someone else, but she'd been completely kidding. Her time in the gazebo earlier this week only confirmed to her that she wanted Conrad, and only Conrad.

"I had someone ask about you too," Jo said, and Glory Rose swallowed nervously.

"I'm not dancing with anyone tonight," she said.

Jo opened her mouth to reply, but a deep bass voice

covered whatever she was going to say. "You're not? That's too bad."

Her eyes flew to the voice she recognized so well, the one she dreamed about, the one she wanted to hear every day. Conrad stood right behind Jo, who shifted to make room for him in their group.

"I was really hoping that I could dance with you tonight."

Fawn squealed and bounced on the balls of her feet. "Yes, you can," she said.

"Fawn," Pearl Jo admonished.

"What? She's dying every day without him; she wants to dance with him."

Glory Rose pressed her eyes closed. Though Fawn wasn't wrong, a hint of embarrassment moved through her. At the same time, she was also kind of glad that Fawn had spoken up, because then she wouldn't come off as too needy.

The line dance song ended, and cheering filled the barn. Glory Rose watched as cowboys started to come off the dance floor and pair up with the women around them. A slow song started, and a man said, "Cowboys, find your girl and join us on the dance floor."

Conrad shouldered his way into the group further, his eyes locked on hers. "Will you dance with me?" he asked.

Glory Rose nodded, praying that her voice would unfreeze so that she could speak to this man intelligently. "Thank you, Jo," he said softly, and oh, how Glory Rose had missed the way he spoke.

She put her hand in his and sucked in a breath, because she'd missed holding his hand as well. She thought of the text that Chloe had once sent him, and she said, "I missed you, Conrad."

He didn't take her far onto the dance floor before he stopped and turned around, drawing her easily into his arms. She wasn't sure if he'd heard her, but as he brought her close and dipped his head so that his breath washed softly across the side of her neck, he said, "I've missed you desperately, Glory Rose."

Tears filled her eyes as she clung to him the way she'd dreamed about. He moved them back and forth on the floor. Glory Rose kept her eyes closed so that she couldn't see who was watching. She didn't *care* who saw her with Conrad. She hoped everyone in town would, so that they would know that he was hers and she was his.

"How set are you on staying here?" he asked.

Glory Rose didn't know how to answer, and before she knew it, Conrad had danced her off the temporary hard floor and right out the back door of the barn. The evening air back here definitely held more heat and humidity, but Glory Rose took a deep breath of it anyway.

"I'm sorry my little break was so long," he said.

Glory Rose finally looked at him. "I was expecting you to call earlier." Her voice broke, and she quickly pressed her lips together, because she didn't want to cry.

"I know, sugar," he said, taking both of her hands in his. "I expected that too, but I learned something on this break that I think is really important."

"Oh yeah?" she asked. "What's that?"

"How to forgive Chloe," he said. "I didn't understand how

she couldn't call me and tell me she was pregnant, even when she explained. It didn't make sense until I was faced with having to say something really hard to the person I loved, and I didn't know how to do it. There weren't words, and every day that went by made it easier to simply not say anything."

Glory Rose searched his face, trying to get all he said to settle into her head so she could make sense of it. Had he told her he loved her?

No, she thought. *He can't....*

"But I can't live without you, Glory Rose," he said. A soft smile came to his face, and she felt it move through her whole body. "I'm in love with you," he said. "And I don't want another day to go by where I don't hear your voice."

Tears spilled down her face then, because Conrad always said the most beautiful things. "Don't cry, sugar," he said. "I didn't mean to make you cry."

He drew her against his chest, where Glory Rose wept for only a moment. She looked up at Conrad, who gazed down at her with pure love and adoration in his expression.

"Will you forgive me?" he asked. "Can we please work together to figure out how to handle our families? Because I want *you* as *my* family, Glory Rose. I *need* you."

He leaned closer and pressed his lips to her forehead. "You are the only thing good in my life. You light up the world, and the stars are not the same without you."

She knew that Sari was a good thing in his life too, and she smiled as she tipped her head back and looked at the man she loved.

"I stand at the fence where the horses are," he said. "And I look up into the hills, thinking about you at Shiloh Ridge. I imagine you there and what you might be doing, and I pretend like I can see you and that you're still part of my life, and I want that so badly."

He took her face in both of his hands. "Please tell me I haven't messed up permanently."

She hadn't said very much, and Conrad finally seemed to have gotten all of the words he needed to say out of his mouth. Glory Rose gazed at him too, this beautiful cowboy who she needed in her life too.

"I love you, Conrad," she said, glad when her voice came out strong and sure. "If you can forgive me for the things I'm going to fall down on, then I want to be yours forever."

Conrad grinned, his face alight with happiness. He leaned closer and rested his forehead against hers. She let her eyes drift closed again as he whispered, "There's nothing to forgive, sugar," and then finally, he touched his mouth to hers in the most electrifying kiss of her life.

Chapter Forty

J J Walker pulled on the ends of his sleeves, bringing them down out of his tuxedo jacket. Daddy started fitting on the cufflinks that he and Ruby had found. His emotions tightened in his chest, but he still managed to say, "They have rubies on them."

Daddy smiled at him, a fast flicker of movement as he looked up and then focused on the cufflinks again. "Aren't they great?"

Ruby had been very tight-lipped about the details of their wedding. She told him that she, her momma, and his momma had it covered, and all he needed to do was wear what she told him to wear and show up when she told him to show up.

JJ tried to do what Ruby said, because she'd been right about his shoulder, and with some massage and therapy, it had healed fully. She never hesitated to come out on the ranch and work with him, though Uncle Micah and Aunt Simone kept her pretty busy at the interior design firm.

JJ had no idea what existed past today. He didn't need to know. He'd have Ruby in his life, and together, they would face whatever life brought their way.

Daddy finished with his cufflinks and then reached up to straighten his tie. That too bore a scarlet color, and JJ raised his chin so his daddy could get his tie exactly right. He wore a red vest as well, and he couldn't wait to see Ruby's dress. Every so often, he'd walk into the homestead and catch a word or two of conversation before the women shut it down. He had a feeling her dress would not be white, and he couldn't wait to see what his Scarlet Princess would be wearing as she walked down the aisle to become his wife.

"I can't believe I'm doing this," he said, a round of panic threatening to choke him.

"Hey, this is a good thing." Daddy brushed his hands along the top of JJ's shoulders and straightened his jacket. "You're doing the right thing." He raised his eyebrows as if to ask, *Right?*

JJ nodded and swallowed. "I love her."

"You know," Daddy said. "I wished I had gotten married a lot younger than I did."

JJ turned and faced the mirror as Uncle Rhett and Uncle Skyler joined them.

"Me too," Uncle Rhett said. "I'm starting to fear I won't live long enough to see all of my kids get married."

"I know Momma is holding on for the same thing," Skyler said, and JJ met each of their eyes in the mirror. He felt quite young to be getting married, and Ruby was four years younger than him. Her parents had said nothing, but he knew they worried about their daughter.

The door opened, and someone called, "Your boutonnieres are here," and set a bucket on the ground before letting the door swing closed again.

Daddy went to get the flowers, and JJ wasn't surprised to see blood-red roses get pinned to all the lapels in the room. JJ had three younger sisters and one younger brother, and he took a flower over to Jason and started attaching it to his brother's jacket.

"You make me want to start dating," Jason said.

JJ flicked his eyes up. "Why don't you?"

"I don't know," he said. "I feel like this town is a microscope."

JJ nodded. "I met Ruby in college." Clara Jean had already gotten married, and she had not left the homestead or Three Rivers until that day. She now lived with JJ's best friend in a rental near Wilde & Organic as they built their house on the family farmland that she had taken over from their uncle.

Jason likewise lived at home and worked the ranch. "There's nothing that interests me," he said. "You had a goal, and you went after it." He tugged on the ends of his sleeves as JJ dropped his hands. "Does it look okay?"

"Amazing," JJ said with a smile. "Conrad made up with Glory Rose, and there are a lot of Glovers?" JJ made it sound like a question, and Jason shook his head.

"I don't think I'm gonna be traveling that road," he said.

"Well, whatever you do," JJ said. "I'll be there if you need me." He lifted his brother's chin and looked straight into his eyes. "And so will Momma and Daddy. You know that, right?"

"Yeah," Jason mumbled, though JJ knew he often felt like he came in third place and would never measure up to JJ or Clara Jean. He wasn't the best at school, and he had caused the most grief out of any of JJ's siblings. Jason turned when Uncle Liam called his name, and JJ said a silent prayer for his brother.

The door opened again, and Grams walked inside. Pure love and relief filled JJ. "Grams," he said, and he went to greet her with a hug. He had to bend down to hug his petite grandmother, and she held him by the shoulders as he stepped back.

"When your daddy and uncles got married," she said. "Gramps would lead everybody in a family prayer."

Daddy joined their huddle. "I hope that's okay, JJ. I asked Grams to come say the prayer before the wedding."

"Of course, it's okay," he said, trying to soothe his nerves to a place where he could hear the voice of the Lord as Grams prayed.

"Let's circle up," Daddy called. "It's almost time for JJ to be at the altar." JJ had no idea what time he needed to be at the altar, but apparently, Daddy had been clued in on all relevant details, and he'd kept JJ on schedule all day.

Ruby had designated the American flag barn as the bridal suite, and JJ hadn't seen his mother since earlier that morning. Ruby wanted a sunset wedding with a big dinner to follow, and JJ had given her a credit card and told her to do whatever she wanted. He and his party had full reign of the homestead, and he moved to Grams' side and took her hand as his uncles, their sons, and Jason joined the throng.

He hadn't put his cowboy hat on yet, and in fact, he didn't even know where it was, but anyone who had, pulled their hat off and pressed it to his chest. JJ smiled around at all the good men in the Walker family.

Standing directly across from him was Tate, and tears flooded JJ's eyes for the first time that day. He loved Tate like a brother, and now he actually was his brother-in-law. Tate nodded, his smile as wide as ever, because the man always looked at life as a glass with only one swallow taken out of it. He worked as hard as anyone JJ knew, and he loved Clara Jean fiercely, and JJ was glad he'd get to have his best friend at his side for a long time to come.

"Dear Lord," Grams said, and JJ hastened to drop his chin and close his eyes. "We're grateful for good weather," she started, and JJ smiled to himself. Grams worried constantly about the weather, and if it even hinted that it might rain that day, she wouldn't leave the house.

"We're grateful for so many good men in our family, and we're grateful that we have found a way to forgive one another when we make mistakes."

"Amen," someone whispered down the line, and it sounded a lot like Conrad. The man had been through a lot in the past year, and JJ admired his strength and honor greatly.

"We're grateful for another wedding in our family," Grams said. "And ask a special blessing on Jonah Jeremiah today. Bless him to have a clear mind and an open heart to be able to feel and see all of the things that Thou hast in store for him. Bless Ruby and her family that they will feel loved and welcomed by all of us."

Grams paused for so long that JJ glanced over to her and found tears trickling down her face. "We're so grateful," she said, her voice pitched up and broken. "For the presence of our dear Gideon that we feel here with us."

Daddy edged closer to his mother and wrapped his arm around her. She leaned into him, her hand in JJ's cemented tightly. "We love Thee, Lord, and ask for any other blessings Thou hast for us. Amen."

"Amen," coursed softly through the room, and JJ didn't dare move, lest he be the one who would break the spirit that had settled over them. Everyone stayed still for a moment, and then someone knocked on the door.

JJ turned toward it, but no one entered.

"That's time," Daddy said, and JJ found himself being swarmed with uncles and cousins. They hugged him and said, "Good luck, JJ."

"We love you, JJ."

"She is so lucky, JJ."

Finally, only JJ, his father, and Conrad stood in the room. JJ took a big breath and blew it out. "This is it."

"Yep, we're giving them another minute to line up," he said. "And then we'll go."

Conrad drew JJ into a hug. "I love you, brother. You have shown me what courage is and how to love, and I am so grateful for it."

JJ clung to Conrad because he loved his cousin, and he wanted nothing more than to be able to repeat the same words back to him. But JJ's voice didn't work the way Conrad's did. He only managed to say, "I love you too," before his cousin stepped back and Daddy deemed it time to go.

He led the way out of the homestead and across the back deck. JJ paused there to take in the transformation of the backyard. "Wow," he said, scarcely believing his eyes. He had been told to stay inside all day, and he had done as requested.

The backyard had been transformed into a tropical paradise with trellises that held up tents and dripped with flowers—all red. He didn't dare to guess the names of all of them, but he imagined that it was every variety Ruby could get to Three Rivers by today.

They came in all shades and tints of red, from the deepest darkest burgundy to a light pink. Chairs had been set up with an aisle down the middle that led to the steps where he stood, and a second aisle that led from the barn, creating three sections of seating that all converged at an altar that had a snowy white top with rubies embedded around the edge to hold it in place.

Every chair had a white cover with a red ribbon tied around the back of it. The ends of the bows fluttered in the breeze, and Conrad turned around and reached for him.

"Come on, cowboy, you're supposed to be down there."

JJ found the energy and wherewithal to walk again, and he stepped down the few steps and onto the plush white runner that marked the aisle. Lanterns sat at the end of every row, and JJ became face blind before he'd taken a single step.

The aisle accommodated three people, and Daddy walked on his left with Conrad on his right, and JJ boxed up his emotions and stored them away so that he wouldn't cry in front of the whole town.

He arrived at the altar and hugged his father and Conrad, who both moved to the side. Ruby had asked Willa Glover to marry them, and she stood out of the way also, her black robes accented with red flowers as well.

JJ flipped his gaze over to the barn where he first detected movement. His mother stood there with a clear line of women behind her, and she reached her hand out. Daddy left the altar and went down the second branch of the aisle to reach Momma. He kissed her cheek, and she beamed up at him with all the love in the world. JJ had loved watching his parents love each other, and they'd set such a good example for him for how to treat his spouse and live his life.

On his right, Jason led the groomsmen down the aisle that JJ had just come down. Jason met Momma and Daddy at the altar in perfectly timed steps. JJ took his mother into a hug and held on tight.

"I am so happy for you," Momma whispered. "She is lovely, and you're so blessed to have her."

"I know, Momma," JJ said, sweeping a kiss along both of her cheeks and letting her and Daddy go stand in the first row. He hugged his brother, and then Ruby's mother and each of her younger siblings.

One by one, they all arrived, the women wearing pure white dresses with scarlet sashes tied around their waists. They wore big bows on the back of their dresses, and they filled the first three rows.

Then everyone turned and looked toward the barn.

Ruby's father and Tate both stood there, a gap between them where Ruby would obviously fit. JJ swallowed and un-fisted his fingers to wipe them down the front of his pants.

The barn doors opened, and Ruby emerged wearing a bright red wedding gown. It narrowed at her waist where she had a white sash, a complete mirroring to what her brides-maids wore.

Her hair, now curled and pinned to the top of her head, bore a crown of diamonds and rubies, and JJ could not contain the smile that filled his whole face. The sleeves on her dress puffed up into near-squares, and they barely seemed to be holding on to her shoulders, where another row of glittering gems held them in place. The neckline scooped and plunged, and JJ did indeed feel like the luckiest man in the world.

She linked one arm with Tate while she held an enormous bouquet of snowy white roses. He kissed her cheek and took the bouquet from her so she could link arms with her daddy. That done, Tate handed the bouquet back to her, and she held it directly in front of her body.

She met JJ's eye. He fell more in love with her then than ever before, her smile radiant on her ruby red lips, with diamonds dangling from her earlobes. She took the first step toward him, and JJ couldn't wait to worship at the feet of his Scarlet Princess for the rest of his life.

Chapter Forty-One

F inn got down from the saddle to open the gate that marked the property line between his ranch and Three Rivers. That done, he led his horse through it, along with the one that Theo and Bubba rode together. He re-secured the gate and swung back into the saddle to finish their ride.

"When we get to the homestead," he told his boys. "You're going to do everything that Grandma says, okay?"

"Yes, sir," Theo said.

"Where you gonna be, Daddy?" Bubba asked.

"I have to go help with the harvest tonight," he said. "You guys are going to sleep at Aunt Libby's. Grandma will be there."

His younger sister had had her baby last week, and she'd only been home for a couple of days after a difficult delivery. She had plenty of help around Three Rivers, but she'd asked Finn to help Rusty lead the harvest this year. They'd only been married through one previous harvest, and Rusty had expressed his gratitude for Finn's help multiple times.

"Is Mama coming for the sleepover?" Theo asked.

Finn shook his head. "No, buddy. Mama's gonna stay home with Dustin."

Edith had finished her book a couple of months ago, and she didn't currently have a new deadline. In fact, she'd told Finn she might not write any more books, and he'd told her she could do whatever she wanted. In the back of his mind, he knew that Edith had more stories to tell. She loved writing, and perhaps she wouldn't pursue publishing as aggressively as she had in the past, but she would definitely keep telling tales.

After another fifteen minutes of riding, Uncle Pete's place came into view, along with the big three-story building of Courage Reins. Finn would house his horses in the stable there, where he would help Paul take care of them. The moment he opened the stable doors and turned back to get his boys down from the saddle, his momma said, "There you are."

"Grandma!" Theo yelled, and he didn't wait for Finn's help before sliding from the saddle. He landed on both feet with a grunt and a stumble, and Finn's heart wobbled in his chest. He refrained from telling his son to be careful because he heard it enough from his mother. Theo didn't seem fazed, and he ran toward his grandma, his face full of sunshine.

Finn reached up and lifted Bubba down, and he too ran toward Finn's mother. She hugged them both at the same time, one in each arm, both of them already talking over each other.

"I'll take them inside," she said. "Rusty will be out in a minute to update you with where we are on the harvest."

"Thanks, Momma."

She took the boys through the stable, and Finn followed them down to a couple of empty stalls, where he put his horses, removed their tack, and brushed them down. He made sure they had hay and water, and he'd just stepped out of the stall when Rusty entered the stable.

"I'm so glad you're here," Rusty said.

"Why?" Finn asked. "What's going on?"

"Our big thresher won't start," he said. "I've had Beau looking at it all day and nothing."

Finn pulled out his phone. "All right," he said. "Let me make a phone call."

"Who are you going to ask?" Rusty said.

"Sammy Glover." He tapped and lifted his phone to his ear.

The line only rang twice before she said, "Hullo, Finn."

"Sammy, we've got a thresher that won't start," he said.

"That's not good."

"No, it's not." Everyone in and around Three Rivers was trying to get their harvest in and their winter crops planted before it got too cold.

"What have you tried?" Sammy asked. "Maybe I can send Gun over."

"Oh, does Gunnison know how to fix tractors?" Finn raised his eyebrows and looked at Rusty.

Rusty shrugged one shoulder. "I didn't know that," he said.

"I've been teaching him," Sammy said. "Just for the past couple of months. He's a quick study. Let me text him and see if he can come up."

"We wanted to mow overnight," Finn said, pressing his eyes closed and starting a silent prayer. "Do you think he could come tonight?"

"Do you have his number?" Sammy asked.

"I've got Link's and Wilder's," Finn said. "But I don't think I have Gun's."

"I'll send it to you," she said. "He'll be thrilled, trust me. He told me the other day he actually prays that our machines will break down so that he can diagnose and fix them." She laughed, and Finn chuckled with her. "I'll get a rundown of what Rusty has tried already," Finn said. "I just got here, so I'm not really sure."

"All right," Sammy said. "I just sent you his number."

"Thank you," Finn said, and he ended the call.

Sure enough, he had a text from Sammy with Gun's contact information. He forwarded it to Rusty and said, "We just need to call him."

He met his brother-in-law's eye and found the fear sitting there. Finn didn't want to tell him that he could do it, though Rusty could absolutely do it. Taking on an operation as big as Three Rivers was no small feat, and Rusty had confessed to Finn privately that he felt like drowning all of the time.

Though he trusted Libby and followed her lead, Finn had told him it might take him a couple of years to understand the rhythm and the land of Three Rivers, but once he did, he'd master it. Perhaps he needed just a little more time.

"How's the baby?" Finn asked, and Rusty's worries dissolved away.

"She's the best," he said. "I hate leaving them at the homestead." He turned and walked with Finn toward the end of the stable. "Is that normal? Did you feel like that with Theo and Edith?"

"Oh, yeah," Finn said. "I think Edith was worried that I would come back, and she would have done something to Theo, because she didn't know how to take care of him."

"Libby never seems to have a confidence problem," Rusty mumbled.

"That she shows you," Finn said, pausing just inside the door. "But I guarantee she's just as scared as you, and she has no idea what she's doing."

Rusty met his eyes again. "You think so?"

"Absolutely. You're that baby's daddy, Rusty. Don't be afraid to take Cora from Libby and take care of her. Libby will appreciate it, and you'll get to show her that whatever she can't handle—you can."

Rusty nodded, a newly determined look on his face. "Thanks, Finn."

He sighed as he looked down at his phone. "All right, let's call Gun and see if he can get out here. If he can't, I don't really need you tonight because you were going to drive that thresher."

"I'll go say hi to Libby and Cora then," Finn said. "And make sure my boys don't terrorize that little girl." He chuckled. "They dang near killed Dustin when we brought him home."

Rusty chuckled too, and Finn led the way out of the stable. He left his brother-in-law behind when Rusty said, "Hey, Gunnison, I have a big favor to ask," and he crossed the lawn and went up the steps to the side deck that he knew so well.

Inside, he found Libby sitting on the couch, Theo right at her side with his brand-new niece, Cora, in his son's arms. Everything in the world felt right in that moment, and pure joy filled Finn from top to bottom.

"Wow, bud," he said as he moved closer. "Stay right there. Let's get a picture for Mama." Edith had been to see the baby, of course. She'd helped Libby every day since she'd come home, but she usually came alone while Finn kept the boys at the farm. Theo was just barely getting old enough for Finn to give him a task and have him do it decently well without his daddy hovering over his shoulder.

He'd been to see his sister's baby as well, and he snapped a picture of Theo and Cora while Bubba crowded in close, a cheesy grin on his face. He sent it to Edith, grinning all the while as he tapped out, *We need a little girl. Don't you think?*

Chapter Forty-Two

Conrad drove slowly over the rise and onto Shiloh Ridge Ranch. He looked left toward Glory Rose's house, though he didn't expect to see her yet. He turned right and pressed on the gas pedal to get out of sight, just in case she came around the corner at that exact moment.

After going straight down the lane, he pulled into the driveway at the Ranch House and then turned into the garage. Judge came outside just as Conrad dropped to the cement floor, and he pressed the button to lower the garage door.

"Howdy," he said, a big smile on his face.

Conrad returned the smile and shook the man's hand before he went up the steps and into the Ranch House with him. "Howdy."

He glanced around at everyone gathered there, surprised this many people fit in Judge's house. He didn't see anyone from his family, but he knew they'd be here. He'd invited his parents, Grams, the triplets, and JJ and Ruby, and they'd all promised to be here in plenty of time.

All he could do now was hope and pray that Glory Rose wouldn't recognize their vehicles—or that it would be dark enough for her not to notice.

Ward stood from the bar stool where he'd been sitting and shook his hand. "Hey, Conrad." He beamed at him. "Come take a look. I think we got it pretty close." He led the way outside with Judge, June, and Dot.

"I'm not going outside until I have to," Preacher said, and someone else told him to not be so grumpy.

"It's not even that windy today," Etta said. "Don't ruin this for Conrad."

Before the door closed, he heard someone else say, "Don't ruin this for *Glory Rose*."

That started some squabbling that the closed door, thankfully, shut out.

"Everyone seems real chipper today," he said to Dot, who shook her head with a smile. "They're fine," she said. "They're getting a free meal out of this, and it's the first engagement we've had in years." She grinned, brightening as she did. "Everyone's really excited, actually."

Conrad grinned back at her, glad when she stepped over to his side and put her arm around his shoulders. "We love you, Conrad," she said. "You know that, right?"

He ducked his head even as he nodded. "Yeah," he said. "I know that." He smiled over to her. "My family's all on their way up too." And that should be interesting.

He focused on the gazebo ahead, his step slowing when he took in what Glory Rose's family had prepped for him.

"What do you think?" Ward asked as he stopped a good twenty feet away and folded his arms.

"I think it's incredible," Conrad said as he came to a stop at his side. "It's even better than I imagined." He grinned over to Judge and June. "Way better than the pictures I sent."

"I told you," June said proudly. "Judge has a way with decorating. He's won the town Christmas festival contest several times."

"*Six* times," Judge said in his dry tone.

"That's several," June said.

"I think you have to get to seven to be several," he argued back.

Conrad grinned at their back-and-forth bickering, knowing they weren't truly upset.

"I saw old man Bickmore took it this year," Conrad said. "Glory Rose and I voted for you."

"Oh, my timing was off on a couple of the songs," Judge said with a wave of his hand. "But I think this is pretty incredible."

Conrad looked back to the gazebo, which had every railing, pillar, and post wrapped in fairy lights. Because the calendar had just turned over to February, it would be dark soon, and those lights would be a beacon of light shining on his future path with Glory Rose.

"Do we really think that Sari can get Glory Rose here?" Dot asked. "She's only four."

"Almost," Conrad said, for his daughter's birthday wasn't

for another three weeks. He'd planned an enormous family party and invited every Walker and every Glover, and he prayed every morning, noon, and night that it wouldn't become the biggest mistake of his life.

"Fawn's there, dear," Ward said. "Remember, you're going to text her, and she's going to help Sari get Glory Rose here for dinner."

"I know. I just worry about them." She hugged herself and looked at the gazebo.

Conrad had sent pictures to Glory Rose's parents of the two of them, as well as Glory Rose with Sari and then the three of them that would become a family unit if she said yes to being his wife. Those had been printed in poster sizes, on foam mat, and attached to the gazebo.

They talked a lot about getting married, and Conrad had deliberately waited through all of the holidays and family parties and Glory Rose's birthday before planning this proposal. They still had a lot to learn about how to put each other first and navigate the landscape of two large families. Even so, Conrad had more confidence than ever that they could do it. Because he loved Glory Rose with his whole heart, and he knew that she loved him the same way. She'd proven to him a couple of times now that he was more important to her than anyone else.

He also knew she wanted to get married in the spring or summer, and that required him to get his act in gear and ask her to marry him before too much more time went by.

He looked over to her mother. "It's enough time, right?"

"I think she would marry you tomorrow, right here at this

gazebo," she said. "But yes, it's only February third. It's enough time."

He took a step away from the group and approached Glory Rose's favorite spot on the ranch. Vases of flowers, which he'd ordered and had sent to June's house, lined the steps up into the gazebo, and a beautiful furry blanket lay on the bench so that they could sit there after the proposal. It would be chilly, and he wanted to spend some time with her as they looked down to Three Rivers, and his farm, and imagined their future together.

His parents arrived, and Conrad grinned as he stepped into both his daddy and his momma. "You made it."

"Wouldn't miss it," Daddy said.

Conrad stepped back. "Look at it."

"It's awesome," Elaine said. "Oh, they put my favorite picture right up front." She led the triplets over to the huge photograph of Conrad, Glory Rose, and Sari that Grams had taken on Christmas Eve.

They looked like a family. A real family, who loved one another and shone with smiles and sunshine and Christmas spirit.

"Should I text Fawn now?" Dot called from the lawn.

Conrad turned and called, "Yep. It's perfect."

Then he left behind the gazebo, wondering if fairy lights and flowers and fur would be enough for Glory Rose. *You're enough for Glory Rose,* he told himself. *She won't even care about the fairy lights.*

She just wanted him, as she had said several times since

the New Year. He rejoined her family and shook Bear's hand and Ranger's hand as they had come outside also.

"I'm still okay to have True Blue in a couple of weeks for Sari's birthday, aren't I?"

"Absolutely," Ranger said. "It's blocked off on our family calendar." He smiled, and he pulled Conrad into a hug. "I wish you'd fallen in love with Fawn," he said with a chuckle. "And I pray every night that she'll find a man as good as you to be her husband."

Conrad nodded and swallowed, his jaw tight. "Thank you, Ranger," Conrad said. "That means a lot to me."

He'd learned so much in the past year when he thought he couldn't learn anymore, but Sari constantly challenged him. He learned more about and leaned more into his own faith, finding forgiveness for himself and also for those around him that had inadvertently or advertently hurt him.

What a blessing forgiveness is, he thought, and then Dot squealed and said, "Glory Rose is putting on Sari's coat right now. Let's get inside."

Everyone else bustled away, leaving Conrad alone. Fawn would somehow separate herself from Glory Rose and Sari, leaving his daughter with the job of bringing Glory Rose to the gazebo so that Conrad could propose.

Minutes ticked by while he stood in the darkening sky, and finally, he heard the higher-pitched sound of female voices. And then cutting through the night, Glory Rose said, "Wow. Look, Sari, Aunt June and Uncle Judge have lights on the gazebo."

He stood just out of the reach of the light, and he watched

as Glory Rose and his daughter came toward him, hand in hand. Love bubbled up from the bottom of his boots all the way to the top of his head, once, twice, again, and again and again.

"Daddy here," Sari said. "My daddy goin' be here."

She had come so far in her speech, and Glory said, "No, baby, your daddy has a meeting tonight, remember?"

"No, Daddy come," Sari insisted.

Conrad took that as his cue to step out of the shadows before his daughter ruined the surprise. When Glory Rose saw him, she froze and said, "Who's there?" She stepped in front of Sari in a protective move until recognition lit her face.

"Daddy!" Sari called.

She ran toward him, and Conrad laughed as he scooped her up in his arms. "You weren't supposed to tell her I was going to be here," he said.

She turned and faced Glory Rose, "See? Daddy here."

"He sure is," Glory Rose said. "What's going on, Mister Walker? I thought you had a meeting tonight."

"I do." He took her hand and leaned down and kissed her. "You just happened to be part of it."

He led her toward the gazebo, and Glory Rose pulled in a breath when she saw the flowers. "Conrad," she said in a warning voice.

"Glory Rose," he said back. "I love you with everything I am, everything I know how to be. Your glory lights up our lives, right, Sari?"

"Love you," Sari said, and Conrad grinned at her.

"Yes, we love you."

They reached the gazebo, and Conrad released Glory Rose's hand so he could pick up the blanket. He sat Sari down on the end and nodded to Glory Rose to sit on the other end. He covered his daughter with the blanket, and as Glory Rose sat down, he knelt in front of her.

"I know I'm obstructing your perfect view," he said. "If you give me just another minute, I'll be out of the way."

Glory Rose did not look away from him. A pretty smile filled her face, and Conrad opened the ring box and gazed at the diamond contained therein.

"As I was saying, your glory lights up our lives. We want you with us in the farmhouse. I'll build you anything off-grid that you want, be that a preschool or a guineafowl enclosure or a penguin pond."

She giggled, and Sari scooted down the bench into her side. Glory Rose put her arm around the little girl, and Conrad forgot the rest of his speech.

"Will you marry me?" he asked.

"Yes," Glory Rose whispered.

"What that?" Sari asked. She got up on her feet. "What you say, Glow-Roe?"

Conrad laughed, and Glory Rose joined him. "I said yes," she said in a much louder voice.

Sari turned around as Conrad had practiced with her multiple times, and she yelled, "She say yes!"

That was the Glover family's cue to break into applause. And boy, did they ever. Not only did they clap, but they whooped and hollered, and Conrad barely had time to slide the diamond ring on Glory Rose's finger before they swarmed the gazebo.

Conrad got swept away by JJ, and he hugged him hard for a long moment. Ruby joined them, and then all three triplets engulfed him as the four of them laughed.

His mother stepped into his arms next, saying, "Congratulations, baby. This is such a good thing."

He accepted all of the congratulations and looked around. "Where's Grams?"

"Right there with your daddy," Momma said. Conrad moved over to both of them, as they'd been his anchors in the stormy seas of life for such a long time.

"You did it, my boy," Grams said.

He swept a kiss along her cheek. "I sure did."

"Get back over there with your beautiful Glory Rose."

"I love you, Grams," he whispered. He hugged his daddy and said, "Love you, Daddy." And then he did what Grams told him to do: He moved to Glory Rose's side.

"Kiss her!" Aunt Whitney called, and Conrad obeyed. Aunt Whitney's camera went *click, click, click* as she captured the moment, and he and Glory Rose pulled apart, laughing and smiling for their engagement pictures.

"Okay," June yelled. "We have dinner inside. Let's go back inside, everyone. It's time to eat."

The crowd started to disperse, and Momma moved over to Conrad and handed Conrad a box of pizza. Pepperoni pizza, pan style, with extra cheese and a sprinkling of oregano.

"Thanks, Momma."

"She is so lucky to have you." Momma pressed her cheek to his and turned to go inside with Grams.

Conrad didn't see who took Sari, but he trusted that she would be safe. He indicated the bench, and Glory Rose took a seat again. He covered them both with the blanket, and as the last noise faded away, they gazed out on their beloved Three Rivers.

He handed her the pizza box, and she gasped as she opened it. "Conrad." She looked at him. "You remembered my favorite food."

"I love you, Glory Rose," he said with a smile. "I'll love you for as long as the day is long, and the night is dark, and the stars continue to shine."

She handed him a piece of pizza, and then she said the best words back to him: "I love you too, Conrad."

* * *

Mm, I love a single dad romance - and the Walkers AND the Glovers! I hope you enjoyed seeing Conrad come into his role as a father, and Glory Rose figure out how to balance her enormous family with her happily-ever-after. I just love them. If you did too, **please leave a review for them on Goodreads, BookBub, or Amazon.**

And keep reading for the first two chapters of the next book in the series, THE COWBOY WHO HEARD HER, featuring the the amazing Mitch, who's starting his deaf academy with the woman he's working with and has a cowboy billionaire-sized crush on, Lacy. **You can preorder it now!**

Sneak Peek! The Cowboy Who Heard Her Chapter One:

Mitchell Glover glared at the text that had just come in on his phone. Yes, he'd gotten the invitation to Conrad Walker and Glory Rose Glover's wedding. It had been on his calendar for months. *Of course*, he was going to attend, and he felt like ripping off a text to his aunt to let her know that.

He'd told his mother he would be there, but he hadn't RSVP'd. He didn't see the point. Glovers far and wide knew about the wedding and would be there. His phone went dark, and he tapped to get it to come back on.

He supposed his aunt's question was valid. Would he be bringing a date?

He immediately thought of Lacy. His educational director and longtime crush had not received an invitation of her own. The one Mitch had gotten had only had his name on it, and he hadn't known—and still didn't know—how to bring it up with her.

Maybe you can just say you need an interpreter, he thought. That had worked a couple of times in the past, first for his uncle's birthday and then for the family Angel Tree celebration that happened every fall. Lacy had seemed to enjoy herself in his presence on both of those occasions, but Mitch hated using her as an interpreter.

He left his office and went into the kitchen, his phone still sitting on his desk. Everything had been going really well in his life in the past several years, and Mitch really couldn't complain. He had dated plenty of women over the years, some deaf and some hearing, and he hadn't liked any of them half as well as he liked Lacy.

He set the air fryer to preheat so he could make the chicken eggrolls he loved. She had found an amazing sweet and sour sauce at the grocery store, and Mitch got it out and poured a little bit into a glass bowl. He added salt, pepper, and garlic powder and mixed it all up, not knowing or caring how much noise he made in the kitchen.

It was almost the weekend, with the Walker-Glover Wedding of the Year tomorrow morning. At first, Glory Rose had wanted to stage it in True Blue, but then she'd broken from family tradition when she decided to get married at the church.

Mitch's mother and Uncle Judge would perform the ceremony together, also something that had never been done. They would then move to True Blue for the luncheon to allow space for everyone to sit for the wedding, as well as have all of the tables and chairs set up for the luncheon without needing time for setup and takedown.

Mitch honestly had not given much thought to his own wedding, and as he closed in on thirty-five, he wondered if he'd ever get married at all. The work he'd been doing to become a Deaf advocate and a fluent Sign Language teacher and speaker had dominated his life for the past decade, and the Academy had been everything Mitch had breathed, eaten, or dreamed about in the past two years.

He put his chicken eggrolls in the air fryer, set the timer, and poured himself a cup of coffee. It was almost four o'clock, and he'd be awake all night if he drank too much. He stirred in some sugar and took his coffee cup to the front porch.

He took a sip as he gazed across the expansive front lawn, the roundabout he'd had put in with a fountain in the middle, and the lane that extended to the corner, where it narrowed to a single lane and led to the highway. All of the fields on the west side of the road had been left open, and Lacy had planted three pounds of wildflower seeds this past spring.

On the east side of the road, two beautiful dormitory buildings had been erected with a smaller, single-story building between them, which Mitch had designed and planned to use as the administrative offices for his deaf academy. He and Lacy had been working tirelessly on it for the past seventeen months, and he had been dreaming about it long before that.

He planned to launch the website and open enrollment the Tuesday following Memorial Day, which sat just another week and a half from now. Lacy had been working all of her contacts in the state, and Mitch had gotten all of his professors and friends from his time at Whispering Paws to spread the word.

He'd originally wanted to provide an academy for ages five and up, but he and Lacy had quickly learned that that would have to be something that they expanded into. He had amended his plans and made fourteen the minimum age.

They had curriculum built and ready to be taught for grades eight through twelve, and then advanced sign language in specialized topics after that. Anyone who enrolled at the deaf academy could also live on site, and he and Lacy had hired instructors for everything already.

The dormitories needed to be finished with furnishings, and they had moved into interviewing Resident Assistants, though he hadn't hired anyone yet. He couldn't until he knew how many people would be living at the academy.

You need a name too, he thought as he sank onto the bench on the front porch. Conrad Walker had built it for him, and his cousin, Clara Jean, had come over and equipped it with a plush cushion and back with pillows. Mitch had sat here many times and thought through things, because the decision fatigue he faced in putting together this academy had been monumental.

He couldn't have done any of it without Lacy.

He drained the last of his coffee as he tried to find a way to ask her to be his date for the wedding. He didn't want to ask her to interpret. That was the coward's way out, and Mitch was done with it.

He wanted her to get dressed up and curl her hair and put

on makeup for *him*. His heartbeat throbbed in his chest, and he looked over as the screen door opened and Lacy herself exited the house.

"Your timer is going off," she said. "I pulled your chicken eggrolls for you."

She gave him a pretty smile, which absolutely devastated Mitch. He scooted over on the bench built for two and patted the empty spot beside him. Lacy didn't hesitate as she moved over and sat down beside him.

Sitting side by side was not ideal for sign language. He had to be looking directly at a person to read their lips, and while he could probably read her hands just fine, she said nothing.

Mitch shifted slightly, and she looked at him. *My cousin is getting married tomorrow*, he said.

She nodded. "Yes, I know. It's been on your calendar for a long time."

Yes, it had been, and he wondered if she'd thought at all about going with him. *There's going to be a lot of people there,* he said. *My momma is officiating the ceremony, and she said she would sign it all for me.*

Lacy smiled, and she looked like a golden angel straight from heaven. She'd cut her hair recently, but it still hung down past her shoulders, and she brushed it back now, as she nodded once again. "That's great," she said. "Then you won't miss out on anything being said."

He'd miss out on plenty, as he always did, and he frowned as he looked out over the academy. He caught her hands moving in his peripheral vision, but he didn't look at her.

His dog sat up and nosed his knee at the same time that Lacy put her hand on his leg. That was how he knew she'd said his name, as Champ had been trained to alert him when someone did so. Without thinking, he covered her hand with his and laced his fingers through hers. He felt more than saw her tense at his side, but she didn't pull away, and he didn't let go.

After several moments of pure bliss, his skin sizzling where it touched hers, he looked at her. She didn't sign as she asked, "Do you need an interpreter to go with you?"

He shook his head because no, he did not want an interpreter to attend a family function with him. His momma and daddy did a great job with sign language, as did Link. Misty got better all the time, and Chaz would be home, and he knew sign language really well.

He couldn't look away from Lacy's positively perfect blue-green eyes. He'd wished once upon a time that he'd been able to attend a deaf school that also taught him how to speak, but he hadn't.

He'd grown up with Signed Exact English until he was eight years old, and then he'd come to live at Shiloh Ridge Ranch. His momma had gotten better and better at sign language, but he'd never attended a specialized school, and he had been the only deaf person in Three Rivers for as long as he could remember.

He managed by typing things on his phone and gesturing, and when he really needed to be able to talk to someone, like at a doctor's appointment, he did get an interpreter. He hated that he had to do everything via video, but it was better than nothing.

He didn't want to remove his hand from Lacy's to be able to speak with her. As he'd explored the option of cochlear implants while living in Virginia, he'd been disappointed to learn that because he had never learned to speak, it would probably take him upwards of twenty years to do so, even after he got the implants.

Mitch had decided against getting them and had thrown himself into learning as much specialized sign language as possible, everything he could about Deaf culture in the United States and the world, and building this academy.

Lacy cocked her head, which was their universal sign for, *what's going on? Talk to me.*

Mitch did it without thought, and he hadn't realized it until Lacy had pointed it out to him. She'd laughed and said she always knew when he was trying to figure out what to ask next, or what to say, or what she had said, because he would cock his head.

Champ had laid back down, and Mitch finally lifted his hand from Lacy's so that he could talk to her.

I don't want you to come to the wedding as my interpreter, he said. *I want you to come as my date.*

Sneak Peek! The Cowboy Who Heard Her Chapter Two:

Okay echoed through Lacy Hayes's mind.

She couldn't believe she'd said that word to Mitch, and now, fifteen hours later, she stood in her slip, trying to decide what she could wear to his cousin's wedding.

She saw the way his face had brightened, and he'd asked, *Really?*

She'd smiled, tucked her hair, and nodded. "Yeah, really."

Then her phone had rung, and it was a call she needed to take from the groundskeeping company that they'd hired to beautify the land and erase all signs of construction around the dormitories.

Lacy had quickly excused herself and gone down the front steps, and by the time the conversation had ended, Mitch had vacated the bench. She'd heard him washing dishes in the kitchen, but instead of joining him, she'd tiptoed up to the third floor in the manor, where her apartment sat.

The wedding wasn't until eleven o'clock, with lunch afterward, and Lacy suspected that no one in Mitch's family would bat an eye at her being there. She'd attended a few family functions over the past year, and they knew her. "Yeah," she told herself, moving a pink dress out of the way. "As his interpreter."

He'd asked her out fifteen months ago and never brought it up again until yesterday. His discipline and his respect of her boundaries impressed her, and she'd been fighting her own feelings for the man for almost a year.

"He's not just a man," she whispered as she lifted a pretty emerald dress off the rack. "Mitch is a cowboy god."

And he was. He had taken mere ideas and shaped them into physical facilities. He'd attended a deaf college for a decade to make sure he had the skills and knowledge to open this academy. He could train dogs to be hearing helpers, and they adored him.

Lacy found herself wondering if he could take her broken and bruised heart and put it back together as well.

She put on the green dress and remembered why she didn't wear it very often. The straps sat a little bit too wide, and she couldn't wear a bra with the dress. That seemed highly inappropriate for a family wedding in a church, so Lacy quickly shed the garment and rehung it in her closet.

Mitch had texted her the details of the wedding last night, and he said he'd come pick her up on the third floor at ten-thirty. She'd brought in a mini-fridge and a microwave for when she didn't want to go down to the kitchen to make something to eat, and she padded out of the bedroom and into her faux kitchen to get a piece of string cheese and a pint of strawberries.

Since she lived alone on the third floor and always kept the door locked, she didn't need to worry about anyone seeing her in her slip.

Mitch had never once come to the third floor, and a quiet excitement began to grow inside her that today would be the first time. He'd held her hand for the first time yesterday, and Lacy had realized how starved for human touch she had become.

Her brother lived in town, and she'd been working with him as the physical facilities director here at the academy for almost a year. But Jacob was not the touchy-feely type of man, and Lacy couldn't remember the last person she'd hugged. Probably her mother, when she'd left San Antonio to make the move to Three Rivers almost eighteen months ago.

Tears filled her eyes, and she quickly brushed them away, as she had already done her makeup that morning. Lacy wasn't normally a weepy woman, and while she'd experienced some very difficult things in her life, the most crushing was the ever-present loneliness that went with her everywhere.

Her phone buzzed on the table, and she flipped it over. *Do you want breakfast?* Mitch asked. *I'm making omelets. I'm happy to bring you one.*

Lacy had eaten the piece of string cheese, but the strawberries still sat on the table in front of her. Her first instinct was to deny the omelet. She had food up here, and she had no idea what to say to Mitch.

You can't hide in your own house, she told herself, and she got to her feet and sent him a text as she hurried out of her rec room and into her bedroom.

Any chance of making it sausage and cheese? If so, I'm in.

Mitch sent back two laughing emojis and said, *Your wish is my command.*

She knew Mitch would deliver too, because he'd never let her down yet. She decided she didn't have time to choose a dress before breakfast, and she quickly shed her slip and stepped into a dark green pantsuit that her sister had made for her before she'd moved. The ribbed knit felt soft against her skin and simulated a warm hug for Lacy. She slipped on a pair of wide-foot sandals and headed downstairs.

For some reason, Mitch liked to play the radio when he cooked, though she'd asked him if he could hear, even a little bit, and he'd denied it. *It makes me feel normal,* he'd told her. *My momma and daddy always listen to the radio while they cook.*

Lacy's heart ached that he needed something like that in his life.

He had no idea how loud he set the radio, and this morning, it seemed to be blasting through the house. She was actually surprised that she hadn't heard it on the third floor.

She entered the kitchen and stepped down the counter to turn down the radio. She could turn it off and he wouldn't know, so she did that. He turned toward her, more hope on his face than she had seen in a long time.

Hey, he said. *Good morning.*

"Good morning," she said back. She took in the mess on the island where he had been preparing ingredients for omelets. The man was a whirlwind in the kitchen, but everything she tasted that he'd made had been delicious. He told her he'd learned to cook in a few community classes here in Three Rivers before he'd moved to Virginia.

I'm doing your sausage right now, he said. *Do you want any veggies in your omelet?*

"No, thank you," she said.

He nodded and went back over to the cutting board where he diced green peppers for himself. He had two pans sitting on the stove, but he hadn't turned on the flame under either of them yet.

Part of her wanted to simply ask him something and have him be able to continue to cook while he answered. But that wasn't a reality for a deaf person.

Mitch had to focus on what he was doing, and that included having a conversation. She could knock on the counter, and he'd feel the vibrations and look up.

It was a very common signal to get the attention of someone who couldn't hear. In fact, Mitch had filled his house with wood, as did a lot of Deaf people and Deaf-friendly places, as wood carried vibrations really well.

Lacy wanted to give Mitch the space he needed, so she waited while he finished with the onions and green peppers, turned back to the stove, and pulled her sausage off, draining it onto a plate covered with a paper towel.

He finally looked at her, and she raised her hand as if she needed him to call on her before she could speak. He did that adorable head tilt, and she asked, "Do you need any help?"

No, I've got it, he said. *You just relax*. He turned his back on her again, lit the flame under the pans, and moved like one of those chefs that cooked at a teppanyaki grill. Here, there. Spatula in his hand, this in the pot, that in the pan, and a few minutes later, he placed a perfectly folded sausage and cheese omelet in front of her. He carried his own plate around and sat beside her.

She looked at him and asked, "Will there be dancing at the wedding?"

He cut off a bite of his omelet and nodded. She wished he would look at her again, but he didn't, and Lacy took the hint that he didn't want to talk. They ate in silence, though everything Lacy did with Mitch was in silence. She could only eat half of her omelet before she felt like she might pop, and she pushed her plate away a couple of inches.

Mitch looked at it and then her. *Are you done?*

"Yes," she said. "You made an omelet for a giant." Lacy grinned at him, glad when he returned her smile. He looked at his plate, where he only had two bites of omelet left. He forked them both up together and then signed with one hand, *I guess I'm a giant then*, and he put them in his mouth while she laughed.

She stood and took his plate, sliding hers on top of it. She looked right at him because he could read lips.

"I'll do dishes."

You don't need to do that, he said.

"I want to." She moved away from him, cutting off eye contact and the conversation at the same time. Two could play his game.

He joined her at the kitchen sink, creating an intimate

space between them as they stood hip to hip. She washed and he rinsed, setting their clean dishes in the drainer beside the sink. As she wiped out the sink and sprayed it with hot water to get it all cleaned up, he set his coffee mug in the dish drainer, and then turned toward her.

She flipped off the water and turned to look at him. He reached up and tucked her hair behind her ear, sending a shower of sparks down her neck and across her shoulder. His other hand slid along her waist and drew her into his chest. He stood about six inches taller than her, and Lacy fell motionless and weightless as he wrapped her up in his arms. Then she remembered how to be a human being, and she hugged him back.

She'd asked him if there would be dancing at the wedding, and as he started to sway back and forth with her, their bodies pressed chest to chest, Lacy whispered, "I want to dance with you today." She drew in a breath. "I want to go out with you."

Mitch pulled away, for she'd clearly alerted him to the fact that she had spoken. His eyebrows drew down, and he lifted one hand to the side and asked, *What did you say?*

Lacy wasn't sure she could repeat the words now that he would understand them. She also didn't want to keep fighting her feelings, and she didn't want to go another eighteen months without hugging another human being.

You don't need another human being, she told herself. *You need Mitchell Glover.*

So she backed up a couple of steps and Mitch let her go. She held his gaze firmly as fear struck through her over and over as a rattlesnake did its prey. Then she raised her hands and drew a deep breath.

"I said I'd like to dance with you at the wedding today."

He smiled. *Okay.*

"And then I said I'd like to go out with you." She watched the smile drift off his face and his expression turn a bit guarded. He looked away, but Lacy held her determination not to be ashamed of what she said.

She simply needed to wait for him to answer.

* * *

What is Mitch going to say? Why isn't he saying it?? Ahhhh! I can't wait for him to get his happily-ever-after and open his academy and all the things!

Preorder your copy by scanning the QR code below with your phone!

The Cowboy Who Came Home: A Second Generation in Three Rivers Ranch Romance™ (Book 1): He's been serving in the military for a decade. She's been quietly grieving a devastating loss. When Finn and Edith reunite in small-town Three Rivers where they grew up together, can their second chance romance provide hope, healing, and the happily-ever-after they both crave?

Scan this QR code with your phone to see this series in eBook, audiobook, large print paperback, or regular paperback:

Be sure to check out the other three series set in the beloved town of Three Rivers too!

Meet the cowboys who started it all at Three Rivers Ranch! Scan the QR code below with your phone to check out this complete series.

Scan this QR code with your phone to see and order this series in eBook, audiobook, large print paperback, or regular paperback:

Seven Sons Ranch in Three Rivers Romance™ Series

Meet the cowboy billionaire brothers at Seven Sons Ranch! Scan the QR code below with your phone to check out this complete series.

1. Rhett
2. Tripp
3. Liam
4. Jeremiah
5. Wyatt
6. Skyler
7. Micah
8. Gideon

Shiloh Ridge Ranch in Three Rivers Romance™ Series

Become a Glover Lover by reading all the Glover Family romance & family saga at Shiloh Ridge Ranch! Scan the QR code below with your phone to check out this complete series.

1. The Mechanics of Mistletoe
2. The Horsepower of the Holiday
3. The Construction of Cheer
4. The Secret of Santa
5. The Gift of Gingerbread
6. The Harmony of Holly
7. The Chemistry of Christmas
8. The Delivery of Decor
9. The Blessing of Babies

About Liz

Liz Isaacson writes inspirational romance, usually set in Texas, or Wyoming, or anywhere else horses and cowboys exist. She lives in Utah, where she writes full-time, takes her two dogs to the park everyday, and eats a lot of veggies while writing. Find her on her website at www.feelgoodfiction-books.com.

www.ingramcontent.com/pod-product-compliance
Lightning Source LLC
Chambersburg PA
CBHW020516110726
47899CB00004B/1131